Come Away With Me

Maddie Please

Published by AVON
A Division of HarperCollins*Publishers* Ltd
1 London Bridge Street
London SE1 9GF

www.harpercollins.co.uk

This paperback edition 2018

First published in Great Britain in ebook format by
HarperCollins*Publishers* 2018

Copyright © Maddie Please 2018

Maddie Please asserts the moral right to
be identified as the author of this work

A catalogue record for this book
is available from the British Library

ISBN: 978-0-00-830521-5

This novel is entirely a work of fiction.
The names, characters and incidents portrayed in it are
the work of the author's imagination. Any resemblance to
actual persons, living or dead, events or localities is
entirely coincidental.

Set in Birka by
Palimpsest Book Production Limited, Falkirk, Stirlingshire

Printed and bound by CPI Group (UK) Ltd, Croydon, CR0 4YY

MIX
Paper from
responsible sources
FSC
www.fsc.org   FSC C007454

For Arthur
For Henry
With much love.

Chapter One

Aggravation

Scotch Whisky, Coffee Liqueur, Single Cream, Sugar Syrup

So, it was Friday night. Six-thirty. I'd got in at half past seven that morning and was still working. Everyone else was entitled to a social life, but not me, apparently. India had left at five on the dot as usual, trilling happily about some party she and Jerry had been invited to. Something that necessitated an extended lunch hour so she could get her nails done. Wouldn't that be nice? No such excitement awaited me when I got home.

I started to clear up; Tim was always very good but India thought she had staff. She'd left a half-eaten prawn sandwich on her desk that was curling gently as I swept it into the black bin liner. Mercifully it looked too revolting to eat, otherwise I would probably have been tempted. I had no willpower. As I went round the office, emptying the bins and wiping crumbs off India's desk, I reminded myself of things I had to do.

I was supposed to be losing weight for India's wedding in December.

I was supposed to be organising her hen weekend.

I was supposed to be looking forward to being her brides-maid.

*

Don't get me wrong; usually I loved my job. But I loved it a lot more before my sister started working there.

Dad took over our grandfather's estate agency in 1998 and it was in a glorious old building in the middle of the high street, next door to the baker's, perfect for foot traffic and the odd tourist to wander in and enquire after a little place in the country. Actually, thinking about it, we'd had quite a few of those recently.

In my teens I used to help Dad out in the office at weekends and in the school holidays, learning how to answer the phone (smile, Alexa, smile), draw up floor plans and conduct view-ings. It was in my blood. The thrill of waiting for an offer to be accepted, of being able to look around gorgeous houses I couldn't afford, pointing out exciting things, like underfloor heating, ten-inch attic insulation or garden water features, never left me.

It was almost perfect, if only Dad had stopped harking

back to the glory times of property when you used to be able to buy a flat in London for buttons and sell it for millions a few years later. Even when we were small he would bang on about getting on the property ladder. It wasn't as though he'd done badly in recent years, despite the property crash in 2008, but he was only too keen to tell stories of the good old days. Perhaps it was because I was three years older than India, but I paid attention and found something I really loved doing.

I started working with Dad straight out of school, never considering doing anything else. Pretty soon, Dad was happy to leave me to run the office while he and Mum took more and more holidays.

India floated off to a polytechnic to do media studies. Heaven only knew what she actually did there. Having never been to uni myself, it seemed her three years away were punctuated with rancid arguments with flatmates, complaints about everything and tearful phone calls for money. The vacations were worse. India spent all her time lounging about the house, eating all the biscuits and having long telephone calls with her friends, which seemed to consist of little more than India saying: 'Yes, no, *no*. Did he? What did she say? No! No! *Honestly?*'

India seemed good fun in those days, maybe because she wasn't my responsibility. She knew loads of people, introduced me to her friends and was an unending source of fabulous gossip. I can remember us enjoying girls' nights in, face packs, pizzas, terrible movies and bottles of wine pinched from Dad's collection. We once watched *Mamma Mia!* while necking back some vintage Dom Pérignon champagne. We got a lot of grief for doing that but at least India took the blame.

I had just accustomed myself to perhaps taking over entirely at the office and reorganising it after Dad retired when India finished uni. She'd failed to get a degree of any sort. This was breezily explained as being down to a 'glitch' in the examinations department that would be sorted out 'eventually'.

She somehow managed to get away with things I never would have – from convincing Mum and Dad that her lack of a degree was the fault of the polytechnic, to having men swanning after her despite showing little to no interest in them.

When India was told in no uncertain terms that she had to get a job, she tried with a very ill grace, which would have been hilarious if only I hadn't been forced to pick up the pieces. There was an internship at the local radio station, which failed because India didn't quite believe there was such a time as seven-thirty in the morning, and if there was it had nothing to do with her. Then came the beauty tester position for the local paper, which unfortunately didn't pan out, as the paper wanted more than 'this stuff is crap' or 'this smells like a farmyard' from her.

Much as I enjoyed my sister's company and hearing about her hilarious escapades, my role in her life gradually changed. Except when she needed cheering up with a good bottle of wine when she was down. Or picking up when her car ran out of petrol.

I'd worked for years learning how to be a good estate agent, getting my qualifications, doing a thorough job and making myself indispensable. But India skimmed the surface of life, getting away with everything, so when she arrived at the office with Dad one Monday morning and flopped down at the desk opposite mine asking for coffee, I shouldn't have been surprised.

Dad patted me on the back and said, 'Look after India, will you, Alexa? Show her the ropes, get her some experience. Mum said you'd be okay with it.'

I didn't quite believe it ... but now, now ... well, to say I was irritated didn't do the word justice. Particularly after Laura's party, when India had apparently been cosying up to my boyfriend. I still hadn't forgiven her for that. Or found out exactly what she was up to.

And then it got worse, because not only did India not do any work, refuse to turn up on time, leave early and expect me to sort out all of her mistakes, she also met Jerry, fell in love and got engaged. Suddenly my younger sister, who, irritating though she was, had probably been my closest friend in the last few years, became a complete nightmare.

From the moment India said yes to Jerry, her phone was filled with Pinterest pictures of wedding place settings, colour schemes, bouquets and sparkly shoes. These days India couldn't be in a room for longer than five minutes without saying, *'Of course, when I'm married ...'* And I was struggling to handle being around her when all she talked about was her wedding day, or Jerry, or both.

Because, like the gilded child she'd always been, India was the one with the wedding coming up and the respectable fiancé and the trendy lifestyle in the cool, loft-style apartment near the river. Conversely, my attempts at independence had failed so spectacularly that when my flatmate had an early midlife crisis and decided to go travelling for a year, I couldn't afford to live on my own any longer. I had to move back home to the end of my parents' garden to 'stay' in their granny annexe. It was supposed to be a short-term thing. So far it'd been over six months.

As I dumped the rubbish into the bin I got a text from Mum.

'India wants pale blue for the tablecloths and pink for the bridesmaid's dress. Do you think you could get into a size twelve by December? The one she especially likes is on sale right now but there's limited stock. And the big sizes have sold out.'

The wedding. Again. I didn't bother replying (They'd changed the colour scheme and dress colour at least three times in the last week. Big sizes? Bloody cheek.) and decided to throw the towel in. It was time for a long bath and a big glass of wine. And maybe an hour without being asked about the stupid wedding ... Was that too much to ask?

*

'Do you know we're known as SKI-ers?' Dad said proudly over Sunday lunch that weekend. 'I read about it in *The Oldie*. We are Spending our Kids' Inheritance – get it?'

'Yes, we get it,' India said, opening the drinks cabinet and pulling out a new bottle of Sipsmith gin. 'Can I take this?'

India and Jerry were visiting for Sunday lunch and we had all enjoyed one of my mother's justly famous roast dinners, but I knew it was only a matter of time before India started raiding the fridge. Old habits are hard to break.

Mum sighed. 'Well, yes, India, but why don't you just buy your own gin?'

Good question.

'I keep getting ID'd,' India said with a pout that fooled no one.

'Oh, don't be ridiculous – you're twenty-six,' Mum said, before her butterfly mind darted off to a more enjoyable subject. 'And getting married in four months!'

'Seventeen weeks yesterday,' India said, beaming from ear to ear.

Next they'd be back on the colour scheme and place settings.

India sent a fond smile across to where her fiancé, Jerry, was sitting happily working his way through a slab of brie.

He looked up and winked. 'Well, I for one can't wait!'

'Poor deluded fool,' Dad said, noticing India trying to slip a bottle of Angostura bitters in her bag. 'India, are you going to leave us any alcohol, or are you planning on stealing all of it?'

India went and dropped a kiss on top of his bald head.

'Oh, Daddy, you can always restock in duty free,' she said, 'when you go to Australia.'

'That's not for a while,' he said, taking the Angostura bitters back.

'So how are the August figures looking, Alexa?' Mum said.

Right. That just about summed up my life at the moment.

My younger sister had infuriated me all week with her untidiness, her inability to use spellchecker and her cavalier attitude to the appointment book, and now here she was again, dominating the occasion, raiding the drinks cabinet and probably the freezer. We'd spend the rest of the day discussing her wedding dress fitting, the flowers, the cake, the bloody flower girls; but I got asked about the sales figures for the family business.

I felt a noble pang of self-pity. Mum had to talk to me about something, I suppose, and at the moment it certainly wasn't going to be my boyfriend or dazzling social life. I had neither. I had loads of friends but in the last few years they'd all been getting engaged or married; now they were busy having children.

'Oh, you know, okay,' I said, feeling a little proud despite myself. 'The three properties on the Bainbridge estate have gone and there's an asking price offer in on Walton House.'

'Excellent, well done, it's been a good year despite all the doom-mongers. I was talking to John Thingy at the golf club yesterday. You know, the tall, thin chap from Countryside Property, and he said they're doing awfully well. He was asking after you. Don't you think you could fancy him just a bit?' Mum said airily. 'You don't want to be living at the end of our garden for ever, do you?'

8

I thought of John Foster with his damp hands and the irritating way he wound his legs around like pipe cleaners when he sat down.

'No,' I said, 'I couldn't.'

'Well, it's a shame. India will be off in no time,' she said, 'and then who will introduce you to people?'

I couldn't remember the last time India had introduced me to anyone significant.

'I'm quite able to look after myself, you know,' I said, 'and I don't need to be palmed off on John Foster just to tidy things up.'

'No, I suppose not. What about that nice Ben with the curly hair? You don't think he might do? Oh well.' Evidently the subject had begun to bore her and she waved a hand at my father to attract his attention. 'Do you know, Simon, I think I fancy a cherry brandy with my cheese.'

'They make a liqueur in Australia from liquorice and chocolate,' Dad said as he went to find some clean glasses. 'I was reading about it earlier.'

'Sounds vile,' Mum said. 'We must try it.'

A mobile phone rang somewhere and we all patted our pockets and looked under things on the dining table to find out whose it was.

'Oooh, it's me,' Mum said and prodded at her phone, standing up to take the call and get away from the noise we were all making. 'Really? Really? Well, that's fantastic! When? When? *Really?*'

She wandered off through the patio doors into the garden, still talking, and we went back to the cheeseboard on the table. India wrestled the biscuits away from Jerry and loaded one up with a pyramid of Boursin, which she then pushed on to his nose. Honestly, they were like a couple of babies.

I tutted and rolled my eyes at Dad but he was busy reading the Angostura bitters label and didn't notice.

'There's a flat coming up on the Park you would like,' I said to my father. He might have nearly retired from the estate agency but he still liked to keep a finger on the pulse.

Dad looked blank. 'I'm not thinking of moving. Am I?'

'You could always downsize, have a nice simple place to look after,' I said. 'Less housework for Mum.'

Not that she seemed to do any; the kitchen floor was really sticky. But then who was I to talk? I hadn't looked at a cleaning product since moving into the garden flat.

Down the other end of the long table, India and Jerry were squabbling over the box of chocolates I had brought for my parents as a gift, ripping off the cellophane with glee, India's dark curls slipping out of the messy chignon she had recently adopted and falling over her face. She had some idea that it might be nice for me to do the same thing when she got married, but my hair – while the same colour as hers – was straight as a poker and unlikely to co-operate.

They looked up as Mum came back in from the garden, her face bright with shock.

She took her cherry brandy and downed it in one.

'You'll never guess,' she said. 'That was someone called Stephen McKenzie about the raffle.'

We all looked at her blankly, waiting for more details. On these occasions Mum was inclined to spin things out as long as possible.

I cracked first. 'What raffle?'

'He had some news; I mean some really unbelievable news that I think is going to make life a bit difficult. I'll have to check my dates.'

'God, Manda, you're not pregnant, are you?' Dad said, a hazelnut whirl halfway to his mouth.

India pulled a face at me across the table.

'Don't be ridiculous, Simon. I mean our holiday dates,' Mum said. 'I'll get my diary.'

Dad grabbed her arm. 'Later. Tell me what's going on first.'

'Well, do you remember the golf club dinner we went to in January? The Founders Day Dinner Dance and Fundraising Extravaganza? Bel Goodwin was doing the tombola and you won a bottle of Liebfraumilch?'

'It was corked,' Dad said.

'Yes, but do you remember Jeff Bosbury-Wallace was selling raffle tickets in aid of Cancer Research? It was a nationwide thing, not just for the golf club. Ten quid each or a book of ten for a hundred?'

'No,' Dad said, pulling the chocolates towards him as his attention waned. 'I don't remember and I hate to break it to you but that's still ten quid each, by the way.'

'Well, I bought a book.'

'What? A hundred quid! You spent a hundred quid on raffle tickets? It's not as though that club fundraiser doesn't cost me an arm and a leg already! Jeff Bosbury-Wallace is a bloody bandit! They should have given them to us for nothing.'

'Have you won something?' Jerry said, being the perfect potential son-in-law and breaking the tension.

'I have!' Mum said triumphantly, sitting back in her chair and sending him a fond look.

Behind her I saw India wander up to the wine cabinet and pick out a couple of bottles. Things like this had started to annoy me over the last few months. I mean, why did she still have to behave like a pigging student? Jerry earned a packet and Dad paid India almost as much as I got. Which was so grossly unfair it was almost litigious.

'So? Well? Are you going to tell us? For God's sake, please tell me it's not more disgusting wine?' Dad said.

'It's not!' Mum said.

We sat in confused silence for a moment until Dad gave her a wide-eyed look.

'So? For the love of God, what?'

'A holiday!' Mum said. 'We've won a holiday.'

'Have we? How marvellous!'

'The first prize was a trip to see Santa in Finland with up to four children. Thank God we didn't win that. Second prize was probably a trip to see Santa in Finland with eight children. Now I'll go and find my diary.'

I think India and I drifted off at this point; our parents went on holiday so frequently that it was no longer of any interest to us. We had even been named for holidays they had particularly enjoyed in their youth: Alexandria and India. They were due to take a month-long trip to Australia soon to visit relatives who lived on the east coast in a place that sounded like Boomerang. Mum had shown us pictures of her cousin and his family, red-faced and cheerful, having a barbeque on the beach and probably in imminent danger of skin cancer.

India came out of the kitchen with a supermarket carrier bag filled with swag. Bloody hell, the place would be stripped bare by the time they left! She did this every time.

'Hey you, that's a 10p Bag for Life, I'll have you know,' Dad said, outraged, not apparently noticing the bacon, tins of baked beans and the dozen eggs.

Mum came back, riffling through the pages of her diary and frowning.

'I thought so,' she said. 'Houston, we have a problem.'

'What?'

'Well, we can't go. We'll be in Australia.'

'When we're married, Jerry and I are going to go to Australia,' India said, never one to miss an opportunity. 'We might go for our first anniversary.'

Dad ignored her. 'Well, can't we swap the dates of the prize holiday?'

'No, it's September 23rd or not at all. Non-transferable, that's what it says.'

'Well, how unreasonable – that's no time at all. Surely we could go a week or so later?'

Mum looked at him over the top of her glasses. 'I know you're a persuasive character, Simon, but I don't think you could persuade the ship to wait for us.'

His face fell. 'Ship? Oh, don't tell me I'm going to miss out on a cruise!'

Dad loved cruising even more than Mum did. They'd been on over thirty.

By now India had collected up an unopened pack of paper napkins, some dishwasher tablets and a new bottle of loo cleaner. If this carried on they'd have to borrow Dad's trailer so they could get all the stuff back to their flat. And it wasn't as though they didn't already have their own Toilet Duck. It was just an ingrained habit with her.

Mum and Dad huffed and argued over the prize holiday dates, and Dad was seriously trying to work out if it would be possible to catch up with the ship halfway through their Australia trip until Mum described the sort of jet lag and expense he would be incurring and he thought again.

I went upstairs to see if there was any shampoo I could take down the garden to my place before India nabbed it. I justified this by telling myself I'd been too busy with showings and keeping the family business in the black to make it to the shops. I could hear my parents still rabbiting on, trying to work out a way for them to take two holidays at the same time, a logistical challenge unheard of even for them. I came back down with some of my mother's overpriced conditioner and a couple of loo rolls. Through the open front door I could see India loading up the boot of Jerry's car with some barbeque charcoal and a box of firelighters. They have a barbeque on their cool roof terrace. Of course they do.

In the dining room Mum was pushing down the cafetière plunger and looking pensive.

'I suppose someone could go,' she said.

'What? You mean I go to Australia and you go on the cruise?' Dad said. 'Well, it's a thought.'

'No, you twit, I mean if *we* can't go ...' She paused and raised her eyebrows meaningfully.

'Oh, I see. Well, yes, I suppose so. We might be able to keep some food in the house for longer than a week too.'

'Simon, come into the garden for a moment,' she said. 'Bring your coffee.'

I had another chocolate and looked at my watch; it was half past four and Jerry and India would be leaving soon, God willing. I watched my sister and her fiancé trying to guess the flavours of the chocolates with their eyes closed and making the other one promise not to trick them with the coffee one.

Jerry would drive them home in his groovy car, to their hip, blonde-wood apartment, and unload their ill-gotten gains before India went to have a long soak in the bath, surrounded by Diptyque candles, and he spent the evening playing on his Xbox. You wouldn't think a hotshot barrister would waste his time doing that, would you? Not that Jerry looked like a hotshot barrister; he was tall, thin and pale, with leather elbow patches on his tweed jacket. I wondered what India could possibly see in him at first, but I had to admit he was extremely funny, very successful, and besotted with her in a way that resulted in extravagant presents and compliments. Who wouldn't like that?

When they got engaged last year they'd started out wanting a small, cute wedding with a few friends and family. Now it had grown into something Prince Harry might have envied, in a country house hotel with a complete year's flower produce from The Netherlands, gauze bags of almonds and embossed scrolls. God knew what it was costing.

I hadn't a clue what I was going to do for the hen weekend. India wouldn't co-operate and I was sick of thinking about it. I was a bit off that sort of thing at the moment anyway, thanks to Ryan. Bouquets for the mothers, the honeymoon wardrobe, four or five tiers for the cake? Not to mention the three flower girls I was supposed to keep under control while necking back as much champagne as possible. And before you ask, no, I wasn't planning to cop off with the best man. The best man was Jerry's cousin Mark, who was delightful, gay, and would probably have done a better job of styling the event than any wedding planner ever could.

'So that's settled then,' Mum said.

We all looked up as they came back in from the garden and India took the opportunity to wedge a chocolate into

Jerry's mouth. He spluttered in disgust and spat it into a paper napkin with a plaintive cry of 'Bunny, you *promised*!'

Bunny?

'What's settled?'

Mum sat down and tapped on her coffee cup with a spoon.

'Dad and I have come up with a solution to this holiday problem. We're going to let you go instead.'

Mum sat back beaming, waiting for our reaction.

'Jerry and me? To Australia?' India said, her eyes widening with excitement.

Over my dead body.

'No, the other one,' Dad said.

'Well, I'm not going to Australia with Jerry,' I said.

Mum tutted. 'You girls can be dense sometimes. You and India can go on the cruise.'

I had a moment's wild excitement at the prospect of a break from what I had been doing for the last few months: sulking in the granny annexe at the end of my parents' garden after that nightmare weekend when my boyfriend, Ryan, and I had broken up and my flatmate, Karen, decided it was the perfect time to go off and find herself in Sri Lanka.

But then work had been so busy recently and showed no signs of easing up, what with showing builders round dilapidated renovation projects or cajoling fussy metropolitan couples who, without exception, thought they wanted country kitchens, wood burners and gardens big enough to keep chickens. They didn't. I mean, have you smelled a chicken house?

I hadn't had a holiday for ages. You honestly couldn't count that trip to Paris last year, when it rained every day and Ryan and I spent the whole time arguing about where to go. Recently I'd been spending most of my time at the office, so this could be the perfect chance for a break, sunshine and perhaps a few cocktails.

This idea was then replaced by the mental image of a boat filled with elderly people, shuffling around a wave-lashed deck on their Zimmer frames.

And finally I registered the utter horror that would be going on holiday with my sister.

Since the engagement we hadn't been particularly good friends, despite what India thought – she seemed pretty oblivious to everything these days. I suppose somewhere deep down I still had affection for her, but nothing I could dredge up on a day-to-day basis.

India looked at Jerry and then at me. From her expression she seemed to be thinking much the same.

'You'll love it. And who knows, Alexa might find herself a nice chap to bring to the wedding. You can treat it as your hen weekend, although it's longer than a weekend, obviously. A hen holiday,' Mum announced proudly, seeming to think it was all settled. She'd been doing this a lot recently – every time she heard us squabbling she would produce a plan to reconcile us and consider it a job well done. Not this time ... I wasn't five any more.

'How long?'

'Twelve days.'

'What! We can't both take twelve days off!' I said.

India's gaze flicked hopefully between Dad and me. 'Can't we?'

Considering it was only August and India had already taken two days out of next year's holiday allowance, I thought it was pretty unlikely.

But Dad had it all worked out. 'I'll get Charlie Smith-Rivers from the Exeter office to pop in.'

'But twelve days?' I said, thinking how much I hated Charlie Smith-Rivers, who always swanned around pretending he knew more than everyone else in the room. And nothing was ever in the right place when he left.

Twelve consecutive days with India. I hadn't spent much time with her outside of work for ages and I was barely managing to get through this lunch as it was.

'Well, that's how long the cruise is.'

'Where are we going?' India said.

'You fly in to New York. Then board the *Reine de France*, sail up the East Coast to Halifax and then back to Southampton across the Atlantic.' Mum read out the itinerary from her phone.

'Wow,' India breathed, her blue eyes wide.

The mental image of the elderly Zimmer walkers faded and was replaced by one of glamorous, fur-swathed Hollywood stars, politicians and Princess Margaret complete with cigarette holder. It was quite possible, too, that Noël Coward would be playing the piano in one of the cocktail lounges. I didn't know why but I seemed to have slipped back several decades.

'That's really generous,' I said, trying to concentrate on something other than absolute panic at being on board a ship, in the middle of the ocean, with my sister. Think of the shoes, I told myself, the evening dresses (I'd have to buy some new ones), gala dinners and sparkly things. Really, given the chance, I could be pathetically shallow.

India leapt up and wrapped her arms around Mum's shoulders.

'Mum, can I borrow your turquoise evening bag, the one with the beads?' she wheedled.

You see? She was no better. I was about to ask the same thing. Perhaps we still had something in common after all?

Chapter Two

The Wet Spot

Dry Gin, Apricot Brandy, Elderflower Liqueur,
Apple Juice, Lemon Juice

Dad took us to Heathrow very early on September 23rd. By then I had parked all my reservations and prejudices about joining a boat full of old crocks with my wedding-obsessed sister, especially after Mum gave me a pretty stern talking-to about being the bigger person, making allowances, blah blah blah. Yes, Mum, okay. So I did my best to think positively. I was firing on all cylinders and ready to go. I mean, if nothing else, we were going to spend a few hours in an airport lounge, complete with free champagne and magazines, before flying to New York. As far as holidays went, this was a result.

After a tearful farewell dinner with Jerry the previous night, India, burdened with a hangover, had spent most of the car journey convincing herself our flight would crash into the Queen Mother Reservoir shortly after take-off, or – failing that – into the Atlantic, where our remains would never be discovered. She'd always been a bit dramatic when it came to air travel. No idea where she got it from, what with our parents spending more time in the air than on the ground these days.

Dad eventually reassured her by promising that if anything happened he and Mum would throw a wreath over the probable crash site and give Jerry the insurance money. There had then been a mild argument about whether Jerry should get my insurance payout too. Once we had agreed Mum and Dad would get my bit and put it towards a world cruise, India calmed down and got into the spirit of things, which was good as we were just coming up to departures and I couldn't wait to get out of the car. Surprisingly, the subject of the wedding hadn't come up once so far. I was just hoping it would stay that way ...

Dad hated lengthy farewells at airports because they tended to make him sentimental, or maybe just jealous? I couldn't think why because, in two days' time, he was due to get on board a massive Emirates plane to fly first class to Australia. Anyway, we pulled up at the doors of Terminal 5 in good time and he practically chucked us out of the car, slinging our luggage on to a trolley before driving off with a jolly wave through the sunroof.

India and I stared at each other for a moment, unused to being left alone together and, to be honest, rather uncomfortable.

'Let's drop our bags and check in first and then head to the lounge?' I said, not sure I sounded as excited as I should have, but determined to make an effort.

India nodded and we went to get rid of our bags. Heathrow was always busy at this time of year, everyone jetting off for last-minute sunshine, so we had to weave around a lot of luggage racks and pushchairs parked in awkward spots, not to mention massive suitcases wrapped in clingfilm. Then India spotted two very elegant representatives from the *Voyage Premiere* cruise line waiting behind a help desk and we dragged our cases gratefully over.

They were glamour personified with those slight French accents that always make people sound sexy and interesting, even if they are discussing the Guatemalan economy or washing-up liquid. In short, tight red suits and dinky little hats like saucers, all set off with silk scarves with nautical flags sprinkled all over them and tied in that careless, impossibly chic, way French women probably learn at primary school.

'Welcome, Miss Fisher and Miss Fisher. Hmm, India and Alexandria; beautiful names. We are delighted to welcome you on the first stage of your exciting journey.'

I watched her fabulously manicured nails typing our details into her computer and waited, as I always did, for her to frown and say I couldn't go because my passport photograph wasn't attractive enough or something. However, all that happened was that she produced some glorious red stickers for our cases marked *Voyage Premiere*. And then she directed us to our private lounge where, as we had hoped, there was free champagne and comfortable chairs where India could nurse her hangover, flick through *Vogue* and text Jerry, and I could watch planes taking off and not crashing at all.

India had already been on a strenuous diet and exercise regime since setting the wedding date and I had fully intended to do the same thing, but it hadn't quite worked out. But I *had* been on a diet and exercise regime for the last three days, which I thought was better than nothing. Although there hadn't actually been much exercise, if I was honest, other than lugging my cases on and off the bed and repacking them. And not much diet either, other than not having some toast and marmalade yesterday morning because I was too excited. Oh well, we couldn't all be a size ten like India, could we?

I had looked at the *Voyage Premiere* website on several occasions, of course, so I knew what to expect. The photographs of our ship, the *Reine de France*, showed a selection of exceptionally elegant couples with marvellous teeth who were always laughing and happy, whether they were tasting wine, eating exquisitely fine-tuned canapés in front of a perfect sunset or relaxing in the Jacuzzi while drinking cocktails. Was that even allowed? Alcohol in a Jacuzzi? Perhaps the clientele of the *Reine de France* were so classy and sophisticated that they didn't get drunk and force each other's heads underwater as most of the people I knew would have done.

In the private lounge we looked around, wondering which

of the other people were going to be on the ship with us. None seemed quite glossy or elegant enough to fit in on board, but then, as India pointed out, in our jeans and T-shirts, neither did we.

'That man over there,' she hissed. 'He looks the sort.'

The man in question was tall, quite good-looking and had a swoop of grey hair that made him look rather distinguished. He was with a two-dimensional woman in black who looked far too bad-tempered for the *Reine de France*. I couldn't imagine her frolicking in a Jacuzzi with a Gin Sling.

Then there were a couple of exotic-looking women who were rocking the big eyebrows, white trousers and perma-tan look. They seemed to have cornered the market in gold jewellery and had six unruly children with them who had taken full advantage of the free refreshments and were busy building a tower with their empty cola bottles. Would they be taking six children on a cruise? Wouldn't they prefer a fortnight on a beach? Or was I being mean?

Anyway, shortly after that one of the women noticed that the flight to Miami was boarding and they began rounding up the children and their numerous backpacks with a great deal of arguing and a couple of well-placed slaps. I guessed they were off to Disneyland and I was glad for them. Twelve days on a cruise ship with a load of old couples on Prozac and intravenous alcohol was no place for a kid in my opinion.

I commandeered their empty table, which overlooked the departure runway. India went to get us some champagne while

I logged into my laptop and surreptitiously looked around to see if I could spot any more potential travellers heading for a cruise. An exceptionally nice-looking man was sitting on his own at the table next to us, typing rapidly into a laptop and occasionally staring vacantly into space. He was wearing a black polo shirt and chinos. Could he be coming on the ship with us? Did he have a thin, pretty wife with him who was perhaps having a manicure somewhere in one of the side rooms? Or maybe his girlfriend was running wild in duty free, buying some last-minute handbags and gold-tipped cruise wear?

Unexpectedly he looked up and caught my eye and I gave one of those eyebrow-raised, tight-lipped smiles you do when you have nothing sensible to say but don't want to appear unfriendly. Instead I think I probably seemed a bit of a prat and he frowned and looked away. Oh well.

Luckily, at that moment India came back with some bubbly and a bowl of pretzels.

'Well, here's to it!' she said and we clinked glasses.

Fabulous. There's nothing quite like chilled champagne at ten-thirty in the morning.

'I hope Jerry's all right,' she said after a few minutes, the corners of her mouth turning down. 'We've never been apart this long before.'

Any minute now we would be on to the wedding and things had been going so well. For the first time in ages it seemed we'd been getting along – perhaps it was the holiday spirit? Or maybe it was the champagne?

'Of course he is,' I said, trying to damp down my exasperation and empathise with how India felt. That's what Mum said – try and see it from your sister's perspective. 'He'll either be in work, being clever and demolishing someone's alibi, or he'll be smashing up concrete bunkers and shooting aliens on his Xbox. It will make him realise how much he depends on you. Absence makes the heart grow fonder, you know.'

'Out of sight, out of mind,' India said gloomily, 'and there's loads of stuff to do for the wedding. D'you know ...'

I interrupted her before we could get on to the table settings, Dad's speech or the flower girls' shoes.

'Too late now, we're here. Buck up, we have pretzels ...' I picked up the bowl in one hand. 'We have champagne!' I waved my glass in the air with the other.

Unfortunately, at that moment, one of the rowdy children came back and crashed into the back of my chair before scrabbling about under the table for some random plastic animal she had left there. My champagne flew out in a graceful parabola and dowsed the man sitting at the next table.

'Oh God, I'm so sorry,' I gasped.

Grabbing a handful of paper napkins I began dabbing at him, but of course they aren't much use for anything except wrapping cutlery, and trying to rub the back of someone's shirt is definitely invading their personal space with knobs on. He did smell rather gorgeous though, some woody-green sort of aftershave. Not that it mattered. I wasn't looking for another man in my life – I'd only just got over the last one.

'It's fine, perfectly fine,' he said in a tone of voice that said the exact opposite. He had unusual grey eyes and at that moment they were fixed on me; very cold and unfriendly. Like ice chips. His voice was deep and attractive with a very slight American twang. I felt quite fluttery and flustered for a moment and stood on one leg looking stupid while he shook some of my pretzels off his laptop, which mercifully appeared undamaged.

'I'm awfully sorry,' I said. 'I was just ...'

I waved my glass in an explanatory way and he flinched.

'It's okay, it's empty.'

'I know,' he said coldly, 'but don't do it again, will you? Should I move perhaps?'

'No, of course not. I will. Sorry.'

I crept back to my seat and ducked my head into my shoulders.

'You idiot! What did he say?' India hissed, pulling me down into my chair.

'Nothing much.'

'He must have said something.'

'He said *you are so much prettier than your sister* and then he asked for my mobile number.'

'I bet he didn't. Did he?' India could be very gullible sometimes.

'No, India. He told me to go away and stop being a nuisance.'

'Hmmm. Well, do you want to go and get some more champagne? Seeing as you chucked your last one over him.'

28

'I didn't chuck it over him; it was an accident,' I whispered urgently, feeling my face flushing with embarrassment.

'Well, you could have chatted him up. He's quite nice-looking.' India twirled her hair round her fingers and looked at him from under her lashes.

I nudged her, stifling a giggle. 'For heaven's sake, India, stop it. You're on your hen holiday and you're flirting with strangers? Really?'

'I wasn't flirting, I was just looking. Watch and learn.'

This was so typical of my sister; she couldn't pass up any opportunity. She'd even been known to flirt with Tim in work and I was pretty sure she scared him to death. He had to have the day off after the last works Christmas party.

'Look, let's swap seats? I'd feel better and I'm sure he would too.'

I went to get some refills and some more pretzels and moved into her chair. I was aware Mr Grumpy was still typing at high speed into his laptop but also watching me out of the corner of his eye. That's quite a skill too, isn't it? Perhaps he was a spy?

After a few minutes Mr Grumpy stood up and packed his laptop away, pulling his damp shirt away from his back and sending me another look.

He called a waitress over.

'Is there somewhere I can get a shower?' he said. 'I need to change my shirt.'

The waitress fluttered a bit and took him away and I tried

to put the image of him doing the aforementioned activities out of my mind. I was thinking he'd look rather marvellous though. Sort of big and rather chunky and ... Oh, shut up, Alexa.

Still, I watched him go with a tinge of sadness. He walked with long strides but an unhurried grace and was the best-looking man to notice me in a very long time. Actually he was the *first* man to notice me for a very long time. It was just a shame it was for the wrong reasons. Though there was still no sign of the wife/girlfriend/significant other, so things could be looking up.

I wondered where he was going. He had missed the flight to Miami by now and also flights to Dubai, Rome, Sydney and loads of other places. I knew this because I had a special app on my laptop. I liked to fantasise about where I would go on holiday ... if I ever had time to go on holiday, which I hadn't for the last four years. As I've said, a weekend in Paris in November in the rain does not count as a proper holiday.

Perhaps he was a businessman travelling alone to some vital financial conference where he would address the World Bank about foreign aid? Or perhaps he was going to present a proposal to a board of shifty-looking venture capitalists for some huge office tower block in downtown Manhattan? Either way he was gone.

India wandered about looking out of the windows and fidgeting while I sat eating pretzels and sipping champagne.

I tried to relax and look cool and not like someone who was in the habit of slinging drinks around.

'Can we go to duty free now?' she said at last. 'It's still over an hour till our flight. I want to find a lipstick to wear at the wedding.'

I resisted the temptation to groan and we gathered up our bags and made our way into consumer paradise, avoiding the huge bears, remote-control helicopters and iPad covers, and heading straight for the make-up. I didn't really mind although I wouldn't have admitted it to my sister. To be honest I'm especially keen on those dinky little palettes of eyeshadows and blushers with the tag 'Airport Exclusive'. There's just something about 'travel-size' products I can't get enough of. Within seconds India found a male assistant to help her. I was just having an enjoyable few minutes playing with a battery-operated pig when she found me.

'Don't wander off like that,' she said furiously. 'You're supposed to be looking after me. Mum said.'

I gritted my teeth. The phrase 'Mum said' had haunted me down the years for as long as I could remember. It didn't hold the same power now though; after all, India was twenty-six and more than capable of looking after herself.

Luckily we heard our flight being called and scurried off to the right gate, oohing and aahing as we saw the bulk of our plane just outside the window. We were on our way.

*

We found our seats, had a slight argument about who would sit next to the window (India won; as she kept reminding me, this was 'her' holiday after all); we pressed all the buttons on the entertainment system; we read the menu card. The plane took off without crashing into the Queen Mother Reservoir so we drank gin to celebrate. Then we had dinner and some wine. Then India started moaning about how much she was missing Jerry so I stuck my earphones in and watched a film about a detective who would have got the case solved far quicker if he had stopped smoking quite so much. When it was obvious I wasn't going to agree how marvellous Jerry was or discuss the colour of the sugared almonds, India curled up on her seat like a cat and had a nap.

I had another little gin and flicked over to the screen showing us where we were. That was a bit unnerving as we were south of Greenland, about as far from land as we could be. I took my mind off it by watching a film about a man rescuing his wife from some unnamed organisation. It involved a lot of explosions and dangling off collapsing bridges; I love that sort of thing. He must have had the upper body strength of Superman and the wife did the whole thing in stilettos and never once smudged her lipstick. Then India woke up and we had some odd cakes and an even odder cup of tea, and then we were descending through the cloudbank to JFK Airport.

I leaned across my sister to look out of the window, hoping for some of those interesting little glimpses into people's back-yards you get when you're coming in to land. There were crowded twelve-lane highways and massive houses and the occasional swimming pool and then car parks and industrial yards full of trucks. I tightened my seatbelt and clung on to the seat arms as if trying to keep the plane in the air for a few more seconds, but suddenly there was a runway and we were down with that terrible back thrust of the engines that makes you think the wings are going to fall off. When we landed I realised I hadn't thought once about work or what Charlie was doing with my in-tray or whether the Masons would complete on Stafford House. This had to be a record. I should have timed it.

The woman in front of us was disobeying the keep seatbelts fastened sign and was already scrabbling in the overhead locker for her hand luggage. Not that it would get her off the plane any quicker, just earn her a dirty look from the flight attendant on the way out.

Chapter Three

Vacation Cocktail

Vanilla Vodka, Coconut Liqueur, Lime and Pineapple Juice,
Egg White, Blue Curacao

Until you stand next to a transatlantic liner the size of
the *Reine de France* you can't imagine how huge they
are. It was sensational to see it coming into view as our transfer
bus pulled up to the quayside. A sleek black hull reared up
out of the oily waters of the dock. There were hundreds of
exciting-looking windows above us and people leaning over
balconies to wave to their friends.

It turned out several people on the plane were going to
be on the trip with us and none of them looked old or infirm
or miserable. They seemed to be just as thrilled as we were
to be joining a liner to sail up the coast and across the
Atlantic.

There had been a bit of a discussion on the transfer bus

as to whether we were allowed to bring our own alcohol on with us. Some said no, others waved innocent-looking water bottles and raised their eyebrows in a knowing way. I guessed it was gin or vodka. Someone else said they knew someone who had been chucked off a cruise for trying to sneak a case of wine on board and we wondered how that might be possible. I mean, you couldn't exactly disguise a case of wine or slip it in under a blanket, could you?

This? Oh, this? Oh, it's just my sewing machine/medicine/art materials.

We negotiated the snaking queues in a hangar-like building where bored-looking women checked our passports and asked if we had any firearms, animals or drugs. Happily we didn't.

On board there were waiters who greeted us with trays of cocktails, which is the way every holiday should start. I took an orange one. India worried for a bit about calories and then gave in and had a pink one. The crowd swept us up to the reception desk where we queued to collect our cabin keys. When it got to our turn, another excessively chic young woman – name badge Marie-France – frowned over her computer screen and did a great deal of frantic typing.

Right, *this* is where we get chucked off, I thought; ever the pessimist. This was the point where she would discover I had an unpaid parking ticket I'd forgotten about or that someone had stolen my identity and opened up an online shop selling explosives and cocaine.

At last Marie-France looked up and smiled.

'So sorry to keep you, Miss Fisher and Miss Fisher. You were booked into cabin 840. A twin with a window? Hmmmm.'

She typed some more and then turned away and picked up a phone. She rattled some French off at high speed and did some Gallic pouting and shrugging.

'They're not going to let us on,' I whispered.

'Shut up! For God's sake, don't start,' India hissed back. 'Honestly, Alexa, we have this every bloody time. You can barely get on a bus into town without assuming you're going to be chucked off. It's just a bit of admin. If there's any problem we'll just wing it.'

India might be scattier than I am but she can be far more assertive in certain situations. Winging it is not something I'm good at. Fixing Marie-France with a steely glare, India began tapping her fingernails on the desk in front of her. Then she began shifting her weight from one foot to the other in a *don't mess with me* sort of way. Marie-France began muttering in French into the phone again.

At last she put the phone down.

'So many apologies. Your cabin is unavailable.'

'See, there you are, I told you,' I said, bending to pick up my bag.

I could imagine myself slinking away down the gangplank and trying to get back to JFK in the rain, a tragic figure with my dark hair in rats' tails around my face; although the

September sun was still streaming in through the portholes so perhaps I was being overly dramatic on this occasion.

'There has been – 'ow you say – spillage and the cabin must be redecorated –'

Redecorated? And *spillage*? What sort of spillage? A dropped breakfast tray? A carelessly thrown bucket of creosote? Blood splattered up the walls?

'– and so we 'ave moved you with apologies for the inconvenience and our compliments. Cabin 1137. Your suitcases have been taken there. We wish you a pleasant voyage.'

Marie-France gave us a charming smile and handed over two keys. I took one before she could change her mind and ran for the lifts, grabbing another cocktail on the way for good measure. A blue one this time.

Cabin 1137 was not so much a cabin as a little suite, with two double beds, a bath and shower room and a small sitting area. Plus a balcony! Be still my beating heart. It was beautifully decorated in shades of blue and pale green with a load of pillows and the option for more if we weren't satisfied as there was an extensive pillow menu. A card placed on the dressing table next to a small basket of fruit advised us our steward would be Amil and he would attend to all our needs. All of them? Really? Poor bloke.

We scurried around, opening all the doors and drawers and investigating the free toiletries in the bathroom, and then we discovered the bottle of champagne in the ice bucket with a note: *Compliments de la Reine de France*. We had that opened in no time flat and were clinking glasses yet again. How had I resisted the siren call of the sea and cruising this long? This was marvellous!

'Let's go out on the balcony,' India said, 'and watch the other people coming on board.'

'Good idea!'

Outside the afternoon was glorious with a dazzling blue autumn sky. Above us planes were still criss-crossing the sky with vapour trails; helicopters were buzzing around.

Many floors below us on the dockside, yellow taxis were hooting their horns at each other and the coaches that were still disgorging people and huge piles of luggage on to the road. A policeman was trying to move vehicles on and we could hear him blowing his whistle and bellowing from our vantage point above him. It was all terrifically exciting. I wished I had some of those paper streamers that people used to throw off the side of departing ships, but I expect these days I would be prosecuted for littering.

India went back inside to scan through the ship's newsletter so we could decide what to do with the rest of the day. I stayed where I was, leaning over the rail and sipping champagne and feeling rather glamorous and sophisticated. I heard next-door's balcony door slide open and someone came out. There was a sort of half-barrier between our balconies but if they leaned on the rail like I was, they'd be able to say hello.

I arranged my face into a pleasant, welcoming expression, ready to be charming. And then I froze.

It was him.

The man from the airport with the grey eyes and pretzels all over his laptop. The one I had chucked champagne over. No! Surely not? It couldn't possibly be! Oh, God.

Perhaps he wouldn't recognise me?

He turned towards me before I could duck out of the way and for a moment I tried to look like someone different, though how I thought that would work I have no idea.

'Oh, hello,' he said, 'you again.'

I gave a sort of comic twitch of my head.

'Me again!' I agreed. I held out my champagne glass a little. 'Holding on tight here.'

'Good,' he said, and then he looked at me for a few moments and went back into his cabin.

Oh, bollocks.

I went back in to find India; she was sitting on the sofa with her feet up on the coffee table, looking at the newsletter and swilling back the champagne like there was no tomorrow.

'Oh, look, someone's just put a note under our door,' she said.

'It's probably our next-door neighbour complaining,' I said and briefly explained the situation.

I went to open the envelope expecting a terse written warning.

'Oooh, marvellous! It's an invitation to the Captain's

cocktail party – seven-thirty p.m. in The Lookout Bar!' My spirits lifted.

'Excellent. Here, have some more champagne to celebrate!' India said, tilting the bottle.

At this rate we were going to sail up and down the East Coast of America on a sea of alcohol, completely plastered.

We unpacked, finished off the bubbly and went off to explore.

There must have been a couple of thousand people on board by now but the corridors stretched ahead of us, almost completely empty. And it was so quiet. Where had everyone gone?

We soon found out. They were at a *Farewell to New York* gathering around the pool on Deck 7. And, yes, there was alcohol involved yet again. I was beginning to wonder if my liver would last out the trip. Perhaps I would go a bit steady and just have some – oooh, Margaritas! I loved those. And Long Island Iced Tea! And some more of the blue stuff! Well, perhaps it would be sensible to eat something too. After all, what time was it, actually? Local time was about five-thirty but in my head it was midnight and it had been a very long day.

We took a plate each and loaded up with canapés that were miniature works of art. Blinis and stuffed sweet peppers and tomatoes, and a very sophisticated selection of vol au vents and tiny pizzas. Never mind the intensive diet and exercise regime. Never mind the hangovers heading our way. Twelve days of eating like this and we were going to have to be rolled off the ship. And the importance of India's wedding dress still fitting her in December wasn't something we should forget. I could just imagine us inserting panels into the sides like Dad said he'd once had done with some 1970s flares.

We said *Farewell to New York* for about half an hour and then decided to go back to our cabin for a breather. That's the thing Mum always said about cruises: there's never a moment to yourself; there's always another party or another show or some interesting classes to hurry off to. I could only assume the travellers on the decks furthest away from the action were going to wear running shoes for the whole voyage.

We went back to our cabin via the shops, where there was a cluster of large American ladies around a special 'Farewell *to New York*' offer on white cardigans with gold anchor buttons and matching white trousers. Much taken with this look, India pushed to the front and hunted around until she found some jaunty white caps with faux braid across the front to complete them. She tried without success to persuade me I should try on the whole ensemble. She was convinced I would have looked amazing. Yes, in a horrific, *Carry On, Captain* sort of way.

'Oh my God; your bridesmaid's outfit,' India breathed. 'How about that for an idea? It would be so incredible! Really retro and different. I can just see it now. And the flower girls dressed in sailor suits.'

Perhaps she had enjoyed one too many Margaritas? I

certainly had. I hurried her away, got her into our cabin and locked the door to stop her escaping.

*

We had a nice sleep for an hour and then, like the Duracell bunny, India was ready to go again. She sat bolt upright in bed, her hair all over her face, and shouted at me. India has never been a morning person, but she doesn't like missing anything in the evenings. I, on the other hand, could give or take a late night ... unless of course it involved pizza, ice cream and Prosecco in front of Netflix.

'Come on! The ship is moving! We'll be going under the Verrazano-Narrows Bridge! We're missing everything! It's seven o'clock and the Captain's cocktail party is in half an hour!'

'Actually it's about two in the morning,' I said blearily, burying my face in my pillow. 'Do we really need another party?'

'Wash your mouth out. Come on, let's get tarted up. There might be some nice men on board –'

'India! You're engaged! You're getting married in a few months!'

'For you. Let me finish, will you! What do you take me for? There might be some nice men on board *for you*. I'm only trying to help!' she said over her shoulder as she riffled through her luggage looking for the perfect outfit.

'I don't want a nice man,' I grumbled, swinging my legs on to the floor. 'I've only just got those CDs back from Ryan.

And yes, I know it's been months, but I'm not in any rush.'

I didn't really want more cocktails either, to be honest. If anything, I wanted a nice cup of tea and a chocolate digestive.

'Well, just a man then,' India said. 'Mum said you weren't to come back without one.'

'What, like a sensible coat for school or a puppy or something?'

India rolled her eyes. 'You can be so boring these days. Come on, get a move on.'

The Captain's cocktail party was in full swing by the time we got there. There was even a bloke in a white tuxedo playing the piano and grinning and nodding at us like Liberace as we came in.

We shook hands with the Captain, who was an imposing old salt with beetle brows and a weather-beaten complexion that spoke of many years before the mast. Then I had some more blue stuff and India chose a gin and tonic that she said could more accurately be called tonic and gin. We soon realised we were part of a select band that had been invited from Decks 11 and 12 only, so we felt rather special and important.

There were several of the bulky American matrons there who were 'golly gosh darned thrilled' to be in close proximity to the Captain and his First Officer, almost as though they were the celebrity remnants of a boy band. They clustered round taking selfies and asking whether he had met any royalty during his time at sea. When he mentioned a Spanish princess and a member of the Swedish aristocracy they looked a little confused and disappointed so he cheered them up by mentioning the Duchess of Devonshire and Princess Michael of Kent and they all started taking selfies again.

Outside the evening was darkening and, in the distance, I could see the lights of Manhattan shimmering and flashing just like every picture you've ever seen of them but more so. It was breathtaking.

'Bloody hell,' India said as we moved to the end of the room, 'look over there! It's her! It can't be!'

I looked to see who she had spotted. A tiny woman in a white sequinned cocktail dress was standing smiling and tossing her abundant red hair about, surrounded by a posse of Japanese ladies who were taking selfies and twittering like a flock of hyperactive starlings. The woman looked familiar, as though we had unexpectedly encountered an old school friend. Who was she?

I looked blank for a moment. Beside me India fidgeted with exasperation at my ignorance.

'It's only Marnie bloody Miller,' she said.

I gasped. 'Marnie Miller? Of course!'

The name was almost as familiar as my own but I couldn't for the moment remember why.

'Marnie frigging Miller!' India said, her voice a deferential whisper.

Then Marnie swished her trademark hair over her shoulder, flashed a dazzling smile and I suddenly remembered. The self-help guru, lifestyle authority, cookery expert, writer and sometime agony aunt? The woman with possibly the most envied lifestyle in the world? *That* Marnie Miller?

I almost wanted to rush over and take a selfie with her too. She was the one celebrity India and I had agreed on. We had devoured her books over the years, watched her on television, tried to make her healthy carob and beetroot brownies, bought her books on Christmas crafts and had even heard her *Desert Island Discs*. I'm not a massive fan of Iron Maiden but if Marnie Miller wanted to take 'Two Minutes to Midnight' with her as one of her eight records, they must have something going for them.

'Bloody hell,' I breathed.

We stood back, watching her signing autographs and posing prettily for her fans. Her impossible to emulate (trust me, we'd tried) red curls were flickering and shining under the lights as only very expensive hair can.

I'd not met many famous people before. Well, I'd seen Alan Titchmarsh when he was doing a programme in Cheltenham about urban trees and I tripped on one of the camera cables and nearly knocked him over. And I saw Helen Mirren riding a bike once. Well, I think it was Helen Mirren.

But to be in the same room as someone as famous as Marnie Miller was a bit different. I just wanted to stand really close and stare at her, which obviously would have been weird and freaky so I didn't.

'I wonder what she's doing here?' I said. 'I mean she wouldn't just be having a holiday, would she?'

'Hardly. She'd be off to Necker Island with Bill Gates and Richard Branson if she wanted a holiday,' India replied, slipping her lip gloss out of her clutch to reapply.

A large American woman in a purple jumpsuit, which had probably seemed like a good idea when she bought it, was also staring at Marnie and had overheard our conversation.

'She's running two courses on the ship,' she said in a loud stage whisper.

'No! What on?' India said, rubbing her little finger over her lower lip, looking perfect once more. 'Whatever it is I'm going to it.'

'I think it's something like Love Your Life,' our new friend said. 'And Your Story. Isn't she wonderful? She gives of her time so freely. She does such a lot of charity work too. Orphans and clean water. The last time I saw her on a TV appeal I cried. I could hardly see my credit card through the tears.'

Down at the end of the room, Marnie Miller gave a merry laugh and hugged one woman who promptly started crying. Wow. It was like one of the gods had come down from Olympus.

'Isn't she just gorgeous?' our companion breathed, shaking her head in wonderment. 'So pretty and *so* unaffected. And a figure to die for too. She can't be more than a size four. Just the cutest thing.'

We all turned to stare at her again for a few minutes and then the crowds suddenly parted.

'Come on,' India said, smoothing down her dress. 'Let's go and say hello.'

46

I wasn't too sure I was ready to be so close to Marnie Miller, but India had always been braver than me in these situations. So I shook my hair back in an attempt to look confident and we strolled across the room towards Marnie, who looked at me, a ready smile on her face.

'Oh, hello, ladies,' she said, smiling with lots of teeth that had probably spent a great deal of time in the company of an orthodontist and a veneer specialist. 'How lovely to meet you.'

Yes, it was definitely her: that very faint trace of a Scottish accent that was so attractive; the flawless skin and pocket rocket figure.

'Lovely to meet you,' India said breathily. She beamed a genuine smile at Marnie, definitely more convincing than my wide grin.

Marnie's face lit up. 'Oh, how amazing! You're from England?'

We nodded and smiled modestly as though we had done something clever.

'We've read your books; we really love them,' India said. 'And seen your series on *Finding Love Without Fear*.'

Marnie's face creased into a gentle smile as though this was the most wonderful thing she had ever heard, although I bet every single person before us had said the same thing.

'How kind of you. Thank you. Did you have a particular favourite?'

I thought about it for a moment. There were so many but then most of them seemed to blur into one.

'I really loved *Marnie's Christmas Crafts*,' India said.

We'd spent several hours trying to make reindeers out of pine cones. I don't think the end result was quite as polished as the picture.

Marnie looked thrilled. 'I loved that too! I have a special place in my heart for that book. And you?' She turned her beautiful turquoise eyes on me and my mind went blank.

'There was one about getting a promotion at work, making sure you didn't get passed over for other people. Was it called *Don't Stop Moving*?'

Her smile faltered for a second. 'Maybe you're thinking of *Don't Stop; Keep Moving*. I think "Don't Stop Moving" was S Club 7.'

'That's it,' I said, feeling pretty stupid.

'One of my favourites,' she said with a delightful crinkle of her nose.

'Could we take a picture with you?' India said, after giving me a not-so-subtle sharp look.

'Oh, of course!'

Marnie turned and clicked her fingers and a small, worried-looking woman dressed in rather droopy clothes came and took India's phone to take some pictures of the three of us. Marnie was smiling in an attractive and controlled way that made the most of her perfect, white smile and India and I grinned like maniacs.

'So what are you doing on the ship?' I asked, trying to regain some dignity. 'Someone said they thought you were doing some courses?'

'I am! Do say you can join me? *Spring-Clean Your Life* has helped so many people come to terms with their failures, and I know lots of people would like to write but maybe don't know where to start so I'm doing a little thing called *Write for Love*. Everyone has a story to tell after all. Love, loss, new experiences, disaster, triumph – it's all there.'

Well, yes, I supposed so, although I was still waiting for the triumph bit to be honest. I'd done a bit of the love and loss recently, with Ryan enjoying *new experiences* with a frankly grubby-looking girl from the building society as well as his mother's Avon lady.

Bastard.

Perhaps if I went to *Spring-Clean Your Life* Marnie Miller would help me focus on the positive things in my life and hopefully clear out the negative. The negative list included: my inability to find a decent man; my terrible ex, Ryan, who I'd allowed to come between me and my sister even before we started working together; living in my parents' granny annexe; and my non-existent social life. Maybe I should focus on the positives instead; it might be easier. My job, which I enjoyed, if you didn't count my sister 'not-working' next to me. An amazing cruise, where I should be making the most of my last holiday with my sister before she got married. My parents, who were in excellent health and at that moment probably at Heathrow waiting for their flight to Sydney.

Spring-Clean Your Life: yes, that's exactly what I needed to do.

India and Marnie were still laughing, talking about the books Marnie had written and what she was planning to write next. I couldn't believe how calm India seemed, and I was still feeling a little out of my depth at being so close to someone so famous when Marnie reached out a little hand and patted my arm.

'Oh, do say you'll come along too, Alexa? India says you were quite good at English essay writing at school. Who knows, we could make a bestselling author out of you.'

Was I? That didn't sound like India.

Bestselling author?

I had a vision of myself smiling modestly for the cameras at the Booker Prize awards evening; signing copies of my book in Foyles; travelling first class to Los Angeles and finalising a film deal.

Yes, that would be a triumph, wouldn't it? Something to make Ryan regret his treacherous trousers.

'Brilliant idea,' I said with a smile, imagining Ryan's stunned face. 'Where do I sign?'

Marnie clapped her hands together in delight, as though having India and me at her talks was all she needed to make them a roaring success.

'Then I will look forward to seeing you in the Ocean Theatre on Wednesday at eleven.'

She looked past me and the warmth of her smile faltered a little.

'Ah, there you are, Gabe. I was beginning to worry.'

I turned to see who she was talking to and saw the man from the cabin next door. The victim of my champagne and pretzel accident. He was looking rather gorgeous in black jeans and a soft grey cashmere sweater that matched his wonderful eyes. He gave a rather tight smile and came to stand next to me, hands in his pockets. My entire body seemed to fizz. I swear I had never been more aware of any other human being in my life.

'This is my dear friend Gabriel Frost,' Marnie said, gesturing towards Mr Grumpy.

'We've met,' he said tersely

'Have you? Hmm. Gin and tonic?' Marnie turned and clicked her fingers at her assistant, who was back in her preferred place, standing behind her boss oozing anxiety. The girl leapt to obey and was back in a few seconds with a lovely-looking drink on a tray, which Gabriel took with thanks.

'Gabriel is working very closely with me this trip,' Marnie said, smiling up at him.

I blanched. Was he her significant other?

Had I been fancying Marnie Miller's boyfriend? Life was sometimes monumentally unfair. For example, Marnie Miller had a successful career, looked a trillion dollars, was petite, sweet-natured, had probably never heard the words hangover or cellulite, definitely didn't own a pair of magic knickers, and on top of all that had Gabriel Frost to keep her warm at night.

Bugger. Sod it. Arse. Rats. Bugger.

And other expletive deleteds.

Not that he was *my* type of course. I've never ended up with good-looking, well-dressed, educated men. I've always landed the scruffbag, moody ones who borrow money from me, sulk when they can't watch football on my television and never remember my birthday. I wonder if I've been short-changed?

Chapter Four

Breakfast Martini

Marmalade, Dry Gin, Triple Sec, Lemon Juice

We'd had a better time than I'd expected knocking back cocktails on deck, not arguing once, and for the first time in ages I remembered how much fun India could be. Then we got our second wind and went off to have dinner in the Champs-Elysées restaurant. This was apparently the budget option; the really posh people were in the Louis Quinze on the deck above us. From the pictures in our guide to the ship it looked as though everything up there apart from the food was gilded. Nothing was served without at least one edible flower on it and it wouldn't have been surprising to learn there were people available to cut up your food for you.

We had been assigned a table with two couples, both of them American and neither of them strangers to the art of speed-eating. No sooner had our waiter brought our food than cutlery was flashing at high speed and the wine was flowing like water.

India and I introduced ourselves and found out more about them.

Marty and his wife, Marion, from Washington, DC, were celebrating their twentieth cruise and their fortieth wedding anniversary. The other couple were Marty's brother Ike and his wife, Caron, all the way from Boise – home to hogs and potatoes and not much else, according to Ike.

All of them were cruise veterans and knew exactly what was acceptable and when it was time to complain.

'This is good enough,' Marty said as he hoovered up his chicken main course, 'but I'm not entirely sure about the afternoon choices in the food court. Two cruises ago I was there when they were down to only three ice cream flavours. You have to watch 'em.'

'I will,' I said, horrified at this possible deprivation.

'Your first cruise?' Caron asked.

'It's my hen holiday!' India announced. 'I'm getting married in December.'

'How perfectly lovely,' Marion said, rather misty-eyed. 'And is your sister your matron of honour?'

'Maid of honour,' India said with a smirk. 'She's not married yet.'

'Oh, plenty of time yet,' Caron said. 'I was nearly twenty-seven before I got married.'

I shot India a warning look, daring her not to tell them I

was twenty-nine already. Unusually for her, she kept quiet.

There was a short discussion about the wedding and then Marion changed the subject.

'You have to get to the Ocean Theatre for the evening shows as soon as you finish your coffee. *As soon as.* Don't hesitate. The best seats go very quickly. No time for aperitifs or a stroll round the deck. You have to cut straight through –' she made an arrow shape with her hands '– and don't stop.'

It was eight-thirty and the evening show was due to start at nine-fifteen. I began to think I should set off now.

'The best seats are on the right-hand side as you look at the stage, about ten rows back. But there's a pillar you need to watch out for. If you get there late, go to the middle of the back; there are always tables with a reasonable view, and of course there are waitresses who stay there if they can get away with it.'

'Waitresses?' India said.

Would the exertion of getting from the restaurant to the theatre mean we needed more food?

'They'll bring you drinks from the bar. And snacks. It's very convenient,' Caron said, as she took a healthy sip of her red wine. 'We'll look out for you, as you're new to cruising. The gin cocktails on this ship are a specialty.'

'Thanks,' I said, wondering, as the waiters brought me a glossy slab of raspberry cheesecake with whipped cream rosettes and chocolate curls, if I would have room for any more drinks before tomorrow night. Or any more anything for that matter.

'And the bourbon,' Ike said, scraping his plate clean five seconds after it was put in front of him. 'The bourbon selection is grand. Back in the day we used to have them out on the deck with a cigar. Nowadays, of course, you'd get thrown off the ship for even thinking about lighting up. It's a great shame. Progress.'

He watched with a hangdog look as his wife enjoyed her dessert, obvious as a spaniel, until in the end she passed him her plate and let him finish it.

'I'm as healthy as a bug in a bed,' he said, hitting his chest with a clenched fist. 'My physician says I have the cholesterol of a thirty-year-old.'

'A thirty-year-old warthog,' his wife growled.

'Now, Caron, honey, just because you have to watch your weight,' Ike said.

'Oh, tell everyone,' she said. 'Tell the whole ship! Why not? You won't be getting my dessert on gala night, I can tell you that for certain.'

Ike winked at me. 'She's a firebrand. Thirty-eight years we've been together. Married on Christmas Eve. I'd have got less for murder.'

'And when you go on the ship's tenders tomorrow to get to Newport, don't bother sitting on the top deck. It's cold and pretty rocky,' Marty said.

'What are tenders?' I asked.

'They're the lifeboats really. They use them when the ship is too big to actually dock.'

'Well, I like sitting up top,' Marion said.

'Yes, but your hair doesn't,' Marty replied.

They bickered on happily through the cheese and coffee and then, just as I was thinking I might fall asleep nose down in the sugar, rose like a startled flock of gulls and chivvied us out past the bowing waiters and proud, Italian profile of the maître d', who wished us a pleasant evening.

Other people in the know evidently had the same idea because there was a well-mannered but insistent tide of people surging the length of the ship towards the open doors of the Ocean Theatre. Our new companions brushed aside our feeble protests that we were tired and settled us triumphantly at a table for six close to the stage. Within moments Ike had ordered a round of drinks and then sat back with a contented sigh to watch the show.

'The dancers are very good on this ship, much better than on the *Roi*,' Marion said.

'The *Roi*?' I asked.

'The *Roi de France*. They're not nearly as good. And last time we came there was a singer – well, he could have given Sinatra a run for his money. Just wonderful.'

Right on time the lights dimmed and there was an excited smattering of applause. The curtains pulled back and a line of dancing girls in bowler hats and stilettos high-kicked on to the tune of 'Cabaret' and whoops and whistles from Marty.

'I'm going to fall asleep if I close my eyes,' I hissed to India. 'I've been eating cheesecake at three in the morning. And now I've got a highball in front of me.'

She pulled a face at me. 'Let me guess; you'd rather be in work?'

'Hardly!' I scoffed. I thought about it and what Mum had said; what was the point of having a holiday if you weren't going to enjoy it?

'Then just roll with it! We can sleep when we get home,' she said, raising her glass and clinking it against mine.

'You're right!' I said and took a slurp of my drink. I couldn't remember the last time India and I had had so much fun together. I shouldn't wish it away. 'Oooh, this isn't bad actually.'

On the stage the male dancers, who were sporting an impressive display of eyeliner as they gamely tried to do Joel Grey impersonations to 'Willkommen', joined the girls, who were busy straddling chairs and tipping their bowler hats.

'I saw this on Broadway in 1998,' Marty said as the routine came to an end and we all applauded. 'I couldn't believe my eyes and I've been in the Army. It was a bit racy.'

'I don't remember you asking to leave early though,' Marion said, tapping the table in front of him.

Marty wagged his head and laughed.

Beside me India had started doing that thing with her head where she was jerking backwards and forwards as she fell asleep. I nudged her with my knee and when that didn't work finished her drink off. Strange. It was usually me having to leave and have an early night.

In the end it was a fun evening. There was no sign of Marnie Miller or Gabriel Frost that I could see. Perhaps this wasn't their sort of thing? Maybe they were *otherwise occupied*? I steered my tired brain away from that scenario and watched as a sharp-looking man in a DJ came on and introduced himself as Francois Du Pont, our compere for the evening. I think by his accent he was more Paris-Texas than Paris-France but Marty and Ike laughed at his jokes while Marion and Caron discussed whether this was the same man they had encountered on the *Destiny of the Seas* two years previously.

Then a singer came on with a selection of songs in tribute to Dean Martin, where he very convincingly almost fell off his stool.

India was properly asleep by that point, resting her head back on the red velvet seat, her mouth open. I just hoped 'Dean' couldn't see her.

The show ended with a rousing dance routine to a selection of Chuck Berry hits, ending with 'Johnny B Goode'; there was air-guitar playing on the part of the boys and some choreographed hand jiving by the girls. It was really jolly good.

As the other guests headed off to the bars and casino, I nudged India awake and we tottered off to our cabin and made half-hearted attempts to get our make-up off. I looked out at the dark sea and the glitter of far-off lights on the coast that was slipping past us and smiled as my head span. Then we both fell into bed. What a day!

*

It felt like I'd had ten minutes of sleep when I woke up. Daylight was streaming through the windows and occasionally I heard people chattering as they walked down the corridor past our room. I lay in bed wondering if the room was indeed rocking or if I had a worse hangover than expected. Then I remembered I was on a ship, which explained it. The tenders were due to take us off the ship and into Newport, Rhode Island, from nine o'clock, and it was now eight-thirty.

I wondered for a few moments if I really needed to see Newport, and then I remembered Marion's comment the night before. Apparently, Newport was 'a darling town', very exclusive and good for shopping and dining, with 'the best handbag shop' she had ever been in.

'India! Get up! It's time to move. Breakfast!' I shouted, chucking one of my pillows at her.

India made a few horrified noises and rolled away from me, but I chucked another pillow that caught her smack on the head and then I went into the bathroom to shower and steal all the complimentary toiletries, which were Jo Malone and absolutely gorgeous. By the time I came out she was sitting up on the side of her bed.

'Breakfast!' I said. 'Hurry up. We can go to the food court self-service. It'll be quicker.'

I threw open the doors to the balcony and let in a fresh gust of salty air, feeling much better after my shower. India fell backwards on to her bed and whimpered.

'Oh God, why do you always have to be so bloody enthusiastic in the mornings?'

'Come on! Remember what you said? Would *you* rather be in work?'

'No,' she said rather pathetically.

'Well then, come on. We could go and see The Breakers; a dream come true for a couple of half-arsed estate agents like us.'

To give India her due, she surprised me. In twenty minutes we were in the food court with trays and India was trying to decide what to eat in order to get rid of her hangover.

All the time, food trolleys laden with new breakfast choices were hurtling through the kitchen doors and out into the food court at frightening speed. There was a group of travellers dithering and fretting to such an extent that I swear we had finished our food and were on our way back to our cabin to collect our passports and ship's identity cards before they had eaten anything.

Newport was indeed glorious, with pretty artisan shops and cafés clustered around the quayside. As we passed a beautiful shop full of handbags, we saw Marion inside with a forlorn-looking Marty. Still feeling a bit fragile, we had decided not to join the tour around The Breakers, the house built for the Vanderbilt family, who evidently had more money than was good for them from the look of the photographs.

Instead we wandered in and out of the immaculate little alleyways around the quay, admiring the jaunty yachting clothes on sale. There was a whole raft of incredibly expensive, impossibly chic, home-style shops filled with every type of throw, vase, candleholder and hand-carved bird necessary to make one's weekend cottage perfect.

Everywhere there were tourists plodding about, pretending they had a boat, and the occasional genuine boat owner who could be distinguished by their good looks, expensive clothes and – in the case of the young girls, at least – constant laughing and glossy blonde hair that needed a lot of flicking.

I looked at them from the weary heights of my twenty-nine years and felt unexpectedly sad. Were they as happy as they seemed? Or had they just not been alive long enough to be disappointed? Would they too one day find their boyfriend, half-naked, sprawled over another woman and then listen to his preposterous explanations about CPR and the Heimlich manoeuvre? I wouldn't go through that again. I'd made up my mind.

Philosophical thoughts put firmly to one side, we went to sit at an achingly stylish wine bar overlooking the sea with the intention of ordering a glass of water and an elegant sandwich. One of Newport's prettiest, blondest, happiest girls came across and introduced herself to us.

'I'm Callie – happy to be your server.'

We thanked her for handing over the menus.

'You're welcome,' she said with a dazzling smile. 'Can I bring you something while you're waiting?'

In the manner of all American restaurants she had already

brought us some iced water, which took care of India's dehydration.

'No, thank you.'

'You're welcome. Would you like the parasol adjusted? The sun's really hot today.'

'No, it's fine, thanks.'

'You're welcome.'

Callie skipped away happily towards the kitchen in her size-four denim shorts and T-shirt. She had a glossy mane of hair caught up in a high ponytail and long brown legs that ended in smart pink deck shoes. She made Olivia Newton John in *Grease* look fat and sloppy by comparison.

'Is she going to say you're welcome every time we say thank you?' India said, watching her blearily.

'I expect so.'

In front of us bobbed millions and millions of dollars worth of boats of all shapes and sizes. There were a few of Callie's clones wandering about on board the one nearest us, laughing and flirting with some excessively handsome young men as they pretended to mop the decks. I felt even older and wearier just watching them. Perhaps I was destined for a cantankerous old age, getting more and more cynical about men and love and relationships until I just didn't bother any more?

I rested my head back on the chair and closed my eyes as, beside me, India glugged back her iced water with a groan.

'Enjoying your day?'

I looked round, rather startled to see Callie showing Gabriel Frost to the adjacent table. Gabriel Frost, here at the same restaurant we were sitting in ... What were the chances?

'Oh yes, absolutely, it's a very pretty place,' I said, rather flustered, trying to smile but probably just grimacing.

'Hey, are you folks friends? Would you care to share a table?' Callie smiled helpfully.

No, actually no. I didn't think I could cope with him sitting right next to me and having to make small talk ...

He hesitated for a moment.

Say no, say no.

'Well, I suppose that might be nice.'

'Hey, that's so cool!' Callie said, topping up our water glasses. 'Small world! I'll bring you over a menu momentarily, sir.'

She gave Gabriel a smile he was not intended to forget and skipped away. I was so surprised I picked up my glass to take a sip, just to have something to do with my hands, and spilled some water on the table. The fizzing was back suddenly. Gabriel took his seat and seemed to fit into the scenery perfectly.

'Not tempted by The Breakers then?' Gabriel said, yanking me out of my thoughts.

'Not really. I think we just wanted to soak up the atmosphere,' I said stupidly.

And seeing as India felt a bit queasy after the ride in the ship's tender – she would insist on going on the top deck despite the warnings – I wouldn't want her throwing up on their inlaid marble floors.

'You're very wise. Some of these tourist places are expensive and very crowded,' he said. 'Have you ordered?'

Callie came back and was standing eagerly on tiptoe next to him, pencil and pad at the ready. That's the other thing about American restaurants: they give you a closely typed, three-page menu without any pictures, and 2.7 seconds later they come to take your order.

'A carafe of red,' I said. *Hair of a reasonably large dog.* 'And some whole-wheat toast with avocado and chilli flakes.'

'Jerry said that was supposed to be good for hangovers,' India said.

'Ideal. I'll have the same, thank you,' Gabriel said. 'And a glass of Pinot Grigio.'

'You're welcome! Excellent choice,' Callie said, wrinkling her button nose with pleasure. 'Can I freshen up your water a little?'

She topped up our glasses to the brim. I couldn't believe it – Gabriel was being chatty, agreeable, nice even. What had happened to the grumpy man I'd met/chucked my drink over in the airport lounge, or our rude neighbour on the balcony? Perhaps he was getting into the holiday mood too?

'Thank you,' Gabriel said.

'You're welcome!' came the inevitable reply, and she darted off again.

'So is this your first trip to the States?' Gabriel asked.

'We've been to Florida and New York before, but yes, this is our first time in New England. It looks beautiful,' I said, waving one hand around me. 'The boats and the sea. And the ... and the boats,' I finished lamely.

Next to me India tried and failed to look bright and alert.

'This is a little overdone for my taste,' he said, 'unless of course you're a boat owner. I know a publisher in New York who has a boat here. He recommends it very highly, but I prefer the Maine coastline, although it's not nearly so pretty. Just big hunks of rock and the sea.'

Hunk is about right, I thought, rather unexpectedly. Especially if he stayed in this mood – I could begin to see why Marnie Miller might have gone for him ...

He sat back in his chair, shrugging his broad shoulders under his turquoise polo shirt. I wondered if he had managed to get the one I'd soaked with champagne laundered.

Callie was back with our drinks and behind her was another equally trim and glossy girl with our food.

We exchanged thank yous and you're welcomes a few times before they left us to it.

'What do you think of the ship?' I asked as Gabriel helped us to wine. If he could do small talk, so could I. Plus, India wasn't being much help, staring down at her plate thoughtfully.

'It's fine. Rather bigger than I was expecting but Marnie was so keen for me to come ...' He tailed off.

Ah yes, Marnie Miller.

'I have a great deal to do. I can't see me doing it if I keep getting enticed from my cabin.'

Enticed? Who was enticing him?

I had an image of Marnie in a silk negligee and rather silly swansdown-trimmed mules, hanging on to his doorframe, luring him out. But then she wouldn't do that, would she? Otherwise they would *both* be out in the corridor ...

Callie was back.

'Is everything okay with your meals?'

We reassured her we were happy and the food was perfect. She looked a little doubtfully at India who was doing her best, but evidently the hair of today's particular dog was a little hard to tame. She was sitting a bit lopsidedly in her chair with a glassy-eyed expression. Even so she was still drinking Merlot with some enthusiasm.

'I hope you'll come along to Marnie's talks,' Gabriel said. 'She's a great speaker.'

How long had they been 'good friends', I wondered. And how old was he? He looked to be in his thirties but I wasn't very good at that sort of thing. Surely Marnie was in her late forties? Despite the veneers and the possibility of cosmetic surgery.

'I think we will,' I said.

'Are either of you writers?'

'Not really, I mean not since school,' I said, kicking India under the table to try and make her a bit more responsive. She took another bite of her food and pulled a face at me.

67

'Alexa was always the clever one,' she said, 'not me.'

'No, I wasn't!' I said, shocked. This was the second compliment India had paid me recently and I wasn't used to it.

'Of course you were.' She looked away. 'Every teacher I ever had told me I wasn't as good as my sister.'

'Really?'

India rolled her eyes.

'That sounds like you had some really nasty teachers! You must come along to Marnie's talks so you can *Spring-Clean Your Life*,' Gabriel said. 'I insist.'

He smiled at me and my heart did a little flippy thing in a very silly way. He really was phenomenally attractive. His turquoise shirt seemed to bring warmth to his grey eyes, and they sparkled as the sunlight reflected off the water.

We discussed Boston, which was our next port, and Maine where his parents had a house on the coast. The way he described it was magical. The view of the ocean and how, in the winter, the force of the waves was astonishing. I could almost imagine the chill winds from Canada bringing snow to hurl against the shuttered windows and picture him walking on the beach, his boots crunching on the icy stones.

We finished our food and the minute the last fork hit the plate Callie was back with more iced water and the dessert menus. India had perked up a bit by now and wanted a warm chocolate brownie with ice cream. Evidently the hangover was abating.

Gabriel's phone buzzed with the arrival of a text message and he read it, frowning.

'The last tender goes back to the ship in an hour,' he said, standing up. 'I promised my mother I'd pick up something for her. I'll see you back on board maybe?'

He was going to buy something for his *mother*? Were there actually men like that in the world?

We smiled and waved him off, watching him go in almost a daze. He really did seem too good to be true, but then I remembered the champagne incident and his icy tone and calmed down. Almost immediately Callie was back with a weighty slab of chocolate brownie, a scoop of vanilla ice cream, and two spoons that she put down in front of us with a sparkling smile and a wink.

'Just in case you need help. Your friend is very charming,' she added, watching as Gabriel walked through the wine bar and out into the sunshine.

'Yes,' I said, 'I suppose he is.'

Ah! But he'd left us to pay for his lunch. Nice one.

Callie topped up our water and brought us some new napkins.

'The check is all taken care of,' she said.

'What?'

'Your friend has paid the check, so no hurry, ladies; enjoy your dessert. It's really good.'

'Bloody hell,' India said, 'we weren't expecting that – were we?'

I sat back and blinked a bit. 'No, we certainly weren't.'

Chapter Five

Rhode Island Red

Tequila, Chambord, Lemon Juice, Agave,
Orange Bitters, Ginger Beer

It was the second night on board and, according to the daily newsletter, tradition dictated that now our non-existent maids had unpacked for us we would be able to don some evening finery. Tonight was going to be the first of the gala dinners. The main difference was the dress code (posh frocks) and the food (five courses instead of four). Blow the diet and fitness routine. After a day traipsing around Newport with only an open sandwich and a glass of red wine to sustain us I couldn't wait.

By now India had completely recovered from her hangover and had a plan.

'I'm going to stick to water and soft drinks from now on,' she said, as we got dressed for dinner that evening.

'Really?'

I paused as I zipped her into her blue sparkly dress. To be fair, her diet and fitness regime of the last few months had paid dividends and she looked amazing, but then she always did.

'Absolutely,' India said, looking slightly martyred. 'It's called pacing myself. And I'm not going to mix wine with cocktails and other random spirits. I might just have an occasional white wine spritzer. But no cocktails before dinner. Well, not every day anyway.'

'If that's what you want to do,' I said.

'You could do the same,' India said, looking a bit less sure. 'After all, alcohol has a lot of meaningless calories and you were supposed to be losing weight before the wedding.'

'Are you saying I'm fat?' I challenged, feeling fifteen again, swatting away my younger sister bouncing around calling me names.

'No, but remember the bridesmaid's dress? I'm just saying you could lose a few pounds,' she said, checking her eyeliner in the mirror before flashing me a look. 'You said you wanted to.'

'Then I'll make sure I only drink meaningful calories in future,' I said crossly. 'Like vintage champagne and twenty-year-old brandy.'

God forbid we should get on to the wedding again.

I clambered into my dress, which was black and unstructured. By which I mean loose. Next to my sister I was definitely the big one, even though I was only a size twelve. Well, fourteen, especially in stretchy fabrics. And occasionally a sixteen if I'm honest. The high street can be so random.

I looked at myself in the full-length mirror and had a moment's doubt. Perhaps India was right? Maybe I should have a small white wine spritzer and some filtered tap water with my meal? Yes, that would be the way to go. Moderation in all things. One day on, one day off perhaps?

Ten minutes later we were making our way towards the Champs-Elysées restaurant, teetering along in our high heels, admiring our reflections in the bronze-mirrored walls. Suddenly we spotted a table next to the window in the Picasso cocktail bar. There was a wonderful view of the sunset over Cape Cod, the colours a dazzling blend of gold and apricot with clouds as fluffy and luminous as Donald Trump's hair. Well, of course, we stopped and sat down to appreciate the beauty nature had spread out before us, and before you could say *zut alors* a bedroom-eyed waiter, name badge Giovanni, had appeared beside us. Three minutes later we were appreciating nature's beauty with a large Gin Sling each and a silver bowl of salted cashew nuts. Perhaps our moderation would start tomorrow.

When we got to our table it was fun to catch up with our new friends and find out what everyone else had been doing. I hadn't realised the people you sat with on your first night were your table companions for the rest of the trip and felt very lucky we had met such a nice bunch. Marion had struck gold in the handbag shop and was proudly displaying an exquisite little evening bag at which Marty was glowering. Evidently her idea of an essential purchase and his were poles apart.

Ike and Caron had been to Newport on a previous cruise but had never seen The Breakers before, and they filled us in on all the details of the gilding, the marble, the furniture and sheer excess of the place until we felt we had been there too, but without the expense, the queuing or the sore feet. I wondered what it would be worth, if it ever went on the market. Imagine doing the floor plans!

As it was a gala dinner – the theme being Sparkle – there was champagne on the table, so that put paid to our evening of moderation good and proper. There was also an excess of sequins and lamé so that the room fairly crackled with light bouncing off the dresses and, in the case of two ladies on the next table, tiaras. I think I stared a bit to start with, finding it a bit OTT, but after a while I thought they were rather snazzy. I mean, why not?

'I rather think I'd like a tiara,' I said, pausing for a moment to let my cutlery cool down. Eating with Marty and Ike did tend to speed things up a bit.

'That's because you're English,' Marion said, looking at me over the top of her wineglass. 'You English are used to such things. I'm surprised you didn't bring one.'

'We don't actually all own them, you know,' I said.

'No? Well, I call that a shame. You should get one. You have the face for it.'

India snorted with laughter.

The face for a tiara? I wondered what that meant. Anyway, I ploughed on with my sea bass with its lemon spume and asparagus tips, while Ike, who had finished his long ago, turned round to see what the next course, which had already been delivered to the tiara wearers, looked like.

'They've got beef,' he said after a moment. 'Looks good. I ordered that to make up for the chicken last night. How about some red wine? Any preference, ladies?'

'No, but we'll buy it. You got the wine yesterday,' I heard myself say. India kicked me under the table and I pulled a hopeless sort of expression. Having a day of abstinence and moderation was going to be difficult.

After dinner the others decided they were going to the casino and we allowed ourselves to be swept along with the tide of people going to the Ocean Theatre for the evening's entertainment. We found a table near the back and prepared to order some water, but somehow found two Long Island Iced Teas in front of us, in the inaccurate belief that they were diluted and therefore not really alcohol.

Onstage there was a tribute to the sixties. The girl dancers bopped and shrugged in white Courrèges boots and the boys were in Beatles wigs – it was terrific. We had just about finished our drinks when the waitress brought over two quarter bottles of champagne with paper straws in them.

'We didn't order these, did we?' India said.

74

'Compliments of the gentlemen,' the waitress said before she darted off.

We looked around to see who was trying to attract our attention but couldn't see anyone other than a couple of stout men two tables away who I thought were waving at their wives.

'Which gentlemen? Have you been chatting random men up again?' I said. I'd been feeling quite friendly towards India; maybe it was all the wine. 'Up to your old tricks?'

'Bloody cheek! What old tricks?' India replied, outraged, completely missing my gentle ribbing and taking it seriously.

'Don't play the innocent,' I said, feeling suddenly annoyed and hurt; after all, I had been trying to be nice, or at least not 'boring', as India always seemed to think I was. The old resentments came swirling up. 'You know exactly what I mean.'

'No, I bloody don't. God, you're such a misery sometimes,' India said.

'Laura's party?' I snapped back. 'You never did explain what happened there.'

We sipped our champagne in tense silence.

*

The following day we woke up rather hungover again, but perhaps not quite as bad as the previous day. Either we had indeed been more measured or we were developing immunity to alcohol. India's irritation from last night seemed to have dissipated; perhaps it had just been a little spat fuelled by too much alcohol and not enough sleep. Or at least that's what I tried to tell myself. In the end it was only another eight days at sea with my sister. I could get through that. Especially with enough cocktails ...

The ship had moored in Boston overnight and, excitingly, was immediately underneath the flight path of Logan International Airport. Like everyone else we went up on to the top deck to watch the huge planes coming in to land and almost taking the funnels off the *Reine de France*.

We had booked the excursion to the town of Concord and enjoyed a nice snooze on the coach before being unloaded in one of the prettiest New England towns for our tour around Louisa May Alcott's house. Having always been a particular fan of hers it was my idea of heaven. India trailed after me grumbling as I ooohed and aaahed at Roderigo's boots and Beth's piano and wondered which of the houses nearby had been the inspiration for Laurie's.

Having tolerated this slight detour into culture, India wanted to shop. So we did the rounds of some of the dinky little stores in which Concord specialises, and bought some excellent knick-knacks and the palest pink cashmere sweater, which India couldn't live without. Before long we found a place for a late lunch and ended up having more wine. And a bowl of fries. And ice cream. I mean really, how did that happen?

The trouble was the wine bars were so sweet and the staff

so incredibly welcoming. Even the menu cards were cute in a retro, Disney-ish way. And everything seemed so reasonably priced. It would have been hard to stop at a cup of coffee when it came with a slab of cake for half-price. And it was damn near impossible not to have two glasses of wine *and* be given the rest of the bottle for free *and* a bowl of fries.

We decided tomorrow would definitely be a day of moderation and healthy eating. I mean, after all, we were going to have a whole day at sea, sailing past the coast of Maine that Gabriel loved so much. Who knew, we might sail straight past his parents' house!

Tomorrow was also going to be the day of Marnie Miller's first talk; eleven o'clock sharp. After that India and I would both be really enthused and motivated and would spend the rest of the day writing in a quiet corner somewhere, far away from other people or waiters or any food or cocktails. We wouldn't stir except for some herb tea and perhaps a handful of quinoa.

Well, that was the plan.

*

Back on the ship India had reread the daily newsletter and discovered there were cream teas and a fine selection of French patisserie available in the Marie-Antoinette Lounge, courtesy of Juan Del Martino, the ship's head pastry chef. Like a pair of Muppets we followed the herd and had even got as far as the doors to the place when I grabbed India's arm.

'We really don't need this,' I said.

Her face fell for a moment and then, as if she had been awoken from a trance, she nodded.

'You're right! What am I doing? I had cake in Concord only a couple of hours ago!'

Instead we went back to our cabin and had a little bit of a lie-down. This then deteriorated into a sleep that saw us waking up at eight-thirty.

'I do not need a four-course dinner tonight,' I said, feeling abstemious and full of good intentions. 'I know I have it in me to be eighteen stone, but I'd rather not.'

'Oh, all right.' India sighed, although I'm pretty sure she agreed with me. She picked up the newsletter and put it into her handbag. 'Let's read about some of the things we can do over a salad in the food court. I mean we've been on board for days and hardly even tried anything – other than the food and drinks.'

'Great idea.' I had been completely captivated by the idea of activities when I was back home, listless and dreaming of my luxurious holiday, determined to make the most of every moment; and all we'd done was eat, drink and wander around picturesque towns. It was time to get down to business – maybe I'd find a new hobby, something I'd be good at ... not like the time I tried to make a patchwork quilt and sewed it to my trousers.

In the food court we went to find a simple green salad and came back with lobster. In butter. With French bread.

'So tomorrow,' I said, once we were settled at a table by the window, 'we have Marnie Miller in the morning. What else can we do?'

India pored over the paper. 'Right, here we are. Dancing tomorrow afternoon at two p.m. Learn the waltz with Omaha dance champions, Peter and Paula. And towel folding at half past three with Jaresh.'

'I can fold a towel already,' I said.

'Into the shape of a swan? Or a monkey? No, I thought not. Looks like there are some groups on board too. Dorothy has some friends and so does Bill W. I've noticed they always seem to have little get-togethers every afternoon.'

'I think the Friends of Dorothy are single gay people and the Friends of Bill W are AA meetings,' I said quietly.

'Really? How marvellous! There's a talk about Fabergé eggs and another one about whisky. There's bingo and then at three p.m. there's adult colouring-in.'

'You're joking?'

'I'm not. There's a talk about Halifax. On the Atlantic crossing we can do fruit carving, learn the foxtrot and go to a talk about the *Titanic*.'

'Now you're joking?' I said.

'Nope, not at all. Listen to this. *That perennially fascinating ship and the voyage of doom towards its tragic end.* Well, that's what it says here. We're missing the entertainment by the way. It was Tribute to Elton John Night.'

'I'll bite back my disappointment,' I said.

'Sarky. And of course we have Marnie Miller first. We will be stimulated, pissed, educated, be able to fold towels into unusual shapes and have dancers' thighs. You couldn't ask for more really, could you?'

'I suppose not,' I agreed, as I mopped up the garlic-butter sauce with my remaining bread.

'Right, shall we go and have a nightcap? My round?' India said with a grin as she pushed her cleared plate away from her.

'I suppose so,' I said. 'What did happen at Laura's party? You can tell me – I won't mind.'

'Oh, leave it!'

Chapter Six

Absolutely Fabulous

Vodka, Cranberry Juice, Champagne

The following morning we woke late and had a leisurely breakfast of fresh fruit and plain yogurt in the food court. While we congratulated ourselves on our discipline and what India had heard was now called 'considered eating', it was a bit forgettable even if the strawberries were cut into cunning fans. We added a spoonful of some grain thing. It looked like something I might have fed to a budgie and tasted of burnt biscuits. It also killed any chances of conversation as we munched through it, jaws aching. We had decaffeinated coffee with skimmed milk and without sugar. It was thoroughly unsatisfying, I thought, but I didn't say anything in case India was feeling happy with getting back on that healthy track.

We then had a brisk walk on the promenade deck that went around the ship, with encouraging notices telling us how far we had walked. Apparently three laps of the deck equalled one kilometre. Did that make me feel better? No, not really.

There were loads of people taking it very seriously though, who were striding out, chests like bellows, arms swinging. One man even shouted at his flagging wife as we passed them: 'Come on, Tessa, keep up. Another two circuits and you can have that doughnut.' It seemed a little harsh, as she was at least eighty by the look of her. If it had been me I would have waited until he strode ahead round a corner and sneaked off to get one without him, and had a hot chocolate too.

*

At eleven o'clock we made our way to the Ocean Theatre where Marnie Miller was giving her talk. There were already ten full rows of people waiting for it to start and Marnie herself was standing at the back of the room having what looked like a very quiet argument with her miserable assistant. On the stage a man in a high-vis jacket was plugging various cables into different sockets and looking doubtfully at the projection screen behind him.

We went and sat on the eleventh row and others joined us. Marnie – famous, successful and charming – was quite a draw. Most of the attendees were women but there were a few determined-looking men too, flicking biros with their thumbs and ruffling through impressive piles of paper. Some were dragging laptops out of smart bags; others had notebooks and pencil cases. A couple, sitting like the class swots at the front, were clutching what looked like full manuscripts. Were they hoping to give them to Marnie to read?

At exactly one minute to eleven Marnie swept centre stage, closely followed by the miserable-looking assistant who was carrying everything: a laptop bag, bottle of mineral water, glass, box of tissues and a cushion.

After a few minutes the screen flicked into life and the high-vis man blew an audible sigh of relief. Marnie turned to the audience, her megawatt smile flashed on and her miserable assistant took the opportunity to scarper stage left. The theatre dimmed a little and someone turned on the spotlights, placing Marnie in an attractive circle of light, her red hair glossy and glowing. She was wearing artfully ripped jeans and a tiny Guns N' Roses T-shirt. It looked a bit odd actually, like a child dressing up in its mother's clothes.

She sat down in the spotlight with a loud sigh, as though she had been doing housework all morning and her back was killing her. By the look of her immaculate hair and make-up I was guessing she had spent a tiring couple of hours in the spa.

'Ladies! And gentlemen – how nice to see you too! Welcome, all of you writers, to our first little get-together, which as you can see is called *Write for Love*.' She waved a hand towards the screen. 'Well, now, do we have any writers in the house?'

There was a bit of shuffling around at this point and some uneasy laughter as several keen types put their hands up.

Marnie smiled. 'I can reassure you; you are all writers. Every single one of you is a writer. There's no doubt about it. Yes, come in, come in. Yes, you *are* a little late but no matter. You write stories, maybe diaries or memoirs, letters, postcards, birthday cards, your kids' homework?'

More laughter.

'A few of you will have written a book: sixty, seventy, eighty thousand words. Others won't have picked up a pen since high school. But you are all writers.'

There was a noticeable straightening of shoulders at this point as people enjoyed the scent of success already, imagining themselves posing with their bestseller or signing autographs in the bookshop.

'The question we need to ask is: are you *good* writers? Do you *Write for Love*? For the love of writing? Yes, do come in, sit down, there are plenty of seats. Yes, yes, over there are a few spare seats. If you want to write solely for yourself it doesn't matter quite so much. But if you want to see your book next to mine in Barnes & Noble or Waterstones, you need to be a *great* writer.'

Marnie carried on in this vein for some time and then started telling us about how she was first published. You could almost feel the atmosphere charging with optimism. I've no idea how she did it. She'd even made me think I could write a bestseller by the time she'd finished her introduction. Was it her personality? The vivacious way she darted across the stage, making each of us, sitting there in the gloom with our laptops, notebooks and chewed pencils, feel we were the most important person there?

To try and get into the spirit I had bought a rather cute notebook decorated with embroidered seagulls and starfish in one of the shops on board the ship, and I opened it and started doodling. I'd bought a very stylish pen too, and some propelling pencils decorated with pictures of shells just to keep the nautical theme going. Perhaps in future years these would become precious artefacts? I could just imagine it.

'Ladies and gentlemen, this is the very notebook in which Alexa Fisher began her writing career on board the Reine de France. *I have several commission bids and there has been interest from around the world, including the Bodleian Library and the Smithsonian. I shall start at twenty-five thousand pounds …'*

I wrote my name in my best handwriting inside the cover and then doodled a flower underneath it. Perhaps this would become my trademark? Maybe there would be a flower on the cover of each book, hidden somewhere for my devoted readers to discover?

She told us about her search for success, how many times she had been disappointed, and then the breakthrough of *Falling into Leaves*, the fifth book she had written while still working full-time in a Worcester building society.

She had been signed by the most successful agent of the day, who had organised a bidding war and a six-figure advance. We could almost feel the stardust falling on us as we sat there.

Then she told us about her wonderful husband, Leo – at this point she put up a picture of them on their wedding day, a golden couple under an arch of white roses in a haze of glamour, and a lot of the ladies cooed and sighed with pleasure. I smiled as well. I'd forgotten Marnie was married; of course she was, and to that golden-haired, blue-eyed paragon of gorgeousness ... Gabriel was just a friend then, which meant he was 'available', as Mum would say.

Oh, stop it, just stop being so pathetic.

I tried to pay attention again and stop remembering Gabriel's dazzling eyes.

This could be you, Marnie seemed to be saying when I tuned back in. You too could be successful, size six and beautifully groomed, with a perfect manicure and a husband with a faultless profile, flashing Osmond teeth and cornflower-blue eyes. Just write that bestselling book and everything will fall into your lap.

'I could do this, I know I could,' India sighed.

'What would you write about?'

'Me, my life,' she said.

Up on the stage Marnie was in full flow.

'But here's my first warning: people's lives can be quite similar sometimes. School, marriage, jobs, the occasional holiday, kids, house decorating; there are a lot of dull days in an average person's life. Even I sometimes have to take a break, sit back and draw breath. I am not just a successful life coach and speaker; I am also a brand. Do you see the difference? I travel thousands of miles a year promoting my work, researching, spreading joy in ordinary people's lives. My readers don't want to read about the days when I'm decluttering my wardrobe. Or meditating on my balcony overlooking the lake. They don't want to know how I look when I'm slouching in my cashmere joggers! They want to escape through my work to somewhere different. Somewhere exciting and new.'

'That's telling you,' I muttered, ''cos your life is really boring and pointless.'

'Oh, shush!' India hissed.

Marnie held up a notebook and pen. 'These two are the best friends of any successful author. Whether you are writing a memoir, a cookery book or a book on Christmas crafts. Now mine just happen to be Aspinal and Mont Blanc but you can jot your ideas down on anything. You might have a notepad from the supermarket. The blank pages in a diary. The back of an envelope.'

'Or I could just scrape in the mud with a stick,' I muttered, earning myself another dig from my sister.

'So how do we find ideas? Where do they come from? That's the question I get asked a lot. Where do I get my ideas? Well, the idea for *Falling into Leaves* came from one day when I was walking to work ...'

Marnie then gave us a précis of all the places where she had stumbled upon ideas: cafés, supermarkets, trains, overheard conversations. All I could think was she went to far more stimulating places than I ever did and overheard a very superior sort of gossip.

Still, perhaps she had a finely tuned ear for that sort of thing?

Then she started speaking about how she had turned into a world-famous self-help guru because so many people wanted to know the secret of her success.

Someone in the front row put a hand up and Marnie faltered for a second.

'Yes, gentleman with the unusual sweater? Do you have a question for me?'

One of the manuscript clutchers next to the stage stood up and gave a rambling description of his own book, engagingly entitled *My Life in Plastics*. He wanted to know if she would take a look. Several people tutted disapprovingly. One of the veterans told him to sit down and there was a sudden heated spat between them that almost threatened to degenerate into name-calling.

Marnie dealt with him kindly but firmly and then got back into the swing.

'You must be able to capture the attention of an agent or publisher or reader in very few words. I know when I wrote *Buying Time*, my fourth book, my agent described it as the best ...'

I zoned out again and drew another flower and a house.

'I thought she was supposed to be teaching,' I whispered, 'not just showing off?'

Next to me India was writing down practically every word Marnie uttered. I reached across and drew a smiley face on her paper and she brushed me away with an irritated hand.

Perhaps I could write a story about a woman who sells her infuriating sister into slavery?

'... that was when Angelina Jolie discussed buying the film rights to *Good Woman, Great Life*, all because the pitch was so accurate. My publisher said that *Marnie's Party Pieces* was the easiest book she ever had to place because I made it sound so easy.'

I thought about putting my head down on the table and having a little nap, but I knew if I did India might put her hand up and snitch on me. Heaven knew she'd done it often enough in the past.

'Miss, Miss, Alexa said she forgot her gym kit but she didn't – she stuffed it behind the radiator in the cloakroom.'

I drew a chimney on my house and then a cat with fangs. Perhaps I would write about a vampire cat and create the bestselling children's book of the twenty-first century, and then JK Rowling and I would be best friends and we really would go on holiday together to Necker Island. No, if I thought about it, that was very unlikely. Some of the audience might have the talent for writing books, but I wasn't one of them.

I realised that Marnie was bringing the session to a close and, next to me, India was underlining something in red. I leaned over to see and I swear India tried to cover it up with her hand. Honestly, how old is she?

At the end Marnie tempted us with the sorts of wonderful things we could achieve if we went to her second talk, *Spring-Clean Your Life*, and offered to meet people in the cocktail bar before lunch for further informal chat.

As we filed out of the theatre I hesitated and looked back. Striding briskly out on to the stage to speak to Marnie was Gabriel Frost. India nearly fell over me.

'What's the matter? Why have you stopped?'

'It's him: Gabriel.'

We watched as he handed Marnie a couple of sheets of paper. She scanned through them and looked up at him. From her expression it was clear all was not well.

She gave a little cry and raised a hand to him in anguish. Gabriel shook his head. His dark hair gleamed under the stage lights and threw his cheekbones into sharp relief.

Marnie turned away and pressed her hands to her face.

'She's not happy,' India said.

'Perhaps she's broken a nail?' I said. 'Or her nanny has given in her notice?'

'Has she got children? She didn't say.'

I looked for a moment as Marnie stood, staring at the floor, deep in thought. One hand was clenching and unclenching against her side.

'I don't know,' I said, 'but somehow I doubt it.'

*

We wandered along to the cocktail bar and found about twenty of our number waiting for Marnie to put in her appearance.

'So where is she then?'

'She did say here, didn't she?'

Unexpectedly Gabriel Frost walked in, his face showing nothing of his feelings. He smiled in a smooth, professional manner and tilted his head to one side sympathetically.

'I'm so sorry, but Miss Miller won't be available as she wished. She sends her apologies and looks forward to talking more with you, perhaps later on? She will try and be in the cocktail lounge before dinner this evening, all being well. Thank you so much.'

The others turned away, muttering, disappointed.

'Well, I suppose we might as well grab a fizzy water while we're here,' India said. 'I'm just going to the loo first if I can find one within a five-mile radius. Wait here. Actually, go and bag that table. I won't be a mo.'

As she left my side Gabriel caught my eye.

'Hello there, Alexa, I wondered if you might be here.'

Blimey O'Reilly! He'd been thinking about me? Really?

'Marnie's not well?' I said, hoping to encourage him to spill the beans.

'Oh, she's fine. Just ... well, something unexpected. Can I get you a drink?'

Oooh, hello!

'That would be lovely.' I looked at the cocktail menu. 'A Crimson Crush, please.'

91

Well, it's got pink grapefruit and pomegranate seeds so that's healthy, isn't it? I mean grapefruit is loaded with vitamin C and pomegranate is a superfood or something.

He went over to the bar to order and I sat at the window table India had pointed out, watching him. The way he moved, how his hands played with a paper drinks mat as he waited. Tall, long legs. He really was rather gorgeous. Lucky Marnie; even if he wasn't her significant other, she got to spend time with him while she and the unfeasibly handsome Leo were apart.

When he joined me at the table we looked out at the sea. It was smooth and a delicious shade of blue, reflecting the brilliance of the sky. Far out on the horizon I could see a boat. A trawler maybe. Nice to think there were other people on the ocean with us.

'I'm sorry if I seemed out of sorts the other day,' he said at last, pulling me out of my thoughts.

Had he? I hadn't noticed. Which time though – the first day I'd met him, on the balcony, or a few days ago, when he'd paid for our lunch? So I decided it was best to stay quiet and see where he went with it.

'Newport is a nice place. Not as good as Maine obviously. In my opinion anyway. I would have spent more time there but I had to shoot off. Marnie was ... well, she needed me.'

I bet she bloody did, I found myself thinking rather unkindly.

'It's fine,' I said, taking a sip of my Crimson Crush and choking a little. Hmm, vodka. Gabriel passed me a paper napkin and I wiped my eyes. 'But thanks for lunch. That was unexpected. And very kind.'

'You're welcome,' he said.

'So is she okay?'

'Marnie? Oh, I don't know. We'll see.'

It was difficult to tell what that meant. Was he bothered? He didn't seem to be. Was that a bit callous? Seeing as they were supposed to be such great friends.

'It was a good talk, I think,' I said, changing the subject and wondering just what Gabriel Frost was doing sitting here with me when Marnie was supposed to be upset about something.

'Was it? Yes, I expect it was. She does these things so well, getting people all fired up. Making them believe their lives can be better if they take her advice. Persuading them that it's easy. It's not, but then nothing worth having is.' Gabriel frowned and sipped his drink.

'So you're a writer too?' I said.

'I write, yes,' he said.

There was a pause while I waited for him to elaborate, but nothing happened.

Blimey, come on, play ball here, stop making this so difficult.

'Marnie's very ... um –' what was the word? *Lucky?* '– entertaining.'

'Yes, I suppose she is. Will you go along to *Spring-Clean Your Life?*' he said.

'Oh, I expect so – India is very keen anyway.'

93

'India is a friend?'

'My younger sister. So she's sometimes a friend.' *And occasionally she's a pain in the arse.* 'This is our last trip together before the wedding.'

'Ah, I see. And when is that?'

'December 2nd.'

'And are all the plans going well?'

'Pretty much there. Although we still need to sort out the flower girls. There are three of them, all under eight, and they keep growing so fast I think we'll have to get their dresses at the last minute.' I couldn't believe I was voluntarily talking about India's wedding. Obviously the alcohol was doing odd things to me ...

'Lovely.' He finished his drink and gave a funny, tight little smile. 'I'd better be going.'

'Oh, okay. Thanks for the drink,' I said to his retreating back, feeling thoroughly confused.

India appeared at this point wiping her hands on a tissue.

'I've just had a hand-cream explosion. Was that Gabriel Frost? What did he want? I hope I didn't frighten him off?'

'He bought me a drink, was asking how we liked Marnie Miller's talk.'

'Well, I thought she was great.'

'Don't you think maybe there was a bit too much about her and her fabulous life and her handsome husband and celebrity friends?'

India shrugged. 'But that's what she sells! That image, that lifestyle. You heard what she said: she's a brand. How do you think she made her millions? Why do you think we were so pleased to see her on the ship? I suppose it's difficult to pretend you look for bargains in the January sales and can do fifty things with mince if that's what your life is like. But she knows a lot, don't you think?'

'Yes, I suppose so.'

'Well, I'm going to have my teeth whitened when I get home. Now are you going to order me a cocktail? I fancy a daiquiri.'

I turned in my chair and looked at her in astonishment. 'Hang on, you said fizzy water. I thought we were supposed to be on a healthy eating kick today?'

'I was only going along with you to give you moral support!'

'You mean I had that bloody yogurt for nothing!' I gasped.

'Well, so did I! I only had it because you said you wanted ... I hate yogurt, you know I do. And fresh fruit when I wanted a smoked salmon bagel?'

'You said you wouldn't get into your dress,' I reminded her indignantly, 'not to mention telling me I needed to lose weight!'

'Rubbish, my dress was hanging off me last time I tried it on. You've already had something pink.' India gave an irritable gesture towards my empty glass.

'That was mainly fruit.'

'Yeah, right.'

India folded her arms and huffed a bit. She looked out of the window at the sea and turned one shoulder towards me.

I'd seen that look so many times over the years. Her furious, silent rejection of me when we had to travel on the same school bus. Sighing and grumbling when our parents read out school reports and realised she was always near the bottom of her class and I was top of mine. I'd spent most of my life trying to appease her and today was no different. And it was her hen holiday.

'Okay, let's have a strawberry daiquiri and then we can go and get some lunch.'

'Okay, if you like,' she said, as though I was doing her a favour.

'And some salted almonds?' I knew they were her favourite.

She shrugged. 'If you like.'

Let's be fair, I'm as weak as water.

Chapter Seven

Passion Killer

Melon Liqueur, Passion Fruit Liqueur, Tequila

We rounded off our day of healthy and considered eating with four courses of French-inspired cuisine and some wine before we went to see the show. This time it was a tribute to the 1940s, something that made the elderly American passengers terribly excited.

There was a large group of Army veterans on board, all wearing matching knuckleduster class rings, grey slacks and baseball caps covered in gold embroidery. They had bagged the tables nearest to the stage, leaving India and I to a table near the back of the theatre, which I didn't mind a bit – it was nice to be away from the scrum to get to the front seats.

The veterans whooped and hollered with delight when the girl dancers came on dressed in very short white naval uniforms and the boys serenaded them with 'There Is Nothing

Like a Dame'. There was then some enthusiastic jitterbugging and acrobatics before a guest singer came on to the stage.

The plunging neckline of her green satin dress meant her substantial bosom arrived in the spotlight a couple of seconds before she did and the veterans went wild. She sang 'Somewhere Over the Rainbow' and 'I'll Never Smile Again' and there was a certain amount of emotional sniffing and eye dabbing from the veterans before they gave her a thunderous round of applause. Even India and I got swept up in the excitement, swapping gleaming smiles, which might have been down to the alcohol we'd just had or the entertainment ... it was hard to say.

Then a young man with a predilection for sunbeds came on and sang 'Some Enchanted Evening' in the woman's face with such force that we could see her hair moving. It was terrific.

The star singers were replaced with the girls singing 'I'm Gonna Wash That Man Right Outta My Hair' while apparently dressed in towels. I was surprised one of the veterans didn't have a stroke.

'Having a good evening?'

I looked up, startled, as Gabriel Frost came over to sit in the chair next to me.

'It's very lively,' I shouted over the cheering as the girls sashayed off the stage. I fluttered a bit. Twice in one day – this was unusual, but also I wasn't quite sure what I thought about Gabriel. He kept disappearing with odd excuses and he kept dodging my questions. It just seemed a bit strange. After being involved with a slippery customer like Ryan I wasn't going to just fall for some snappy line, and for that matter I wasn't even sure why Gabriel was hanging around with us ... Didn't he have other people to speak to?

Gabriel raised a hand and two of the waitresses at the back of the theatre raced each other to see who could get to him first. Perhaps they thought he was a good tipper or maybe, like me, they thought he was gorgeous. He was certainly a more attractive prospect than the veterans.

Up on stage the noise levels subsided for a while as a juggler did his best with five coloured rings and then tried some plate spinning. Bearing in mind the boat had started doing a bit of rock and roll he did very well.

'I was going to order some champagne, if you would care to join me?' Gabriel said.

He seemed more cheerful than he had been earlier, and looked relaxed and rather scrumptious in a soft blue shirt and black jeans.

'We were supposed to be having a day of healthy eating,' India said. She tapped on the table with a finger for emphasis. I wondered whether she actually needed more alcohol. Did I for that matter?

'Goodness me, I am impressed,' Gabriel said, eyebrows raised.

'The important word was *supposed*,' I said, 'but we don't seem to have been particularly successful, so yes please.'

He laughed and within a few minutes the speedier of the

two waitresses had produced three glasses and an ice bucket of champagne.

'What are we drinking to?' India said.

'Oh, I don't know, how about friendship?' Gabriel said.

We clinked glasses.

'No Marnie this evening?' I said.

Gabriel shook his head. 'No, she's having a difficult day. Some unexpected news.'

'Nothing too bad I hope?' I said, hoping he was the sort who could be encouraged by a bit of gentle sympathy into sharing further details. He wasn't.

'We'll see,' he said. 'How are you enjoying the voyage so far?'

India started telling him how much she was enjoying it and I took the opportunity to do what I had been longing to do: have a really good long stare at Gabriel Frost.

His face was half in shadow, the stage light harsh on the left side of his face as he turned towards me. No wonder the waitresses had practically fought each other to serve him. A strong jawline, straight nose, full lower lip ... which was supposed to hint at a passionate nature, wasn't it? His hair was dark and glossy. He was probably the best-looking man I'd ever seen. Even if he had been both tetchy and evasive. It almost made up for his changeable nature. Almost.

'And how about you, Alexa?'

He turned to me and I felt a bit hot and silly for a moment. I took a sip of my champagne.

'Oh, it's really nice.' *Nice?* I cringed as the word left my mouth. 'I mean it's great. A lovely boat ... I mean ship. We're looking forward to doing the dance lessons, aren't we, India? India?'

I suddenly realised India was doing her trick of falling asleep, bolt upright and still clutching her champagne glass. I shook her.

'What? What? I wasn't asleep. Was I?'

'Yes, you were.' I took the glass from her before she dropped it. I thought she was supposed to be the night owl?

India looked at me blankly for a moment. 'I think I'd better go to bed. Thanks for the champagne, Gabriel,' she said with a sleepy smile, before turning to wink at me. 'I'll see you later.'

She staggered off while, onstage, the dance troupe started 'Boogie Woogie Bugle Boy'.

'Shall we go somewhere?' Gabriel said, raising an enquiring eyebrow at me.

I nearly fainted. What on earth was he suggesting?

He laughed. 'Sorry, that came out wrong. I just thought it might be nice to find somewhere quieter. I can't think straight in all this noise. I think it's warm enough to sit out on deck. I mean, if you'd like to?'

If I'd like to?

#Stupidquestion.

I picked up my champagne glass and my evening bag. Who said I couldn't live a bit dangerously? Sure, I wasn't certain I liked him enough for a relationship, but who said anything about a relationship? Even Mum had said I should try and find a man ... Well, she didn't say I had to keep him – did she?

'Oh, okay,' I said, playing hard to get.

That's me all over. Why can't I take a leaf out of my sister's book for once – play it cool and get men slavering all over me? I mean, isn't that what flirting is all about?

We left the theatre and went out on to the promenade deck. The very last of the sunset was fading over the coast far out on the horizon. He found a table and two cushioned steamer chairs for us in a sheltered alcove and we sat with our feet up watching the silken sea slip past us.

'So, how are you enjoying the trip?' I asked him.

'Oh, it's fine. But I now have a lot of work to get through.'

'What are you doing? Did you say you were a writer?'

'No, not really. I work for Marnie; I'm more of a behind-the-scenes sort of guy. So, what brings you on board this ship? What do you do, Alexa?'

I drew breath and hesitated. This, in my experience, was where things tended to go wrong, as I don't have an off button when I'm asked that sort of question.

I finally broke up with my boyfriend, Ryan, on Valentine's Day when he gave me a card with the wrong name written inside, and since then I have had zero social life as I'm too busy avoiding him. This was shortly after I caught him shagging the tart who he now lives with, half a mile away from me, and who is six months pregnant. My sister – who I've only recently discovered also made a play for him at Laura's party – is about to get married to a successful and charming barrister who has friends called Monty and Lola and Quentin. They live in a hip industrial-style apartment overlooking the river that is almost unbearably chic. I'm living in the granny annexe at the bottom of my parents' garden. And on top of that –

I realised he was still waiting for my answer.

'I'm an estate agent. I think you call them realtors in America? Selling houses, you know? I know a lot of people don't like estate agents but it's a brilliant job. I mean, what could be more exciting than finding people their first home, or the house of their dreams?'

He laughed. 'Everyone needs a realtor at some point.'

'Doesn't mean you have to like them though, does it?' I said with a grin.

'Well, people don't like paying for something they think they could do themselves. But could they really be bothered to go round the streets, knocking on doors, looking for houses for sale? Would they take the photographs or draw the floor plans? And what if you wanted to move abroad? How would that work without realtor sites?'

I raised my glass in tribute to him. I felt suddenly clever and glamorous, sitting out on the deck of a beautiful ship drinking champagne with possibly the world's handsomest man.

I bet he didn't throw his balled-up socks under the bed or sit in his boxer shorts eating cold baked beans out of the tin like Ryan had. I bet he wouldn't tell me I looked like a cross between a black pudding and a failed Kardashian sister when I put some old leggings on to do the gardening.

I suddenly wondered what Gabriel Frost looked like with no clothes on and blushed in the darkness.

I sipped my champagne again and calmed down.

'Thank you for those kind words. Have we sailed past your parents' house yet?'

'I don't think so. That's on the coast of Maine. But we've passed Massachusetts.' He gestured towards the rail. 'Back there in the dark is the glamorous playground of old Cape Cod with its sand dunes, salty air and quaint little clapboard cottages that cost over a million dollars.'

'Really?'

'Oh yes, and the closer you can get to Nantucket and Martha's Vineyard the more expensive it is. My parents' house is just where the land ends and the sea begins. It's wonderful, especially when you get past Kennebunkport and the coach-loads of tourists hoping to see George Bush surf fishing.'

'I'd like to go to one of those places on the coast you read about, where there are weather-beaten, salt-grimed fishermen sitting on the dock complaining about the weather and the tourist boats. And there are lobsters in a tank, and you pick one and they cook it for you. I've seen pictures in *National Geographic* in my dentist's waiting room.'

'That's very poetic.' He laughed.

'I might chicken out when it came to it,' I said.

I held out my empty glass and he refilled it.

'There's a place I know just like that where the quay is built into the rock and there are only a few fishermen with their own lobster pots. They bring the catch to a place called Ken's Hut. They give you a plastic bib and some metal tools and a bowl of melted butter,' Gabriel said. 'It's absolutely delicious. There are only about six tables and they have blue-checked plastic cloths with cigarette burns, and storm lanterns when the weather is good enough. You can even eat outside in the summer. There's the prettiest view over towards the island and of course there's a lighthouse –'

I watched him, his face relaxing into a small smile of pleasant memories. The breeze from the sea ruffled his dark hair.

Was there a Mrs Frost? There had to be. Did he have a wife and some adorable children back at home who even now were missing him? Mrs Frost would be tall and slender. She would be an athletic, Nordic blonde with piercing blue eyes and endless legs. The type of woman who cared nothing for fashion or flashy cars. Who would decide to go for a run *for pleasure*, didn't need to diet and had never heard of something called 'considered eating'. She'd do that *hygge* thing that's so popular at the moment, with cashmere throws and pale wood everywhere, and blue and white enamel mugs of hot choco-late. No, scrub that; every time I'd ever had a drink from an enamel mug I'd burnt the skin off my top lip. She'd be a great cook and a marvellous hostess and wouldn't hide emergency chocolate at the back of the wardrobe like I did.

They would have beautiful children, carbon copies of their mother, probably bilingual, naturally tidy, who never asked for junk food or complained about school, or fought on the floor screaming like India and I had done when we were young.

'You're very quiet,' Gabriel said.

'I was just wondering –' I shut up just in time and tried desperately to think of something to say '– how many eggs they use on a ship this size.'

He blinked back his surprise that I should be thinking such a thing.

'Dozens I expect. Perhaps there are hens down below deck furiously laying, day and night.'

'I hope not – that would be cruel.'

He raised his eyebrows. 'But you wouldn't mind plunging a lobster into a pot of boiling water?'

'Well, I wouldn't do it *personally*, of course.'

He chuckled. 'I often wonder if the lobsters nudge each other to the front of the tank and try to stay at the back and look unimpressive.'

I laughed with him and then put on a funny voice. '*Pick him, I've not been well!* Do you think that sounds like a lobster?'

He laughed again. 'Exactly like a lobster!'

I put my hands up and made them into pincers. '*Look at my claws. They're tiny. Pick him over there!*'

Gabriel spluttered into his champagne. He looked so care-free, I wondered if this was the real Gabriel: the relaxed, happy man with the childish sense of humour.

'There you are, Gabe! I've been searching this ship for the last half-hour!'

We both looked up. It was Marnie Miller.

Of course it was. She came clip-clopping along the promenade deck towards us in her high-heeled, satin evening shoes, a pashmina wound round her tiny shoulders like a child wrapped in a blanket.

Gabriel stood up. 'I thought you'd turned in?'

'No, I have not turned in. I've been looking for you.'

She suddenly registered that I was there and her tone changed; it was subtle but unmistakeable. 'I was worried. You naughty thing.'

'No need,' Gabriel said. 'We were just enjoying the sea air.'

'And champagne!' Marnie said. 'How lovely!'

I stood up from my steamer chair; the comfortable, warm mood of the evening had gone now.

'Would you like to join us?'

I think, under the circumstances, ninety-nine point nine, nine, nine per cent of women would have said, *Ooh no, I can see you're having a lovely chat. I don't want to interrupt.*

Not Marnie Miller.

She sank gracefully into my chair and pulled her pashmina more tightly around her.

'I'd love some champagne,' she said with a sweet smile.

'Of course.'

Gabriel went off to find another glass and Marnie directed her beautiful eyes at me.

'Have we met?'

'I was in your talk this morning: *Write for Love*. I thought it was really great.'

'Did you? How super of you to say so. You never know how these things are going to go. I mean I've done this sort of thing so often but sometimes I'm just – well – the girl from Worcester, wondering if I'm good enough. Does my lifestyle advice really help? Am I really and truly a success around the world?'

She tilted her head to one side and gave me a sad, beseeching look.

'I should have thought you knew that by now? You've sold billions of books.'

'Yes, but inside my head I'm just little old me. Struggling to get my head around life. Wondering if I'm useful. Wanting to be a success.'

'But you are,' I said, slightly irritated by her rather transparent attempts to be humble while fishing for compliments. 'You're a terrific success. You have thousands of readers, you do television seminars and magazine articles about decluttering and improving your life, you have fantastic reviews on Amazon. I mean, you're on this ship because people want to learn from you.'

'I'm still the silly girl with the untidy desk.' She was off on one now, I could tell. 'Little Marnie Keogh with the skinny legs who was never picked for the netball team, or got cards on Valentine's Day, or had a boyfriend. Sometimes I wonder if people really do like what I have to say or if they're just being kind.'

I fell into her trap, irresistibly baited by her hunger for praise and flattered that, for some reason, she was confiding in me.

'Why should any of that matter now? People admire you. You're pretty and gracious and everyone loves your books. They buy them in shops and supermarkets and airports all over the world. You must help a lot of women every day.'

She looked at me, her lower lip trembling a little. 'Yes, you're right. Thank you so much. I do, don't I?'

Mercifully, at that point Gabriel returned and poured out a glass of champagne for her.

'Thank you, darling,' she said and sipped it, hunching her shoulders up with pleasure.

I had the ungracious feeling that she needed a good slap.

'Right, I'm off to bed,' I said.

'Oh, must you?' Marnie murmured unconvincingly, looking at Gabriel as though she wanted to eat him.

I think I was just jealous.

'I really must,' I said, draining my glass. The champagne tasted flat and bitter now, not nice at all. I slunk off to bed in a right old mood.

Chapter Eight

East India

Cognac, Grand Marnier, Maraschino Liqueur,
Grenadine, Angostura Bitters

The following day we were going to be at sea all day and planning to spend some time enjoying the onboard activities. For one thing there were dance lessons with Peter and Paula, who were planning on teaching us ballroom dancing. God help them.

First of all we had breakfast. India tried a nice healthy option of whole-wheat granola but said the noise she made eating it was too much for her and gave up halfway through, pushing the bowl away.

'I think I'll stick to quiet food today,' she said, looking rather pale and fragile. She had already expected me to acknowledge her bravery for even being up and dressed. 'Why did you let me have that champagne after dinner last night? That was when the rot set in.'

'It's not my bloody fault! Oh, it wasn't the Strawberry Daiquiri then? Or the Martini? Or the wine?'

'Stop shouting, for God's sake. Today I'm sticking to the controlled eating,' she said, 'and I'm going to find something else for breakfast.'

She wandered off to look at yogurt and fresh fruit and came back with two jam doughnuts and a vanilla milkshake.

'Pardon my French but how controlled is that?' I said.

'This is a medicinal doughnut,' she said. 'Shut up and leave me alone.'

I left her hunched over her carbohydrates and went off for a walk round the deck on my own. It was a bit colder outside as the ship sailed north, but it was very refreshing. The sky above was pale blue with wisps of cloud scudding in from the sea. I had been pleased how well India and I had been getting along. I needed to give her and her hangover some space otherwise it was only a matter of time before our morning bickering turned into something much worse.

I found a sheltered spot where there were thoughtfully placed chairs in between the orange bulk of two lifeboats. Ten minutes later, apparently unable to leave me alone, India appeared and sat down.

'So, last night...' she said, flopping down beside me. 'Gabriel Gorgeousness. What was going on there?'

'Nothing, he just wanted company, I suppose. Marnie Miller said she wanted an early night. We were just the first people he saw.'

India gave me a look. 'So you don't think it's because he fancies you?'

'No, don't be ridiculous!' I said, my brain spinning with the possibilities.

'Of course he does! You don't think he's been following you around for no reason, do you? Do you think it was a coincidence he turned up in Newport to have lunch with us?'

I blinked at the prospect. But, to be fair, India's radar was far better attuned to this sort of thing than mine. I allowed this thought to sink in.

'You fancy him too, don't you? I know you. You always settle for the slightly grubby types with few prospects and no table manners, when you prefer the good-looking ones, but don't think you stand a chance with them.'

'What? Where did that come from?' I said, a bit taken aback by this sisterly psychoanalysis. 'I'm not you. It is possible to go through life not fancying every man I set eyes on, you know.'

She wasn't listening. 'He might be just the thing to get you over Ryan the Bastard. Get yourself *over* Gabriel Frost instead, so to speak. Get you back in the saddle. A moonlight stroll along the deck; he invites you into his cabin *for coffee*. I mean, it is next door to ours after all. You wouldn't have to go far in the morning, would you? Or in the middle of the night if he snored.'

'So you're encouraging me to have a swift bonk, are you? Honestly, India, you're about to get married – you should be full of romantic yearning not encouraging mindless sex between virtual strangers.'

She laughed and it almost felt like old times. 'There is something to be said for it.'

'I bow to your superior knowledge!'

'But I bet it wouldn't be mindless. I bet he'd be really good in bed.'

'India! You're almost a married woman. And by the way I don't need to get over Ryan the Bastard as you so delicately put it. I got over him in ten minutes.'

'Rubbish.'

'I did!'

'No, you didn't. You were still moping about and sulking months after you found out what he'd been up to. And when you heard his new girlfriend was pregnant you were inconsolable.'

'Well, I thought he might have been, you know ...?'

'The One? Don't make me laugh,' India said. 'He was never good enough for you. He was always a bit shifty.'

Good enough for me? Since when did India worry about that sort of thing? She'd been so wrapped up in Jerry and the wedding I was surprised she'd even noticed Ryan and I had broken up.

'Well, you've had your share of unsuitable sods over the years. How did you know Jerry was The One?' I said, trying to shift the focus away from my obviously terrible taste in men. 'He wasn't the sort I thought you would go for.'

She thought for a moment and looked rather soppy and wistful. 'He came over for dinner, and he brought Lindt chocolate. Three giant bars rather than a poncey box because he said you got more chocolate for the money. Which is true, isn't it? And Sarah and Lucy were there and they started talking about Uri Geller and what happened to him and how he used to bend spoons.'

I frowned. 'Yes. How is this relevant?'

'We tried sticking spoons on our noses and Jerry was the only one who could do it, and then we found out he'd wedged it on with a Dairylea triangle. And the spoon fell off and I looked at him with cheese on the end of his nose and I knew. He was The One. I know he might not be the best-looking bun in the window but he makes me happy and he's kind and thoughtful and funny.'

'Wow,' I said, a bit gobsmacked. This was not the sort of thing my sister usually said. 'That's amazing.'

There was no doubt about it – my sister had been a bit of a bike in her teenage years. There was always some drama, some boy throwing pebbles at her bedroom window in the small hours, occasionally the unexpected creak of the stairs in the middle of the night. Twice there were pregnancy scares; once a jilted suitor threatened suicide. I can think of a few reasons for throwing myself off the Clifton Suspension Bridge, but I have to say my sister isn't one of them.

Now, of course, all that was forgotten and she had morphed seamlessly into a wholesome fiancée and paragon of virtue. But I knew where all the bodies were buried so to speak. I knew exactly when, with whom and where she first had sex (her sixteenth birthday with Simeon Palliser in his parents' gazebo) because she couldn't resist telling me she'd done it before I had. Perhaps that didn't help our relationship either.

'Well, that's the sort of man you should have. Not Jerry, of course, because he's mine. But someone who makes you feel like that,' India concluded.

'Ryan thought Frankie Boyle was funny,' I said gloomily.

'Case proven, m'lud. I'm going in now and I shall have a hot chocolate. With marshmallows.'

'Is that really a healthy option?'

'Dunno, I just want one. Are you coming?'

I nodded. We made our way to the food court and got two hot chocolates, one with marshmallows and one without because I think they taste like old pencil rubbers.

'Perhaps you just overthink things?' India said, continuing her thoughts on my situation. 'You're the clever one after all.'

I laughed. 'Says who? I never went to university. I didn't get a degree.'

'Well, neither did I if you remember,' India said.

'What *did* you do for those three years?'

India laughed. 'I had a lot of fun, got pissed and involved with some people I'd have been better off avoiding. I certainly didn't do any work.'

'Yes, that's pretty much what I thought.'

We sat watching people milling around, having either a late breakfast or an early lunch. It was always funny watching the more dedicated eaters panicking when something new was wheeled out of the kitchens. They would be quite happy with their muffins, fruit and cereal, and then pancakes, crispy bacon and croissants would make an appearance and they would almost spin off in confusion.

'I think I could get used to living on a cruise ship. Everyone's nice to you, the scenery changes every day and you don't have to do any cooking or housework.'

India snorted. 'Ah, but what about when you had children? There aren't exactly good schools or cub packs on board, are there?'

'Well, no. But if there were enough kids, you could form one.'

India delved about for the marshmallows at the bottom of her mug with a teaspoon. 'How many kids would you need to form a cub pack anyway?'

'Five? Six?' I said. 'I don't know. And what if one of them was a girl?'

'Difficult.'

I came to my senses. 'India, we can't afford to live on a cruise ship. Why are we even worrying about it?'

'Ah, but if you married Gabriel Frost you probably could afford it,' she said. 'He looks rich. I expect that means you'll put him off soon.'

After that we wandered about, looking in the shops at the duty free stuff. There were some incredibly expensive bottles of whisky and teddies wearing knitted jumpers with *Reine de France* embroidered on them. Then we went to have lunch in the Hawaiian Bar next to the pool, an exciting-looking place with fake palm trees and very blue water.

We found a table where we could watch people getting in and complaining about the air temperature. (I didn't think the *Reine de France* could be held responsible for that.) The water was so warm it was steaming. And it was September after all.

'What shall we have?' India said.

I perused the menu. 'It's pizza or pizza.'

'That's not very Hawaiian, is it?' she said.

'It is is if you put pineapple on it. Allegedly.'

India thought about it. 'No, I don't fancy that. Pizza should be pizza. Anchovies and olives.'

'Well, let's have that.'

A waiter in a Hawaiian shirt and board shorts came over to take our order. I think he had been specially selected for his golden-haired beachboy look. He was tall and tanned and young and lovely as the song goes.

'Me name's Liam, I'll be looking after you? I'll get that order sorted, and to drink, ladies?' he said. He was definitely Australian by the sounds of it. Every sentence seemed to end with a question mark.

I was about to ask for some iced water but the abstemious one on the controlled eating diet plan got in first.

'Two lagers,' she said. 'Large ones.'

'Two lagers? Good choice? I'll get right back to you?'

'Thanks?' India said as he walked away. She leant across the table. 'You can tell by the way he's swaggering he thinks we're watching him.'

'Well, you are! Stop it!' I said to India.

'Just looking – what do you think Jerry would look like in a Hawaiian shirt like that?'

'Look, can we stop it with the Australian verbal tick? Jerry is not a Hawaiian shirt sort of bloke.'

Liam, the beachboy, returned with our lagers and a cheeky wink.

'Here you go, ladies? Your pizzas won't be long?' He put down two enticingly frosted glasses and tucked his tray under one arm. 'First cruise with us, is it?'

'Yes, first cruise full stop actually,' I said while, beside me, India sank nearly half her drink and let out a happy sigh, wiping a foam moustache away with the back of her hand afterwards. She can be classy my sister.

'You won't find better than the *Reine de France*,' Liam said. 'I've worked on them all? This one is proper good? Been to any of the activities?'

'We're going to the Peter and Paula dance classes later,' India said.

'Aw, they really are the dog's bollocks? I mean really?'

118

If he carried on asking unanswerable questions I was going to hit him.

'Gosh, I'm really hungry,' I said, looking over his shoulder in the hope that our lunch might appear. He took the hint.

'I'll go and look?'

India watched him go and shook her head at me.

'You're turning into a real grouch?' she said.

'I am not! And stop doing that.'

'What?'

'Turning every sentence into a question.'

'It's Gabriel Frost, isn't it? You were just the same when you met Ryan and you didn't think he'd noticed you. And when you met Tom what's-his-name. He took four days to phone you back, and you were like a bear with a sore bum.'

I spluttered my outrage. 'You were never more wrong! Gabriel who? I mean really, I don't know where you got that idea from.'

'Okay, if you say so.'

'Anyway he's with Marnie Miller, isn't he? Who could possibly compete with her?'

India looked thoughtful. 'But he's not with her, is he? He works for her – there's a difference.'

Beachboy returned with two pizzas the size of bicycle wheels; if they were thin and crispy the deep dish ones must have been like airbeds.

'There you go, ladies? Enjoy?'

'Thanks.'

'Can I freshen up your drinks there?'

'No, we're fine thanks.'

'Do you want mayo? Ketchup? Black pepper?'

I resisted the urge to wrap my pizza round his craggy, smiling face and sipped my lager.

'No, nothing thanks.'

'Side order of fries? Green salad? How about some hot sauce?' Liam was almost desperate now.

'No, honestly. We're okay.'

Nor did I want some olives, garlic bread, banoffee pie or ice cream.

'Well, you know where I am if you change your mind? I'll be seeing you?'

He stood and span his tray on one finger for a moment, distressed he couldn't think of anything else to bring us, and then he wandered off, straightening a couple of chairs as he went.

'Well, for heaven's sake,' I said.

'He fancied you,' India said, wrapping a massive slice of pizza into a roll and stuffing the end into her mouth.

'Stop trying to fix me up with someone. Just because you're all loved-up and off the market!'

India smiled smugly. 'I'm right though. You're sex-starved.'

'Oh, shut *up*.' I laughed.

'I'm right.'

Chapter Nine

Waltzing Matilda

Passion Fruit, Dry Gin, White Wine,
Champagne, Ginger Ale

Thanks to the length of the Versailles Ballroom, Peter and Paula looked to be in their thirties at first glance. Close up they gained twenty years. Even so they were a well-preserved couple, trim in the way that only a lifetime of strenuous exercise and discipline can guarantee. They were dressed in sharp, unattractive dance outfits that owed a great deal to the colour tangerine. Peter wore a shiny grey suit with an orange shirt and spotted tangerine tie. Paula was a riot of carroty ruffles, sequins and tulle. Neither of them seemed able to stand still. Peter twirled Paula round and presented her in front of him as though she was a stuffed toy at a funfair stand. Both had rictus grins. I wondered if they smiled in their sleep. Or maybe once the bedroom door had closed behind them their features collapsed into sullen misery and they had to massage the feeling back into their jaws.

'And *so*, ladies and gentlemen, Paula and I are delighted to welcome you to our World of Dance.'

Peter span and twirled Paula around in front of him and she smiled as though only gelignite would stop her.

'Dance is our life, ladies and gentlemen. We met through dance; we love to dance. We can think of no better exercise or hobby. You can dance in anything, anywhere. In leisure suits and T-shirts. In slacks and sweaters.' Peter's eyes glinted with something akin to frenzy as Paula carried on pirouetting. He gestured with one hand to the young men lined up against the wall. 'Some of the crew are here to assist if there are ladies without partners. All of them are competent dancers – you need have no fear. Dance, ladies and gentlemen, dance for pleasure and health!'

'He's freaking me out,' India muttered. 'Is he on something?'

'Now who's being grumpy? They're just filled with the Joy of Dance!' I said. India trod on my foot making me yelp.

'Ah, a volunteer!' Peter said, holding out a hand towards me.

'Oh, thanks so much,' I muttered to my sister out of the corner of my mouth.

I stepped forward to take Peter's outstretched hand and he tried to whirl me round, but unfortunately I didn't spin as well as Paula in her satin dance shoes. The rubber soles of my trainers stuck to the floor and I ricocheted off on to the bunions of a stout Army veteran, baseball cap jammed over his eyes and standing a little too close to the action.

'Hey, lady, watch it!' he grumbled, hobbling out of my way.

'Sorry,' I gasped.

Peter grabbed me and held me in a rigid dance hold, one hand flat against my back, the other holding my hand up above shoulder height. I hoped I wasn't too sweaty.

'This is the basic frame. I want you all to find yourself a partner and copy us. Paula will help you.'

It was really weird standing with everyone watching us, in close proximity to a man I'd never laid eyes on before. It felt oddly intimate and yet at the same time Peter was ignoring me, shouting instructions over my head to the others. I wondered if he could feel any rolls of fat escaping from under my bra and I took a deep breath and tried to stand up properly. I bet Paula didn't have a spare ounce of flab.

I sneaked a look up his aquiline nose.

India had been paired up with one of the other men in the room who looked oddly familiar. Someone in crisp chinos and a clean white shirt with his blond hair smoothed down into some sort of order. It was Liam.

I sent India a questioning look and she grinned and shrugged.

'And *so*. Listen to the music; the waltz is the easiest of all the ballroom dances. Just listen to that lovely beat. And *one* two three, *one* two three. Make that box, make that box.'

Peter shoved me back in a rigid line, his knees clashing

against mine. I tried to follow him, make myself dip and sway like he did. I must have looked like a sack of spuds as we moved across the floor, close to the open doors at the end of the room.

Peter suddenly saw something that irritated him enough to let go of me and I trotted on alone for a few moments, hopping from foot to foot with the vector force Peter had left behind.

Suddenly Paula appeared and thrust me towards a spare man. I looked up, completely red in the face, and gasped; it was Gabriel, looking as flustered as I was.

'Making new friends? You might not be the right height, but you should be fine to waltz. Come now, no time to waste, join in.'

Paula wove off, luminous in her orange outfit, adjusting an arm here, an elbow there; flashing around the dance floor like Donald Trump in a frock.

Gabriel was struggling not to laugh and I could feel my red face heading towards beetroot.

'I'm sorry about this,' I said, feeling a complete fool. It would have been one thing if Gabriel had sought me out, but quite another for me to be foisted on him. I mean, look at him – all six gorgeous feet of him ...

'Why?' He chuckled as we tried to follow the steps together. 'I've been up for hours trying to get through some new work, and then I thought, sod it. So I came to see what all the fuss was about – not that I anticipated this though.'

I blushed furiously and was looking around for my sister

when Gabriel suddenly turned us around and I found myself glancing back up at him. Gosh, he was pretty incredible to look at.

And that was when I realised that while I couldn't waltz, he could. Gabriel steered me out from the central maelstrom and into the calmer waters where we could make the box. I fixed my eyes on his grey sweater and tried to count. I wondered where my feet were in relation to his. It would be too embarrassing if I trod all over him.

'Don't look down,' Gabriel said, laughter in his voice. 'Look at me.'

Now we all know how hard it is to look at someone when you fancy them but don't actually know them that well. He was certainly over six feet tall to my five feet four, and in the end I fixed my eyes on his chin and wondered if I had in fact died and gone to heaven. It might have been an accident that we ended up dancing together, but oh my, he even smelled wonderful, of warm wool and expensive aftershave. We moved around the room to the rather cheesy music – I think it was Engelbert Humperdinck at one point – and suddenly I realised I was actually waltzing. Well, I hadn't seen that coming!

I looked around to find India so I could make a funny face at her and share my triumph. She was still with Liam. They stood looking at each other's feet and giggling. I thought Peter had assured us the male staff could dance? There seemed to be a lot of silliness going on over there.

'I didn't have you down as a dancer,' I said at last.

'No? Why ever not? I love dancing,' Gabriel said, edging me expertly over to an empty part of the dance floor. I was beginning to enjoy myself. Now was that because of the dance or the partner?

'You seem far too serious. I didn't think this would be your sort of thing at all.'

'Well, you did say you'd be here,' Gabriel said.

I felt rather giddy at this point and bit my lower lip to stop myself squeaking my delight.

He was here because *he knew I was going to be here too*?

Really? I didn't think I'd ever been so flattered in my life. Not to mention thrilled and astonished. But maybe he was just saying it? I tried to tamp down my excitement.

'Oh,' I said, sneaking a glance. He was looking down at me, a smile on his lips. He seemed pretty sincere.

'Wait till we get to the Argentine tango,' he said, a chuckle in his voice.

'That's not going to happen any time soon,' I said firmly. 'I've seen *Strictly*.'

He laughed.

For a moment I tried to imagine myself in a scarlet beret and tight black satin dress, split up to my knickers. I'd have a cigarette drooping from one lip and one high-heeled foot on a chair as I tried to be a sultry gaucho chick.

'The opportunity to do you serious damage with a load of unguarded ganchos and kicks would be frightening.'

'Perhaps we could attempt the Charleston?'

126

'Well, I could do the funny faces and falling over I expect.'

He laughed again. 'I bet you could too! It's almost worth trying.'

Over on the other side of the room, India was at least dancing now, not fooling around laughing with Liam. In fact, as they swept past, they seemed to be doing rather well.

'Having fun?' India yelled over the noise of many shuffling feet and Vera Lynn and 'The Anniversary Waltz'. 'You naughty thing!'

'I don't think your sister approves,' Gabriel said after a few moments.

'Approves of what? Of me? I stopped caring what India thought years ago,' I said, wishing it was true.

'What are you doing after this?' Gabriel asked. Was it my imagination or had he slowed down a bit.

'Towel folding,' I said.

'You're joking?'

'No. Haven't you got back to the cabin to find a couple of towel swans on the bed?'

'Well, yes, but it doesn't mean I want to do the same back home!'

'Wouldn't your wife be impressed?'

Clumsy or what? I'd seen him hanging around with Marnie and, to be honest, there was no evidence anything was really going on. But maybe that was because he had a wife at home ... or a girlfriend. I really didn't like to think he could be a cheater too ... not after Ryan the Bastard.

'Possibly,' he said, and my heart plunged. 'If I still had a wife.'

If I still had a wife. So there had been one at some point.

Peter and Paula were now dancing in the middle of the whirling couples, showing how it should be done and shouting advice. At that moment there was also a public announcement about someone who had missed the lifeboat drill and Peter had to shout to make himself heard over that as well as Elvis and 'Are You Lonesome Tonight?'

'My right hand here, you see? Hand flat against the lady's shoulder blade,' he bellowed.

Everyone was gradually slowing to watch until only Peter and Paula were dancing. They ended with a triumphant flare of Paula's skirts and an extravagant wave of one arm as Peter dipped her backwards. We all applauded.

'So, next time we will be doing the quickstep,' Peter said. 'We hope to see you all here. Paula and I will be giving an exhibition of the American Smooth this evening before the dancing.'

'Well, we can't miss that,' Gabriel murmured, and I swear my insides sort of flipped over. His arm was still around me and the feel of him was making me light-headed. I didn't understand; I barely knew the man and already my stomach was doing cartwheels.

India was pushing her way through the crowd towards me, Liam hot on her heels.

'Liam says he can get a pass for me to go on the bridge,' she said. 'I'll see you at the towel folding?'

'Yes, fine,' I said, a bit startled for a moment.

I watched as she hurried out after Liam, snaking their way through the group of Army veterans who were blocking the doorway and talking about their time in Germany when Elvis was there. I wondered what to do. Should I follow her? Should I go back to our cabin? Go to the bar?

Gabriel ran a hand through his hair.

'Fancy grabbing a drink?'

'Would I? You bet,' I said. Spending time with the *unmarried* Gabriel Frost wasn't something I was going to miss. 'If you're sure?'

'I wouldn't have asked you if I wasn't,' he said with a grin.

Was this actually happening? Men didn't generally ask me out in daylight or when they were sober.

I followed him to a small, informal wine bar, yet another place I'd not found before. It was on the top deck with a wonderful view over the stern of the boat. There were just a dozen or so tables with blue leather chairs and crisp white napkins.

We were shown to a fantastic seat overlooking the sea, where I could watch the wake of the ship swooping away in a continuous foam-topped wave many feet below us. The sky was a dull grey with the threat of rain in the clouds. I could see another huge cruise ship far out to sea, heading in the other direction. I expected it was filled with tourists like us, enjoying their journey back from Halifax, eating too much, going to talks about the *Titanic*.

Don't mention Marnie, I thought, repeating it to myself like a mantra.

I would not spoil the moment by asking where she was.

I wouldn't even talk about her lecture.

Don't mention Marnie.

Don't even think about her, or her next talk, or ask what he was to her.

Or what she was to him.

Talk about something else.

Don't mention Marnie.

The waiter pulled out my chair and I sat down.

'So, how is Marnie?' I said.

Doh.

Gabriel shrugged. 'I think she'll be okay.'

'She's enjoying the trip?'

'She does a lot of these things – it's a passion of hers. Ships and cruises.'

'Lovely. And her husband? Doesn't he ever join her?'

Oh, for heaven's sake, woman. Shut up!

Gabriel didn't reply but handed me a menu card. Behind him the waiter stood, pen poised.

'What shall we have? What do you fancy?'

Well now, there's a question.

What do I fancy?

All sorts of rude thoughts whirled round my head. I said the first thing I saw on the menu.

'Just a glass of red wine. And some olives. Please.'

'Good choice. I'll have the same.'

Gabriel handed back the menus and poured me some iced water from the jug on the table.

'So now then, towel folding? Tell me about that?'

I laughed. 'Don't you think it would be fun?'

'I suppose so. I've not thought about it.'

'Well, come along then, join in.'

The waiter arrived with our drinks and there was a bit of napkin flourishing and bowing before we could carry on the conversation.

'So why don't you?' I said.

Gabriel hesitated. 'I have work to do.'

'Yes, what is this work that keeps you so busy?' I said, suddenly bold.

'Oh, just paperwork.'

'So are you a writer?'

'Well, yes and no.'

I frowned. 'Fiction or non-fiction?'

Gabriel tilted his head and his eyes sparkled with amusement. 'Now that's a very good question!'

'Huh?'

He laughed. 'Sorry, Alexa, I'm teasing you. I'm trying to make it sound more interesting than it really is. I've been working as part of Marnie's team for a few months. I'm doing some of her legal work. She has a lot of different areas where she needs to protect her interests. Books, magazines, interviews, this trip. And ... well, never mind.'

Ah, a lawyer. I couldn't think what to say. I mean it wasn't as though he was going to start discussing juicy cases he'd known or naming people he'd successfully sued.

'You sound a bit American,' I said instead, steering the conversation wonderfully again. Really, I was getting into this flirting business for once.

'No, I was born in England, but my mother is married to an American. I spent a week with her here at their house in Maine before this trip. It's a beautiful state. And you? You're enjoying a break from work?'

I nodded my head. 'Oh yes, but I enjoy work too. I always knew I would follow in my dad's footsteps. He took over my grandfather's company and, well, from the moment I left school – even before then – I helped him in the office.'

I tailed off. No one, not even Ryan at the beginning, had asked me about work. But Gabriel nodded his head, encouraging me to continue.

'That moment when you know you've helped a couple or family find their perfect home. You can't beat it. That place they've been searching for. Perhaps wondering if they can afford it or whether they'll sell their own house in time. It's nice to be part of their journey. The young couple starting out, the retired lady wanting somewhere easier to manage, the couple expecting their second baby. They're all different but they all want the same thing. Somewhere to call home.'

'You make it sound very rewarding, and you're so

enthusiastic. I love that.' Gabriel had a look on his face I didn't really recognise.

I was surprised at myself. I never really talked about work like that to anyone. To everyone else I just pretended it was any old job, nothing important ... but really, well, I did kind of love it.

'What else do you do? Do you write?'

I laughed. 'No, despite what India said, I'm not in any way cut out for that.'

'So what do you do in your spare time?'

I took a sip of my wine to avoid answering. Let's be honest, these days I had a lot of spare time. The longer I thought about it the more I realised I couldn't think of a sensible answer. I also realised I had a bit of olive stuck between my front teeth, which was of course elegant and attractive in the extreme.

I didn't have a husband or family to look after. I didn't even have a home of my own to decorate or tweak. There wasn't much need to fold towels into swans at the moment.

'I read, I cook.'

Well, that might have been stretching the truth just a bit. I used to cook when Karen and I were sharing a flat and we had a proper kitchen with an oven and induction hob and actual cupboards and worktops. Now I was living at the end of my parents' garden in the granny annexe, I had what might politely be called a kitchenette. And who bothered actually cooking for one anyway? Plus, going out with 'friends' was an old memory. Most of my friends had kind of disappeared off the radar now they were married and had kids. I couldn't remember the last time I met up with any of them – there was always something they were rushing off to. I shook my head, to brush away the creeping feeling of failure. Still, there was one area where I was a success.

'What I'd really like to do is expand the business,' I said, voicing something I hadn't mentioned to anyone. 'We get a lot of enquiries about smallholdings and places people can keep chickens or live the good life. I'd like to start a department just handling those things.'

'That sounds fascinating. People really want to do that?'

'Oh yes. They have plans to buy somewhere big enough to keep a few sheep or goats. Perhaps a rescue donkey. It's all good stuff and very well intentioned. I do wonder sometimes if they really know what they would be taking on. Perhaps we could advise on that too?' I added thoughtfully.

'And planning the wedding,' he said.

'Oh, the wedding,' I said.

I looked out at the waves and thought about the wedding. There was still a lot to do, stuff that, as bridesmaid, I should be sorting out. I gave a heavy sigh.

'Yes, this trip is supposed to be our hen thingy. It's not really working out like that though. All we seem to be doing is drinking cocktails.'

Gabriel looked puzzled. 'I thought that was what you were supposed to do on your hen weekend?'

I laughed. 'Yes, you're right. Anyway we get to Halifax tomorrow and then we set off across to England.'

'Are you looking forward to it? The waves on the Atlantic can be very impressive sometimes.'

'I love that!'

He grinned. 'Me too.' He held out his glass to me and we clinked them together. 'Here's to being a good sailor!'

We carried on in companionable silence for a while, watching the seabirds diving and swooping around the back of the ship. Gabriel shifted in his chair.

'What are your hopes and dreams then, Alexa?' he said.

My hopes and dreams.

I didn't have a clue. No one had ever asked me that.

'I suppose I hope my parents will carry on in good health. That my sister will be happy. That one day I will ...'

'What?'

'I don't know. I just sometimes wonder.'

'Wonder what?'

'Well, what it is I do that's so wrong?'

I stopped, horrified at myself. He didn't need all this ridiculous soul-baring. I hardly knew him and I'd already gone off on one about the magic of being an estate agent. *God!*

'I'm sure you don't do anything wrong, Alexa,' he said after a moment.

'Apart from chuck champagne over people at airports?' I said, trying to lighten the moment.

He grinned. 'Oh, I've forgiven you for that. You do realise I thought it was very funny, don't you?'

My heart did a little judder. 'I thought you were furious.'

He shook his head. 'It was all I could do to not laugh out loud. Your face was a picture. But you need some dreams for yourself, you know.'

I turned back to my wine, wanting to change the subject. I was finding it increasingly difficult not to stare at him with his mesmerising grey eyes and his muscular shoulders moving under the cashmere sweater. I could remember how it had felt to have his arm around me, my hand on his as we moved to that awful music. Oh dear, not only did I fancy him something rotten, but I was starting to like him too.

Stop it. Stop it. *Stop it.*

Chapter Ten

Sidecar Named Desire

Calvados, Apple Schnapps, Lemon Juice, Sugar Syrup

So. Towel folding.

No, I didn't know why I was going either. Particularly when, with a little bit more courage on my part, I could have spent a couple of hours with Gabriel, drinking wine, laughing and getting to know him better. He was, after all, the first man in a very long time I could honestly say I'd fancied. And why wouldn't I? He was, even without the benefit of two large glasses of Merlot, gorgeous.

His voice was warm and low; he had impeccable manners; he didn't bolt his food and then ask if I needed help finishing mine. He didn't eat with his mouth open or look at other women with his mouth open either. He didn't burp, fart or pick his nose. Have I known men who do such things? Yes, of course I have – Ryan did all of them and more besides.

I can remember being out for dinner with Ryan once to celebrate my birthday. (I'd organised it, booked it and paid the deposit by the way.) He deliberately ordered three courses that were different from mine so he'd effectively have more choice. Then he swapped his whitebait starter (bleugh) for my pâté. He ate half my steak. And then, when he'd finished his apple pie, he dug into my Eton mess. And he drank most of the wine. And half my Calvados on the pretext of never having tried it. And then claimed to have left his wallet behind. And did I say anything? No.

Anyway.

I caught up with India in the vast glass and gilt atrium where she was looking at the leaflets advertising excursions in Nova Scotia.

'Where have you been?' she said, sounding very aggrieved. 'You're supposed to be looking after me.'

'I can't do that if you go off without me,' I said snappily, feeling a little put out. 'I wouldn't have minded going to see the bridge either. But we're not joined at the hip, are we? Where have you been?'

'Looking for you. Liam had to go back to work after we went to see the Captain on the bridge. It was brilliant. It's the best view on the ship.'

'Good. I wouldn't want him to be steering if he was stuck behind a pillar or anything.'

'And there were loads of dials and switches. I thought there would be a big wheel to steer with but there wasn't.'

'There aren't any sails either.'

'Very funny. So where have you been?'

'Having a drink. With Gabriel Frost.'

India's mouth dropped open. 'No! Really?'

'We went to a little wine bar at the back of the ship.'

'Wow! And?'

'And what?' I was in far too good a mood to let India's prodding get to me, and I was enjoying myself. We hadn't bickered like this in ages. It was nice – kind of.

'Well, is that it? There must be something more than that?'

'Not really. I asked if he wanted to come to towel folding and he didn't. And I asked if he was a writer and he said he was sort of looking after legal work for Marnie. But obviously he couldn't go into details.'

'You're useless!' India said, just like she always did.

'But I did find out he's not married.'

'That's something. But is he all loved-up with Marnie?'

'I don't know. I didn't ask. They work together.'

India rolled her eyes. 'No wonder you're still single,' she said waspishly. 'Come on, it's five minutes to towel folding. We'll just have time to get there if we hurry.'

*

Towel folding had already started by the time we got there. It was almost exclusively women. Evidently towel folding didn't hold the same appeal for men as writing a bestseller or learning to waltz.

Jaresh the towel folder extraordinaire was standing in front of a pile of white towels, his hands busy as he created something that looked like a towel croissant but turned out to be a crab. Personally I thought he cheated by sticking on two cartoon eyes at the last minute. I mean, who was going to keep a stock of plastic eyes in the house for those last-minute touches when you were expecting guests? No, nor me.

Anyway, then we had a go. India, of course, was good at it, and won a prize of some cartoon eyes and a face flannel from an impressed Jaresh. She also received some pretty poisonous looks from a couple of Army veterans' wives.

Then we watched him make an elephant from two towels. I had more luck with this and mine stood up too, which is more than India's did. Finally he showed us how to make a monkey from a bath towel and a flannel. After sticking on more googly eyes he hung it from a coat hanger. That would frighten the crap out of your unsuspecting guests. By then of course I was in a mood.

I was fretting about Gabriel and properly starting to worry about my future – something I hadn't really done before.

My hopes and dreams.

Was I going to end my days in the granny annexe at the bottom of my parents' garden? Bloody hell, I was pushing thirty. My best years were behind me. Weren't they?

If I'd had Wi-Fi I would have googled to find out for certain, but on board ship it was an expensive extra. And how shaming for the ship's IT expert to know I'd been looking for *Am I going to die alone eaten by cats?* or *Why don't any men fancy me?* If he told the rest of the crew they would all snigger at me.

I stopped and looked at India, who was still wrestling with her monkey's legs, and suddenly I needed her to answer something, a question I'd been too afraid to ask my blunt-to-a-fault sister.

'So why am I still single? What's the matter with me?' I asked and instantly regretted it.

India looked up and pushed a wisp of hair out of her eyes.

'Are you meaning anything specific or just generally?'

'Oh, thanks so much. I meant why can't I get a man? Why can't I be like you are with Jerry?'

'Don't you dare!'

'I didn't mean specifically Jerry, you clown. I meant why can't I get a bloke? A nice bloke?'

India pulled her monkey's paws out a bit further and shrugged. 'I dunno. Because you always go for the gits?'

'I don't!'

'Well, Ryan was a git and so was Tom. I don't know why you put up with either of them.'

'But I didn't know about Ryan and that woman till it had been going on for weeks. I think I was the last person in England to know,' I choked out, not wanting to go back to that moment. God, it had been embarrassing.

India gave a sigh of exasperation, unravelled her monkey altogether and started again.

'You turned down John Foster.'

'Wouldn't you?'

'Depends how desperate I was feeling. And thingy with the hair. What was he called?'

'Narrow it down a bit?'

'Blond, gormless, a bit of a piss artist.'

'Ben? You make him sound so attractive now you've said that,' I said, folding my towel into a small square.

India put her mangled monkey down and sighed, fixing me with a meaningful look. She looked pretty serious, and perhaps even just a bit frustrated. I gulped.

'There's nothing much wrong with you, Alexa. You're reasonably okay. And –' her expression became rather perky '– you have Gabriel Frost after you.'

'He's not after me. He was just passing the time while Marnie was busy having some part of her painted or massaged.'

'Look, Alexa, are you ever going to see Gabriel Frost again? After this cruise?'

'No, I doubt it.'

'Then go for it.'

'Go for what?'

'Jeez, you're slow. Have a bit of fun. It's a masked ball tonight, isn't it? So we'll get dolled up and go for some excitement,' she said, as if it was the most obvious solution in the world.

'What if he's not around?' I said slowly, the idea of being rejected burning in my stomach.

'He will be, trust me. And you can pretend to be someone else if you have a mask on, if that makes you feel better.'

'Who am I going to pretend to be?'

India pulled a face. 'Well, not Theresa May or Princess Anne obviously! I mean you can just be a bit mysterious. Flirt a bit.'

I thought about it. 'Oh, okay. I suppose.'

Flirt? Me? Maybe with a mask on I could try? This whole thing was starting to sound a bit exciting, and wasn't that just what my life needed right now? It wasn't like Gabriel Frost would look at me twice in the real world. I mean the chances of us meeting at all had been infinitesimal. This being flung together on a ship thing might just be working for me.

'Now help me make this monkey, then we'll go and get started on your eyebrows.'

'What's wrong with my eyebrows?' I said, startled.

'You should have two separate ones. I've been meaning to say something for ages.'

'Can we have a cocktail first?'

India sighed. 'Yes, if it makes you happy.'

*

We had two. A cheeky Margarita and then we read the cocktail menu carefully to see which one was the strongest. We ended up with something called Mary Queen of Scots that seemed to be nothing but several different types of rocket fuel diluted with a cherry that lurked at the bottom of the glass like a dead sea anemone. And then we went back to the cabin to start beautifying. I needed all the fortification I could get, especially if she was plucking my eyebrows – which turned out to be far more painful than she'd told me it would be.

'So, which dress?' India asked, her speech somewhat hampered by her setting rejuvenating face mask.

'Black sequins,' I said, similarly encumbered. 'I'm saving the bigger one for later, when I've expanded after eating my way across the Atlantic. What about you?'

'Turquoise? And Mum's evening bag.'

I nodded. I was feeling quite excited actually. It was nice to be here with India, even if she said things I didn't like, or maybe just didn't want to hear. For the first time in years it felt like we were normal sisters, getting ready for a night out. Maybe this cruise wasn't such a bad idea of Mum and Dad's after all. Or perhaps it was the umpteen units of alcohol sloshing around my bloodstream? It wasn't just warm, fuzzy feelings towards my sister; I could even imagine myself slinking about, flirting with the waiters and being rather outrageous, while at the same time irresistibly remote and mysterious. India was right – I should have some fun, get out more. I'd wasted enough time being all wounded and crushed by Ryan and his shitty behaviour.

Bastard.

*

We reached the dinner table just in time. Our table companions were already there, masks on as befitted a masquerade ball. Caron looked very chic in blue velvet, Marion in red satin and Ike and Marty in rather snug DJs.

'Well, aren't I the lucky one, sitting with all these beautiful ladies?' Ike said as we came to sit down.

I looked around the room. There was soft music playing. Each table had candles in huge, glass storm lanterns. The room, normally bright with chandeliers, was dimmed, throwing a mysterious glow across the room. The contented murmur of people enjoying the excitement of this enigmatic evening was everywhere. But Gabriel wasn't there.

The tables were set with crisp white napkins, the cutlery sparkling silver. A woman walked across the room, allowing everyone to admire the bead-encrusted gold dress that shimmied around her slim figure. I felt suddenly dull in my black sequins and looked up through my mask to see India watching me, her eyes dancing with amusement.

'Hmm, flashy!' she murmured. 'And so unsubtle.'

Instantly I felt better.

But Gabriel wasn't there.

The meal was wonderful, and it went on for ages. We had wine and liqueurs and coffee afterwards and the room grew hot and the laughter noisier.

'I need to go to the loo,' I said, pulling my napkin off my lap and putting it on my plate.

'Want me to come with you?' India said, looking wistfully

145

across the table to where Ike had just opened a bottle of brandy and was sharing it around with a generous hand.

I shook my head. 'I'll be back in a moment.'

I went to the cloakroom and washed my hands, letting the cold water run over my wrists. Looking up into the mirror I barely recognised myself. India had done a great job with my eye make-up. And my eyebrows looked pretty good too, despite the pain and all the yelping. My eyes were huge and filled with secrets behind the mask. I walked back towards the dining room, my high heels catching in the thick pile carpet. Then I hesitated for a moment. In front of me through the double doors was a wonderful snapshot of people enjoying themselves, dressed in their finery, the occasional gleam of jewellery glowing in the candlelight. I needed some fresh air. I needed to be outside, out there under the dark sky and drifting clouds.

I pushed the door to the promenade deck open; the air outside was wonderful. It was cold and crisp, and scented with the sea. I pulled my wrap around my shoulders and went and leaned on the rail. Below me in the darkness I could hear the ocean rushing past as we steered north towards Nova Scotia. Walking towards the stern, where there was shelter from the wind, I stood leaning back against a bulkhead for a moment, feeling the ship moving beneath me.

There was someone else there, as somehow I had known there would be.

Someone looking at the sea; tall and broad-shouldered, wearing a DJ, the black bow tie loose under his collar.

It was as though he had been waiting for me and now he could feel my eyes on him and the waiting was over.

He turned and looked at me for a long moment and then walked towards me, his dark hair gleaming in the starlight above us.

Reaching for me, he pulled the mask off my face and dropped it on to the deck by my feet. Then he grasped my arms and pulled me to him and suddenly his lips were on mine.

I could feel his hands running down my back, pressing me in to his body, melding me against him. I was weak and breathless. Giddy with triumph and surprise.

He held my head between his hands and pulled away, looking down at me.

'If you only knew,' he said.

'Gabriel,' I whispered, my heart thumping wildly.

And then he kissed me again, deeper this time, greedier, his need urgent.

He held me against him, my body fitting so perfectly against his. I could feel the cool fabric of his jacket, the heat of his body underneath it, the hardness of him. He wanted me and I wanted him, in a way I had never, ever desired a man before. I wanted so many things. To fuel his passion, his need, his hunger. I wanted to always feel like this.

'Tomorrow,' he said, his mouth against my temple, 'I must –'

And then he stopped.

Must what?

He held my arms against my sides, his fingers biting into my flesh, and gave a low groan of frustration.

'I wish,' he said, 'I just wish things were different.'

He walked away from me then, leaving me cold and trembling. A sob of disappointment rose in my throat. My exhilaration was replaced with utter despair.

It was a long time before I could move. The ship ploughed on into the darkness, the clouds above flying against the wind and thickening so the stars were blotted out and the night grew darker still.

I went back into the smothering warmth of the ship, thanking a waiter who held the door open for me, smiling at the maître d' as he escorted me back to my seat and arranged my napkin across my lap with a flourish.

Ike passed me a glass of brandy and I drank it, not tasting it at all, just aware of the fire of the liquid as I swallowed.

India was laughing, her face flushed and pretty in the candlelight.

She raised a questioning eyebrow at me. I think I smiled, but I couldn't feel it on my face. I was frozen with shock.

'You've lost your mask somewhere,' she whispered.

I reached up and touched my cold face.

'Oh yes,' I said, 'so I have.'

'What's the matter?' India said, concern in her eyes.

'I'm fine,' I lied, trying to rub some feeling back into my hands.

'You'll tell me eventually; you might as well tell me now.'

I thought about it. She was probably right but even so ...

'Not here,' I said.

India's face brightened. 'Flip, that sounds interesting.'

She drained the last of her brandy and Ike reached over to give her some more.

'Cheers, Ike!'

'You too, darlin'?'

I put my hand over my glass. 'No thanks, Ike, bit of a headache.'

The party had evidently started in my absence. Marion and Caron were talking about going dancing and Marty was trying to persuade them to go to the casino.

'So you weren't outside pushing the lovely Marnie over-board?' India said, leaning towards me.

'Someone's fallen overboard?' Caron said, blinking across the table, her nose twitching with the scent of excitement. 'Well, how terrible. Ike, we should tell someone.'

'No, Caron, no one has fallen overboard,' I said, foreseeing a full-scale alert and the ship turning round. 'Look, India, not now – later.'

Our companions had decided against that night's show because the crew were basing the evening on *Mamma Mia!* and Ike and Marty refused point-blank to go. Apparently they had been to the stage show in Boise and hated every minute. They had also been forced to sit through the film countless times at home. Enough was enough.

'We thought we would just stay and chat this evening,'

Marion said, gesturing for the waiter to come over. 'Honey, this brandy is giving me heartburn. Let's have something else. How about –'

The waiter stood patiently while Caron and Marion went through the cocktail list and tried to decide what to have.

'Irish coffee,' Caron said at last.

Marion gave two thumbs up. 'Brilliant, let's order four. The boys can carry on with the brandy.'

I was beginning to understand why the ship was filled with older people: their livers must be seasoned travellers too. I tried to protest but Caron was having none of it and four large coffee glasses appeared within minutes followed by four glasses of Frangelico, which Marion had been reading about and fancied trying.

My head was splitting with too much alcohol, the late hour and the remnants of my shock. I couldn't think properly. India was now having a rambling argument with Marty about American politics. Which was a bit weird because I didn't think India knew anything about politics, American or otherwise.

'Yes, but the electoral votes system,' she said, tapping her coffee glass with a teaspoon, 'that's what I don't understand. And the importance of loss aversion? How does that work then?'

Blimey! She would be explaining the offside rule next. Living with Jerry was obviously having quite an effect on her.

Marion looked a bit flummoxed and nudged Marty. 'Over to you, Idaho's answer to Tim Russert.'

The conversation veered off American politics and on to the ethics of zoos – don't ask. Then we realised the waiters were methodically clearing the tables and extinguishing the candles so the darkness of the dining room was gradually creeping towards us. There were only half a dozen tables left with people chatting and drinking while the waiters lurked around the dark edges of the room like the Nazgûl in *Lord of the Rings*, waiting to pounce and sweep the tablecloths off.

'I think I want to go to bed now,' I said. I looked at my watch; it was after midnight.

India dragged herself up from the table and tottered after me, weaving backwards and forwards along the corridor, eventually taking her shoes off.

'So,' she said, tugging at my arm, 'tell all. What's happened?'

I put my finger to my lips as we were nearing our room. After all, Gabriel was probably next door. Would he be crossing the Atlantic with us, or would he, like a lot of the American travellers, be getting off at Nova Scotia and touring Eastern Canada?

Maybe he would return to his mother's house in Maine with its view of the waves crashing over the rocky coastline? Perhaps he would stand and watch as the *Reine de France* sailed down the Gulf of Maine and out into the Atlantic. Would he think of me or would he have forgotten about a drunken kiss on a warm September night and a girl who had melted against him, oozing desire from every pore?

We got back into our cabin and India went into the

bathroom. After a while she opened the door; the tap was running and I could hear her brushing her teeth.

'I went outside on to the deck for some fresh air –'

'Can't hear you,' India shouted from the bathroom. 'Wait a minute and start again.'

The taps ran again and India dropped something and swore. Then she came out in her pyjamas and flopped on to the bed.

'Now tell me everything,' she said, 'and don't leave out anything.'

'I went out on to the deck for some fresh air and it was lovely. Cool and dark. And he was out there. Gabriel Frost.'

India gasped and lifted her head off the pillows for a moment.

'You're kidding?'

'No, he was standing by the ship's rail as I knew he would be. And he saw me and didn't say anything; he just came towards me and kissed me. I mean properly kissed me. Not a peck on the cheek to say hello, but a full-on snog. And I liked it, India, I mean I really liked it. And then he said he wished things were different, and something about tomorrow, and then he kissed me again. And then he just went and I couldn't move for a bit. You know? I was sort of frozen with the shock or something. And then I came in again and I couldn't think straight. All I could think of was: why? Why did he do that? Was he drunk? Did he do it on purpose?'

There was no reply. I looked over at my sister; of course she was fast asleep, zonked out cold.

'India!' I hissed. No response. I threw a pair of socks at her and she grumbled at me in her sleep and turned over.

Bloody typical. I'd listened to just about every detail of her romance with Jerry from the day they met in B&Q. She was looking for sandpaper to try out some furniture-distressing effect and he was looking for floor wax because he'd dropped coffee on his glamorous, loft-style apartment floorboards. Now, for the first time in years, I had something decent to share with her and she'd gone to sleep.

I pulled the duvet over her and went to brush my teeth. As I lay down I thought about Gabriel, asleep in the room next door. I put my hand up to touch the wall behind my pillows. Perhaps he was just the width of the wall away?

I woke a couple of times during the night, needing the loo or a drink of water. Each time my brain started up again, thinking about Gabriel, remembering how he had looked, what he had said to me, the feel of his shoulders under my hands.

Chapter Eleven

Hair of the Dog

Honey, 12-year-old Scotch Whisky, Single Cream, Milk

The following morning I got out of bed at seven-thirty, desperate for a cup of tea. It felt as though I had hardly slept at all. The air in the cabin was hot and stuffy and stank of alcohol – hardly surprising really considering the previous night. India was fast asleep and snoring like a rhinoceros, one arm thrown over her head, as relaxed in sleep as a child.

I showered and dressed and went out into the quiet corridor. I wanted to be alone and I was greedy for my memories, wanting to relive the previous night.

The air was colder here and I shivered in my thin shirt and jeans. I saw Ike and Marty in matching Chicago Bears jackets striding towards the stern. They must have been made of strong stuff considering how much alcohol they'd shifted the previous evening. I went in to find a cup of tea, or preferably two. My mouth was dry and my hangover only just under control. Why did I keep doing this to myself? Apart from anything else, India and I were going to end up spending all our money on the bar bill at the end of the trip, and there were still six days of transatlantic crossing ahead.

I found a seat by the window, away from the bickering Army veterans and their endlessly hungry wives, and drank my tea, wondering what to eat. It's very hard to think properly with a thumping headache.

The veterans were sitting in a large group in the middle of the dining area with a huge pile of hand luggage, backpacks and video cameras. It looked as though they were leaving the ship and taking full advantage of the breakfast – stuffing fruit, bottles of soda and muffins into their bags with no hint of shame.

In the end I had a croissant and apricot jam, scattering flakes of pastry over a wide area. Then I had some more tea and sat looking blankly into the far distance. I supposed I should go and wake India up but I didn't have the energy. If I did I would have to chivvy her into her clothes and towards breakfast and paracetamol, and make a fuss of her, when all I really wanted to do was sit by myself and think about Gabriel.

The ship was slowing to a halt now, and the quayside buildings moved infinitely slowly past my window. Ropes were thrown out to men on the quayside and soon passengers would scurry away from the ship to explore the new delights of Halifax. Refuse lorries began to unload the trash and other vans started to load more food into the ever-hungry belly of the ship. How could there be so much folded and baled cardboard coming off? We'd only been on for a few days. It was as though there had been a delivery of vast magnitude, of new beds or washing machines or fridge freezers. And where had all those bottles come from? The ones that were crashing into the skips? Ah yes, in retrospect most of them were probably ours. It gave me the shivers just thinking about it.

Right, from now on I was going to stop eating so much and deffo stop knocking the booze back. Definitely.

I finished my croissant and dabbed at the crumbs on my plate with a damp finger. I felt a bit more human now. I needed more tea and then I'd be fine. Perhaps I should have another croissant? With black cherry jam? Or possibly one of those maple pecan ones? A tray of them had just been wheeled out of the kitchens and the veterans would spot them in a moment and snarf the whole lot up in seconds. I almost got up, ready to sprint across to grab one.

No. I would be disciplined and sensible.

I got a fresh mug of tea and sat looking out of the window. The gangway had been opened and people were starting to drift on to the quayside. Occasionally there was a group, scurrying after a tour leader, heading for a bus to take them off on a coach ride somewhere else.

Suddenly I saw a familiar figure on the dockside in front of Pier 21. No, two familiar figures. I squashed my nose against the glass so I could see better. Gabriel and Marnie. He was carrying a small case and she was standing in front of him talking nineteen to the dozen. If I hadn't known better I would have said they were arguing. Gabriel turned away and Marnie touched his sleeve. Then she put her face in her hands. I watched as Gabriel slowly hugged her, rubbing her back, and they stood there for a few seconds, not moving while the other passengers who were leaving the ship for a day out dodged past them. She looked up at him, her face pale in the bright sunlight, her lovely red hair spilling over her shoulders.

What the hell was going on? After last night, I felt even more confused.

Perhaps something had happened to the sainted husband, Leo?

No! Perhaps he was dead or lying seriously ill in a coma and Marnie was about to hurry to his bedside with Gabriel on call to comfort her.

Or maybe Gabriel had made a pass at her and she was letting him down gently. *I fear I can never be yours for I love another and will always love him.* Hmm, suddenly she was talking like a Jane Austen heroine. I could almost see the sprigged gown and shy bonnet.

Oh hell, what if he had made a pass at me because he was frustrated in his pursuit of Marnie? *Or* what if he'd been drunk and mistaken me for her? I'd had a mask on! Yes, that was it! That's why he had come across and kissed me.

No, don't be ridiculous, I told myself; Gabriel would have had to be out of his skull on magic mushrooms *and* had a bag on his head to confuse the two of us, mask or no mask.

And he'd ripped off my mask first thing, so unless he was blind drunk …

The two of them moved along the quayside. He had one arm around her little shoulders as he guided her towards the terminal building.

Well, bloody hell, what was going on? Was he leaving? My thoughts were tumbling over each other in my need to make sense of this. Was she trying to persuade him to leave her alone and find love elsewhere? Or maybe she was using his mobile to ring the hospital and find out if her husband was going to live? I ran over to the counter, grabbed another cup of tea and snaffled the last maple pecan Danish from under the quivering nose of a woman in a tartan tracksuit who almost growled with disappointment. Then I returned to my seat and pressed my head against the window again so I didn't miss anything. I stayed like that, eating my Danish pastry and drinking tea until I was desperate for the loo. But of course I didn't dare go in case I missed anything.

'Well, here you are! I've been searching everywhere for you. What are you doing?'

I looked up to see India about to sit in the seat opposite mine. She had a tray of breakfast: two mugs of black coffee and a bowl of fresh fruit.

'What are you looking at?'

India stared out of the window with me, watching a man far below push a trolley full of cardboard boxes towards the ship. I wondered what was in them? Exotic vegetables or more wine maybe? Or edible flowers to scatter in this evening's salad?

'I'm watching them,' I said.

'Who?'

Let's be fair, India looked as rough as a badger's bum. She was pale, tinged with green around the edges, and her eyes were – as my father would say – like two rissoles in the snow.

'Gabriel and Marnie.'

India sipped her coffee and hunched over the table, her hands tucked into the long sleeves of her sweatshirt.

'What about them?' She frowned and held up one finger. She blinked slowly, trying to organise her scrambled brain. 'Hang on, you told me something last night, didn't you? Something about Gabriel Frost. Now what was it?'

I didn't reply. India carried on drinking her coffee and giving the occasional groan. At last she pushed the bowl of fruit away and went to find some toast and marmalade.

'Are you okay?' I said, moved at last to pity, despite her falling asleep during my confession last night.

'No, not really, thanks for asking,' she said caustically. She took a bite of toast and chewed, her eyes closed. 'I think I might be coming down with something.'

'What? Cocktail-itis?'

'Is there such a thing?'

'No, I'm being sarcastic. But there is such a thing as chronic liver damage. I think we could both apply for that. It's a good job we don't go on cruises often. I don't think I could take it.

No wonder Dad is so keen. I want to know what they're doing.'

India shrugged. 'Having a cup of tea? Or a glass of absinthe? God, ghastly thought. What does absinthe taste like?'

'No idea and I don't think I want to know.'

'What were you telling me last night anyway? You were droning on and I fell asleep. Something about Gabriel Frost? Do you know, I think there's something going on with him and Marnie. I saw them together last night. I was going to the loos outside the dining room and they were in the atrium place. I could see them over the balcony. Looked like they were arguing.'

'Really?' I pulled back from the window to look at my sister. She had finished her first piece of toast and was buttering a second. 'So what did they do?'

India shrugged. 'She was talking, and then he pulled out his phone and checked something. Then he walked away and she followed him. I bet they were off for some illicit sex.'

'Rubbish. She's married to the most wonderful man in the world. Don't you remember her telling us?

'There's a picture of her with Leo Miller on their wedding day in the reception area. They had a load of white doves released just after they were pronounced man and wife. I rather like that. When Jerry and I get married ...'

'Oh yes, I'd forgotten you and Jerry were getting married.'

'God, Alexa, just because you're not the one getting married! Do you have to be so frigging miserable about it?' she snapped.

It was the first time she'd ever spoken to me like this.

The basic unfairness of her attitude was overwhelming. All the times I'd cleared up after her, made excuses, done her work. I'd smoothed over her airheaded mistakes, worked into the evening many times because she wouldn't.

I couldn't stop myself. Suddenly all of her selfish actions, her rudeness, her self-absorption and now this ... Well, I couldn't stop.

'Oh, for God's sake, India, I've heard about little else other than your wedding for months! You've had half your mind at work and the other half on Pinterest. You leave the office in a state; you're uncooperative and flaky. People complain about your mistakes and your lateness. All you care about is what you're going to wear, what Jerry said, what it will be like once you're married. I'm bored with it. Not everyone wants to hear every little detail about some ridiculous day. The rest of us have lives too you know. The world keeps turning. Meanwhile I have to do my job and most of yours as well.'

'Well, I'm terribly sorry to take up your valuable time with the most important day of my life,' India snapped. 'If you ever do find anyone desperate enough to marry you, perhaps you'll understand.'

'It's not the most important day of your life,' I said, pretty much shouting now, which I was ashamed of, but somehow couldn't stop. 'It's only one of them. Getting married isn't the be-all and end-all you know.'

'Said the expert!' India shouted back.

A tense silence fell and I looked back out of the window.

We'd never talked to each other like this – well, not as adults. I'd bitten my lip, bottled up all of my feelings on the subject, and just grinned and grimaced through the endless monologues. Sat through meals with my parents when Mum seemed unable or unwilling to talk about anything other than table settings or whether India should have a long veil or a short one. Looked at pictures of flowers, vase shapes, the fonts for the invitations, been asked for my opinion on the wedding list.

I wanted to storm off, my hangover still hovering over me and the news about Marnie and Gabriel making me feel raw and edgy. But I stayed where I was, trying to get control of myself. There was no point having a loud argument in the food court. I had even noticed some of the Army veterans and their wives looking over, which was mortifying.

'What were you going to tell me?' India suddenly said, surprising me.

But I just didn't have the energy and changed the subject to something safer.

'What are we going to do today?' I said, trying to pretend our snappy argument hadn't just happened. I didn't feel any better, to be honest, since offloading my feelings. Guilt was starting to creep in.

India looked blank. She too seemed to be trying hard to move on and pretend nothing had happened. 'What time is it? Half past eleven? There's fruit carving in half an hour.'

'Fruit carving?'

'I've always wanted to do that.' I wasn't sure if she meant

it, but I let her get away with it – maybe she just wanted to get away from me.

'Really?'

'Oh yes, absolutely.' She nodded enthusiastically. She was definitely putting it on. 'The picture in the lobby shows an apple carved to look like a swan and a melon that looks like a shark. Perhaps we could go out after that?'

I began to feel as though I had been dropped into a parallel universe.

'You go to the fruit mangling and I'll go and have a wander around the town. I could do with a bit of exercise.' It was the perfect time for a break. It was obvious we needed some time apart. I needed to do something on my own otherwise this tension would return, and next time I might not be able to stop myself. Even though I was angry, I realised I didn't want to hurt my sister, not really ...

'Okay. I'll see you later,' she mumbled. 'I think I need a shower. I smell like a brewery, don't I?'

'A bit, yes.' At least this was something we could agree on.

*

I went back to the cabin with her to fetch my passport and passenger card so I could get off the ship and safely get on again. I felt rather deflated all of a sudden; we weren't really talking now, and I'd thought we were getting on better than we had for years. It was as though all the booze and partying had brought our frustrations with each other to a head. Either way I was certainly tired. It would be good to have a break and be on my own for a while. I needed to think.

I went down to what passed for the ground floor of the ship, or rather the water floor. A gangplank led to the quayside and I passed through the shadows of the security scanners and out into the sunshine of Halifax. I blinked a bit and looked at the street map I'd been given. There were a couple of pink double-decker tourist buses waiting at the end of the quay as well as a glossy-looking coach. The veterans were standing next to it smoking, while their wives supervised the loading of their luggage into the vast cavern underneath it.

So the veterans definitely were going off to eat their way through Nova Scotia next. Well, that was a positive; it would mean the rest of us could get to the coffee machines without having to queue for half an hour while they filled four mugs each.

I strolled past them in the direction of a rather nice-looking group of cafés and wine bars.

I walked on along the seaway, enjoying the sunshine on my shoulders. To my left was the everyday thump of building work, to the right the sparkle of the water. What would it be like to live here? There were pretty old houses interspersed with high-rise blocks. There were cafés and bars. Ice cream parlours and seafood shacks. There was maple syrup and something called poutine.

A coach roared past me in a cloud of dust and off towards

more exciting places and fast food. I sat on a handy bench, cleverly constructed from old crates, and tried to think about India and my life when I got home. But I couldn't concentrate; all I could think about was Gabriel.

It was a long time since Ryan and I had split up and I was lonely. I wasn't the most *gorgeous* creature in the world. Men didn't fall over at the sight of me but I was okay – quite reasonable on a good day when I made a bit of an effort. Why couldn't I find someone, and be happy? Why did I keep sabotaging relationships before they had even started? What was the matter with me? Why had Ryan shacked up with a girl who never seemed to wash her hair? Why had he shagged his mother's Avon lady? Someone had told me she was at least fifty. Perhaps their skincare products really were that good?

And while we were on the subject, why didn't I now, at nearly thirty, have a decent and forgiving relationship with my sister? Were we going to continue to irritate each other? Were we destined to grow further apart as the years passed? Would we ever be friends? Was it too late? I mean, what she'd just said ... well, it hurt. *Someone desperate enough to marry you.* It was a low blow even for India on her worst day. Surely she knew how upset I was about Ryan, and well, now the whole Marnie bloody Miller/Gabriel situation. God, I needed a break from men. I really did. But that kiss ...

I stood up and attempted to stride away from my thoughts, passing a girl in a very short pink kilt who was playing the bagpipes – this was, after all, Nova Scotia. I came to a cluster of craft shops; perhaps I would find something there for Mum before I spent all my money on overpriced cocktails?

I went in to look around. There were several people I recognised from the ship who had evidently had the same idea. They were snapping up keyrings and pottery bowls like they were going out of fashion. There were some incredibly expensive glasses and some rather cute felt owls. Mum was keen on owls and woodpeckers. I picked out one with a quizzical expression and bought it.

I waited while the shopkeeper gift-wrapped it because I had made the mistake of telling her it was a present for my mother. Dissatisfied with the look of it, she started again, this time adding tartan ribbon and a feather. And a tartan gift tag. By then there was quite a queue forming behind me and I had to stop her from redoing it a third time by pretending the ship would leave without me. Reluctantly she let me pay and I bolted out through the door and straight into Gabriel Frost.

'You're here!' I said, shocked into idiocy.

'Yes, I'm here,' he said, and I felt my stomach do that flip thing again, even though I told it sternly not to.

'I thought you might go to see Eastern Canada.'

'I've seen a lot of it already,' he said thoughtfully. 'It's very nice but I don't need to go again.'

'But I saw you. From the window.' Oh, I am so smooth sometimes. 'I wondered if you were leaving,' I finished stupidly.

He looked a bit unsure of himself at that and I was curious

at the change in him. He always seemed so confident when we were together ... well, aside from when he was forced to dance with me, but he'd found his footing there quite quickly.

'Well, I was. But then something happened and I changed my mind,' he said, sounding a little hesitant.

'Oh.'

I immediately put this down to Marnie and her impressive powers of persuasion, but on what basis did I think that? What had I been watching from the ship? The more I tried to think it through the worse things got.

I realised we were still standing in the shop doorway, effectively blocking it. Not only were there people wanting to come out with their stuffed owls and keyrings, there were people wanting to go in too.

Gabriel took hold of my elbow and steered me on to the pavement.

'Are you busy?' His eyes flashed at me and he smiled.

I felt my legs rock a bit. Who knew eyes had that kind of power? Who knew a smile could make me want to fall into his arms?

'No.'

I wanted to say something clever or funny and make him laugh again, but my head was spinning a bit from the fight with my sister and all of this new information about Marnie.

'Would you care to join me then? A glass of wine? There's a very nice place just up two blocks.'

'Oh, okay then.' A glass of wine never hurt anyone, I told

myself, knowing that wasn't the reason I was feeling hot all over again.

I followed him into the cool, welcoming interior of the Olde Cape Breton Bar. We were shown to a table with a red-checked cloth and unlit candles stuck into wax-encrusted wine bottles. Gabriel handed me a menu card, our hands brushing, and I had to stifle a whimper.

'The crab cakes are good,' he said, oblivious to my internal struggles. Maybe I was sex-starved, as India said. I was certainly behaving like a complete idiot.

'Great,' I breathed and attempted to read the options. The words swam in front of my eyes. Perhaps I needed glasses?

'And a crisp white wine?'

'Absolutely.'

I mean, it's not as though I haven't sworn every day for the last week to lay off the booze, is it?

A gum-chewing girl with purple hair came out to take our order without any fussing or annoying *you're welcome* stuff and a few seconds later brought our drinks. Over the bay the open sky was clear blue, and it was warm and pretty, sheltered from the wind coming in off the sea.

'So, how are you enjoying life on board?' Gabriel said, holding out his wineglass for me to clink.

'It's amazing,' I said, glad he was sticking to safe territory. 'It will be hard to top this ship.'

'She's a beauty,' he agreed, 'and Halifax is a great town. My aunt used to have a house here and we visited her most summers.'

'We?'

'My parents, my brother and me. Morgan lives in Oxford now so he doesn't get to this side of the pond too often.'

'Gabriel and Morgan; your parents went in for great names, didn't they?'

Gabriel laughed. 'Morgan was almost called Raphael, so he thinks he got off lightly.'

'And what does he do in Oxford?' I asked, thrilled to be learning more about Gabriel. He'd always seemed so closed off on board the liner, but here he was being open and honest, telling me things without much prompting at all.

'He's a Professor of Advanced Mathematics.'

'Crumbs.'

He laughed, his eyes lighting up. 'Yes, I know! He's enjoying a mathematics conference in South Africa at the moment; having a marvellous time, so he says.'

'A marvellous time at a mathematics conference,' I said thoughtfully. 'How does that work? I can't imagine there are many jokes to be had there?'

Gabriel chuckled. 'Apparently there are but only they understand them.'

The gum-chewing girl returned with our crab cakes a few minutes later. Apparently it was a small portion; even so there were three of them nestled on a large dressed salad, accompanied by a basket of sourdough bread. It was all delicious.

We talked about the ship and the efficient crew and the food. All the time I wanted to ask him so many questions.

Why did he kiss me? What did he mean when he said he wished things were different? How come one minute he was leaving the ship and the next he wasn't? And what was going on with him and Marnie?

But I didn't ask any of those things. I suppose I felt too shy and, for once in my life, I was trying to watch what I said.

He asked me more about my work back in England and the small estate agency came alive for me again when I was telling him about it. It sounded somehow interesting and cute, especially now I had some distance from it. I almost missed the day-to-day ... almost. Put that on one side of the scales and Gabriel Frost on the other and there was no contest. He laughed at all my stories about unreasonable clients and seemed genuinely interested in everything I told him. And I was suddenly bold enough to take a selfie of us, the sea blue and sparkling behind us. But not brave enough to ask him the two questions uppermost in my head:

So why did you kiss me? Did you know it was me?

'Would India mind if I took you out to dinner this evening?' he asked suddenly. Was this it? Was he asking me out properly? Was this going to answer all of my questions? 'I'd rather eat somewhere else. Just for tonight? I'm booked into the Louis Quinze restaurant but, well, I could do with a change. There's a very good place on the top deck, near the bow. Quite small and I'd have to book if you fancied it. Thai cuisine, if you like that sort of thing? I mean it wouldn't be inappropriate, would it?'

What an odd phrase. I felt even more confused, but I wasn't going to say no.

'That would be lovely. India is doing fruit carving at the moment.' I caught his expression. 'Yes, I know. I'll tell her when I get back. She had a very late night; I wouldn't be surprised if she's gone back to bed.'

Was I blushing? I was sure I could feel myself blushing.

I'd mentioned bed.

I suddenly remembered the moment last night when I had reached out to touch the place behind my pillows, wondering if he was just the other side of the wall. I took a sip of wine to steady my nerves and cleared my throat.

'I'd love to. I'm sure India can manage without me for one night. I mean for one evening.'

I wasn't going to be out *all night*, was I?

Gabriel gave me a look and his grey eyes were twinkling with amusement.

'Then it's a date. I'll see you in the atrium at seven-thirty?'

'Fine.'

We had a date!

I could hardly speak, let alone eat. What would I wear? I had no idea. For a mad moment I thought perhaps I could buy something on board the ship, then I remembered the phrase *cruise wear*. Gabriel would be less than impressed if I turned up in a jaunty nautical blazer with a white canvas skirt embellished with gold buttons. I'd have to think again.

Chapter Twelve

Brandy Alexandria

Cognac, Crème de Cacao, Single Cream,
Umbrella, Cherry, Sparkly Stick

Back on board the *Reine de France* I made my way to our cabin. On the way I ran through what I could say to defuse the tension between India and me. Perhaps I should apologise? Perhaps she would. Unlikely, but there was always a first time. I was in a state of juddering nerves by the time I opened the door, only to find her asleep in bed. She turned over and looked at me rather blearily.

'Oh, it's you. Is it breakfast time?'

'We had breakfast hours ago, India.' I sighed, thinking how little she'd changed from the girl who could drop off to sleep anywhere and everywhere but stay up all night when it suited her. 'It's nearly five-thirty. You've missed most of the day. And I have a date!' I trilled, trying hard not to feel too elated.

India processed this information, her fingers just showing over the edge of the duvet like a mouse's paws. She frowned.

'Who with?'

'Gabriel Frost.'

She jerked a bit and was sufficiently impressed to raise her head.

'You're kidding! Did he say anything?'

'Well, we didn't resort to semaphore or sign language if that's what you mean. We had lunch today and he asked me then.' I was glowing, I could tell. It also seemed that this information had helped us blow over our cross words from earlier and I was quite pleased. Even though nothing had been resolved, I knew I didn't want to fight with India. Not now anyway. I had Gabriel to think about ...

India stuck her lower lip out. 'This holiday is supposed to be about me, not you shagging random men. Mum said ...'

Anger shimmered through me and I had to hold on to my temper, which was already quite unpredictable following our row.

Tersely I responded, 'I'm not shagging anyone, and weren't you the one who told me to do exactly that? Even Mum would say you can spare me for one night, wouldn't she?'

India sat up, looking thoughtful. 'Well, Gabriel Frost seems okay. Really nice. Not that I would know of course. I mean, just because he's attractive doesn't mean anything, does it? We don't really know him, do we?'

'India, come on. It's one dinner and we can have cocktails

before I go. It's not like you don't have lots of people to talk to at our table.' I could hear myself pleading, whining – great, so grown-up! And had I really just asked permission from my younger sister to go to dinner with the first attractive and interesting man I'd met in ages? When she'd had her first date with Jerry she'd blown me out of the water without a second thought as I remembered.

But India wasn't listening any more. She stretched and turned to look out of the French windows.

'Is it really five-thirty? I've slept nearly all day. But I did have breakfast, didn't I? I'm sure I did. I had some toast and, oooh yes, I went to the fruit carving. You should have come too. I tell you what, it was brilliant. There was one of the chefs there, in a tall white hat like they wear on TV. And he had a knife so sharp it could shave a gnat's whiskers. I can now make a peacock out of a cantaloupe melon and a Father Christmas out of a strawberry. We could do that for the reception, couldn't we? That would be so cool!'

'No, India, because we would have to do about two hundred on the morning of the wedding. I don't think that's a very good idea.' Back to the wedding already – why was I not surprised? But I didn't say anything.

She wrinkled her nose in thought. 'Mmm, perhaps not.'

She swung her legs out of bed and pulled on her dressing gown.

'Marion and Caron were there too; they said they make lilies out of tomatoes all the time. I'm not sure I believe them.

They were going to show me at dinner this evening. Look, if you want to spend the evening with Gabriel that's okay. Where are you going?'

'Some Thai place he knows about on the top deck. I have to meet him at seven-thirty.'

'Hang on, you thought he was leaving the ship,' she said, turning back towards me abruptly, her hair flying in all directions.

'He changed his mind.'

India laughed, her eyes glinting. She was starting to get into the spirit of it. 'Oooh, did you beg him to stay? I can just imagine you grovelling and pleading.'

I was mortally offended. 'No, India, it was nothing to do with me. It was actually something to do with Marnie. They were together when he was leaving, remember?'

She sighed. 'No, I can't. Oh yes, I do. Perhaps I've caught dementia or something. They do say alcohol knocks off brain cells, don't they? Or was that cigarettes? So did those Army veterans get off?'

'They did. They were all herded on to a huge coach with their seven tons of luggage and were off to tour Eastern Canada and look for fast food. Have you heard from Jerry by the way?' I said offhandedly, hoping it would distract her long enough so I could find the perfect outfit for the evening. Normally bringing up Jerry started a fifteen-minute monologue at least.

'WhatsApp,' she said, looking a little dreamy. 'And an email he forwarded from the florist accompanied by a rambling, panicking message. Though what he thinks I'm going to do about the merits of Peace roses versus something else that might or might not be available in December when I'm mid-Atlantic I don't know.'

That was short, so I went with the blunt approach.

'Right, I need to start getting ready and decide what I'm going to wear. Dress or trousers? You're good at this sort of thing; I need your advice.'

India loved being asked for her advice and she thought about it. 'Dress.'

'Blue patterned or the pink linen one?'

'Blue – the other one will crease like mad if you're sitting down all evening. And if you spill anything on it, it will look rubbish, whereas on the blue one it won't show. And then when you put it back on in the morning, it won't look like a limp rag, which the pink one will.'

'India! What do you mean, *put it on in the morning*? I'm going to have dinner with him and that's all. I'm going to be sophisticated and witty and charming. I'm not going to spill anything down myself. I'm not going to sleep with him!'

'Really?' she asked airily, as if she knew something I didn't.

'Yes, really!'

'I thought you fancied him?'

'I do, but that doesn't mean I'm going to drop my crushed, food-splattered, pink linen dress on his bedroom floor.'

'More fool you then. He's in the next-door cabin, isn't he?

I'll bang on the wall if you make too much noise and keep me awake.'

'India, just shut up for once. I'm nervous enough as it is. I'm not going to keep you awake because I'm not going to sleep with him.'

'If you say so.'

'Oh, shut *up*!'

'You shut up.'

I got my revenge by locking myself in the bathroom, having a long shower, doing my make-up in front of the illuminated mirror and ignoring my sister's desperate pleas for the loo. It almost felt like old times. I started singing.

*

At seven-thirty-one I arrived at the atrium where I had agreed to meet Gabriel. I thought I'd play it cool, keep him waiting and arrive late, but in the end I couldn't do it. Instead of strolling slowly to the lifts and arriving in a calm and collected state, I almost trotted there and was a bit out of breath.

'You didn't have to rush,' he said. 'I knew you wouldn't be caught in traffic or anything.'

I laughed and tossed my hair a bit, wondering if he would notice I had been messing about with my heated rollers. In the restaurant an Asian girl in a silk robe greeted us. She was really tiny, like a child playing at dressing up. I'd read about size-zero people but never actually seen one in the insubstantial flesh before. I bet she could wear Ladybird clothes if they still made them. I felt like a hippopotamus next to her. She did a lot of charming bowing and smiling and then led us to our table and brought iced water and menus.

'What would you like?' Gabriel asked as he glanced at the menu.

I pretended to study mine very hard so that I didn't stare at him any more than I had already. He was looking particularly handsome in a dark blue shirt and chinos. What on earth was he doing with me in my Primark dress and ASOS shoes?

'Um, I don't know really. I mean I like Thai food – well, everyone likes Thai food, don't they? But I'm not – well, I don't know what the dishes are called. I mean Pad Thai, is that something? Thai? Um?'

Yes, my campaign to be sophisticated, witty and charming had got off to a great start.

'Is there anything I can help you with?' He leant forward and I could smell his aftershave, or maybe that was just him. Oh God.

I clutched the menu card and brought it up almost to my nose so my mind didn't wander on the topic of *things Gabriel Frost could help me with*.

'I like noodles and green curry,' I said, dredging my memory banks for things I could say about Thai cuisine without looking a complete prat. 'Look, perhaps you could order for both of us. I like it hot and spicy.'

Oh, what was I saying?

And let him order *for me*?

I must have been in a biddable mood.

Never in my life have I allowed a man to order for me, not even when Chris (who had an A-level in French) and I were in France and my bloody-minded attitude meant I ordered a whole boiled crab on a bed of spinach and raw garlic by mistake.

Anyway, I handed back my menu with a calm smile to the tiny waitress and waited to see what would arrive. The first thing to materialise was a bottle of champagne swiftly followed by some tiny canapés.

'I hope you don't mind; I love champagne and I thought it might be nice to celebrate,' Gabriel said.

What are we celebrating?

'Lovely,' I said.

Think calm thoughts. Don't say it, don't say it.

'What are we celebrating?'

Duh.

'The wedding perhaps,' he said.

'The wedding? Crumbs, I'd almost forgotten about that,' I said.

Gabriel laughed.

'God, you fascinate me,' he said, holding out his glass to chink against mine.

'I do?'

He laughed. 'You seem so calm most of the time, very

179

together. And then out of the blue you say something crazy like that. It's beguiling.'

Beguiling. That sounded very sophisticated and chic. Not like me at all.

I gave a small, modest laugh and sipped my champagne.

You can't do both and I choked a bit as the champagne went down the wrong way. I gulped hard to keep the choking to myself. Then of course I realised how klutzy I was being and wanted to laugh. I took another sip of champagne and calmed down.

'So where do you usually live?' I asked.

'I spend a lot of time in New York at the moment, but my base is London. I never seem to be in the same place for very long. I have two daughters from my marriage. They live most of the time with Elsa in London. They visit me at my apartment in New York or we meet up at my parents' house in their school holidays. It's not ideal but we make it work.'

Elsa. That sounded a bit Scandinavian, didn't it?

'How old are they?'

'Beatrice is ten and Amelie is eight.'

'Lovely names.'

I mentally chewed over the next question I could ask him. *Why did you get divorced?*

What does Elsa do?

I didn't have to try. Gabriel wanted to tell me.

'I spent too much time on my career. Elsa found someone new. It was as simple as that. We were civilised about it.' He shook his head. 'Let's be honest, it was awful. But we're doing our best for the girls. It's the most important thing after all.'

We carried on investigating the little dishes of appetisers for a few tense minutes. But I'm not one to leave a silence unfilled for long.

'You mentioned earlier that you were leaving the ship and then you didn't. What changed your mind?'

He looked at me with his beautiful grey eyes, clear as water. 'You did.'

What? I thought it had something to do with Marnie – but me? Well ...

'I did? How? I mean what happened?'

He looked down and moved his cutlery an infinitesimal amount.

'I've had some of the most difficult months of my life. One day I might tell you about it. And you made me laugh when I seriously thought I'd never laugh again. And the next night, when I went out on to the deck to escape the masked ball, I started to think about you.'

Oh God, I think I'm going to pass out.

Here on the floor. Right this minute.

I'm going to go all limp and slide down under the table, dragging the tablecloth and all the cutlery with me.

'I realised you were different from any other woman I'd ever met. And then suddenly you were there. Standing in front of me. I couldn't stop myself; I had to kiss you. It was unforgivable, but I hope you can forgive me?'

'Sure.' I meant this to come out as a confident laugh, but it sounded like a croak.

After all this sort of thing happened to me all the time.

Bloody hell.

'That's okay then.'

The waitress came back and Gabriel ordered some dishes while I twirled my champagne flute, nearly dropped it and stared out of the window at the darkening sea. The girl gave him a rather flirty look from under her lashes and went away with a demure smile.

'So this meal is by way of an apology.'

Colour me confused.

'Apology for what?'

He tilted his head at me, his eyes dancing in the candlelight making me feel all bubbly all over again. 'Have you been listening to a word I've said?'

'Some of them.'

The rest of the time I've been remembering what it was like to kiss you.

'I shouldn't have done it. I had no right to.'

'To what?'

'To kiss you.'

'Oh that! I didn't mind! I mean –'

At that moment the waitress returned with an even tinier and cuter companion and several pretty porcelain dishes filled with more food. Some of it was spicy, some was slightly sour, and all of it was delicious. All hope of finding out just what

Gabriel meant disappeared as he told me all about a trip he'd taken to Thailand some years ago. As we ate he talked about the street food and described the white beaches and clear blue seas he remembered. It sounded wonderful.

I could just imagine us, walking along the edge of the sea, hand in hand as the sun set in a blaze of crimson and gold. I would be wearing a white linen kaftan over a bikini because I would have lost two stone and been to the gym twice a day for a year. Gabriel would be bare-chested and rippling with muscles and there would be candles glowing in the warm dusk and possibly a four-poster bed draped with white silk curtains at the end of the beach where we would –

'And all the details sorted out? I'm told these things can take a lot of planning.'

I lurched back into the present.

'Yes, yes,' I said, trying to latch on to what he had been saying. Honestly, I have the attention span of a beetle sometimes. 'What things?'

'The flower girls? You said they were still growing?'

'Oh, them. Yes, they are. I think I'll have to ask their mother to sort them out. She's my cousin.'

'So. This is an exciting time?'

'Well, yes it is. I can't wait to cross the Atlantic.'

Gabriel frowned. 'I meant the wedding. It must be exciting for you.'

'Exciting? The wedding? Gosh, no, not particularly; it's just a lot of list making and nagging people at the moment. I'll be glad when it's over to be honest. I mean it's been dragging on for a year; it will be nice to talk about something else for a change.'

'Oh, I see. Well, that's refreshing I suppose. What does the lucky groom do?'

'Jerry? He's a barrister and goes to London a lot for expense-account dinners with judges, but I only ever see him eating Pot Noodle or playing on his gaming console and shooting people. He's very funny and terrifically kind but I think he would drive me mad eventually. He never takes the bins out in time, or gets his car serviced until the engine is smoking, and then he thinks it can be fixed by shouting at it. And it's the devil's own job to get him to make a decision about anything. Do you want more coffee, Jerry? Oooh, now I'm not entirely sure. *Possibly*. I could shake him sometimes.'

Gabriel shook his head. 'So why do you want to marry him?'

I blinked at him. 'I don't want to marry him.'

'But you're getting married on December 2nd. Don't you think you should tell him he's driving you mad?'

The penny dropped with a loud clanging noise, like a hammer in a metal bucket. I felt quite giddy.

'I'm not marrying him. India is.'

'I thought this was your hen weekend?' Gabriel looked confused. It was just as adorable as I had imagined.

'Yes, it is. For *India*,' I explained. 'India and Jerry are getting married on December 2nd. I'm the bridesmaid and list compiler.'

184

'So you're not getting married?'

'No.' I almost shouted it. 'No,' I added a bit more quietly.

'And you're not engaged? You don't have a significant other?'

'No. I did have a significant other but he turned out to be an insignificant other who was shagging the Avon lady.'

He spluttered with laughter and dabbed at his mouth with his napkin, while I wondered just why I had brought that up. But somehow the painful memory was subsiding and I giggled a little too.

'*What?*'

'Forget I said that.' I was blushing now.

'Okay. I'll try.' But he winked at me and I felt myself go even redder as I tried not to burst out laughing. He'd thought *I* was engaged; he'd thought *I* was getting married!

'And the plans for the wedding are going well, by the way,' I said, looking to change the subject as I marvelled at how well this date was turning out. 'The dress, flowers, cake and other stuff are all booked. India is getting married in the village church. She wanted a marquee in the garden at home for the reception but that's madness in December so it's at The Manor House down the road from my parents'. I think it will be really lovely.'

'And where are they going on honeymoon?'

'I've no idea. Jerry is supposed to be sorting that but he's so indecisive and forgetful they'll probably end up going to Blackpool.'

Gabriel looked thoughtful. And then he reached across the table and put his hand over mine.

'So if I said I wanted to kiss you again, you wouldn't object?'

He was stroking the back of my hand with his thumb and I thought I was going to faint.

'You knew it was me last night?' I asked quietly.

He looked up, surprise flickering in his eyes. 'Of course I knew it was you!'

'Oh. Only I had the mask on and it was very dark ...'

Gabriel kissed my fingers. 'I knew it was you, Alexa.'

I tell you what, I'd heard the phrase *a bolt of desire shot through her* but I'd never felt one before. It was *exactly* like an electric shock. I wouldn't have been surprised to see sparks coming off the ends of my fingers or a smoking patch on the tablecloth under my hand.

I couldn't think of much else to say after that, and that's really not me at all. I mean I can talk 24/7 on occasions, but this had sort of struck me dumb.

We finished our meal and the tiny waitresses fluttered around us like bright butterflies but we hardly saw them. At least I didn't. Gabriel took my hand and led me out on to the promenade deck and into the fresh evening air. He found two chairs in a quiet corner that had rugs on them as a defence against the chill and brought us two large glasses of something fiery and aromatic. It might have been brandy. God knows what it was, but it was good.

We sat very close together watching the foam of the ship's wake disappearing into the darkness behind it and he took my hand and kissed the tips of my fingers again until I thought I really was going to swoon, and I'm not the swooning type.

I could see the lights of some coastal town growing faint as the ship steered away from land and headed out towards the wide expanse of the Atlantic ahead of us. Coming up were six days of the crossing that would take us back to Southampton and real life.

Meanwhile, as I sat feeling the chills of excitement running up and down my spine, I came to a decision: I was going to do this. I was going to go for it.

Whatever 'it' was.

If Gabriel was attracted to me, why would I pretend I didn't feel the same way? And Marnie Miller? Well, what about her? We were all adults here. Marnie already had the perfect husband, didn't she?

Chapter Thirteen

Hot Passion

Vodka, Passion Fruit Liqueur,
Cranberry Juice, Orange Juice

We sat there for some time and didn't really speak much. Occasionally we saw a boat far out to sea with its lights twinkling. Other people were walking along the promenade deck, taking the air, perhaps enjoying the thought that we were all at the start of something new.

The ship had stocked up on more wine and ducks and jam or whatever was needed, we were all safely on board and we had cast off the ropes from the quayside. It was rather symbolic. The ship was setting off on an adventure and so was I.

'I'll never forget this moment,' I said, and I turned to look at him, at the symmetry of his beautiful face.

'Why particularly?' I could hear the laughter in his voice.

'Because I know what's going to happen; what I want.'

He leaned over, pushed my hair to one side and kissed my neck. 'I know what I want,' he said, his voice very low. 'I want you. I want to touch you.'

He looked at me and I smiled. 'That's what I want too.'

Suddenly he stood up, pulling me to my feet, and held me against him, his hands on my waist. 'Are you sure, Alexa? Are you really sure?'

I nodded. 'Oh yes.'

His breath was warm on my cheek and he kissed me, a dozen kisses as light as feathers along my cheekbone until he whispered in my ear, 'Oh, Alexa.'

We walked back into the warmth of the ship and along the corridor to the lifts almost in a dream. He waited until we could get into one on our own and as the doors closed he turned to me and pushed me back against the mirrored wall. And God, he kissed me.

His body was hard against mine. His fingers encircled my waist and moved up to my breasts and he groaned with desire against my mouth as I melted into him.

We reached his room in a few steps. By the time he managed to open the door I had pulled off his tie and undone most of the buttons of his shirt. His chest was warm and smooth under my hands. I had never felt this way before, a crazy woman tearing at a man's clothes. It was so unlike me. Luckily the cabin stewards weren't around.

Once his door was open he didn't turn the lights on but

walked backwards towards the bed, taking me with him until at last we fell together on to it. He pulled the blue dress off over my head and I pushed his shirt from his shoulders. I didn't think I had ever in my life behaved like this. All I knew was that if I didn't feel him inside me very soon I might die or scream or something.

Perhaps India was right and I was sex-starved? Was this how drug addicts felt, waiting for the next high? Desperate and burning inside. Not caring what time it was, what day it was. Wanting something so much that nothing else mattered.

Then he was above me, his body crushing me underneath him. I wrapped my legs around him and pulled him towards me.

This wasn't lovemaking or romance and neither of us was pretending it was.

It was lust, it was sex, it was fast and hot and hard and bloody marvellous. I'd never felt anything like it in my life. I heard him gasp. He gave a breathless groan against my hair and then everything seemed to stop and the room rocked. I know I cried out and his hands were hard on my body, his fingernails scraping as he trembled against me.

I could feel his mouth moving against my throat. 'God, oh God.'

He bit my neck softly, his teeth grazing the skin.

My arms fell back; I felt wonderful. Powerful. At last.

*

Time passed. I've no idea how long we lay there. I could feel life in every part of my body, from the tips of my fingers to the roots of my hair. Now I knew, now I understood.

At last he pulled away. 'Alexa? Alexa.'

I could hardly breathe. 'Oh wow.'

'I hope ... I wanted to show you –'

I put my fingers over his lips. 'Sssh.'

I could still see his silhouette above me in the darkness and I reached up to touch him. He rolled on to his side, pulling me with him.

'That was incredible,' he said. He gave a shuddering sigh. 'I've wanted to do that for quite some time.'

I didn't know what to say. I mean, obviously, I'd had sex before with various, ultimately unsuitable, people and sometimes it had been okay and sometimes quite nice really. Once or twice it had been a bit more than that. But this was something different.

I had no expectations that he would fall in love with me or think I was worth spending time with because ... well, for understandable reasons. I didn't wonder if he was going to be a significant person in my life, because he obviously wasn't. I lived in a small, slightly dull market town in England, running an estate agency with my sister and timid Tim, a bloke who liked to wear acrylic cardigans, still lived in a two-bedroomed, terraced cottage with his aunt and probably always would.

Gabriel was a high-powered lawyer who worked for Marnie

Miller, the lifestyle guru and all-round superstar, and went to Ken's Hut to eat lobster. He lived between London and New York and Maine. He had two daughters to think about. There wasn't really any room for me in that mix – I could see that only too clearly. And yet …

So, this was purely about sex. And I thought we had done it jolly well.

He bent his head down to my breast and kissed it, making me shiver.

'Your skin is like silk.'

I stretched my arms above my head and he ran one hand down the length of my body. I felt very wicked and wanton and, for the first time in my life, sort of erotic.

'God, you're beautiful,' he said.

I pressed my lips together so I wouldn't say something stupid and wound my fingers through his hair. I wondered how I compared with other women he had slept with. Actually I realised I didn't really care about that either.

If Gabriel and I were simply going to have a six-day affair based on the sort of activity we had just enjoyed that would be fine by me.

Maybe.

I would not do what I usually did: ruin things by letting my thoughts scatter in all directions like an upended basket of kittens. I would not start going all soppy with thoughts of love and commitment and wondering what sort of dress I would wear or what we would call our children.

'I'd better be going,' I said.

'Really?' He sounded disappointed.

That in itself was exciting, and in a way it gave me courage.

I raised myself up on one elbow. 'I think so. India will be wondering where I am.'

'Yes, of course. But you could stay if you wanted to? It might be – you know – rather nice?'

Nice? *Nice?*

I was tempted. Very tempted.

I looked down at him. Bloody hell, there was no other way to put it: he was fucking gorgeous. Hair tousled on the pillow and the most attractive amount of designer stubble. He ran one finger down my arm, making me quiver. I could just imagine how it might be if we untangled ourselves, curled up in bed together. We'd fall asleep and maybe we would wake in the night and I would feel his hands on me again. Then he would roll me over, pull me on top of him and we would make love again –

No, hang on a minute, we wouldn't. We wouldn't 'make love'; we would shag each other senseless until morning. Then he would order champagne and strawberries for breakfast from room service and put the Do Not Disturb sign on the door. And India would eventually guess where I was and thump on the door asking if I was okay, and was I coming to the line dancing?

Perhaps at lunchtime India and I would go to the food court together and sort of coincidentally run into Gabriel.

And he would join us and India would watch him looking at me with hunger in his eyes and afterwards she would ask me what the hell was going on. And perhaps that evening we would meet up and walk hand in hand into the restaurant and the maître d' would smile at us, recognising our new romance, and lead us to a secluded table for two and Gabriel would reach across the table and drop a Tiffany diamond the size of an ice cube into my champagne ...

No, he wouldn't.

We'd see each other somewhere, perhaps in the theatre when Marnie Miller gave her next talk about being an internationally famous everything, goddess and all-round know-it-all. Gabriel would casually spot me in the audience and wink at me and perhaps come across to say hello and palm me a note asking me to meet him somewhere or come to his cabin at ten-thirty, and I would go and we would do some fabulous things involving ice cream, chocolate truffles and a blindfold.

Crumbs, actually I quite liked the idea of that. I'd better give that some more thought.

No, I wasn't going to get ahead of myself, was I? Not this time.

I shook my head and leaned over to kiss him. How wonderful that I could kiss this gorgeous man and he would kiss me back. That was enough. It wasn't anything more than a very glamorous holiday romance. And there was nothing wrong with that, was there?

At the end of it I would go back to work and so would he and that was that. I'd hoard my memories and sometimes I'd allow myself to think about him. Would he think about me? Perhaps one afternoon when he was walking across the beach below his parents' house he would see a boat far out at sea and reflect on this trip and try and remember my name. And then maybe his daughters would run up to him with a strand of seaweed or a shell and he would forget me.

Suddenly, unexpectedly, I felt the prickle of tears. I needed to get away or I would make a complete fool of myself.

'No, I'd better go. Seriously, India will worry,' I said cheerfully.

And in a way I knew that was true. She had seemed a bit disappointed not to have dinner with me tonight and I was starting to feel bad about that. It was her hen holiday after all ...

'Okay,' Gabriel said, pulling me back to this moment, in his bed.

He sounded rather sad actually. Then he reached up and touched my face, pulling me back down to kiss me, a sweet, soft kiss that almost made me reconsider.

But no.

There, I'd averted disaster. I was cool with this. We'd had a jolly good session and we were dealing with it in a grown-up way. No awkwardness or blushing. No need to say anything embarrassing.

I scrabbled about looking for my clothes, which were

scattered around quite a wide area. We'd been a bit frantic with the pulling off and chucking around activity. When I eventually found one of my shoes in the bathroom and my knickers under the bed, I got dressed as quickly as possible in the dark.

'I'll see you tomorrow?' he said, still sitting in the crumpled bed.

'I'm not going anywhere,' I said with a casual sort of laugh.

I nearly said *well, see you around then* but even I'm not that stupid. I hesitated in the doorway and blew him a kiss before closing the door quietly behind me.

*

When I walked into the room next door I wondered if India would be able to tell right away what I'd been up to. For one thing it had been months and months, not that she knew that. Perhaps if I were lucky she would be asleep. But as I creaked the door open I saw she was in bed watching television and drinking white wine out of a glass tumbler.

'Nice meal?' she snapped after a moment.

'Excellent,' I said, trying to keep it light. 'Thai things. Spicy and sour at the same time. And all prettily tweaked and decorated with flowers. It really was lovely. And then we had some brandy out on deck; it was great. We had fun.'

'Yes, I can see that.' She gave me another look as she reached for the wine bottle and topped up her glass. 'Want some?'

'Um, I don't think so. I'm a bit tired actually.' I gave a bit of a fake yawn and a stretch by way of emphasis.

'Yes, I bet you are,' she said, rather terse.

'What?' I said.

'Nothing. So, did you get on well? I mean did he snog you?'

I tried to sound nonchalant. 'Well, yes, a bit. And yes we did get on okay. Gabriel is a very nice man. He's really good company. I like him. I think he likes me.'

'Yes, that's a bit frigging obvious.'

'Why?'

She took a sip of wine. 'Because you've got your dress on inside out.'

Right, so unless I was a lot cleverer than I had been in the past, that looked like ruining any chance I might have of playing it cool.

India would now pester me for details then complain I was giving her too much information. Then she would make some pointed comments whenever she saw him like: *here comes your boyfriend, Alexa*. Eventually I would have to strangle her with her own belt or lock her in a cupboard, otherwise she would be dropping innuendo and suggestive comments all over the place like the contents of a split beanbag.

'Have I?' I said, trying to appear nonchalant, while desperately trying to think of a way this could have happened innocently. It was the first time I was playing it cool and I didn't want my sister to spoil it. Honestly, I just had to go six days without ruining anything and I couldn't think of one damn reason why this dress would be inside ... Maybe I could say I'd spilt something on myself and gone into the loo to turn my dress inside out? No. It was like that when I went out and neither of us noticed? No.

'So go on then. What happened?' India said, turning off the television and fixing me with that look that had usually had me confessing to something I'd done when we were kids.

'We had a really lovely dinner,' I repeated, trying to keep my voice even. 'I told you.'

'And?'

'And then we went back to his cabin and shagged each other senseless.'

India spluttered into her wine and laughed. 'Don't be ridiculous. What really happened? I bet you spilled something on yourself.'

Hmm.

I was on the horns of a dilemma here. Slightly surprised I had indeed acted like a sex-starved wanton but at the same time hurt my sister didn't think I had it in me to be the target of someone's lustful urges. I mean I'm not that bad. I've had my moments. Quite a few of them only an hour ago.

'Yes, you're right. Thai green curry. All down the front.' I nodded, lying through my teeth.

'I knew it. You're hopeless.'

I went into the bathroom and looked at myself in the mirror for a long moment. It was very hard to concentrate; to remember what I was supposed to do.

Perhaps I really had been shagged senseless?

I cleaned my teeth and brushed the tangles out of my hair.

India turned her light out and gave a happy sigh. 'Jerry sent me a lovely text. He's really missing me. He can't wait till we get back.'

'Only six days to go then,' I said.

Lying in the gloom I thought back over the evening. What I had said and what Gabriel had done. I could feel myself blushing. He must have fancied me. I certainly fancied him but then I expected every woman on board did.

'So are you seeing him again?' India asked.

'Seeing who?'

'Very funny.'

Chapter Fourteen

Fog Cutter

Light Rum, Cognac, Gin, Lime Juice,
Cherry Brandy, Sugar Syrup

The following morning I woke up feeling a bit disorientated. India was already in the shower, crashing about
and probably using up all the shampoo and conditioner so I
would have to make do with what little was left.

I relived the night before all through breakfast. India had
been thoughtful over her scrambled eggs, American bacon
and pile of buttered toast, while I'd stuck to fresh fruit. Perhaps
I was imagining myself rolling around on Gabriel's bed again
and didn't want to risk the term *beached whale* coming up.

'We ought to have our photos taken,' India said out of the
blue. 'There's a proper photographer on board. You don't need
an appointment.'

We bickered for a few minutes about whether this was a

good idea or not, and then India played the guilt-trip cards of this being 'her' holiday and 'Mum said'.

'Oh, all right,' I said at last. Peace at any price.

'You'd better put some make-up on then,' India said, 'and a clean shirt. And hurry, there's a talk on later about Fabergé eggs.'

I darted back along the corridor and up in the lift to our cabin. The steward had been in, bringing order to the chaos we had left with clean towels and sheets and emptying the bottles out of the bin.

I found a clean shirt and made some attempts to improve my make-up before I made my way back to find India. The long corridors were surprisingly empty as people went off to talks and activities. Today was also *Creating Fruit Platters to Delight Your Guests* and *Napkin Folding to Delight Your Guests*.

As the lift doors opened someone grabbed my arm and pulled me inside. I started to yelp, and then realised with a prickle of excitement it was Gabriel.

'I've been thinking about you,' he whispered.

I felt like a spy or someone mysterious, having an assignation in a dark corner. It was a good job there wasn't anyone else in there with us.

'How did you know I was here?'

'Luck. I saw you leaving the food court. You're driving me mad,' he said with a choking laugh.

'I have that effect on lots of people,' I gasped back.

I don't think we meant the same thing.

He kissed all my lipstick off, his hands on my bottom, pulling me hard towards him. He certainly was pleased to see me – I could tell that.

A disembodied voice told us we were arriving at the third floor and the lift doors pinged open. Gabriel took a deep breath and let me go.

'Where are you going?'

'To find India. She wants us to have a photo taken.'

He smiled. 'Then you'd better put some more lipstick on,' he said. 'I seem to have smudged it.'

I nodded and gave what I thought was an enigmatic smile. And what was that other thing he'd said? Beguiling.

Then he reached out and touched my hand, his eyes creasing in concern. 'Are you sure you're feeling all right?'

So, that's not how you do enigmatic or beguiling then.

'Fine!'

I'll admit it, I was feeling pretty amazing as we walked back through the ship. Occasionally his fingers would brush against mine or he would put one hand into the small of my back as he guided me through a crowd of people queuing up to go into the *Napkin Folding* talk.

We got to the food court and Gabriel turned, his hand on my arm.

'Have fun,' he said.

I watched him hungrily, remembering what he had felt like last night as we had made love –

No, I meant as we had shagged each other.

For the first time since I'd come on board, I could feel the ship moving, rocking from side to side. I suppose it was the rougher seas as we headed out into the open ocean away from the shelter of the land. It made me feel slightly odd.

*

We had our picture taken; it didn't take long.

Chin up, ladies, and smile. Lovely. Look at me. Look at each other.

I knew what the result would be; India would look photogenic and gorgeous and I would look slightly strange. I never seemed to know what to do with my face. Still, if it made her happy.

Then we fed our coins into the machines in the casino. I lost all mine and India won ten dollars. That figured. Then we went to mooch about, finding new places we had missed up to now. There was an amazing observation room with floor-to-ceiling windows where we watched the ship nosing through the waves. It was wonderful.

All I seemed to have done recently was eat and drink too much. I suppose if I hadn't been so bone idle I could have gone into the gym and asked one of the terrifying trainers there to sort out my burgeoning flab. I could have gone striding out around the deck with all the other walking nuts in their eye shields and made-to-measure trainers; ten circuits equalled one glass of wine, or so someone had said.

I wasn't sure if it was true or not. If it was I'd need to spend the next thirty-six hours walking non-stop to make up for what I'd already had.

We didn't do ten circuits of the ship but we had our lunch-time drinks just the same. And a brie and cranberry panini. And a bowl of fries. Never mind fitting into my bridesmaid's dress, I'd have trouble fitting into my car at this rate.

'I want to be a writer, just like Marnie,' India said, her eyes focused on her future fame, riches and book signings in Foyles. 'I mean how hard can it be? Really? Marnie can do a book a year and the last one sold over half a million copies. If she only got one pound for each book that's half a million quid. I could do that.'

'What are you going to write about?' I said.

India began to look misty-eyed. I bet she was imagining herself in a few years stepping out from Marnie's shadow as a writing expert and celebrity with designer clothes and sharp little shoes.

'I'll think of something. I'm going to write down a plot this afternoon. I'm going to devote every single waking moment to it from now on.'

India usually had trouble finishing writing a shopping list so I thought this might be a stretch too far but I wasn't going to dampen her enthusiasm.

'That would be really good,' I said.

'I'm not going to let *anything* or *anyone* distract me until I've got it done.'

India crammed the last two fries into her mouth and mopped up some salty crystals with her finger.

'But I thought we were going to *Fruit Platters to Delight Your Friends* at two-thirty?' I said.

I'd decided to join India at this event as she had complained about being 'abandoned' yesterday evening, and we'd missed the Fabergé talk. Plus it was worth trying to mend fences with her. We weren't going to have any excursions to distract us from our issues for the next few days, so it would be better if we got along.

'Well, after *that* obviously,' India said, linking her arm through mine. 'I'm not going to turn into a complete bore. And anyway I might want my main character to *provide* a fruit platter to delight her friends at some point in my book. So it's research actually.'

'You're right, good thinking.'

*

The fruit platter thing was really good I have to admit. The chef was another of the inscrutable-looking ones with a towering white hat and I don't think he spoke much English apart from saying *very good* or *yes*. There were large mounds of fruit of every colour, shape and size, and some small oval dishes for us to use, and we were shown how to arrange all sorts of things in an attractive and enticing way. Afterwards we were encouraged to take our platters back to our cabins but by then India and I had eaten most of it anyway so we didn't bother. I thought it unlikely we would be doing it again any time soon if I was honest; well, not without a good dollop of ice cream.

'I think I need a nap,' I said, feeling distinctly full and a bit tired. But then I'd had a bad night's sleep what with *one thing and another* so it wasn't really surprising.

'Well, I'm going to the library to write out my plot,' India said, looking industrious, and I realised I hadn't seen her this fired up about anything other than the wedding in a long time. It was good for her, and for me.

'Oh, okay.'

'Don't you want to come with me?' she asked, a bit puzzled. 'You can be a bestselling writer too.'

'I'll have a nap first,' I said, stifling a yawn, 'and then I'll join you.'

I went to get the lift up to the eleventh floor. I reached my cabin and was about to close the door behind me when Gabriel's door opened.

'Oh, hello,' he said.

We stood and looked at each other for a moment, my heart thundering.

'What have you been doing?' he asked at last.

'*Fruit Platters to Delight Your Friends*,' I managed to say, just before he reached out and touched my mouth with one finger and I shuddered.

Then he took hold of my hand and I went willingly into his cabin. 'Come in here and tell me about it.'

He locked the door behind me and started unbuttoning my shirt. I watched his hands, busy on the little buttons, before I reached out, grabbed his belt and pulled him towards me. I could feel the heat from his body.

He leant over me, his eyes hovering over mine for an excruciatingly long second, before he kissed me. 'You taste of strawberries. *Fruit Platters to Delight Your Friends?*'

'I think we could delight each other,' I said, as the wanton part of me I'd just discovered took over.

I saw his eyes flash, before he lowered his head and softly bit my shoulder. 'I think we could too.'

Twenty seconds later we were naked on the bed together. No preliminary chitchat or *would you like something to drink? Tea or Coffee? Iced water?* No messing about with *how was your day?* We didn't say another word; we just took off our clothes and got down to it. It was fast and furious and fantastic. I'd never known anything like it; it was even better than last night. And I swear, as I cried out, he groaned my name.

I held his head against my heart and ran my fingers through his hair. A sudden wash of feeling flowed through me. Call it tenderness or care or concern for him. I wasn't sure. He was kind, clever, passionate, handsome, interesting and successful. How could any woman look for something else when she had this? Suddenly I could sense the sadness within him, the loneliness, the need. A restless searching for something. Perhaps a wish to be valued as a man, for himself. The emotions I had felt in the past were nothing compared with this moment. I was in deep trouble.

'Wow,' he said at last.

'Mmmmm,' I agreed and closed my eyes.

For two pins I would have fallen asleep, but I couldn't do that.

I made to get out of his bed, only for him to pull me back, curving his body around mine. I liked the feel of that and gave a little murmur of pleasure.

Then, without meaning to, we fell asleep, and when I woke up there were people outside in the corridor, going back to their cabin, laughing, someone stumbling and exclaiming, *Miranda – these bloody shoes!*

It was a good job I wasn't going to see Gabriel again after this week because it would have been terribly embarrassing. Everyone knew the rule of unattached sex was for the sex to happen and then you left. No hard feelings and no expectations. But, well, Gabriel had wanted to hold me. So maybe this was different for him too. Oh, God, stop! This was a fling, a holiday romance based on something I didn't understand. It wasn't going to blossom into something else, was it? We would not in forty years' time be interviewed for a programme called *Holiday Romances that Lasted a Lifetime* on an obscure television channel. I needed to get a grip!

Never mind; there were many ways to spend an hour in the afternoon and this was undoubtedly the best I'd known. I bet I used up thousands of calories too and it was far more fun than pounding around the promenade deck ten times in an eye shield.

I couldn't stay there, no matter how much I wanted to, because of the whole *this isn't a relationship, it's a bit of fun* thing. But also because, if I did, there would be dozens of unanswerable and embarrassing questions from India. I couldn't think which would be worse.

'I must go,' I said.

Gabriel turned his head away. 'Oh. Why?'

I didn't know what to do for a second. Did he want me to stay? Or go? Had he enjoyed me as much as I had enjoyed him?

I collected my clothes and pulled them on. He pulled the duvet over himself and watched me.

'Alexa.'

'Yes?'

'I want you to know, I –'

'What?'

'Marnie ...'

I looked at him for a second but he just shook his head.

Of course; we were having a fling. He didn't want Marnie to know. She was his employer after all. I wasn't expecting him to propose or anything. I mean it was just sex.

I took a deep breath. 'You needn't worry; you don't need to explain. We're just having fun, aren't we? Anyway, I'll see you.' I made myself smile at him. 'That was great.'

Great? What sort of word was that? My whole body was

tingling and pulsing with pleasure. I wasn't sure I could walk straight. Great didn't nearly cover it.

He looked at me. 'Yes, it was.'

'Well then. I'd better –' I made some vague gesture. 'Sorry about the … you know?'

The bed looked as though we'd been fighting and his cabin could have been the scene of a burglary.

Gabriel's clothes were all over the place. We had knocked a shade off one of the bedside lamps and the fruit bowl had fallen on the floor, the fruit scattered under the bed. A vase of silk flowers had tipped over and the decorative glass pebbles inside were falling down the back of the sofa cushions. The steward was going to weep when he saw it.

'It's okay,' he said, a smile playing on his lips.

I checked I had my shirt on the right way round and went back to my cabin. Thank the gods, India wasn't there. I went into the shower and used all the new selection of toiletries and then sprayed myself with her perfume and sat wrapped in a bathrobe on the balcony, thinking. The thinking process was helped by a very large gin and tonic from the mini bar that I think counted as medicinal.

It was getting chilly and I knew I wouldn't stay outside for long, but I wanted to be there in the cold air, knowing Gabriel was only a step away in the next cabin. Maybe he was asleep, still with my sweat on his body, or he could be showering. Either way I would have given a lot to be in there with him.

I thought back to what we had been doing and blinked a

bit. I'd never been like this in my life. I mean when I was with Ryan we had done a bit of role-play to try and spice things up, but the outfit he had bought me was nylon and very scratchy so I couldn't wait to get it off. And while we're on the subject, would anyone else in the Western world find dressing up their girlfriend as a nuclear power station worker sexy? No, I didn't think so either.

But this? Chucking myself at someone I hardly knew? What on earth had come over me? Apart from an exceptionally attractive and sexy man I mean.

Chapter Fifteen

Atlantic Breeze

Light Rum, Apricot Brandy, Galliano,
Pineapple Juice, Lemon Juice

I got dressed and went to find India. She was supposed to be in the library but that was full of Americans looking for Sudoku books and jigsaws of the *Titanic* and buying souvenir keyrings and baseball caps with *Reine de France* embroidered on them. I eventually found her sitting in the bar next door in a big leather armchair with her feet up on a footstool, her laptop open. She had a cocktail and some salted peanuts on the table next to her. I flopped down in the adjacent chair.

'Oh, hello. I was wondering where you had got to,' she said. 'I've got on so brilliantly you wouldn't believe it. I've got the whole story mapped out and I'm just trying to think of names for my main characters. It's not as easy as you might think. Have you had a nice nap?'

I hesitated, thinking about it, and then realised one of the waiters was already homing in on me, rotating a round tray balanced on his outspread fingers. Now was neither the time nor the place to go into details.

'A nice nap? Absolutely!'

The waiter flipped a paper coaster down on the table in front of me and waited, his head tilted politely.

'What are you drinking?' I said.

India looked at her drink. 'An Atlantic Breeze – it seemed appropriate.'

I turned back to the waiter. 'I'll have what she's having,' I said and then of course was convulsed with giggles remembering that scene in *When Harry Met Sally*.

'Are you quite all right?' India said, giving me a hard stare.

'Yes, great.' I mopped my eyes with a paper napkin and tried to calm down.

India carried on typing for a few seconds and I took some deep breaths and tried to wipe my mind of the rather startling images of Gabriel and what we had been doing with each other less than an hour previously.

'Your drink, madame.' The waiter was back, all sloe eyes and snake hips. He put my luminous cocktail down on the coaster and fussed about with a napkin and a bowl of nuts.

I think he was trying to send me an engaging look but I didn't have the energy or inclination to respond.

'Can I get you *anything else*, ladies?' he said with a definite hint of seduction in his voice. 'My name is Pascal. You only 'ave to ask. I am at your service.'

It was five-thirty; I had a rather nice glass of rocket fuel in front of me, the prospect of another fine dinner ahead. I might need a lot of things but a flirtatious episode with a rather oily French waiter wasn't one of them. And I was not at home to Mr Suggestive, thanks all the same.

Pascal wandered off with a dissatisfied Gallic pout.

'So what have you been doing? Did you find out about the talk on the *Titanic*?'

'Hmm? What? No, I forgot.'

India sighed in exasperation. 'I did ask you to find out. We'd better not have missed it. I'm sure it's sometime tomorrow. Someone told me it's really interesting.'

'Liam, I suppose?'

'No,' India said with an exaggerated eye-roll, 'forget about him.'

'Yes, well, you're spoken for. I'm supposed to be looking after you. And protecting you from people like him.'

'Oh, beak out of it,' India muttered.

'Well, you shouldn't be flirting.'

'I wasn't, believe me. The day I take advice from you on how to behave is the day I throw in the towel.'

'Right! How would you feel if Jerry said the same thing to

his friends when he's enjoying the fleshpots of Wolverhampton?'

'Jerry wouldn't dare!' India said furiously.

'Well, nor should you,' I said. 'Now tell me about your plot?'

The situation was mercifully defused and India looked pleased I was showing some interest. I decided I was going to keep a closer eye on Liam in future.

'Well –' she scrolled back through her notes '– it's going to be about a girl who can't find Mr Right and has been out with all sorts of unsuitable men. A bit like you. But then she meets a man on the Internet or she might meet him some-where else. I haven't decided. And he's not what he says he is. But then nor is she. He claims to be a solicitor – you see I can get all the legal jargon from Jerry to make it sound real-istic – when in fact he is a duke. Or possibly an earl. Which do you think sounds sexier? I can't think of many dukes who are hot stuff. I'll have to google them when we get home. Earls sound younger, don't they? And the heroine is an estate agent because I know all about that ...'

'You do?'

'Very funny. But she says she's a party planner because it sounds more interesting. And he asks her to organise his mother's eightieth birthday party and of course she doesn't have a clue. He's expecting a marquee and catering for two hundred and she turns up with some sandwiches in clingfilm and a Victoria sponge with Smarties on the top. And it all goes incredibly wrong but in the end it's fine. And she in return asks him about problems she's having with her lease and her shitty landlord and of course he gives her legal advice that's completely wrong because he doesn't have a clue either.'

'So what happens?'

'Well, they all live happily ever after of course. And she gets to marry a duke or earl and moves to live in his castle. With a load of servants and a walk-in wardrobe full of really cool clothes.'

'Excellent.'

India smiled happily.

I thought about it.

'I read about a duke the other day in the papers. He had to move into a cottage on his estate and open his stately home to the public because of crippling death duties. Your duke doesn't have a castle with a leaking roof he can't afford to repair? Or a mad aunt in the attic who thinks she's about to be married to her fiancé who actually ran off with the house-keeper twenty years ago? And is there a bad-tempered butler who is stealing the family portraits and selling them on eBay?'

India took a deep breath. 'No, none of those things.'

'I know, he could have a completely crazy ex-wife who lives on the estate in a house at the end of the driveway with seven terriers and an Italian riding instructor?'

'No, he doesn't –'

'And a rakish younger brother called Piers who is always trying to murder him so he gets to be the duke? But the duke doesn't realise it and he's continually allowing himself to be lured out on the lake in a leaking rowboat or up on the roof in force nine winds? He could have a sister called Petula who's a raving alcoholic and sets fire to the drawing room curtains with a cigarette lighter. '

'Um –'

'I can see it all now. His mother – the dowager duchess – is the Spanish society beauty Berengaria, who now looks like Maggie Smith in a mantilla. But she's had oodles of plastic surgery so her face is so tight she can't sneeze. And she lives in the best rooms in the castle, which by rights should be our heroine's, but the dowager refuses to move out because the previous duchess made a deathbed confession that she had hidden some priceless emeralds in the room during the war but can't remember where. So the dowager wanders about at night in her dead husband's hairy dressing gown looking for the secret panel, and all they can hear is a ghostly tapping. How about this then: the duke is desperate to provide an heir to the family fortunes so he and the heroine spend every other chapter shagging each other senseless in every room in the house, gradually getting more and more rude and experimental. You could add in some spanking and bondage, couldn't you? Isn't that what the English aristocracy go in for?'

India looked confused and a bit annoyed.

'No, that's not what I planned at all.'

'Oh. Sorry.'

'My heroine is going to be called Devon or McKenzie, something really modern, and the hero is Alfred or Arthur or something. And he's really handsome and looks like Tom Hiddleston with black hair. And he rides a big grey horse round the estate and has a chocolate Labrador called Treacle.'

'Excellent. Sounds great. Could you keep in the spanking?'

'No! God Almighty! Our *mother* is going to read this!'

'Well, she won't mind.'

India's eyes were round with horror. 'I'd die of embarrassment!'

'Why? You never know, perhaps Dad liked it?'

'Don't be disgusting.'

'You're such a prude! They must have had sex at least twice,' I said, but I was also rather surprised by what I was coming out with. I never talked like this, or at least I never used to. Since being on board this ship I seemed to be getting a bit more confident ... or something anyway.

Sipping my cocktail I relaxed as the alcohol, diluted with more alcohol and some splashes of fruit juice, worked its magic.

India struggled with the idea.

'But they're our parents.'

'Yes? And your point is?'

'I have to say you're pretty interested in sex for someone who isn't getting any!' she said witheringly.

I wasn't thinking fast enough. 'Oh, you think?'

Her eyes narrowed. 'You have something to tell me?'

'No, no, absolutely not.' I took another long pull at my

drink and coughed a bit. Drinking cocktails through a straw was always a bad idea.

I looked across at India and suddenly found I couldn't meet her gaze.

'Hang on! What have you been up to?' she said.

'Um, nothing.' I could feel myself blushing.

'Um, nothing? What does *um, nothing* mean? Bloody hell, you haven't been going off with Pouting Pascal, have you? Is that why he's being so friendly? You're disgusting!'

'No, I haven't. Give me some credit. Look, I'll tell you when I feel ready.'

India laughed disbelievingly. 'You're not getting away with that! I told you all about Jerry and stuff, didn't I? Even the bit when he suggested the handcuffs and the judge's outfit.'

'Ooh yes, did you actually get round to doing that?'

The handcuffs had been a source of much hilarity at the time when India had ordered them off Amazon, but then it had all gone a bit quiet and I never did find out what happened.

'I ... I'll tell you if you tell me what you've been up to.'

It was a stalemate.

'You go first,' I said.

India snorted. 'Not likely. What have you been doing?' Her face suddenly dropped with shock. 'It's not Gabriel Frost? It can't be him? Surely?'

I did a bit of huffing. 'Why not?'

'You've had sex with Gabriel Gorgeous Frost? When for fuck's sake? When did you find the time?'

I was suddenly rather pleased with myself.

'Well, let's just say after *Fruit Platters to Delight Your Friends* I went back to the cabin to have a nap and I didn't,' I said.

'In our cabin?'

'No, his.'

India gasped. 'Well, thank God for that! You are joking? You sly cow!'

'And last night.'

'And last night? When I was in bed next door? I was watching the Disney Channel! And you were next door? Screwing Gabriel Frost? So you didn't spill curry down yourself?'

I could see the waiters were beginning to edge a bit closer, pretending to wipe the tables and straighten the chairs.

'Er, could you speak up a bit, India? They can't quite hear you.'

India sat open-mouthed for a moment. 'You're not making this up?'

'Ferrets bite me if I lie.'

'Bloody hell. And? What was it like? Why didn't you tell me?'

This was the first time my sister had shown any interest in my sex life for a very long time. I was enjoying this, having something to say, something interesting as well.

'It was all a bit sudden actually. And it was –' I tried to think of the right word '– it was brilliant.'

'And this afternoon? How did that work then?'

'I told you, I was going back to the cabin for a nap after the *Fruit Platters to Delight Your Friends* session and he opened his door and invited me in, so I went.'

'Just like that?'

'Just like that.'

'Wow.'

I sipped my Atlantic Breeze and India looked at me in astonishment, processing this new information.

'Wow,' she said again. 'So when are you seeing him again then?'

I shrugged and tried to look casual. It was ages since I'd had one up on my sister and I was thoroughly enjoying it.

'Don't know. I suppose we have a few days till we get to Southampton. We'll fit something in. So to speak.'

'Well, don't let me stop you,' India said, suddenly getting slightly shirty. 'Look, you don't really think Jerry would – you know – flirt with other women?'

'Not if he knows what's good for him. Now tell me about the handcuffs and the judge's outfit.'

Chapter Sixteen

Titanic

Vodka, Martini Bianco, Galliano, Blue Curacao

'Was the *Titanic* the ship that couldn't sink? Contrary to popular belief it was never claimed so at the time. It was, however, possibly the most beautiful, most sumptuous ship ever built, where every last detail was of the highest quality and life was luxurious. Unless of course you were in steerage and had to share two bathrooms between seven hundred people. Your journey was far less enjoyable and in fact even your chances of survival were less certain. If you were a woman in steerage you had only a twenty-five per cent chance of survival. If you were a man you had little chance at all. In fact more men travelling in first class survived than third-class children.'

'Cheery,' India muttered next to me.

'Imagine sharing a bathroom with three hundred and fifty people,' I muttered back.

222

'It's bad enough sharing one with you.' India looked round the theatre rather obviously. 'So where's Gabriel this morning?'

'No idea, I'm not his keeper.'

'Perhaps he's tending to Marnie Miller's needs.'

I bit down the swell of annoyance this caused me and tried to look indifferent.

'You're trying to look indifferent, aren't you?' India said.

'I'm not trying to look anything!'

At this point the woman in the seat in front turned and glared at us.

I nudged India's arm off the armrest between us and we had a bit of an undignified scuffle.

Down on the stage, the speaker – a very tall, gaunt man with glasses and a hunched posture that spoke of many years ducking under low doorways – was still going on about the *Titanic*. Behind him was a picture of the ship as it steamed away from the Irish coast towards its doom.

'The ship was due to dock at New York on April 17th 1912, but, as we all know, she never arrived. She struck an iceberg three hundred and seventy miles south southeast of Newfoundland and sank in two hours and forty minutes. The exact location is believed to be forty-one degrees north, forty-nine degrees west. We will be passing this spot at approximately midday today.'

He clicked a remote-control device and the picture behind him changed to the iconic photograph of the ghostly bow of the *Titanic* bathed in an eerie blue light. He paused for dramatic effect and stared out at the audience. There was a collective gasp from a large party of Americans and even the sound of restrained sobbing from someone. It seemed a bit of an excessive reaction to me; it had sunk over a hundred years ago. A bit late to cry about it now?

'And why does the *Titanic* provoke such interest, all these years later?' the speaker continued, pacing the stage. 'It wasn't the first disaster at sea. It wasn't even the greatest loss of life although 1,517 people perished. In 1865 a Mississippi riverboat exploded killing 1,800, but could you name it?'

'So are you going to see him again?' India whispered.

'Who?'

'Gabriel? Are you going to see him again?'

I shrugged.

'Well, don't let me stop you. I'm off to see Peter and Paula later to learn how to foxtrot,' India said. 'And no, I won't be flirting with Liam or anybody else for that matter. If you want to spend the afternoon shagging each other's brains out then feel free.'

The woman in front turned and glared at us again. I held out an apologetic hand and pressed my lips together.

'We know John Jacob Astor and Benjamin Guggenheim died, but so did one-year-old Gertrud Klasen in third class, and two-year-old Helen Allison in first class.'

The theatre was filling up with people shuffling along the rows towards the middle so they could see the slides more easily and appreciate the scale of the disaster, the remains of which were apparently 12,500 feet beneath them. Or at least they would be later that morning when everyone was enjoying coffee and bagels in the food court and had already forgotten about Millvina Dean who had survived the disaster aged three months.

'Spotted him yet?' India whispered.

'I'm not looking for him,' I said, 'I'm just looking around.'

'Perhaps he's looking for you? Wanting to drag you off again to slake his untameable lust.'

'I'm not going to respond to that on the grounds that it might make me want to clout you with my seagull-decorated notebook,' I said.

'Ha! So you do care? All that bollocks about just having fun. You fancy him!'

'Of course I fancy him, India. Or I wouldn't have had sex with him, would I?'

'The water temperature that night was minus two degrees Celsius. Few would have survived more than fifteen minutes. But the ship's baker was rescued after two hours, claiming his survival was due to whisky.'

'So are you going to, y'know?'

'I think that comes under the category of mind your own business,' I snapped.

'I told you about the handcuffs and the blindfold,' India said crossly.

'And Milton Hershey of Hershey Chocolate had reservations to sail but cancelled them at the last minute. In fact the

225

tragedy could have been worse. The ship was equipped to carry three and a half thousand passengers but there were only two thousand two hundred on board that night.'

'I think you're scared, that's your trouble. For some reason you prefer to latch on to the losers and wankers like Tom and Ryan. And remember that idiot Chris? The way he mucked you about? Anyone else would have kicked him into touch after five minutes but you put up with him for six months. And you never did get those vinyls back, did you?'

'He said someone nicked them.'

'Sure they did. He flogged them on eBay you mean.'

'Oh, shut up.'

India snorted. 'You know I'm right.'

Down on the stage the speaker had found a laser pointer and was indicating the fatal flaw in the *Titanic*'s design. Something about bulkheads and the water getting in over the top.

I nudged India. 'Chris was a loser. You're right about him and he was rubbish in bed too.'

'Well, there you are then.'

'He called me by his ex-girlfriend's name on more than one occasion and he had a thing about whipped cream that wasn't always convenient. Good job I wasn't dairy intolerant. Ryan was reasonable, but he liked to watch the football over my shoulder while we were having sex. That was a bit off-putting.'

'Good grief.'

'And I have the sneaking suspicion Tom was bisexual; he was very interested in my make-up'

India snorted into the sleeve of her jumper and shook with silent laughter. Eventually she calmed down and took a deep breath.

'And Mr Gorgeous?'

I sighed.

India giggled. 'That good, eh?'

I sighed again. 'Brilliant. Some men know what they're doing and some don't bother trying. Some of them are better at other things perhaps?'

India pulled a face. 'What, like servicing the car or peeling spuds? Who cares about that?'

'I'm trying to be fair,' I said.

The woman in front of me turned round again, exasperated, and I realised that most of the people around us were quite blatantly listening in to our conversation.

'I'm *trying* to listen to this man talking about the *Titanic*,' the woman said. 'I don't want to know what Chris or Tom did in bed.'

Someone further along, a woman with extravagantly coiffed blonde hair and evidence of several face-lifts, made slightly annoyed grumbling noises.

'Well, I was interested,' she said. 'I was hoping to pick up some tips.'

'The whipped cream?' her neighbour said.

'My second husband always wanted to do that but it's full

227

of calories. I said no, Burl, there's diabetes in both our families. Not unless there's a low-sugar version.'

The annoyed woman in front of us gave a strangled scream and stood up, edging her way along the row past a lot of people's knees and handbags.

Down on the stage the speaker looked up, shading his eyes from the spotlight.

'Sorry, is there a problem out there? Can't you hear me?'

*

After we nearly fell out of the theatre giggling, there was a brief lull between activities and we went to find some lunch in the wine bar up at the top of the ship where Gabriel had taken me. I half hoped he might be there but he wasn't. There were a couple of men already on the bar-stools: one with a Stetson and tooled leather boots to identify him as a Texan, the other in a Boston Red Sox T-shirt. They were steadily working their way down a bottle of Sailor Jerry and, by the backslapping and laughter, had clearly been doing so for some time.

India perused the cocktail list and decided, in view of our recent public disgrace, that we should have a Dirty Martini to celebrate. It was jolly nice too, very bracing. I was beginning to see the wisdom of a cocktail that was alcohol mixed with alcohol. It wasn't pretending to be anything other than a stiff drink. It saved time.

We went to sit in a corner away from prying ears and

anyone who might have witnessed our rapid exit from the lecture. Once the waiter had left us with our cocktails and a bowl of peanuts we relaxed.

'Seriously. This Gabriel. What are his intentions?' India said.

She took a handful of peanuts and started crunching, her expression alert to what information I would let slip. She looked clear-eyed and very pretty and far healthier than her alcohol intake over the last few days should have allowed.

'His intentions? You sound like an outraged maiden aunt, not a woman who's had carnal knowledge of her fiancé while he was dressed as a high court judge in Batman boxer shorts and no trousers, and while she was handcuffed to the bed. I still can't get over that.'

'Well, you wanted to know. You shouldn't have asked. Seriously, what's going on, Al? I know what's going to happen – you talk the talk and can't walk the walk. You're saying it's just mindless sex and no strings and you're having a bit of a fling but you're not like that. We both know it. You go all soppy and fall in love. By the time we get off the ship in Southampton you'll be planning the wedding and then there will be tears. It's taken you long enough to get over that shit Ryan. I don't want you getting hurt like that again.'

I looked at her in surprise. This was very unexpected.

'Good God, India, when did you start to care about the state of my heart? You're serious all of a sudden.'

'Well, maybe I am. I'm getting married soon. Who's going to look out for you then?'

'Yes, I do know you're getting married soon; you remind me on a regular basis. And when did you ever look out for me? I was always the one looking out for you,' I pointed out with strangled outrage. But India just shook her dark hair over her shoulder and waved her hand.

'I mean does he even know where you live so he can send you flowers? Does he even know your surname so he can google you? Did he wear a condom so I know you didn't catch any diseases or get pregnant?'

'That's definitely mind your own business. Would you tell me if Jerry did?'

'Well, of course he doesn't, but then I'm actually trying to get pregnant. Or was.'

It took a moment for this comment to register. I put my drink down suddenly, feeling shocked. What?

When had India jumped from weddings and twinkly table settings to serious thoughts about children?

'Oh. What do you mean *was*? I didn't know that,' I said, feeling even more removed from my sister than I had before we got on the ship. We used to tell each other these kinds of things – the big things – and she hadn't even mentioned this. This was huge.

'Well, I don't tell you everything, any more than you tell me,' she said. Suddenly she looked away. 'I'm not pregnant by the way – before you ask. I wouldn't be knocking back all this booze if I was. And it's looking like it might be harder than we thought.'

'Have you had tests? I mean – you know?'

India looked out at the sea and then shrugged. 'I expect we will. I'll be sure to let you know when Jerry goes to give his sample,' she finished a bit waspishly.

I knew my sister well enough to know she was seriously upset. I reached over and rubbed her arm and she ducked her head towards me to show she appreciated the gesture.

'Seriously, India, if there's anything I can do?'

'Oh, you know, we'll sort it out. I'm sure we will.'

It was suddenly blindingly obvious why my sister was so obsessed with the minutiae of her wedding. It was giving her something to focus on, so she could avoid dwelling on the other, far more significant matter.

She picked up her Dirty Martini and gave me that look that said please don't ask me any more questions. So I gulped mine back too and had to suppress a coughing fit. Then I stuffed the last of the peanuts in my mouth.

'I suppose we should be going to the dance classes soon,' I said, searching for another topic of conversation and not peppering her with questions I was desperate to ask. I could see she'd already spent enough time worrying about this. She needed something normal, to have some fun, and I could help there. 'It's one o'clock already.'

India smiled at me then and picked up the cocktail menu.

'Well, there's time for another quick one, don't you think? Let's have a White Lady.'

'What's in that?' I asked, relieved she had moved into safer waters and we were still okay, or as okay as two sisters who were trying to mend their relationship could be. One day at a time. One cocktail at a time.

'Just a little bit of gin,' she said with a wicked twinkle. And I gave a laugh. It was going to be lethal, but maybe that's just what we needed.

The ship gave a sudden definite lurch as India went up to the bar. The weather was worsening. Outside we could see spray drenching the windows and, beyond, the lowering grey skies. The waiter laughed and made a grab for an ice bucket that was sliding towards the edge of the bar.

'Whoa there, the forecast said it was going to be a bit bumpy once we headed out. Batten down the hatches!'

I had always thought of myself as a good sailor. I'd even coped pretty well with a gale in the Bay of Biscay, but then I'd never been on the Atlantic. This was going to be interesting.

We went to Peter and Paula's class after lunch in the ball-room. Two cocktails or not, the weather was getting rougher. This time the dominant colour for our dance masters was turquoise. A turquoise satin shirt for Peter and matching sequins and ruffles for Paula.

'The foxtrot!' Peter declaimed, spinning Paula round in front of him. 'And not just any foxtrot – we are going to teach you something called the *American* foxtrot. As with so many things, America took a good idea and improved it.'

'What, like turning chips into curly fries or pasta into mac and cheese?' I said.

232

India nudged me. 'Sssh!'

Peter was still talking. 'You've all heard of slow, slow, quick, quick, slow? Well, here is where you use it. It's simple, effective and easy to learn. Promenade twinkles, fallaway twinkles and closed twinkles with a promenade-closed ending can all come later. For today we are back to the basic steps and the sway and glide of one of the most versatile of dances.'

There seemed to be a shortage of male partners this time. There was certainly no sign of Liam.

India and I did what we could, grasping on to each other's elbows and treading all over each other's feet, but it was increasingly difficult to glide and sway attractively when the ship was ploughing through what felt like quite significant waves.

'And glide and glide, feet relaxed and rocking. Walk through the music and glide, and glide and slowly, slowly,' Peter hollered over the music.

After a few minutes of stumbling around and treading on each other we gave up.

'Wow, I don't think I should have had that White Lady,' India said as we made our way to the edge of the dance floor. 'I think I need a sit-down.'

We sat down on a couple of the gilt chairs that surrounded the dance floor. India leaned her head in her hands and groaned a little.

'But this ship has the most sophisticated stabilisers anywhere on the high seas,' I said, paraphrasing the ship's publicity literature. 'You can't be seasick?'

'Okay, I'm not. I just need a rest. Don't you feel it?'

'No, not really. Just a bit of movement.'

'I think we need to go up to where I can see the horizon, don't you?'

'Okay, if you think it will help.'

We made our way up to the promenade deck and went outside into the fresh air. This in itself was not straightforward. The doors to the deck were very heavy and were being kept closed by a force seven gale outside that wanted them shut; one of them swung back, making me rock even more.

Eventually we made it to the sheltered area at the back of the ship where we could see the angry grey waves crashing away behind the ship. There were also an outdoor pool and a hot tub there, both of which were roped off with 'Danger Do Not Enter' signs on them. They seemed a bit unnecessary to me. We watched mesmerised as the water in them slopped and crashed about with the motion of the ship, spraying the contents over the side. It was very impressive. Anyone even considering going in would have to be certifiable.

'I think I need a cup of tea,' India said rather weakly.

This in itself was startling; India never drank tea.

We struggled with the doors again to get back inside and found her a cup of tea and a piece of cake that she couldn't eat.

'Are you sure you're not pregnant?' I said.

'Definitely not; I think I'm seasick.'

There were lots of other people with the same suspicion.

Even some of the diehard food court regulars were sitting looking steadfastly out of the window with only a glass of water for company.

I left her there, clinging on to the table, and brought back some seasickness pills.

'The pharmacist says either stay up and look at the horizon or go to sleep,' I said.

India took her tablets and finished her water.

'Bed,' she said. 'I think that would be best. I'm going to bed.'

'Do you want me to come with you?'

'Not unless you feel ill too?'

After she'd gone I sat and finished her piece of cake – always tidy, that's me. Then I went off for a wander. Even after all this time there were parts of the ship I hadn't seen yet, including a spa, a casino, a gym and a cinema. Marnie was due to give another talk tomorrow morning but the only thing going on now in the space between afternoon tea and cocktails was a talk in the smaller of the two lecture theatres on the ship's catering. Well, at least it would mean a nice sit-down. I went in and found a seat near the back. A stout chef in his whites was already talking.

'The Champs-Elysées restaurant routinely serves seven hundred and fifty covers per sitting. The ship has its own bakery and pastry departments. I am the executive chef and one hundred and two chefs work under my supervision ...'

I was aware someone was edging along the row of seats

towards me and I looked up with a polite smile. It was Marnie Miller and she was smiling too but in a rather odd way.

She sat down next to me and crossed her legs elegantly.

'... the ship loads dry and frozen goods every ten days. Dairy products and fresh seafood every week. There is a permanent provisions team of nine people who load and distribute throughout the ship's galleys and bars ...'

'Hi,' I said.

'I'm glad I caught up with you. I want to talk to you,' Marnie whispered back.

I didn't answer. Something about this – I wasn't sure what – made me feel very uneasy indeed.

'... the ship has nine bars and eight different places to eat. Every day seventy pizzas, three hundred English scones, and two thousand canapés are consumed. On this transatlantic crossing we expect to use over thirty tons of fresh fruit and vegetables, twenty thousand litres of fresh milk and over thirty thousand eggs ...'

That answered the egg question then. I would have to tell Gabriel next time I saw him.

'I need to have a quiet word,' Marnie repeated, her voice hissing serpent-like in my ear. 'It's in your own interests. I think you should listen. It's about Gabriel Frost.'

Chapter Seventeen

Bitches' Brew

Grand Quinquina, Genever, Vodka, IPA Beer

I didn't move for a while. Next to me Marnie was also still, but it was a sort of rigid, listening immobility that was unnerving. At last the chef stopped talking about pastry and bread making and how many different sorts of cheese there were on board (twenty-one) because he had encountered a technical hitch with the projector. The images of cases of wine being trundled on board the ship had frozen. Golly, there were a lot of them.

There was therefore a bit of a delay as a harassed-looking crew member in a blue boilersuit came on to the stage to try and sort things out, pushing buttons and turning the projector on and off while the chef looked at his watch and muttered.

Marnie reached across and touched my arm with her teeny tiny hand. 'I want to help you, Alexa. You're playing with fire. It would be wrong of me not to say something.'

I looked at her. 'I don't know what you're talking about,' I said at last.

Marnie pulled a sad face and patted my arm again. 'I think you do. I know it's embarrassing but I know what he's like.'

'What who is like?' I said, playing for time.

'Gabriel. Gabriel Frost.'

Down on the stage the chef was starting to get rather annoyed judging by the colour of his face. The original crew member had been joined by two others and all three of them were pressing buttons and sighing and pointing at the side of the stage.

Marnie stood up and gestured for me to follow her. Which, sheep-like, I did.

She walked out towards the cocktail bar and ordered two drinks. I'm not sure what they were except they were pink and rather vicious. Something to do with Polish vodka and raspberries I guessed.

'Now then,' Marnie said. She took a deep breath and looked across at me, her beautiful eyes sympathetic and sad. 'I know Gabriel Frost is an attractive man; we're all girls here, aren't we? We can say it like it is. But you need to be careful. I don't think you know what you're doing.'

How old was I? Twelve?

'What do you mean?' I said with a careless little laugh.

'I think I know what's been going on; I'm not blind. I know Gabriel has been making a fuss of you, knowing you to be a bit of an innocent. He can spot things like that.'

238

Innocent? I don't think so.

I shook my head and frowned. 'And?'

'I guess some might say this was none of my business.'

'Yes, they might,' I said sternly, wishing I was almost anywhere else.

She sipped her cocktail and put the glass down on the table before she spoke.

'He's only recently divorced. I mean a man as good-looking as that would have been married, wouldn't he?'

I tried to look nonchalant and thought back to the Nordic blonde I had imagined with the beautiful children and the cool, laid-back, exquisite life. Well, I knew that wasn't true any more.

'So?'

'So he likes to find women like you, naïve women who are impressed by him.'

I took another gulp of my drink. It was icy and very strong. 'And?'

'He's very charming, isn't he? He's well known for it. Hell, he even tried it on with me when we first met.' She laughed. 'But our relationship is strictly business. The thing is, when he's got what he wants, he loses interest.'

'How do you know this?'

She gave a funny little laugh. 'I know Gabriel. He's bright and clever and drop-dead gorgeous, isn't he? You were tempted, weren't you? He made you think you were different, didn't he?'

'Well, yes ...'

Marnie's expression hardened and I knew I'd made a mistake. She had been fishing, guessing before, but now she knew.

'His wife – and those poor children caught up in it all. Both of them needed therapy after everything. And Elsa was such a sweet person. She didn't deserve what she put up with. And I've got to tell you, his divorce was supposed to have been very unpleasant.'

Her voice had dropped to an appalled whisper.

I reeled back, horrified, and Marnie nodded. 'I'm afraid so. Elsa was gorgeous, terrifically bright and attractive. I think that's what Gabriel couldn't bear. That other men found her attractive. He was always accusing her of something. She was so lovely.'

'Was? Did he kill her?' I gasped.

Marnie shook her head and her red hair span out like a flame. 'No, goodness me, nothing like that. Oh, *Alexa*, it's just so hard to talk about. Sure, Gabriel's a great guy, but he isn't ready to move on. He's still hung up on Elsa and you can't honestly think ... well, let's just say I've seen him do it too many times to count and I just wouldn't want to see it happen again,' she said, looking sad.

I sat stock-still, my heart rapidly speeding up, as I tried desperately to believe that all I felt for him was lust: nothing serious. But, God, that was a lie.

However, looking at Marnie's searching eyes, I held it all together. I couldn't bear for her to know what I felt. So I coolly shrugged my shoulders. 'It's nothing serious,' I said, trying to sound strong.

She reached out and touched my hand, her tone dripping in sympathy. 'Be careful.'

I could feel the disappointment settling in my stomach like a stone. I realised that despite my best efforts I had been doing what I always did. Imagining that this particular man, *this one*, could be it. The love of my life, someone I met and fell for who fell in love with me. That magical moment when everything went right for a change.

In years to come, when people asked us how we'd met, he would reach for my hand and smile and we would remember my chucking champagne over him. Hmm, no. Perhaps we would have to remember something else. Like that moment on deck when he kissed me and my legs went all wobbly. The man I had been waiting for.

And now it didn't feel like that any more. I didn't feel attractive and exotic; I felt a fool. God, I was an idiot. I should have known better.

'Hey, are you coming along to my next talk tomorrow? *Spring-Clean Your Life*? You might find it useful.'

I blinked a bit and forced a smile to my lips. I wasn't going to give her the satisfaction of seeing she had got to me, not on any level.

'Yes, sure. India has a bit of seasickness at the moment though. That's where she is, sleeping it off with some medication. Hopefully she'll be okay.'

Marnie gasped and reached into her handbag. 'Look, I have just the thing! Take these – they're brilliant. And don't worry about giving them back. I have some spare ones in my suite. They are the best for seasickness.'

She handed me two wristbands and explained how they worked – something to do with pressure points or ley lines; some sort of voodoo. I wasn't really listening. And then I went back to our cabin to see how India was getting on. My feet seemed heavy and tired now. All the excitement had gone. Instead of walking past Gabriel's door with the little thrill of anticipation that he might be there, that he might open the door and give me that smile, I was apprehensive, worried in case he did.

*

India was propped up on her pillows sipping some water.

'Where have you been? I'm bored,' she said, her lower lip pushed out in a resentful pout.

I shut the cabin door behind me very quietly.

'I went to a talk on the ship's catering.'

'Sounds fascinating,' she said sarcastically as she lifted her head tentatively off the pillow, before letting it fall again.

'It was quite interesting actually; did you know the ship gets through six tons of chicken a week? And two tons of sugar?' I said, keeping my tone as light and encouraging as I could. I'd developed that voice to use at work when a house sale had fallen through at the last minute. I needed to be impartial, unemotional but helpful. It was the only thing I could think of doing at the moment.

'Strangely enough I didn't know,' she said.

'And on the average seven-day cruise sixty-two thousand alcoholic drinks are consumed. That's over four alcoholic drinks per passenger per day. And that's eight times as much as normal,' I continued, feeling my voice getting strained as I tried to keep hold of my emotions.

'Yes, that sounds about right,' she groaned.

I looked over at her. She did still look a bit peaky.

'How are you feeling?' For a second I stopped thinking about Gabriel and the conversation I'd just had with Marnie. I held out the wristbands. 'I saw Marnie and she sent you these. They're supposed to work on seasickness.'

'Wow.' India's eyes widened as though I was giving her an unparalleled treasure. 'That's kind of her.' And I had to admit it kind of was.

She slipped them on to her wrists and sat up looking thoughtful.

'Yes, I think they are working. I feel much better already. I must thank her. Where did you see her?'

'In the talk on catering. She's giving another talk tomorrow morning, wanted to know if we were going.'

'Well, yes! Of course! After all we are besties now,' she said with a smile, shaking her wrists at me with a flourish to display the bands.

I wandered around the cabin, picking up clothes and making half-hearted attempts to tidy up.

'What's the matter?' India said.

'Nothing.'

'There's something, I can tell.' India got out of bed and pulled on her dressing gown. 'Yes, I'm definitely feeling better. That's brilliant. Sometimes the old ways are the best. Now what is it?'

I took a deep breath. 'Marnie came looking for me and she warned me off Gabriel.'

'What? Bloody hell. What a cheek! Really?'

'She talked about his ex-wife. She said he was just using me.'

'Wow.' India looked thoughtful. 'I'd say that was none of her business, but well, you did know there had to be a catch, right?'

'God, I'm such an idiot. I fell for it again.'

'Oh, Alexa,' she said. She put her arm around me awkwardly and we sort of hugged for a bit. We'd never gone in for a lot of hugging.

'I know, I know, I'm an idiot,' I said, through tears that had suddenly started flowing down my cheeks. I brushed them away angrily. What was the point in crying?

'Don't be silly; of course you're not an idiot. I mean you always do get your hopes up, don't you? But is that a bad thing? To hope for something lovely?' India said, handing me a tissue to mop my eyes. 'Look, what time is it?'

'Six-thirty,' I said mournfully.

244

'It's time we got dolled up. Isn't it the Black and White Ball this evening? There's no need to stay here and feel sorry for yourself. So what if Gabriel's not the forever guy for you; who cares when there are plenty more fish in the sea?' she trilled, throwing a sequinned gown at me and making me almost smile. India was right, wasn't she? It wasn't the end of the world, but somehow I couldn't get rid of this sick feeling in the pit of my stomach. I'd thought this time was different.

I hadn't known I felt so strongly about Gabriel. I hadn't seen this coming at all. Perhaps we might have concluded our six-day fling with no hard feelings and I would have got over it.

He would have gone back to his life and I to mine. I would sit at my desk opposite Tim, eating Polos, answering the phone, selling houses and working out floor plans. Gabriel would sit in a house overlooking the ocean. I would go to the bakery up the road for a sandwich. He would go to Ken's Hut for fresh lobster. I would be at the end of my parents' garden watching the trees lose their leaves. He would wake to see the waves crashing over the rocky coastline.

It wasn't as though I was going to bump into him in the high street going into Boots. I didn't even really know what he was actually doing on the ship. He'd said he had intended to leave when we got to Halifax but he hadn't. He'd stayed on board. Because of me. That's what he had said. I'd been so thrilled too, so incredibly flattered. But was that really the truth?

245

Now everything was different. I was being made to look and feel an idiot. I was being tricked and used. Buggeration.

'Yes,' I said at last and stood up. 'Let's go for it. Let's get our posh frocks on and go for it. There are only three days left until we get to Southampton. It's still your hen celebration. I'm not going to let this spoil things.'

India's eyes were still filled with concern, but her face brightened. 'Atta girl! Come on, trowel on that slap, do some smoky eyes and get your frock on. The Fisher girls are going out!'

*

We got to the Champs-Elysées dining room without stopping for a cocktail for a change. If we were indeed drinking eight times our normal daily alcohol intake, perhaps it was time to calm down a bit before our livers detonated. India was elegant and floaty in a black chiffon maxi and I think I resembled an oven-ready chicken in a sequinned cocktail dress that was a bit tighter over the arse than I remembered.

Our table companions were already seated, the men in their DJs, Caron in black velvet and Marion in a sequinned top and long skirt. She tugged unhappily at her sleeves.

'This seems to have shrunk. Does anyone else notice their clothes have shrunk? This skirt is digging in too.'

Marty exchanged a look with Ike.

'It's the sea air, honey. It always does that. Something to do with the salt. That's what I read; it was in the Sunday

246

supplement about six months ago. It causes the cloth fibres to shrink and tighten up. It said when you get back home things will return to normal.'

'Is that so? Well, good heavens! They should warn people,' she said as she trowelled butter on to a warm bread roll.

'Good evening, girls.' Ike looked up at us as we arranged ourselves in our chairs. He really was such a nice man and I realised how lucky we'd been with our seating. The four of them would help keep my mind off things, I was sure of it. 'Where have you been?' he continued heartily.

'Oh, here and there,' I said vaguely, sitting down and grabbing for my napkin before the waiter could come along and start flourishing it over my lap like a conjurer. Things that had seemed so special when we first got on the ship were now becoming tedious.

Caron leaned towards us across the table, her up-do sparkling with a diamante pin and a feather. 'Did you go to the talk on the *Titanic*? Wasn't that just amazing? I said to Marty, I wonder if we would have survived if we had been on board? If we'd been in steerage I bet we wouldn't. Although there wasn't that business of locking the poor people downstairs while the rich people got off like they did in the film. But then there was that little girl in first class who drowned. Now how on earth did that happen? I wanted to ask the speaker but we were late for something – lunch I expect – and Ike wouldn't wait.'

She'd barely taken a breath and I found myself smiling.

This really was perfect. What with the way Ike ordered wine and Caron talked, I wouldn't need to think at all. I looked across at India to make sure she was okay. She was chattering away nineteen to the dozen with Marion and examining another of Marion's dinky little evening bags with what looked like genuine pleasure. In the soft light from the dimmed chandeliers and candles in the middle of the table my sister looked very pretty. I felt a sudden surge of affection for her and something new: admiration for her courage.

'Well, that speaker must still be on board somewhere,' Ike said, cheerfully winking at us. 'I bet you could track him down.'

'I will! I'll find him,' Caron said, a determined glint in her eye.

I couldn't hold back a little smile. I almost pitied the poor chap and imagined him scurrying away from Caron, darting anxious looks over his shoulder before finding himself cornered behind a lifeboat, stuck explaining himself.

The wine waiter came over with our half-finished bottles of wine – all five of them – and fussed about, filling up our glasses and bringing carafes of iced water. The menu looked even more extravagant than usual with seven courses plus palate-cleansing sorbets and the ever-present threat of spume, jus and edible flowers over everything.

'Just two more days,' Marty said, looking wistful, 'and then we get to Southampton. It's been such a great voyage.'

'I can't wait to see Southampton,' Marion added between

sips of red wine. 'We've been to London, of course, and we liked that, but this is the first time we've been to England.' I nearly laughed but then realised she wasn't joking. 'We've seen the film about it on the ship's TV. It looks a quaint little town, a real English sort of place. We have the Hamptons in America where all the wealthy people have summer homes. Is Southampton like that?' she asked, turning around to India and myself.

I stopped myself from rolling my eyes and took a deep breath. 'Well, it's –'

'Absolutely,' India cut in, nodding her head. 'It's full of history and buildings and stuff. And it's near the New Forest where Henry the Eighth used to meet up with Anne Boleyn and a couple of his other wives, I expect. There's a motor museum near there too. It's probably really interesting.'

I looked at India in shock. I mean I don't really know much about history, but I'd thought India definitely didn't know much about anything. Then I remembered her arguing about American politics the other day. What else had she been suddenly coming up with? Never mind; either way, this India was definitely different from the India I remember.

'Well, is that so? How marvellous!' said Marion, looking thrilled. 'We love that sort of thing, don't we, Marty?'

Marty nodded back at her, his eyes full of excitement. 'And we thought of a day trip to Scotland while we're there. I mean it's not far, is it? I'd like to see Edinburgh.' He said it to rhyme with iceberg.

'Scotland?' I spluttered. 'How long are you in England?'

'Two days,' he said happily. 'We have a transfer to London, a tour bus around Hampton Palace and somewhere else – Windsor Palace I think. And then we fly home the following night. And it's not as though we have to get over the jet lag, do we? That's another good thing about cruises.' The other three nodded at this and raised their glasses. India and I shared a glance.

'Plenty of time then,' India said. I could tell she was trying hard to hide her laughter, but I knew her too well. I pretended I suddenly needed to take a sip of water and nearly choked while trying to keep a straight face.

'Have you been?' Caron asked, forking into her seared scallop starter, which had just arrived on the table. As always the food looked incredible and I was surprised to find I was actually hungry, so I started to tuck straight in too.

'I went to Edinburgh once,' I said between mouthfuls. 'I've never been so cold. But then it was November.'

'I wonder why all the men wear skirts then,' Ike mused, scraping the last of the jus off his plate and casting an enquiring eye towards Caron's plate.

I spluttered into my wineglass and caught India's eye. This was going to be fun! And shockingly I hadn't thought about Gabriel once ... Oh, now I'd spoiled it.

Chapter Eighteen

Penicillin Cocktail

Honey Water, 16-year-old Malt Whisky,
Ginger Liqueur, Lemon Juice

The theatre was quite crowded when we got there the following morning; obviously a lot of people were keen to take advantage of the opportunity to share in Marnie's fantasy. We found seats at one of the less popular tables to one side of the stage. I had an obstructed view but I didn't actually mind. It was almost a comfort to have a pillar I could hide behind if the need arose. After our chat yesterday I wouldn't have minded no eye contact at all. But India had pointed out that there was no use hiding in the cabin and I needed to get out there sometime. Even so I could see her waiting in the wings with her perpetually dejected assistant standing holding the bags and clipboards.

Bang on the dot of eleven o'clock Marnie tossed her hair

back, put on what I realised now was her professional smile and came out from the wings to a thunderous round of applause. She looked marvellous in a chic sea-green dress that subtly accentuated her curves and contrasted with her shining red hair. Her glorious legs were on display in sheer tights and spiky nude stilettos.

'Oh my, isn't she just adorable?' someone said nearby as the applause died down. 'I'd give ten years of my life to look like that. She's got everything, hasn't she?'

'Brains, beauty, talent,' an elderly woman agreed with a sigh, 'and a gorgeous husband. How is one woman so lucky?'

'I was talking to someone who says she gets you to throw out all your old clothes and then arrange what's left alphabetically or something,' said another.

'I bet she works like a dog,' someone chipped in.

I was getting a bit weary of all this Marnie Miller adulation if I was honest. After all she was only a phenomenally successful and beautiful woman with a considerable personal fortune and probably better contacts than I could even imagine.

Okay, she had a glorious Cotswold manor house and a penthouse flat overlooking the Thames. So what?

Her husband, Leo, was a man blessed with good looks and a successful career and a substantial bank account of his own. What was all the fuss about? She'd seemed so different the few times we'd been alone together, but then again she had given India those bracelet things and that had been kind. And warning me off Gabriel ... well, I didn't really appreciate it at all. It was only supposed to be a fling on my side too. But I suppose that might also have been a generous gesture on her part ...

God, was I just a horribly jealous and unattractively mean-spirited person? Perhaps I should rethink things as part of my personal spring-cleaning? I'd read somewhere once that you should try not to say anything unkind, untrue or unpleasant. Perhaps I should think about that a bit more?

Marnie held her hands up to encourage us all to silence and things gradually settled down.

'*Spring-Clean Your Life*,' she said. 'Now how do we do that? Why do we need to do that?'

Next to me India was already scribbling in her notebook. Right, so this was the time when I would concentrate on gleaning pearls of wisdom from Marnie, not just sit with my mouth open wondering how much her shoes cost. Although they did look suspiciously like Jimmy Choos. I'd have to google them when I got the chance. And that dress was absolutely gorgeous. I bet she didn't go to high street stores and riffle through the sale rails like I did. I thought I looked okay, in new jeans and a T-shirt (two for twenty quid, which for me is pushing the boat out a bit), although the jeans seemed to have shrunk since I bought them, which was very annoying. Maybe it was that sea air Marty had mentioned ... or the seven courses from last night?

I shook my head and wrote the date at the top of a fresh page and looked up at her, switching into student mode.

'We need to engage in our own lives, don't we?' Marnie continued, striding across the stage. 'Too often we are preoccupied with other people. Our children perhaps or our spouse. Or our grandchildren. Our bosses if we have them. Their needs come before ours. We want to please them, don't we? But what about *you*?'

She pointed out into the audience and you could have heard a pin drop.

'What about you? Your dreams, your strength? Isn't that important too? More important perhaps than the best way to handle a difficult aunt or the man at work who never makes coffee.'

I glanced over at India as I finished writing down 'What about your dreams?' Hadn't that been something Gabriel had asked me? Did I have any? India was writing so fast that I wouldn't have been surprised to see smoke coming off the paper. So I turned back to the stage and waited for Marnie to continue, trying to empty my mind of Gabriel. I needed to think of my dreams ...

'Everyone has dead weight in their lives,' Marnie was saying, looking intently out at the audience and fixing some of them in the front row with a stare. 'Things that drag them down. Think about how you feel on a Monday morning when you're battling on to the bus to go to work. I know how that feels, because that was me once. Are you positive and upbeat, ready to give one hundred per cent to the day? Or are you still going over an argument you had on Saturday with the woman who stole your parking space?'

I stopped writing and looked up sharply. God, I did that: every snippy comment from India, every time she didn't finish up her work and I had to finish it for her. I carried that resentment around for days. Why did I do that?

'You must learn to use your energy positively for your own good. Be optimistic, think about the way you can make every day the best it can be. Rethink your career goals.'

Career goals. Did I have those? I'd told Gabriel I wanted to expand the business but I hadn't given it any thought in months. I certainly hadn't done anything about it. The only things I'd concentrated on were getting to the end of each month ahead of my targets and being annoyed with India when she didn't. Now I knew where her mind had been focused I felt terrible. I had always just assumed, after all of my hard work over the years, that I'd take over the family estate agency, but did I really want that? And could I spend the rest of my life just trying to beat my own targets? Would I turn into a boss who was crabby and frustrated with what I'd failed to achieve?

I wrote down *smallholdings*, and then added a very curly question mark.

'Eliminate toxic friends. Don't waste time with people who bring you down. Who pretend to be on your side when, deep down, you know they're not. Surround yourself with positive influences. Be a positive influence on others. And ladies, that includes men!'

There was a general chuckle from the audience at this

point. I looked around sharply, trying hard not to think about Gabriel.

You know I want you. Don't you?

His deep voice flooded my mind and I cringed. I'd put up no more resistance to him than a kitten to a tidal wave. Other girls and women didn't seem to get into these situations. Why was it always me? I looked over at India. She'd always had men chasing after her, never giving them the time of day until Jerry. In her teens she had played one boyfriend off against another. And now look at her. Engaged, about to marry someone she was obviously head over heels for. Someone who loved her back in the same way. Who was the fool here?

And what had I done? I'd been attracted to a man, had sex, which was supposed to be no-strings-attached, and then fallen for him, when I absolutely shouldn't have. And now, here I was remembering how it had felt to be undressed by him, how he had touched me.

Alexa. My God, Alexa.

He must be a bloody great actor to fake all that stuff. And it *really* hadn't felt like he was pretending. He'd seemed genuinely keen. He'd seemed to need me. Or I thought he had. Could a man kiss me like that and do those things and not actually mean them?

He made you think you were different, didn't he? Didn't he?

Marnie's voice echoed in my mind and I felt sick. She was right … he had made me feel different, but so had Ryan and Tom and, oh, that ghastly boy whose parents owned the petrol station who had kissed me behind the youth club, promised me he wouldn't tell anyone, and then by lunchtime the following day everyone in school knew.

I told myself to snap out of it. I was giving up the chance to learn how to change. I needed to listen. I scrubbed my eyes as subtly as possible, so India wouldn't notice. Marnie was still talking, so I clicked my pen again and prepared to write.

'There is nothing wrong with investing time and money in yourself; it's worth your while. There is nothing more important in your life than your wellbeing. Your health, your peace of mind.'

I liked that idea. I could do more of that, definitely. Keep up the two separate eyebrows thing for starters. And get my nails done occasionally.

Marnie took a sip of her water, allowing her point to sink in before fixing the audience once more in her stare. 'Now let's use an example here, for any of you struggling to relate to what I'm talking about. For example, let's think about someone who doesn't look after themselves, who doesn't listen to advice, someone who doesn't *Spring-Clean Her Life*. She never learns, this girl! Perhaps her new boss is a racist or a man she fancies is commitment phobic. She does nothing, just allows herself to be pulled down by their negativity. Everyone knows the man is bad news – perhaps a friend tells her – but this girl refuses to listen to advice.'

Hang on a minute.

I looked over at India who was still scribbling.

Could she be talking about me? Using me *as an example in her lecture? Surely not!*

Marnie continued, 'We all know someone like her. We might be her ourselves, even if we don't want to admit it. I want to tell you, her, anyone who is feeling like this might apply to them, you are only steps away from finding the way forward. All you need to do is *Spring-Clean Your Life*.' She paused before smiling broadly at the audience, her arms wide. 'You need to believe that you are better, greater, stronger and amazing. You are worth someone's time and you shouldn't accept anything less than commitment. I'll repeat that because I think it bears repeating. You are all amazing. I'm not just talking about romantic relationships here, but honestly, if a man doesn't go out of his way to make room in his life for you, if he's reticent and wants to keep the relationship a secret, what are you doing? Would you let another friend say yes to being treated this way?' She glared at us and I could feel my heart pounding. 'No!' she shouted out and I gasped.

Marnie was right. Oh my God, she was so right. I mean what did I know about Gabriel? Barely anything if I was honest. And he'd wanted to keep our fling/relationship/whatever you call it a secret from Marnie. And I'd let him. I held my breath for a second, letting this sink in. I'd done this with Ryan, letting him talk his way out of cheating on me for months, and Tom, who just took everything from me ... No! No! I wasn't going to do that again.

I looked up at Marnie, feeling determined to listen up now.

I needed to *Spring-Clean My Life* and I really was going to do it this time!

Marnie was strolling now. I must have missed a bit. Her arms were folded, the headset microphone nestling against her cheek like a stray Rice Krispie. When she reached the end she turned neatly on one heel and strolled back. This time her hands were splayed out in front of her as she continued.

For the rest of her talk she covered everything from wardrobes, to friendships, houses and handbags – she had a view on all of them. Get rid of this, have more of that. Kick out anything that wasn't either beautiful or useful. (Wasn't that the mantra of the Arts and Crafts movement?) Give stuff away, especially anything you hadn't worn for a month. Considering I usually lived in jeans and a selection of old T-shirts that would mean slinging out everything else. Even the nuclear power worker outfit. For some reason that was still rolled up at the bottom of a chest of drawers in my bedroom. Hmm. Why on earth had I kept that? That would be the first thing I'd chuck out.

Then she was on to more: declutter your desk (mine was always pretty tidy, so I felt quite smug about that, but I sent India a meaningful look and she stuck her tongue out at me). Declutter your mind (I bet mine looked like an old attic full of rubbish and broken chairs, metaphorically speaking). Clean your house (I wrote down *buy new Hoover bags*). Clean your brain. Sleep more, eat more consciously, drink more water. Be productive. Get up, move around; endorphins make you happy.

Comfort food never brings much comfort. Sit down, don't forget to rest. Take the TV out of your bedroom. The list went on.

By this point I'd stopped writing everything down. I didn't think I needed it. I mean I could remember to do this. Stop doing that. Cut out snacks, don't eat sweets, stop drinking so much (something I'd think about when I got home), quit smoking (I didn't smoke but I gave myself a tick for that one anyway). Eat more vegetables, recycle things. Don't fidget, do your homework, clean your teeth, sit up straight.

Then suddenly I could tell there was a shift in Marnie's voice. She lost her ordering-around voice and became warm and cuddly. She told us about Camp Spring.

The penny dropped; of course, chucking out old T-shirts wasn't enough. If you really wanted to change you needed to go to a Marnie Miller-run boot camp somewhere in Illinois where, for a five-hundred-dollar down payment and the rest in monthly instalments for the rest of all time, Marnie's *Spring-Cleaners* (she actually did call them that) would thrash you into shape physically and mentally. I bet they used wire brushes and megaphones. Well, I definitely wouldn't be doing that, but I couldn't discount everything she'd said ... No, I'd had my realisation. I could see it clearly now. I'd been a pushover and I wouldn't be one any more. I was worth more! I deserved more! I was amazing. Well, sometimes. A bit.

Marnie had started talking about inner beauty and colonic irrigation, which were apparently linked, and India returned to her frenzied scribbling.

260

Up on the stage Marnie was back in full flow after making her sales pitch.

'Now you know how to *Spring-Clean Your Life* I can hear some of you asking yourselves: does everyone need to change? Will nice people succeed? Do all the annoying people need to get what's coming to them? Of course not, life is rarely that simple, but we all need to think about who we want to be. It's up to us to change; no one else is going to do it for us.' She left this thought hanging and took another sip of water.

Then she launched into full flow again, having a go at fast food, plastic bottles, micro beads, the state of the oceans. There was a ripple of laughter through the audience at something she said and Marnie waited for a moment for it to fade. And then, standing on the edge of the stage, she turned and looked me straight in the eye, a small smile on her face. Ah well, that answered the 'does she know I'm here?' question. But instead of shrinking back I stayed where I was. I was going to be the new Alexa, not someone who shrivelled away and let other people take over my life, dictating how I felt and letting their issues ruin my day. No, that stopped here!

'Now we come to the final thing to consider,' Marnie said, having glanced at her watch and seen that time was passing probably faster than she'd anticipated. 'The question you must ask yourself a dozen times a day. The thing you want versus the thing you need. You see there is a difference, isn't there? You may *want* a bag of doughnuts, but perhaps you *need* to go to the gym?'

More polite laughter.

'Perhaps you *want* that relationship but you *need* to step back and stop kidding yourself. Maybe you *want* that man, but you *need* to run a mile.'

I looked up; Marnie was slowly striding along the stage with her back to me.

In the wings I could see Marnie's assistant checking her watch. I wondered if she listened to these lectures and dreamt of being someone else, something else. Funny how she must have heard this stuff a lot and yet still looked so downtrodden.

I must have been daydreaming for longer than I thought as Marnie was suddenly saying how much she had enjoyed the trip, how wonderful it had been to meet so many interesting people and that she wished us all the best of luck with our writing. If anyone wanted to buy her books she had a few left to sell and would be happy to autograph them. At this point the glum assistant wheeled on a trolley laden with paperbacks and there was a surge of interest from the audience, sensing a great last-minute gift for someone.

I straightened up, ready to join in the applause before India and I went to find some lunch. I had so much to tell her. And there he was. Gabriel Frost. On the other side of the theatre. He was leaning against the exit door, a muscular figure in a checked shirt and dark jeans. His arms were folded and he was looking over the audience.

For a moment I had the mad thought that he might be looking for me. But no, of course he wasn't – he was only using me. I knew that. I gave myself a stern talking-to to remind myself of my new determination to change and be strong. But he did look so delicious over there ... *Stop it.*

'God, wasn't that brilliant?' India breathed, and I nodded, maybe not as enthusiastically, back at her.

I had really enjoyed my euphoric moment, but really the rest of it sounded like a mishmash of every other self-help book I'd ever read. India wanted to join the queue so she could buy Marnie's latest book and get it autographed, so I arranged to meet her in the food court and went out almost at a jog trot to avoid Gabriel. Keeping my head down I scurried past a queue of passengers talking to the reception staff about booking a second voyage and taking advantage of the fifteen per cent discount on offer. I wondered how much this holiday would have cost us if Mum hadn't won that raffle. A lot I was guessing.

Chapter Nineteen

Ginger Frost

Vodka, Ginger Liqueur, Orange Juice,
Lemon Juice, Sugar Syrup

That night dinner went on for hours as there were speeches and prizes to be shared out in between courses. Yesterday we'd been given a list of awards to vote for and our steward Amil had excelled himself over the last twenty-four hours trying to impress us. He'd left extra chocolates on our pillows, rose petals scattered over the beds and terrified both of us with a towel bat hanging inside the bathroom.

Apart from the award for best cabin steward, there were prizes for best bar manager, best cocktail waiter, best wine waiter, best talk, favourite dessert, prettiest cake, dog with the waggiest tail. Okay, I made the last bit up but you get the picture.

Our maître d' was presented with a silver tray for twenty-five years service with the cruise line and then there was a long procession of crew members coming forward to be rewarded with a scroll and a handshake from the Captain. Actually it was the first time we had seen the Captain since we came on board. Perhaps he had been too busy steering the ship and pandering to the richer passengers in the suites? Anyway it was reassuring to see he was still on board and he looked as tall and capable as ever, still plastered with gold braid and shiny buttons.

Meanwhile everyone seemed in high spirits, looking forward to the dance and the late-night show that was billed as *A Tribute to Space Travel*. It seemed a bit weird to me, but India was busy sloshing down white wine while I was equally busy with some Barolo that Marty had bought before deciding it gave him gas.

Our steward Amil won a prize and we all cheered and whooped for him. I think he won because India and I collected all the voting cards that had been left outside the doors on our floor and put his name on all of them, but I could have been wrong.

Anyway, he was a jolly good steward and deserved to win. One morning when I'd been too tired to leave the room we'd got to chatting. He hadn't seen his family in Sri Lanka for five months and winning this award would give him a week's leave next time they docked there. I mean, who wouldn't vote for that!

At last we were served with our dessert, which was a bit like a Baked Alaska – but far more sophisticated and successful than the time I had tried to make it with a slice of Arctic roll, some egg white and a blowtorch – and then the maître d' came forward from his cubbyhole by the dining room door to announce the next round of winners.

'And the award for the best informative talk –'

He paused for dramatic effect and, over on the far side of the dining room, there was a crash as someone dropped a tray of dishes and everyone cheered. Well, you do, don't you?

'Do you think it will be the *Titanic* one?' Marion asked, eyes gleaming after she'd polished off Marty's glass of wine.

'Well, it's not a shoe-in. The talk about great maritime disasters was good,' Ike chimed in. 'I voted for that one.'

'The talk on catering was interesting,' I suggested. 'Do you know the ship gets through six tons of butter on a transatlantic crossing? Or was it six tons of chocolate? Anyway, thirty thousand eggs – that's definite.'

'You're kidding?' Caron said, suitably impressed.

'I could get through six tons of chocolate given half a chance,' Marion said proudly. 'My physician told me my sugar levels were so high he dared me to eat pumpkin pie last Thanksgiving. He absolutely dared me.'

India grinned at me. We really had enjoyed our dinner companions and I wondered what dinners once we got home would be like. Me back to my microwave meals and India to dinner with Jerry, who, while very nice, wasn't quite as entertaining as the four in front of us.

'He knows what a whalephant you used to be though, doesn't he?' Marty said between mouthfuls of dessert.

'I was not!' Marion said indignantly. 'A few extra pounds maybe. You are! You're the one who's a hog. Wonder what he would have said if he'd seen you with your snout in the trough over the last few days. Keeping an eye on the calories, were you? More like inhaling them, I'd say.'

'You got it straight up, Marion,' said Marty, reaching over and taking the last spoonful of her dessert, causing her to screech with fury and the rest of us to burst out laughing.

Meanwhile the maître d' was waiting for the noise to die down and fixed us all with a beady eye.

'Prize for the most appreciated and informative talk was unanimous. *Spring-Clean Your Life* – by the very talented and beautiful Miss Marnie Miller.'

The double doors behind him opened and Marnie entered the dining room, a vision in sleek black velvet that showed off her toned shoulders and arms and probably cost more than my entire wardrobe. She turned to the maître d' with a modest smile, mouthing *I can't believe it* while we all clapped. He presented her with a small, silver-framed picture of the ship, and she blushed prettily while he bowed over her hand.

'Thank you all so much,' she said, turning to address us. 'This means the world to me. Really, I can't believe it – you're all so lovely, so kind.'

She went on for a while, smiling and thanking everyone as though she'd won an Oscar. I zoned out for a bit and then zoned back in again with a jolt.

'Of course, to my dear friend Gabriel Frost, who has been such a great comfort to me in the last few days. I don't know what I would do without his love and support. Gabe, come out here!'

Gabriel had evidently been standing just outside the door, and he came forward looking quite embarrassed. Marnie sidled up to him and ducked underneath his arm so that it rested on her shoulder. She looked up at him adoringly.

Well! I felt India's hand reach out for mine on the table and give it a squeeze. Gabriel had his arm around her and she was snuggling in and giggling like a schoolgirl. I felt cold, sick, all kinds of feelings that I desperately wished I didn't. I'd been trying all day to be more confident, stronger, not giving in to the yearning to speak to Gabriel. Maybe end up in his bed ... I tried to stop my eyes from filling.

'He's very handsome,' Marion said, looking at Gabriel dreamily. 'Why didn't I meet a man like that when I was out there looking? Instead I ended up with an ex-Marine who calls me a whalephant and steals my desserts.'

Marty flapped a hand at her, looking around for more leftover dessert. 'You wouldn't have me any different – you know you wouldn't.'

Onstage Marnie was examining the framed photograph of the ship as though it were a missing Raphael and favouring the maître d' with a brilliant smile.

'So very proud and happy,' she said, and he bowed over her hand again while darting a venomous look at the waiter who had now cleared up all the broken china and was scuttling past them at high speed.

They stood there having some official photographs taken and little by little Gabriel backed away. He looked around the dining room and of course he saw me. I held my breath, having a clever and witty conversation with him in my head that resulted in him walking away crushed and ashamed. Gabriel touched Marnie's arm and whispered something to her and then – oh God – he walked towards me.

'Hello, watch out,' India said in a stage whisper and then instantly looked uneasy. Immediately of course the others on our table were on high alert.

'Well, introduce me, why don't you?' Marion drawled at me, completely misreading the look of panic in my eyes that I was sure everyone could see.

'Good evening, everyone; hello, Alexa,' Gabriel said and my mouth dried up, all the clever repartee with it.

'Mnah,' I replied wittily.

'Lovely to see you again,' he said. He stood next to me, looking unspeakably gorgeous in his DJ, quite easy and relaxed while I was as taut as a piano wire. 'I was wondering where you'd got to.'

Was he? No no, I need to be strong. He just wants one more night …

'Oh, you know, I've been here and there. Mostly there. Or here. I can't remember,' I gabbled. There, that would teach him to mess with me!

269

'Are you going on to the dance after dinner?'

'Oh, I don't –'

But before I could finish Marion had leaned across me and held out a hand.

'Marion Kowlowsky, and this is my husband, Martin.'

'Marty,' Marty said, his cheerful, ruddy face grinning up at Gabriel.

Everyone shook hands and was introduced. Ike and Caron asked how he had enjoyed the crossing. There was a bit of routine ship talk about the smoothness of the ocean, the impressive cuisine and high quality of the evening entertainments, and then Ike pulled a spare chair forward from a vacated table and encouraged Gabriel to join us.

'Well, just for a moment.' He looked up at Marnie who was still busy being charming. There was a cluster of guests around her taking photographs and asking her to sign their menu cards.

Ike – incapable of letting the table be alcohol-free for more than thirty seconds – ordered brandy all round and then dropped the question into the pond.

'So, Gabriel, what's your line of work?'

Gabriel sipped his brandy and flicked a look at me.

'I work for Miss Miller. Part of her support team.'

'And what do you do?'

You have to give it to them: Americans aren't shy of asking awkward questions even on five minutes' acquaintance. He'd be asking Gabriel what car he drove or how much he was paid next.

At last Gabriel gave a funny little smile.

'I'm doing some legal work for her at the moment.'

'What sort of lawyer?' Marion asked pleasantly. 'Do you do that high-profile, "counsellors, please approach the bench" courtroom stuff?'

Gabriel laughed and I felt my body fizz all over. 'No, nothing like that, although I sometimes do go to court if I can't avoid it.'

'So do you handle divorces? I might be needing one if Marty keeps on with the smartass comments!'

Everyone laughed and Marty reached across, lips puckered to kiss his wife's cheek.

Gabriel finished his brandy and stood up, his face very still. Glancing over his shoulder at Marnie he turned back to us with a placid smile back in place.

'So sorry, I'd better get back. Delightful to meet you all. I hope we'll meet up later on in the ballroom?' he added with a glance at me, and I just about managed a strangled smile before he walked away.

'Oh surely!' Caron called after him with a throaty chuckle. 'You can count on it! I might want some free advice too!' Ike gave her a friendly smack on the arm and they grinned at each other.

Gabriel rejoined Marnie, who was dealing with her last eager fan, and they left the dining room soon afterwards.

'A lawyer,' India said, turning to me. 'That's not what you told me. Was it?'

'Oh well, I mean, I think so. He said legal stuff ...' I said, feeling rather odd inside.

The maître d' then started awarding more scrolls and awards to crew members, there was more clapping and whooping, and I watched as Marty finished up the cheese that had been left on the table.

'He's very fine-looking, very charming and so handsome,' Marion crooned, glancing slyly at her husband.

'All men look handsome in an evening suit,' Marty said waspishly.

'Hmm, yes, most of them,' Marion responded with a withering look in his direction.

*

I would quite happily have made my excuses and gone to bed but there was no way I was going to be allowed to. India was feeling particularly devilish and practically put me in an armlock when I tried to escape to the lifts.

'It's our last gala night on the ship,' she'd trilled as I attempted to escape. 'We aren't going to give up our night of fun just because of him, are we?'

I hadn't had much choice after that. So when Ike and Caron went off for half an hour to feed the hungry slot machines in the casino, the four of us carried on to the ballroom.

It was still decorated with black and white drapes and harlequin masks from last night's ball, and there were Peter and Paula, about to do an exhibition dance. Paula's hair was slicked back into a severe bun and Peter looked like a rather dangerous spiv. I guessed it was going to be a tango.

Marty quickly found us a table and we unloaded our wraps and handbags and waited for the fun to start.

A bottle of champagne in a silver ice bucket arrived swiftly afterwards and I decided I could have a good time.

'Well, where's this from?' Marion asked, having ascertained it was nothing to do with anyone in our party.

I knew who loved champagne.

'I hope you don't mind?'

It was Gabriel, standing by the table, one hand on the back of the chair next to mine. I swear the back of my neck was prickling.

'Why, thank you, that's very courteous of you. Come and join us!' Marty said with an expansive wave.

I tried to object. The prospect of spending the evening with him looking as gorgeous as that and to have him directing all his very masculine attention at me was too frightening. I was only just starting my whole determined, strong thing. I didn't think I was practised enough to withstand him.

'Oh, I'm sure Mr Frost doesn't —'

'I'd love to,' he interrupted and sat down next to me, his knee touching mine. The warm drift of his aftershave was like an electric shock.

'You don't mind?' He made a small, questioning movement of his hand, his eyebrows raised.

'No, of course not,' I said, trying to sound careless.

I had a sudden, hot flashback. Remembering how his body had felt under my hands. His breath on my neck. His voice in my ear.

Great. Just great.

Peter and Paula span, twirled and twitched their heads in fine tango style, her fingers splayed out like starfish. Peter pursed his mouth with macho determination and in a dramatic, trembling finale bent Paula back over one arm, her face a slash of scarlet lipstick under the spotlights.

There was a moment's silence and then a thunderous round of applause. Marty and a few others stood up, cheering and whooping, and Marion laughed and clapped her hands with glee.

I felt rather than saw Gabriel lean in towards me. He touched my arm and I looked at him.

'I have to see you,' he said, his words hidden under the noise of the audience's approval. I shook my head and looked away.

In the spotlight Peter straightened up and Paula did some spinning and twirling.

Marty was still applauding, slowly sitting back down again.

'Did you see that? Good as anything you'll see on TV. Who says I'm wrong?'

'I have to see you,' Gabriel said again, his voice low and urgent.

'I don't know,' I said, feeling muddled. 'I don't know.'

The excitement of the exhibition tango over, the band began to play generic dance music and couples eagerly flooded on to the dance floor. Gabriel took my hand and steered me away from the table into the shadows at the edge of the floor. I should have resisted, but it would have been 'making a scene' and, if I'm really honest, I wanted to go with him. One night, that was what India had said. Even though, right now, she was staring at me with her mouth wide open, I gave her a look that said – I don't know what I'm doing. But by then he'd put one arm around me and we had begun to waltz as if it was the most natural thing. I've no idea if it was waltz music, that's just what we did. One two three. Making the box.

For a while we didn't talk. Looking up out of the corner of my eye I could see the clean line of his jaw, his beautiful throat, the crisp white collar of his evening shirt.

'Where have you been?' he asked.

'I've been on the ship of course. I could hardly be anywhere else.'

'You know what I mean,' he said.

We shuffled on for a while, endlessly making the box and one two three-ing.

I could feel his hand against my back. His touch made me tremble. It was a miracle I could stand up.

'I want …'

I looked up at him. 'What? What do you want?'

Gabriel looked down at me; he looked at my mouth and his grey eyes darkened.

'You know I want you. Don't you?'

Not to see *A Tribute to Space Travel* then? I didn't answer. I couldn't hear the music any more. I couldn't think properly.

'I can't bear the thought of not seeing you again.'

'You'll be going back to London,' I said, 'or New York.'

'Yes.'

'I'll be going back to the annexe at the end of my parents' garden. We have no future together. This isn't going to go anywhere. I don't know why you're bothering.'

'Alexa?'

And that's when it happened. I suddenly stopped caring. I knew there was no future, but oh God, I couldn't give up one more night. I'd be strong tomorrow. Tonight I'd have what I wanted and what I needed. Because sometimes doing something bad for yourself was the right thing to do.

The band played on, cheesy dance tunes. The room filled up with couples, laughing and swaying together to the music. Gabriel and I moved further away and stood in the shadows, not pretending to dance any more, just looking at each other with a terrible need. And then he kissed me.

Chapter Twenty

Lovelight

Cognac, Campari, Cinnamon Sugar Syrup,
Red Vermouth, Chocolate Bitters

Something had changed between us.

Gabriel took my hand and held my palm to his cheek before looking at me with a question in his eyes. There were things I could have said and things I could have thought but I didn't remember any of them. All I knew was I wanted him just as much as he wanted me.

We went to his cabin then, walking up deserted corridors and stairwells. Somewhere there were people; hundreds of people. They were in the bars, the casino, in the theatre and on the dance floor. They were talking and laughing and arguing and getting drunk but we walked silently to his room and he closed the door behind us and took me in his arms and there was no one in the world but us.

This was different.

He sat down on the bed and pulled me towards him, his hands around my waist. He buried his face in my breasts and I felt his shoulders tremble under my fingertips.

'Oh, Alexa,' he said, 'forgive me. I've been such a fool.'

'Don't say anything else,' I said softly, looking into his eyes and pushing away the ever-present hope that he'd love me back. 'We don't need to talk.'

I took his face between my hands and bent to kiss him. Then somehow I was on the bed with him, astride him. I pulled the bow tie undone, unbuttoned his shirt, and ran my hands over his warm, smooth chest. I could feel his heart beating with the same steady rhythm as my own.

He gently pushed me over on to my back and pulled my dress off over my head. Then he kissed me again, his mouth moving down my throat. This time there was no hurry, no urgency, none of the frantic desperation of last time, just patient tenderness that lured us on towards the most intense pleasure. He watched me, his eyes glowing above me in the shadows as he coaxed me and took me beyond that to a place of absolute peace. A place where I was relaxed and safe, but suddenly, unexpectedly, I wept, shaking in his arms, the tears running down on to his pillow.

He held me, stroking my hair back from my face, and kissed me.

'It's all right, it's all right,' he whispered. And I knew that in some ways it was. He might not love me, he might not really need me, but I would get over that, somehow. I wasn't going back. I could take what he gave me, cherish it and stride forward without him. Not all experiences needed to be for ever.

He pulled the covers over me and we slept. I don't think I could have moved if I'd wanted to. And fool that I was, I didn't want to.

I woke and it was still night, the ship ploughing on towards England and the end of this adventure. There was a full moon gleaming through the windows. I looked across at Gabriel, seeing his profile dark against the paler light reflecting off the ocean. I lay awake, thinking, wondering about how much had changed since I boarded this ship. How twelve days, which had seemed such an agonising eternity to start with, had flown by. I couldn't believe what a difference less than two weeks had made. I'd never felt different before, special. But somehow, right now, I really did. This wasn't just a passing thing; I knew this new me was a better me. Sure, I was going to have to work at it, but wow, I felt wonderful. Maybe I was in control of my life at last.

I slid out of bed, collected my things as best I could and – thank God – found my evening bag and cabin key. Then I put on one of the towelling robes still hanging untouched in Gabriel's bathroom and went back to my own bed next door.

I crept in, praying that India would be asleep and stay that way. I didn't know if I wanted to talk about it all right now. In the morning I could brazen it out, maybe just put my disappearance down to a bit of confusion, alcohol, misunderstanding ... oh, I don't know. Hopefully something would occur to me. Not that she would buy it.

I climbed into bed as quietly as I could and pulled the duvet up under my chin. I lay very still, trying to guess from India's breathing if she was awake, asleep, comatose or had been angrily waiting for me to turn up. I couldn't tell. After a few minutes I began to relax and turned on my side as I always did, waiting for sleep to come and blot out the memories of Gabriel touching me, stroking my arms, kissing my toes and murmuring my name.

A little whisper came across the room from India's bed. 'Are you okay?'

I swallowed hard. Was I okay?

'Yes, yes, I'm fine,' I said, hoping I could hold on to that feeling of strength.

'Gabriel?'

'Yes.'

'Are you sure you're okay?'

'India, I'm good,' I said firmly, because I could tell she was worried. 'Sorry if I woke you.'

I heard her turn over and the rustle of her bedclothes.

'S'okay.'

After a few minutes I heard her familiar snore and knew I was alone with my thoughts.

It was like being a teenager again, remembering what he had said, how he had looked and the scent of him, which seemed to cling to me even now. He had touched me and pulled me hard against him, moving with me in the darkness as I cried out my wonder and pleasure.

He made you think you were different, didn't he? Didn't he?

What had I been doing? Using him? Having him? Shagging him? Fucking? Screwing? What did people call it?

I sighed, heavy with my thoughts; longing for the sleep that evaded me.

Damnation. Damn everything.

As the minutes ticked past, the warm, snuggly afterglow began to fade and a new uncertainty settled in my mind.

When he's got what he wants, he loses interest.

I just hoped I was strong enough to deal with it. Perhaps the first thing I would have to do was declutter my mind of Gabriel Frost. Sweep all these memories into the equivalent of a locked trunk and leave them there.

*

When I woke up again it was nearly nine-thirty. India was still asleep in the other bed, one arm thrown up over her face. Soon we would start to sail up the English Channel towards Southampton. Soon we would be back on dry land with our luggage and our memories, waiting for Jerry to come and drive us home.

He doesn't know your address; he doesn't know your phone number.

281

No, and he didn't bloody ask for them either, did he?

'Bollocks,' I said out loud.

'Let me guess,' India said. 'Gabriel Frost?'

'Yep.'

India turned over in bed and looked at me. 'You twit,' she said.

'I know. I'm a bloody fool.'

'Did you have fun?'

I sighed. 'Oh my God, yes. That's the trouble; he's so frigging fantastic in bed. I don't know what he does or how he does it but – wow.'

We were both silent for a few seconds. India picked up her phone and checked to see if Jerry had messaged her.

'Oh well, just chalk it up to experience,' she said. 'You've never done something like that before – a no-strings-attached night?'

'I suppose not.' Had it really been as no-strings-attached as I'd wanted it to be?

'And don't do it again.'

'No, I won't.'

*

We decided to have a more formal breakfast in the Champs-Elysées restaurant to finish off our final day. I didn't really fancy negotiating the scrum of the food court as the American contingent, sensing the approach of Southampton, were getting increasingly excited and noisy. As we passed the doors we could see some of them loading up their backpacks with bottles of water and muffins. I think some of them were expecting to see Land's End or Stonehenge from the top deck of the ship. I wondered if Ike and Marty were still planning on going to Scotland for the day?

The Champs-Elysées restaurant was a haven of quiet and tranquillity in comparison. The maître d' showed us to a lovely table where we could watch the sea slipping past. We stared out, wondering if we would be able to see the coast of Ireland, but in the distance there was a haze across the water.

I looked at the menu. 'Fresh fruit and yogurt?'

India nodded thoughtfully. 'Ye ... no actually. I want a full English with two fried eggs, black pudding, sausages and then white toast and Marmite to follow.'

'Good idea. I'll have the same,' I said.

'I'm glad we kept up our healthy eating plan,' India said, unfolding her napkin and grinning at me.

'Have you had a good time?' I asked, suddenly worried. It had been her hen holiday after all.

'Of course I have,' India replied. 'To be honest I wasn't sure I would. You know, cruises are something I usually think are just for old people who play shuffleboard, whatever that is. But it's been great. And it's certainly been much better than going to a rented house with a gaggle of other hens. At least you didn't make me wear a pink sash or L plates. I mean we've got along okay – not that we don't usually, but twelve days together is hard for anyone, right?'

'India, I think we can admit that we've not been getting on as well as we used to.' Wow, where did that come from? I was braver than I looked. 'But I do think this trip has been good for us.'

She nodded. 'But how are you?'

I shrugged, attempting to be dismissive. 'I've been a twat, I know that, so we don't need to talk about *him* any more, do we?'

'Him? Gabriel Frost? Not unless you want to?' she said, concern in her eyes, and I smiled falsely back, because I did – that was the trouble.

I was as bad as India wanting to talk about her wedding. I wanted to talk about Gabriel Frost all the time.

I wanted to sit in a comfortable chair with a blanket around my shoulders, a mug of hot chocolate and a new pack of chocolate digestives on a table next to me and think about him. I wanted to go over every conversation we had shared, contemplate how he had looked, remember how he had touched me and made love to me ...

No, he hadn't. I wasn't going to think like that. It had been enjoyable but meaningless sex. We had been shagging. Bonking. Screwing. Fucking. Hadn't we?

Suddenly I wanted to cry. I felt like covering my face with my stiff white napkin and howling. I could almost picture myself sobbing, inconsolable; the tears running down my face and leaving a damp patch on my black T-shirt. India would be worried. She'd pat my hand, then come and put an arm around me, and finally probably slap me about a bit to stop me from becoming hysterical. It would absolutely ruin her last day and her abiding memory of our trip would be taking me to the ship's doctor to be sedated. So, I took a deep breath.

India fidgeted a bit with her napkin. 'Today I'm going to work on my bestselling novel.'

'I think that sounds like an excellent idea.' It would give me plenty of time to think about Gabriel, in very specific detail ... Oh, what was I even thinking!

Thankfully the waiter returned with our breakfast and some coffee, which I pounced on with relief. Perhaps I was just caffeine-light at the moment? That was why I couldn't concentrate on anything.

I stirred some demerara sugar into my cup as a sort of brave, self-medicating gesture, while convincing myself it was healthier than white, and sipped my coffee. Where was Gabriel having his breakfast? Had he ordered room service perhaps? Or gone to the Louis Quinze restaurant for rich people and enjoyed caviar on toast or something equally ridiculous? Did he like coffee or tea in the morning? Or something weird like rooibos with liquorice?

Did he have any hobbies? Did he follow baseball or American football? Did he like his steak rare or well done?

I didn't really know anything about him at all. What a fool I was. I mean I hadn't even asked him any of those questions. Just spent my time staring at him ...

'I'm looking forward to seeing Jerry again,' India said. She paused to give me chance to roll my eyes at her as I usually did when she mentioned Jerry or the wedding. This time I didn't. 'I've really missed him.'

'Good. You're marrying him in December so it's just as well,' I said jokingly and she threw a sugar packet at me.

'I'll have to get back on to the wedding as soon as we're back. Sort out those flaming flower girls. And you too I suppose. I mean did we ever decide what you were going to wear?'

I topped up my coffee and added more sugar. 'Nope.'

'Blue or pink? Or peach?'

'I've no idea. You kept changing your mind,' I reminded her.

'I did, didn't I? Well, what do you want? I'll let you decide. No, I won't. You'd turn up in jeans and a Zara T-shirt knowing you. How about lilac?'

'Over my dead body.' I grinned.

'Green? No, green is supposed to be unlucky ...'

She was on a roll here and, knowing my sister as I did, I could zone out a bit and not miss anything. Plus my brain still wanted to talk to me about Gabriel Frost.

There were so many things about him that I didn't know. I mean basic things like what sort of car did he drive? Did he work from home or did he go to some glass and steel offices filled with clever women in sharp suits who watched him through narrowed eyes, waiting to pounce?

'... terrific in orange with orange gerberas. Or even purple?

That would be unusual, wouldn't it? Sort of Christmassy too. Oooh, I know ... a dark forest green? And the little flower girls in crimson ...'

Did he like baths or showers? Did he use moisturiser? What side of the bed did he sleep on?

'... brown, a sort of plain chocolate colour, you know?'

Perhaps he liked extreme sports? Did he like Marmite?

'Alexa, are you listening?'

'Hmm? Oh yes, of course. You want me to wear Marmite.'

'*What?* No, I didn't say that,' she said, looking at me like I was mad. 'I was just thinking about darker colours. We'll have to go shopping. I mean as a matter of extreme urgency.'

I know what India on an urgent shopping trip meant. Flat shoes and a double-shot espresso for starters. Then a determined route march through every shop in town with bridesmaids dresses. We would have lunch at a wine bar where if you bought two glasses you got the rest of the bottle free. So the afternoon would go a bit blurry and we would end up buying something monumentally unsuitable that would need to be returned the following day.

'Yes, great,' I said with an enthusiasm I didn't feel.

The waiter brought us more toast and some annoying little sachets of Marmite that needed the Incredible Hulk to rip them open. If I ever went on another cruise, which was unlikely considering the cost, I'd be sure to take my own pot with me. But I'd probably be stopped at customs where they would impound it and throw me off the ship.

'And then we'd better see if Mum has sorted her outfit. Perhaps she could come with us?'

It was going to be bad enough going *urgent shopping* with my sister. The prospect of also taking Mum along was very worrying. The last time we went shopping with her was when she needed a smart outfit to go to Ascot. We ended up buying some champagne flutes, a pair of wellingtons with pictures of spaniels on and a new padded gilet for gardening. She's easily distracted is our mother.

'Yes, let's do that,' I said.

India looked at me. 'Are you okay, Al? I mean you don't seem quite with it.'

'I'm fine. Just a bit, you know ...'

'It's that bloody man, isn't it? He's really upset you. I'm going to give him a piece of my mind when I see him. Messing with my sister and upsetting her like this!'

I looked at her startled.

'No, please don't, I'm fine. I've been thinking about Marnie's talk – spring-cleaning my life sounds exactly what I need to do.'

'Well, okay, but if I see Gabriel bloody Frost ...'

'Forget about him. I'm going to,' I said.

'Really?'

'Absolutely. I'm going to just chalk it up to experience, like you said. It was just a bit of fun after all. We were both consenting adults.'

288

India snorted. 'Well, you were both consenting. I'm not sure I'd always describe you as an adult.'

'Oh, thanks. Always have to have the last word, don't you? What time is it?' I said, distracting her.

'Ten-twenty. Why?'

Because I could do with a drink. A double brandy. Or a stiff gin? No, I didn't need a stiff anything.

'We should be going soon,' I said chirpily, 'if you want to get a good place in the library.'

We finished our breakfast and left the restaurant past a few bowing and smiling waiters. They probably wouldn't be quite so cheerful when they saw how much butter I had managed to smear on the tablecloth.

Chapter Twenty-One

Suffering Bastard

Bacardi, Martinique Light Rhum,
Curacao, Sugar Syrup, Lime Juice

I left India in the library looking very determined and indus-trious, then I wandered around the ship for a bit taking in all the sights I could before returning to the cabin to do a bit of desultory packing. In the end I got into bed and had a nap. India came back to our cabin some time later, her laptop tucked under one arm and an expression of fierce enthusiasm on her face.

'I've done nearly a thousand words,' she said.

I sat up and pushed my hair out of my face. 'Wow, that's impressive.' Or at least I thought it was. It sounded a lot anyway.

I swung my legs off the bed and waited for a moment for everything to settle. I felt decidedly odd and my mouth was like the Gobi Desert. I had never been very good at sleeping during the day. I tottered to the bathroom to get a drink of cold water, while in the main room India was still wittering on about something, but to be honest I didn't pay much attention. I had a quick search for some paracetamol but seemed to remember we'd finished those days ago.

Instead I ran some cold water over my hands and held them to my hot face and looked at my reflection in the mirror over the sink. I looked really crap.

I came to a decision – I wasn't going to think about, talk about or look for Gabriel Frost any more. I could be sensible about this, couldn't I? I had enjoyed a bit of a holiday fling and that was all there was to it. People did this all the time, didn't they? That's why there was such a problem with teen pregnancy and STIs. At least I was on the pill. I'd better get myself checked out though, just in case. What a thoroughly depressing thought that was. I went back into the cabin where India had barely drawn breath.

'... and that's the best part about it. I said what I thought. Which quite often you don't, do you? I mean think of the right thing to say at the right time. I can't think of the number of times I've wanted to say something pithy and clever to Jerry's sister and it's only come to me at three in the morning. I swear I am not going to cave in to pressure and have her as a bridesmaid. Jerry keeps dropping hints and I keep ignoring them. I mean why would I ...'

Ah, we were back to the wedding plans. Okay. I could

handle this. It wasn't the end of the world, and obviously it was a big deal to my sister. I could listen and nod.

'So we are going to the show tonight? After dinner?' India asked suddenly when I didn't say anything.

'Yes, sure. Of course. Don't let me drink anything tonight though. I'm turning into a right lush.'

'But it's our last night!' India said, her face creased with confusion. 'Don't be such a killjoy. We'll be back home tomorrow afternoon; you can go on the wagon then. I can't wait to see Jerry. I hope he's remembered to take the bins out. He's quite capable of forgetting and letting it all pile up. And they only collect every fortnight so we'll end up with a month's rubbish in the hallway if he's forgotten. And then we'll get a stiff note from the residents' committee. And he never recycles properly either.'

India carried on chattering while she brushed her hair, fixed her make-up and chose her outfit for the evening. We still had all our packing to do; we had to leave our cases outside the cabin by seven o'clock.

'I'm going to wear some smart trousers and this shirt,' India said. 'What do you think?' She held up a navy blue shirt patterned with white birds.

'Yes, fab,' I said.

'What are you going to wear?'

'I don't know, that grey blouse? Or the pale blue tunic and leggings?'

Oh, who cared? It didn't matter, did it?

'Are you okay?' India said.

She came and sat next to me.

'Yeah, just a bit. You know. A bit tired. I know I shouldn't be but I feel a bit ... Oh, nothing really.' I forced a smile to my face. I was being a selfish cow. We had one more evening together before we got home and India got swept away by Jerry and the wedding took over everything again.

'Okay, I'll wear this,' I said, and I pulled out a dress that I always packed but never wore. It was flowery and rather short, two things I tended to avoid as a rule.

'Great. And I'll put some heated rollers in your hair and we'll have a laugh, okay?'

'Brilliant,' I said. And I tried to sound as though I meant it. This holiday had definitely done something right: my sister and I were getting back to how we used to be. Not all the way there, but getting closer.

I now realised that, despite her prickly nature, India was still protective of me and could be unexpectedly kind. Maybe our relationship could improve after all?

India rubbed my arm and was about to say something, but then decided against it.

That evening we got to our usual table in the Champs-Elysées restaurant to find Marty, Ike, Caron and Marion already seated and tucking in to the basket of assorted bread rolls. Our waiter had long since realised it wasn't worth taking them away.

'There you are, girls,' Marty said. He passed me a card.

'That's our address; if you're ever in Washington, DC, look us up. I've written Ike's on the back. Though why anyone would want to go to Boise I can't imagine.'

'Hey! Nothing wrong with Idaho! No other state has *World Famous Potatoes* written on the car plates,' Ike said.

'And there's a reason for that,' Marty muttered.

India was busily writing our address on the back of another of Marty's cards, and he tucked it carefully into the pocket of his jacket. That in itself was rather touching, seeing as India and I had been just a couple of sisters sitting at their table, drinking their wine and getting variously merry, pissed and shit-faced.

'Do you know Idaho law forbids a citizen to give another citizen a box of candy that weighs more than fifty pounds? Don't you think that's interesting?' Ike said.

Caron tapped his arm. 'The menu, honey. The waiter's coming over. And let's order some wine; I haven't had a drink all day.'

'You don't count that Martini before lunch?'

She flapped a hand. 'Oh, that ...'

It might have been the last night on board but the meal was as excellent as ever. It was going to be a bit of a shock to my system when I got home and reverted to my toasted sandwiches and tins of soup.

I'll admit, at the start of the holiday, I had been a little concerned to find out we would be sharing a table with four strangers, but it had proved a blessing, especially this evening when I didn't feel like talking much. The other four were great talkers, had opinions on everything and didn't mind sharing them.

They discussed the ship, where they were going for their next cruise (Alaska) and gave us more details of their children (one son each, both in the Army). All I had to do was sit there and nod and smile and occasionally ask a question. When we got on to India's wedding plans we were treated to a blow-by-blow account of Marion's son Kyle's short, ill-fated marriage to Chanisse, who seemed to give new meaning to the term high-maintenance.

All the time I was battling with a stubborn little part of my brain that wanted to think about Gabriel. Every few minutes I had to give it a talking-to, and a metaphorical slap, so that I stopped thinking about the curve of his mouth, the way his eyelashes rested on his cheek when he was sleeping, the feel of his ...

Shut up. Okay? Just stop it.

Half a bottle of Cabernet Sauvignon and a large Cointreau later we went to see the last evening show, the much-anticipated *Tribute to the Sea.* We made our way along the corridors, crowded now with guests enjoying their evening to the full.

We passed the casino, whose doors were temptingly open. Inside, the battery of fruit machines were flashing and jangling, promising all sorts of massive payouts. Beyond that a sultry-looking girl in a tight black dress stood behind a roulette wheel, flicking the ball around. Marty tried unsuccessfully to persuade Marion he would just be ten minutes before he was dragged away from all the excitement and forced into a seat around our favourite table in the theatre.

Of course, within minutes, a waitress came across and Ike bought a round of drinks. I didn't want anything, except to lie down in a dark room, but I ended up with a Fish House Punch, which tasted better than it sounded. India had one called Nelson's Blood, which was very orange. That's all I can say about it.

Shortly afterwards the lights dimmed and the curtains were pulled back to reveal a stage decorated like the ocean bed. The girls toddled on somewhat hampered by their mermaid tails and the boys for some reason were dressed like extras from a Jean-Paul Gaultier perfume ad in stripy jumpers and sailor hats with red bobbles. Very strange.

Anyway, they launched into a rousing chorus of 'Surfin' USA' followed by 'Under the Boardwalk'. It was great for getting us in a jolly mood and the audience was soon clapping along and knocking back cocktails in fine form.

Then the curvaceous singer brought her bosom back onstage, this time in a blue fishtail dress with a ruffled lace underskirt to suggest waves. It was really clever. She gave us 'Love Letters in the Sand' and, rather oddly, 'Mull of Kintyre'. Anyway, by the time she had finished, the stage had been redesigned as the deck of a pirate ship and the dancers came on dressed to match. Then there was a juggler who did a turn with some plastic (I hope) starfish. And more dances and songs until the place was rocking. I was slightly rocking too because, somewhere along the line, I had shipped another cocktail decorated with umbrellas and sparkly cocktail sticks (they should take those out; I poked myself up the nose with one and it really hurt) and India was standing in the aisle dancing; at least I wasn't doing that. I didn't seem to be in the mood.

At last the director of entertainment came out, his bald head gleaming under the spotlights, and thanked us for being so wonderful. He hoped to see us again soon and we all sang 'Auld Lang Syne'. Which again was a bit otherworldly as by then all the dancers were dressed as French matelots. Anyway, they had done their best and I for one felt sudden gladness to be going home, mixed with sadness that our adventure was at an end.

*

We got back to our cabin to find our cases had been taken and Amil had left us a final towel crab and some extra pillow chocolates.

'I wonder how Mum and Dad are getting on in Australia? We'll probably never do this again,' I said sadly as I lay in the dark a few minutes later.

'Thanks ever so much for everything. I didn't think it would be this fun, not really. But it's been good, hasn't it?' India said, still chewing her chocolate. 'You've been great company. You made sure we didn't miss anything and you got me paracetamol, and you joined in with everything and we got pissed together. That's all I needed.'

Flipping heck. I heard her unwrapping her second chocolate. I suppose as the more sensible sister I should have demurred and told her to go and clean her teeth but I couldn't be bothered. I was probably wiping what was left of my make-up on to the clean pillowcase so who was I to lay down the law?

'It's been fun,' I agreed. 'All those people who think cruises are for old people are so wrong.'

'Well, we thought that too,' India said, 'when we heard about the trip.'

'Yes, I know but …' I tried to organise my thoughts but failed.

'And we thought we'd be seasick. I only was once, do you remember? I had to lie down.'

Yes, and look where that had got me, I thought.

Gabriel in his DJ, his bow tie looped around his neck. Coming across the dark deck to kiss me.

Gabriel holding me in his arms as we tried to dance when all we wanted to do was make love …

No, that's not what we did.

Oh, sod it. Who cared? It didn't matter now.

'And we learned to make towel swans. And what was the other thing? Strawberry Santas? You can't put a price on that.'

'No, you can't. And no one misbehaved or made an exhibition of themselves. Well, not that I saw anyway,' I said.

There was a long pause when I thought India must have gone to sleep. After about five minutes, as she rustled about trying to get settled, she spoke again.

'Actually I nearly did,' she said.

'Did what?'

'I nearly misbehaved.'

I sat up in bed and looked over at her in the gloom.

'*What?*'

'What happens on a hen holiday stays on a hen holiday, right?' India said sternly.

'Okay,' I said nervously, 'what have you done? Did you break something? Insult someone?'

'No. Do you swear never to tell anyone?'

'Yes, okay.' This was like old times: promises, secrets – the scaffolding of sisterhood. I nearly grinned. 'So? What did you do?'

'I nearly made a fool of myself. And you'll never guess who stopped me.'

My thoughts were now spinning like balls in a tombola. 'For heaven's sake, India, what have you done?'

'Nothing, that's the point. But I nearly did. I nearly got into an awkward situation with Liam.'

'*What?*'

'You know the narrow staircase outside the casino and we wondered where it went because no one ever went down there?'

'Yes.'

'It leads to the staff quarters. Remember that day I was really hungover and we had breakfast and I was going back to bed and you were going to look around Nova Scotia? On the way I bumped into Liam. And he asked if I fancied coming to see around where the staff lived. There's a bar down there apparently. And like a muppet I said yes, and then I thought perhaps I shouldn't, and then he grabbed me and was being all funny and pulling me down the stairs and Gabriel saw what was happening.'

'Bloody hell! What happened?'

'Gabriel took me back to our cabin and made sure I was okay. He gave me a bottle of water and some aspirin. I felt such a complete fool. Didn't he say anything?'

'Not a word.'

'Wow,' India breathed. 'You promise you won't tell anyone?'

'I promise.'

'Thanks.' I heard her shifting about again as she pulled the duvet up. 'I wish things hadn't turned out the way they have. He seemed like such a decent guy.'

Me too, I thought.

'Go to sleep, India, you'll see Jerry again tomorrow.'

She gave a little excited squeak and I felt a twinge of jealousy. 'I can't wait. Night.'

I was beginning to drift off to sleep when there was a subtle rustling sound; the noise of paper being pushed under our door.

It might be a note from Gabriel. Apologising for the way

he had behaved? Maybe he was inviting me next door for a quick farewell shag? I had to know. Could I sleep knowing it was there, lying just inside the door on our blue, wave-patterned carpet?

Okay, I cracked. I couldn't help myself; I got out of bed and went to fetch it. It was a large white envelope, thick and embossed. My heart thumped in my chest. Not just a note then, a really long letter? I even considered opening the cabin door to see if he was still outside. Or maybe he'd left some red roses? Or some chocolates? Or a balloon? Don't be ridiculous, I told myself, where would he get a balloon?

What did he have to say? I put the light on in the bathroom and ripped the envelope open. I pulled out several sheets of paper, headed with the cruise line's distinctive crest. A curly crown held aloft by an angel.

What?

Of course.

I could have cried.

Why on earth would my tiny pea-brain imagine for one second that it might be a passionate love note from Gabriel? Let's be honest, it was more likely to be an invitation to the next Royal wedding.

It was our bar bill.

There were five and a half sheets filled with close-typed entries. Pages and pages of it and hundreds and hundreds of pounds too, totted up drink by drink, bottle by bottle, over the last two weeks. Red wine, white wine, champagne, cocktails, aperitifs, liqueurs. And this list didn't include the drinks other people had bought for us. They would be automatically deducting the amount at midnight unless we wanted to query the bill or any part of it. Like we would have been able to remember?

You wouldn't think two women could get through so much booze and not end up in intensive care, would you?

Bloody hell.

Chapter Twenty-Two

Blue Moon

Dry Gin, Liqueur de Violette, Lemon Juice, Egg White

The following morning I woke with the usual foggy feeling of too many late nights, too much rich food and far too much alcohol. Looking at her rather pinched, grey expression, I think India felt much the same. Outside, instead of the usual calm, quiet ambiance, we could hear people hurrying up and down the corridor, the occasional thump of a bag against our door and once or twice a distant laugh as people shut their cabin doors for the last time and went trundling off with their hand luggage in search of breakfast.

Without really speaking much, India and I got dressed, packed up the last of our hand luggage and swiped what was left of the Jo Malone toiletries from the bathroom. Another notice had been pushed under the door with details of how to disembark. It sounded very efficient, with people being asked to go to the theatre at specific times. We had to be there at ten-thirty and we had two red stickers to identify us.

We made our way to the food court. India found a table and I brought back some coffee and a selection of Danish pastries and muffins. Let's be honest, we didn't need them, but by that point it was habit. Or to put it another way, we were being greedy. What difference would one more meal make?

We sat placidly munching and people-watching. Some of the passengers were already clearing the food from the display cabinets with the speed and efficiency of a pack of Velociraptors. A lot of people seemed to look the way we felt: sort of tired and lethargic after so many days of jollity and overindulgence. And there was just a muted rumble of conversation, enlivened only when there was a minor disturbance somewhere by the area dealing with hot breakfast food and we heard a plaintive cry of '*My bacon, I think you'll find, buddy!*'

The coast of England slipped slowly past with its coves and beaches and hotels and oil storage depots. It was strange to see buildings and other boats again. I think we had the same sort of out-of-it feeling you get when you've been in hospital for a few days and someone comes to drive you home.

Then the ship slowed down, we stopped for a moment, there was a deep and distant rumbling somewhere far below us and we began to turn. It seemed the Captain was going to take us into the dock backwards. Speaking as someone who finds it hard to parallel park even when the rest of the street is empty, that's just showing off in my opinion. Inch by inch we backed into our parking space or whatever it's called. Left hand down a bit. It was exactly ten-thirty. Considering we had travelled 3,365 miles, I think that was pretty impressive.

'We'd better go to the theatre,' I said, checking our disembarkation paperwork again.

India waved a hand dismissively. 'What's the worst they can do if we *don't* go to the theatre at ten-thirty? Not let us get off? Make us sail back to New York? Clap us in irons and put us in the bilges? Chill out.'

I shrugged. She was right. We had another cup of coffee and watched an elderly man ramming bottles of water and several sausages wrapped in paper napkins into his little wheeled suitcase. We have plenty of food in England, I wanted to say. Just because of Brexit, doesn't mean there's nothing to eat.

Another white-haired traveller I took to be his wife appeared, balancing several bread rolls and slices of cheese on a plate.

India went off and returned with two bottles of water and two vast slices of carrot cake.

'What on earth are you doing?' I said.

'I don't know, it's just what everyone else is doing. Herd mentality.'

'So if everyone stays here for the next couple of hours and then starts eating lasagne and garlic bread, you'd do that too?'

'Well, I might. Do you think Jerry is waiting for us?' India looked a little misty-eyed at the prospect.

'Knowing Jerry he will possibly have been on the quayside since dawn, or he might be at Bristol Airport, or he might have forgotten to come at all.'

'He's hopeless, isn't he? I do love him,' India said, taking a bite of cake.

The quayside was gently sliding into view with several workers in boilersuits and hard hats looking up at the vast bulk of the *Reine*, waiting for her to stop. Next to them were various articulated lorries parked up in a line waiting, presumably, to unload stuff. They'd need to get rid of our rubbish first, probably another huge amount of cardboard and bottles. I wondered if they would roll their eyes at the sheer amount or whether it was always like this. Other people would be congregating somewhere, waiting to board the ship before sailing off this evening. Back to New York perhaps, or south to Spain or Africa?

I watched the lorries for a few minutes while I picked chunks off my carrot cake and wondered if it was too early for a drink. I mean I'd quite enjoyed the Fish House Punch last night. And it had fruit in it too, so it couldn't have been that bad. On the other hand there had been something called a Hemingway Breakfast that involved absinthe, rum and marmalade, among other things.

I wondered if Ernest Hemingway really did have that for his breakfast. I imagined him sitting in his house in Key West, surrounded by his six-toed cats and empty Martini glasses. The day I'd had that one, India had enjoyed a Dutch Breakfast, which had advocaat, gin and Galliano. It came garnished with a slice of orange too, and they're full of vitamin C.

For God's sake, what was I *thinking*?

I stood up.

'Come on, let's go. It's nearly eleven o'clock.'

India sighed. 'Oh, all right then, Mrs Nag. I bet you any money we'll just have to sit around for hours waiting for something to happen.'

We picked up our bags and went out into the atrium. Suddenly there was an announcement over the public address system.

'*Would Miss India Fisher and Miss Alexandria Fisher please make their way to the theatre immediately where staff are waiting to assist them in their ten-thirty disembarkation process. That's a* **ten-thirty** *disembarkation.*'

We exchanged panic-stricken looks and set off at a brisk jog.

*

After dealing with some uncharacteristically frosty *Reine de France* employees (how were we to know they only had five hours to clean the entire ship and remake all the beds?) we went through customs and back down the footbridge where we were reunited with our luggage in a cavernous, wind-blasted hangar. And there was Jerry in the same washed-out red cord trousers and Black Sabbath T-shirt he had been wearing the last time I saw him. He had been waiting for us since half past seven and had brought a welcome-home balloon, a bottle of champagne and – his preferred present for all occasions – a bag of jam doughnuts. At the sight of them, India burst into tears and Jerry had to spend a few minutes hugging her and rubbing her back and calming her down. Meanwhile I sat on my suitcase watching our fellow travellers reunite with their friends, climbing on to luxury coaches or cramming their cases into the inadequate boots of taxis.

My eye was suddenly caught by a very shiny black stretch limo parked illegally in the No Waiting area. And then Marnie Miller and her assistant appeared from the terminal building, followed by a porter with their luggage piled up on a trolley like something out of a 1950s travel guide. Marnie whipped off her sunglasses (it wasn't even sunny) and got into the limo, swiftly followed by her assistant who was relegated to the front seat with the driver.

And oh, looky look. My mouth dropped open. Gabriel Frost in a sleek, dark, lawyer-y suit. Getting in beside Marnie, disappearing from view behind the dark windows with her.

Bastard.

Eventually India calmed down and stopped snivelling. Honestly you would have thought she'd been *Two Years Before the Mast* not just away for twelve days on a luxury ship.

'So are you all right? Did you have fun?' Jerry kept asking, his face creased with worry. It was as though he wanted us to say *no, it was awful.*

Behind him I saw Marnie's limo escape through the dock gates with a dramatic sweep, as though it had been embarrassed to be in such close proximity to anything as chavvy as a coach.

'It was fantastic,' I said, 'great cabin, loads of food and drinks. Entertainment, lectures ...'

Jerry hugged my sister again and they rocked from side to side, enjoying being back together again.

'I'se missed ooo so much, my yittle Bun-bun,' he said in the sort of silly voice hotshot barristers use when talking to their fiancées in public places.

'I've missed you too, Jerry,' I sighed.

Jerry turned, confusion all over his face. 'Awfully sorry, Alexa, I meant India. Although I did miss you too of course. Oh, you're being funny.'

Let's be honest, driving home after any holiday is always pretty rubbish. Okay, you have all those lovely memories and loads of pictures on your phone, some of which in my case were a teeny bit obscured at the top because I'd bought a new phone case and the hole for the camera lens was in the wrong place. But anyway the only *other* things you have are a bag full of dirty washing, a load of sugar sachets in the side pockets of your handbag and, on this occasion, some *Reine de France* biros, because every time I was asked to sign a bar slip, I made a point of keeping the pen. I had loads too. How did that happen?

India sat in the front passenger seat next to Jerry and they held hands on the gear stick all the way home, except when Jerry was distracted by India squeezing his thigh and nearly ran into the car in front of us. My bet was that, while I was going to spend my evening unpacking and doing laundry, Jerry and India were going to be in their groovy loft-style apartment, at it like rabbits. Perhaps that's why he called her Bun-bun?

Funny isn't it, looking at Jerry – who when he's not wearing his work clothes looks like a shambling wreck – you really wouldn't think he had a high-octane sex life. And that business with the handcuffs and the judge's wig and the salad cream – well, it will take me a long time to forget that. Oh well.

I had a snooze, my head pillowed on one of the bags that didn't fit into the boot. We did seem to have bought a lot of things. I only remembered buying my mother a stuffed toy owl. What was all this other stuff?

I woke up when we were nearly home to find Jerry and India were now talking full-time as though they had been inhaling helium out of balloons.

'I missed my Bunny,' Jerry said, 'lots.'

'Just lots?'

'And lots and lots and lots,' Jerry squeaked.

'I missed ooo just as much.'

'Really?'

'Really really.'

'And cuddles. I missed cuddles,' Jerry said. 'I fort I would go crazy without ooo.'

'And that, m'lud, is the case for the prosecution,' I said, sitting up.

'Oh, so you're awake,' India said.

'You're round the bend the pair of you,' I said.

'She's just jealous,' India said. 'She hasn't got a boyfriend.'

'Erm, I don't think so,' I said, 'and if I did I wouldn't talk like a demented baby on speed.'

'Gabriel Gorgeousness?' India prompted.

'Who he?' Jerry said, his ears pricking up.

'Alexa had a shipboard romance,' India said confidingly, 'but shipboard romances stay on the ship. And now she's all miz.'

'I am not all miz, I am perfectly okay about it. There's no need to make up stories.'

'I forgot to tell you! Marnie Miller was on the ship giving talks on writing,' India said. 'I've decided I'm going to write a bestseller. I've already written nearly two thousand words. It's all about a girl who falls in love with a duke . And she makes cakes and has a mad friend who runs a teashop and there's going to be a village fete and some hidden treasure. I'm going to plot the whole thing out and make a fortune.'

'Sounds wonderful, Bunny,' Jerry said, slowing down as he negotiated my parents' driveway. The potholes were no better I noticed.

I found my house keys and let myself in. It was unnaturally quiet and tidy with them away in Australia. There was a pile of post to be picked up from behind the front door; quite a few travel brochures, I noticed, and several glossy catalogues for cruise lines including a huge new one for the *Reine de France*.

I flicked through it with India leaning over my shoulder, stabbing at the pictures and saying things like, oooh, I've been in that room. We had dinner there. See that table? That was where we sat.

The pictures were stylish and exciting with more glamorous alpha couples laughing all over everything. They were giggling by the pool as they sipped brightly coloured cocktails (looked like two Piña Coladas to me), chuckling as the wine waiter showed them a bottle of Bollinger, beaming happily as the tall-hatted chef offered them a plate of elaborate desserts. Then there was a picture of two of them in the spa having a couples massage, eyes closed and blissfully smiling as they presumably anticipated some rampant sexual activity later on in their massive, flower-strewn suite. There were even two towel swans in the middle of the vast bed and chocolates on the pillows. I found myself hoping Amil had hung a towel monkey inside their wardrobe so it would frighten the crap out of them later. Bastards.

India went off to check if there was anything interesting in the freezer she could nick for their evening meal and then had a quick scan through the drinks cabinet.

'D'you want this vodka?' she said, waggling a new bottle at me.

'No, but I expect Mum will when she gets home,' I said rather stiffly. I was tired, that was all. I had a headache; I needed a wee and a shower. And I really wanted five minutes' peace and quiet away from Jerry and Bunny who were evidently in the mood for a bottle of champagne and some bedroom gymnastics. Perhaps he would get the handcuffs out or they could play barristers and defendants and talk about taking each other's briefs down?

I stopped India from taking the Angostura bitters, again, and shooed them out. They didn't take much shooing, and then I locked up and went down the garden to the granny annexe. It was exactly as I had left it, even down to the screwed-up crisp packet in the bin and the book left open on the sofa. The laundry basket was still overflowing and I'd forgotten to buy milk and bread on the way home. Instead there was the inflated yogurt and liquid cucumber plus an opened packet of sliced chicken I'd forgotten about that was almost a new life form. I went back up the path to my parents' house where there was civilisation, ice in the freezer and three different sorts of gin.

I ran myself a hot bath and poured in a good dollop of my mother's Chanel bath oil for good measure. Then I soaked in the bath for an hour with a gin and tonic made in a half-pint beer mug. I couldn't stand it any longer; I would have to let myself do it. I lay in the scented water and thought about Gabriel.

Bloody sodding everything.

He'd been everything I liked in a man. Or I thought he had been for a few days, which was longer than some of my previous relationships, which, let's be honest, were three-legged donkeys from day one even though I clung on to some of them like grim death.

Gabriel had been handsome, well-mannered, charming, solvent (if the limo was anything to judge by), intelligent (he did say he was lawyer) and fantastic in bed. Not necessarily in that order of course. And despite the champagne slinging at our first meeting, he'd seemed to like me too. I think. Or at least he'd found me attractive enough to take to bed. And then of course, just as I was starting to go a bit silly over him, I'd found out what he was like. Divorced (not that it mattered) and, if Marnie was to be believed, not as straightforward as he seemed.

He had been sensational in bed. But did that matter? Was that really significant? Was he always sensational in bed with every woman he managed to persuade to join him?

Probably.

But was anything about it meaningful?

No, probably not.

Oh well, what did matter? That I had found him sexy and irresistible or that we had enjoyed each other's company? And he'd saved my sister from a scary situation. That had been quite something. I wished I'd known so I could have thanked him.

I finished my gin and tonic and got out of the bath. Then I went and poured another drink and sat and sulked in front of the television for a couple of hours watching some crap programme about life in the country and a charity's battle to save some frigging beetle.

I suppose I should have gone back to my own bed at the end of the garden but it was dark outside now and raining. So when I had exhausted the rather restricted choice of TV channels my parents were happy to live with, I went up to my old room and switched on the electric blanket while I cleaned my teeth.

The *Reine de France* would have left Southampton by now, taking another fifteen hundred passengers off on an adventure. Someone else would be sitting at 'our' table. Amil would be fashioning towel swans for another couple. The boys and girls of the dance troupe would be flashing their eyes and teeth at a new audience. I wondered if they were doing the tribute to *Cabaret* again and firing up a different group of elderly gentlemen?

I got into bed and lay looking at the painted bookcase under the window that still held my battered collection of childhood paperbacks. Pony stories, boarding school adventures, and a whole shelf of unrealistic romances where the girl (bright, kind and lovely but misunderstood) takes her glasses off and the handsome boy dumps the class flirt, falls in love and proposes.

I wondered what Gabriel was doing. Had he gone to a

hotel? Was he unpacking his cases and sending his clothes to the laundry?

I thought for a moment I was going to cry. Perhaps it was the gin; it has that effect on me sometimes.

Chapter Twenty-Three

Cobbler

Sherry, Maraschino Liqueur, Sugar Syrup,
Pineapple and Orange Juice

I woke up the following morning feeling completely disorientated. Where was I? I wasn't on board ship. I wasn't in the flat I had shared with Karen. I wasn't in the dull little bedroom in the granny annexe with its louvered wardrobe doors and striped curtains that didn't quite close. I seemed to have slipped back several years to my childhood and finding *In the Fifth at Malory Towers* facedown on the floor didn't help either.

What day was it? For the life of me I couldn't work it out. I went to find my phone and realised it was Saturday. Thank heavens. I wasn't due into work until Monday; everyone had assumed we would need the weekend to get over our jet lag. (Of course we didn't have jet lag, the ship's time had gone forward by an hour every day to take care of that.)

I went downstairs to find a carton of long-life milk in the pantry, took some bread out of the freezer, made toast and tea and took everything back up to bed. I had things to do and, following the diktat from Marnie Miller's talk, I certainly didn't *need* any more alcohol; I *needed* to unpack my badly packed cases and get my laundry done. And then go shopping for some food. And do a load of domestic stuff. A day of unparalleled boredom stretched ahead.

I was tempted to phone my sister but India would probably still be in bed frolicking around with Jerry. I guessed she wouldn't welcome a call from me complaining about having no fresh milk.

I thought about yesterday morning, waking up on the *Reine de France*. Was it really only yesterday? It felt like an age. I remembered the endless stream of breakfast foods that appeared every morning in the food court. The variety and choices. A cross-faced woman complaining in shrill outrage yesterday morning because there weren't any blueberry muffins. The numberless polite and smiling staff who took all the debris and washing up away.

I sat up in bed, looking out at the wet garden, munching my toast and trying to get motivated to do something other than feel a bit sad.

Ridiculous. For heaven's sake buck up.

I'd had a great couple of weeks; I'd seen parts of New England I'd never expected to see. I'd had some lovely meals and explored the world of cocktails. I'd learned how to fold towels into elephants and arrange fruit. I could waltz badly and foxtrot worse. I'd not been seasick or contracted food poisoning. I'd had the best sex of my life. Now that's what I called a holiday.

I dressed and went to sort out my laundry, shoving the first load into Mum's washing machine. Well, she had washing tablets and I didn't. She even had ironing water and I didn't know she ironed.

I thought about my parents, still out in Australia enjoying temperatures over eighty degrees and checking under the loo seat for poisonous spiders. I sat hunched on a bar-stool with another cup of tea in my mother's immaculate kitchen, every-thing working, everything to hand. Washing tablets, bin liners, toothpaste, gin. The family joke, that my mother was the most disorganised, domestically resentful woman in the world, was such a farce. She obviously wasn't.

A thought of shocking magnitude hit me and I sat up a bit straighter. Would I ever get to be as orderly as she obvi-ously was? Did it come with time? You forgot to buy loo roll once too often and suddenly some fifth gear kicked in and you became an adult with shopping lists and a proper purse with money-off coupons in the back? Was this a *Spring-Clean Your Life* moment? Yes, it was.

I was nearly thirty and I was still living with my parents. India was a few weeks away from her wedding and becoming Mrs Jeremy Sinclair and probably nine months away from motherhood (or at least I hoped she was). Despite this we both still had keys to our parents' house and thought nothing of taking food out of the freezer or alcohol and barbeque charcoal and shampoo. My mother had even been trying to address the problem of my lack of a boyfriend by suggesting monumentally unsuitable candidates from the golf club. It was time I wised up and stopped drifting.

What would my parents have thought of Gabriel Frost with his grey eyes and broad, muscular shoulders and his voice and his clever hands and the way he smiled, how he had nibbled my neck, his tongue brushing –

Shut up, Alexa. This isn't helping.

Instead of leaving my mug in the sink I washed and dried it and put it back in the cupboard. Then I tidied up my bedroom and changed the sheets and put the dirty ones plus the towels I'd used (and left on the bathroom floor) into the washing machine. There wasn't a cabin steward to take care of it and it would be unfair to expect my mother to clear up after me.

Then I went back to the granny annexe and, for the first time, found a notebook and actually made a shopping list.

*

I went back to work on Monday. It was cold and raining and, as is often the case after an hour, it felt like I had never been away. Charlie Smith-Rivers, the branch manager from Exeter, had been holding the fort and it showed. The office was tidy, there were no in-trays filled with bits of paper or mosaics of Post-it notes across the top of every computer screen.

He held out a sheet of paper to me as I struggled out of my coat.

'I just wanted you to see what's been going on,' he said with a wolfish smile, 'while you've been dancing around the pool in your bikini.'

I took the sheet of paper and scanned through it. There was no doubt he'd done a great job in our absence. But it didn't make him any less irritating. He was the sort of man who wore a cravat in his leisure moments and referred to his wife, Irene, as 'the little girlie'.

'Don't be daft, Charlie, I've been to New York, Nova Scotia and then across the Atlantic. Not exactly bikini territory.'

He turned round as the door pinged. 'Ah, how wonderful, and here is the blushing bride-to-be!'

Blimey, India was on time for once.

She came in, dropped her umbrella in the stand and sat down with a heavy sigh at her desk.

'Hello, Charlie,' she said, 'I thought you were back in Exeter this morning?'

Subtle subtext: why are you here annoying us?

'Just wanted to welcome the weary travellers home again,' he said, rubbing his hands. 'Ha ha ha, and now you have the wedding to look forward to. He's a lucky chap, your Jerry. Youth is wasted on the young, eh?'

'Thank you so much, Charlie, I can see you've done a

fantastic job.' I waved the sheet of paper at him. 'All this progress in such a short time. I think we ought to have a team meeting, India,' I said, fixing Tim, the other member of our staff, who was cowering behind his computer screen, with a meaningful look.

Tim rolled his eyes, ducked even lower and started madly typing.

We finally persuaded Charlie to leave after half an hour, India almost forcing the door closed on his questions about the wedding and had she missed Jerry and was it nice to be back together again?

Tim looked out over the top of his screen. 'Has he gone?' he asked.

I watched Charlie saunter down the road and into his ancient Bentley.

'He's gone.'

'Thank God, the last two weeks have been a trial, I don't mind admitting. My aunt says I'm not sleeping properly.'

I looked at my watch; it was nearly ten o'clock.

'Poor Tim, let's get some doughnuts and then start our meeting,' I said.

'No!' India yelped. 'I've put on five pounds! Haven't you? I'm like a big fat tub of lard! I'll never get into my wedding dress if I carry on like this!'

She sat up straight and pulled at some non-existent flab around her middle.

I hadn't actually dared get on my own scales but undoubtedly my work trousers were a bit tighter than I remembered them being. But I actually wanted and needed a doughnut. I hadn't had any breakfast because I'd been awake for most of the night and of course fallen into a deep sleep round about six o'clock.

I slipped Tim a fiver and sent him off to the bakery down the road, with India's call of *nothing for me, thanks* echoing in his ears.

I started reading the hundreds of emails that had lodged in my inbox during my two weeks away. As usual there were dozens of stupid fake coupons for shops I never went into and a couple of notifications about my long-lost uncle/aunt/friend/work colleague who had died in Poland leaving me a fortune/gold mine/artwork/house. Jolly careless my long-lost relatives.

I even had a frisson of anticipation, wondering if Gabriel had sent me an email.

Of course he hadn't. He didn't know my email address. Duh.

Across the other side of the office India was snorting with amusement at some of her emails. I expect they were from Jerry with a load of lewdness and shared advertisements for wedding lingerie, concerning which he'd been more involved than India had expected.

'He's such a fool,' she murmured. 'Honestly, he's supposed to be in court this morning. What's he doing sending me this stuff?'

'More balconette bras and thongs?'

'I'd be trussed up and oven ready in some of these,' she said, 'and, let's be fair, if he thought I was wearing *that* one he'd be completely unable to concentrate. D'you want to see?'

'Um, no thanks, Indie, I'll pass if it's all the same.'

We locked eyes and giggled. Things had definitely changed. I could feel it in the air and even after a rotten night's sleep I felt happier, lighter.

The phone rang and India answered it. By her expression I thought I could guess who it was. An incredibly annoying couple who wanted to buy a house they couldn't afford, who thought the vendors might eventually be persuaded by their rather insulting offers.

There was a pause while Mr Harvey wittered down the phone at her.

'Well, the Mitchells had three valuations and they all agreed ... no, it's not a conspiracy ... yes, you're right, it is an expensive property, I will agree ... the trouble is ... the trouble ... the trouble is they are in no hurry to move ... yes, but sometimes life isn't fair. Right, I'll get back to you as soon as I can.'

At that moment Tim came back through the door with a nice-looking brown paper bag with grease stains already seeping through it.

'Doughnuts,' he said. 'Two of the little beauties.'

'What! Didn't you get me one?' India pouted.

'Of course I did, only teasing. I never listen when you tell me not to buy you cake. I got six actually.'

I went out to make coffee in the kitchenette and when I got back they were both on phone calls.

I sat down at my desk and suddenly felt that awful, deflated, post-holiday feeling you get on the first day back in the office. When you realise it really is all over. That I was back to real life and the cumbersome beast lumbering towards us that was my sister's wedding.

Having taken two phone calls, India now felt able to start googling bridesmaids' dresses. She found outfits for the three flower girls pretty easily and then she started looking on my behalf. Which meant that nothing got done because she was too busy waving me over to come and look at what she'd found. In the end both of us were googling bridesmaids' dresses and Tim was answering all the phone calls. After an hour or so we found a few possibles and India decided I would need to go out on Saturday and try them on.

I clicked off the myriad pictures of flouncy, frothy, slinky and downright ghastly dresses India had been suggesting so that I was only left with a generic news page open. And there she was. Right in front of me. Marnie Miller on the front page of the news. Looking all sad and pouty.

I gave a strangled scream and India looked up.

'What?'

'It's Marnie bloody Miller! In the news.'

'Well, she often is,' India said, annoyingly calm under the circumstances.

I had clicked on the thumbnail to get the full story and yelped again.

There she was, in a demure grey dress with a white ruffled collar, her red curls tamed into a neat chignon so it looked strangely as though her head was being served up on a platter. And next to her, in a sharper than sharp lawyer-y suit, was Gabriel Frost.

'You are not going to believe this,' I said as I scanned down the page. 'You are not going to frigging believe this.'

I didn't quite believe it either.

'Well, what is it?' India said. She was about to come across to see when her phone rang.

I took advantage of my sister being distracted for a few minutes to read the full story and my heart plummeted like a plummeting thing. I could feel my mouth drying up – with shock I suppose.

'Well?' India said after a few minutes.

'I don't quite believe what I've just read,' I said.

India took her phone off the hook and came racing across the room to look over my shoulder.

'*What?*' she said after a few dumbfounded seconds.

'I know!'

Tim looked up from investigating his second doughnut, sugar all over his chops. 'What? What's happened?'

'Marnie Miller is getting divorced!' I nearly shouted.

Tim shrugged. 'And this should mean something to me?'

I took a deep breath.

'Marnie Miller, you must have heard of her?' Tim nodded. 'Well, she was on our ship, giving talks about writing and spring-cleaning your life and getting rid of all the negative influences. If you did as she said you could be successful and happy and fulfilled. Not as totally fabulous as she is, of course, because she's a brand not a human being, but pretty damn close.' Tim looked bored at this point, so I got to the main event. 'She was going on and on about how lovely her life was, how she had a gorgeous husband, Leo. How they had met and fallen in love, how perfect their life together was. This golden couple with their bloody gorgeous houses and shoe racks and their boat in the British Virgin Islands. Honestly it was like *Hello!* magazine on steroids. Well, it looks like they're getting divorced and we had no idea!'

'Good heavens,' Tim said, his Adam's apple bobbing.

India held up one finger. 'She did have her lawyer with her. That should have been a clue, shouldn't it? Gabriel Frost: he specialises in family law, which someone else said meant *divorce*. Of course!'

By now I was just googling Marnie Miller/divorce to see what would pop up. What popped up was another article from an American newspaper with a picture of Marnie Miller trying to hide her tears behind one hand as she made her way from her fabulous London penthouse flat into a blacked-out, waiting limo. And there was Gabriel with her, one arm around her, the other hand held palm out towards the camera in the classic protective pose.

'International bestselling author and lifestyle expert Marnie Miller was tight-lipped last night as she left her London pied-à-terre. Rumours that she and her husband, Wall Street banker Leo Miller, were to divorce have been circulating for some days and were confirmed by a brief announcement from her lawyer Gabriel Frost (*see picture*). Heartthrob bachelor Mr Frost, one of London's most high-profile and admired lawyers, has been her constant companion in the last few weeks and was with her when she arrived on the *Reine de France* at Southampton last week.'

So it was true? Wow.

I suddenly felt very cold and rather sick.

So 'heartthrob bachelor Mr Frost' really had been stringing me along. I bet he'd been making a fuss of me in order to take his mind off Marnie. I read on.

'My client Marnie Miller and her husband are to divorce after six years of marriage. They are saddened that their relationship is to end in this way and will remain close and loving friends. Miss Miller asks that her privacy be respected at this very difficult time.'

Close and loving friends? What was all that about then? Would Leo Miller want to remain close and loving friends when his wife had been screwing her frigging lawyer? I felt sudden tears prickle behind my eyes. What a sod! Surely that was unprofessional behaviour? He might get struck off or something.

I clicked on a number of pictures and greedily read everything I could find about Marnie and Leo, her golden-boy husband. There were loads of stories about them. Pictures of them at charity dinners, film premieres, launch parties and book tours. Always staring into each other's eyes with a penetrating, loving gaze that seemed a bit much considering recent developments. There were loads of pictures of their wedding, which had been celebrated in California overlooking the Pacific Ocean at dusk. Even the sky had co-operated with a stunning sunset bathing the happy couple in golden light. Two snow-white doves obligingly circled in the air above them without crapping on anyone. It was all picture-perfect.

But now it had all come crashing down. I still didn't understand it. Even in the last few days Marnie had insisted she and Gabriel were just friends; she'd still been on about how wonderful Leo was and how happy they were. Perhaps she had got back to London and found Leo in bed with the housekeeper? Or the chauffeur? Or both of them? Crumbs.

A screwed-up ball of paper hit me on the head.

'Are you actually going to do any bloody work today?' India asked rudely.

Well, I like that!

Chapter Twenty-Four

Simple Truth

Rum, Pineapple Juice, Honey Syrup, Grapefruit Juice,
Campari, Sage Leaves

On Friday evening I was planning to go home after work and do the ironing. But instead India and Jerry took a break from practising for their wedding night and we went out for a drink together. It was kind of fun, chatting a bit about the wedding, but mostly laughing at Jerry's terrible impressions and India trying to remember all the names of the cocktails we'd tried on the ship.

Halfway through the evening we met up with Katie and Fliss – a couple of self-important paralegals from Jerry's work who pretended they wanted to hear all about the cruise and the holiday. What they really wanted to do of course was have a good long stare at India and try and work out why Jerry was marrying her.

Mum and Dad were due back soon from Australia, the cruise all seemed a long time ago, and I wasn't really in the mood for a big night for some reason. Still, by then we'd had a couple of glasses of wine and India and I had obediently dished up some funny stories about the places we had seen and the people we had met.

We talked about Marty and Marion and Ike and Caron. We showed them pictures on our phones of Newport, RI and Boston harbour with the plane whizzing overhead, and the wooded slopes of Nova Scotia. There were pictures of our lovely cabin before we messed it up, of New York and that fabulous skyline.

We had photographs of some of our meals, and nearly all the fancy desserts. Yes, I know it's pathetic to take pictures of your dinner but we couldn't help ourselves. We had selfies of the two of us in our evening dresses and one where we had been pulling funny faces in front of a chocolate fountain. And one in Boston where I had menaced India with a lobster and she had nearly fallen off her chair.

But we didn't mention Gabriel.

Then we talked about Marnie Miller and showed everyone the photos we'd had taken when we first met her at the Captain's cocktail party. I looked hard at that flawless face as she stood smiling between us. With the wisdom of hindsight of course ...

'Wow, she's so frigging cool,' Fliss said in a sort of breathless, admiring voice. 'Look, she's got a Birkin bag and that dress is Prada, I'm sure of it. What was she like?'

I took a sip of my wine and left it to India to describe the brand that was Marnie Miller. What was Marnie Miller like? I wasn't sure any more; her personality had been so powerful and inescapable. I'd gone through so many different feelings: awed, idolising, uncertain, and finally, after the recent news, pretty unimpressed. Perhaps I had been the one in the wrong? Or maybe I was the only person in the universe no longer fooled by her?

After India had waxed lyrical about Marnie for a few minutes, we showed everyone pictures of breakfast at the food court with glistening stacks of Danish pastries and fruit carved into clever shapes. Then the towel elephants on our beds and the gala night ice sculpture of the *Reine de France*'s iconic angel, which had been pushed around the dining room on a trolley to applause and cheers.

But we didn't mention Gabriel.

There were a few dark, unsatisfactory photos of the theatre shows and a couple of Peter and Paula spinning and twirling in their sequins. There were several of India leaning over the ship's rail, her dark curls blowing in the breeze. And one of me with a startled expression pointing at something in the water. That was the day I thought I saw a killer whale but it had just turned out to be part of a white plastic bucket and a clump of seaweed. Still it might have been a killer whale, you never know.

Then there were the shots of various cocktails we had enjoyed. There seemed to be rather a lot of those if I was honest. Something in a hollowed-out pineapple decorated with tiny glittery umbrellas, a clever layered thing that shaded from pink to palest yellow and a massive Long Island Iced Tea that had nothing to do with tea and everything to do with five different sorts of alcohol.

'Oh wowser, who the frig is *that*?' Katie said suddenly, grabbing my phone.

I looked. It was the selfie I had taken of Gabriel and me that day in Nova Scotia when we had shared lunch. The same day he had frightened Liam away from India. I had been wondering why Gabriel had kissed me and asked me to dinner that evening. I'd thought I was in heaven.

'Oh, just someone on the ship,' I said, trying to sound careless. 'I can't really remember.'

India reached over and swiped his picture away. We shared a brief, knowing look.

All the memories came flooding back. I had the awful feeling that I might cry if I mentioned him. I wanted to bury my thoughts of him, not to rake over them.

'So apart from him the boat was full of old relics, I bet,' Katie said, her lean, intelligent face furrowed with pity.

'No, not at all! I mean there were some older people on board but we met lots of nice people; not many kids that I saw, but then we were in the bars most of the time.'

Katie giggled. 'I can just imagine it. A lot of Zimmer frames lined up outside the dining rooms and mugs of Ovaltine at eight-thirty!'

Katie and Fliss laughed, leaning up against each other for support, the brilliance of their humour having apparently sapped their strength.

'No, it wasn't like that at all,' I said with all the passion of the converted. 'It's a five-star hotel taking you somewhere new every day. You should go.'

Fliss rolled her eyes. 'Sweetie, I'm not *nearly* old enough to go on a cruise!'

'You don't need to be old ...'

'Well, my parents went on a cruise once, down to Madeira I think,' Katie said. 'They said there was nothing to do but eat or play bridge. The weather was foul and Ma was seasick. She said never again. I can't imagine anything worse.'

I sent Katie one of my looks. If there was any justice she should have combusted on the spot, leaving a small pile of ash and a lot of melted hair extensions.

Katie finished her drink and looked around with a dissatisfied expression.

'Well, I'm sure you had a lovely time; it's just we'd prefer to go somewhere where there's a bit more talent. Skiing is good for that, loads of hunky men with lots of money. Or flotilla sailing in the Caribbean – I've heard that's a good hunting ground too. Remember that girl we were at school with, Lee or Fee? Fee, that was it. She went flotilla sailing in Bermuda and nabbed a hedge fund manager. They had the best wedding ever. At some stately home place near Bristol. It was fab. I think they're getting divorced now, but it was a fab wedding. I wore a fab blue dress from ASOS. It looked exactly like a Victoria Beckham tunic, I mean *exactly*.'

I looked at my watch; it was nine-thirty and I faced a fifteen-minute walk home in the rain.

'So when's the wedding?' Fliss asked my sister.

'Three weeks tomorrow,' India said, a glow in her cheeks.

'So no wedding bells ringing for you, Alexa?' Katie asked airily. 'No *plus-one* to take to the wedding?'

I could tell by the tone of her voice she thought both things were unlikely. *Well*, I felt like saying, *actually I had a passionate fling with possibly the handsomest man you're ever likely to see.* That *man*. But of course I didn't. I just gave a careless laugh. After all, what was there to tell? And my plus-one on India's wedding day was likely to be a stroppy three-year-old flower girl.

'And is everything sorted out?' Fliss asked.

'Everything except Alexa's dress.'

Everyone turned to look at me and Katie swept a long look over my figure.

'Hmm,' she said, 'that's going to be fun.'

I sucked my stomach in and forced a bright smile to my face. 'We'll be going shopping on Saturday. There are a couple of possibilities.'

'Really? Okay,' Katie said, sounding surprised while pouting sexily over her straw and giving Jerry a sultry look.

'God, is that Benedict Cumberbatch over there!' I exclaimed.

Katie whirled round, choking on her drink, and spent the

next few minutes spluttering, eyes streaming as Fliss thumped her on the back.

'Oh well, better be going,' I said airily.

* * *

We went shopping.

It wasn't what I would describe as fun.

India might have put on and triumphantly lost a few pounds but I had a new, larger bottom as a souvenir of my holiday. I needed to *Spring-Clean My Food Cupboards* as a matter of urgency. Now I knew I wasn't as slim as my sister – I had half her willpower and twice her appetite – but I didn't deserve this. Did I? Hmm. But I'd been making strides in the rest of my life: cleaner brain, cleaner house. I'd thrown away a disastrous suit and was feeling a bit more productive and together.

'What on earth are you *doing* in there?' India asked, obviously frustrated as I grappled with yet another dress. 'I mean does it look okay?'

As I couldn't get the zip done up the answer seemed to be no.

'Having a teeny bit of a struggle,' I said, thanking God there was a lockable door between us, not just a curtain, 'but it's not my colour anyway.'

'Blue? Blue's not your colour?' India said, incredulous. 'Half your wardrobe is blue. Well, try the other one.'

The other one was pink and had a crossover top, which I know is supposed to make the most of one's shape, but in this case it made me look as though I was trying to hide a couple of intercontinental ballistic missiles down the front of my dress.

'No,' I said after a few minutes of trying to arrange myself. Perhaps I had put it on the wrong way? Or back to front? Perhaps it wasn't the right style?

'Oh, for f's sake – look, try the flowery one then,' India said. There was a moment's pause and then: 'I bet I know what the matter is. You said you were going to lose weight before the wedding and you haven't, have you?'

'Shout a bit louder, India,' I muttered.

India knocked on the door. 'Look, it really doesn't matter. I'll just get a bigger size from the rail.'

'Oh yes, because I really want to be the fat bridesmaid on the end of the line,' I said.

'You're not fat,' she said rather too loudly.

'I'm never eating again,' I said crossly.

'Yes, that may well be the case but let's just get this dress sorted out. We haven't got long. Three weeks.'

'I know that, India!'

'Perhaps some magic knickers might help?'

'I've got magic knickers on *already*,' I said through clenched teeth. 'I can hardly breathe as it is.'

India sighed. 'Come on then, let's go and try somewhere else.'

'What like Millets or the camping shop?'

'No, that's not what I meant. Stop it this minute; you've got a gorgeous figure, much better than mine.' My jaw did drop at that one. 'I mean let's go further up the high street and try the shops in the arcade. There are a couple of new ones there. You never know,' she wheedled, and I gave in, because I knew we needed to find a dress; as much as I joked about it I couldn't wear jeans and a T-shirt.

I struggled into my clothes and came out of the changing room, red-faced and sweating.

'Shall we have coffee?' India asked gently. 'Just give you time to get your breath back?'

'No, I'd only have a cake and make the problem even worse,' I grumbled, still unable to shake my grumpy mood brought on by ill-fitting dresses that made me look like a sausage roll.

'Well, I'm parched; these shops are far too hot and everyone knows wedding dress sizes are based on Chinese women or something. Don't take any notice. I know we're going to find something fabulous today.'

We made our way to our favourite café, a place I adore as it's smothered in bunting and fairy lights with vintage china on the tables. India enjoyed hot chocolate while I had a cup of herb tea that tasted of something green and unpleasant.

'Just calm down,' India said kindly, 'we'll find something; we've hardly started looking yet.'

'I'm fine, I'm just annoyed with myself,' I said, sipping my

338

hot grass water. 'I have no one to blame but myself – that's the worst part.'

'Look there's still time. You could lose a few pounds before the wedding but that really doesn't matter. Let's just find something you like.'

'Or I could just put a bag on my head and turn up in my PJs and a dressing gown.'

'Now you're being silly.'

'Anyway the bridesmaid is supposed to look shit, then the bride looks better. And everyone will be looking at the flower girls anyway. Do you actually need me? I mean I wouldn't mind if you changed your mind.'

India gave me a look. 'Don't be ridiculous; of course I want you as a bridesmaid. In fact I'd rather ditch the flower girls. What I was thinking of, agreeing to have them in the first place, I don't know. They are without doubt three of the most irritating and silly little girls ever. Poppy and Scarlett are far too full of themselves and Maudie, while very photogenic, is still in nappies.'

The three little girls were going to be in cream silk dresses with palest gold sashes, dinky little kid leather shoes and flower halos so I knew India was trying to be kind. 'Oh, they're not; they are sweet, and they're going to look adorable.'

'And so will you, you wait,' India said, a certain steely look in her eye. 'We're going into shops where we don't normally go and we'll look with new eyes. We'll force them to have something, just by sheer willpower. We'll do some blue-sky thinking. We'll think outside the box. The perfect outfit is out there somewhere and we are going to find it! *Yes, we are!*'

She high-fived me with a battle cry of '*Team Fisher, yay!*'

India had seriously considered buying an outfit of white canvas, gilt-buttoned Nauticalia when we were on board the ship, so I had my doubts. Still, we went off for round two of pavement pounding and rack shuffling with new enthusiasm. Well, once I had stopped feeling a bit weird because of the grass tea, which was repeating on me rather unpleasantly.

I began to wish we were in America again where the larger customer is catered for and the customer service is far more ingratiating. In the next shop we went into the assistants actually laughed when they found out what we wanted.

'A bridesmaid's dress? Size fourteen, or possibly a sixteen? *Today? Really?*'

The two, thin (probably size eight) assistants peered at me and then at each other.

'Yes,' India said, grabbing hold of the back of my coat as I tried to edge towards the door. This sort of thing always got her riled. India fixed them with her best steely-eyed look and they shrivelled. 'I know you can help us –' she peered at their name badges '– Jodie and Sara. After all, your company slogan is *Right Dress, Right Time*, isn't it? Well, this is the right time, we just need the right dress.'

'Yes, but she hasn't got the right ...' The thin, huge-eyebrowed assistant didn't complete the sentence. Anyway, after India had hinted that we were guests at a *very* high-profile wedding, which might be featured in *Hello!*, the two girls did their best. To be fair they had some nice things in there and if only they had stocked the Right Size we might have had some success.

We pressed on with a new sense of purpose and I even began to enjoy myself a bit. We were a challenge. We were loud. We were annoying. We tried on loads of things that might have worked but weren't quite right. We began to lose the plot a bit and stray into outrageous. I even tried on a pair of dungarees with a frilly chiffon blouse underneath. (It looked quite good actually.) I think by then my blood sugar was dangerously low and I was distinctly light-headed so we went and had lunch.

Following the mantra you might as well be hanged for a sheep etc., I had a large glass of red wine, a chicken wrap and we shared a bowl of chunky chips. And then, realising we really did have to focus on the job in hand and were running out of options, we annoyed a woman in our biggest department store by finding the perfect dress, which they didn't stock in my size because it had been discontinued. Then we went down to the far end of the High Street where there was a selection of charity shops, bookmakers, ice cream shops and amusement arcades. We stood outside the dress equivalent of the last chance saloon. *Mary Dell*.

Mary Dell was the sort of shop I thought had disappeared years ago along with milliners, corsetieres and furriers. There were some dull-looking wedding dresses in the window, protected from the non-existent sunlight by blinds made from orange cellophane.

'I can't go in here,' I said.

'Why not?'

'Because it's the sort of place Mum would go in. No, Grandma. And come to think of it she'd probably be pretty reluctant.'

'Well, yes, after all she died fifteen years ago –'

'Yes, okay, Miss Pedantic.'

Inside there was a slightly strange-looking woman dressed in a dark blue dress with pins stuck into a pincushion on her wrist. Behind her was a terrifying woman in black with a tape measure around her neck and *Miss Dell* on her name badge.

'Do you have an appointment?' Miss Dell asked.

'No, sorry, I didn't know ...'

'Hmm.'

She looked into a large green leather diary on a shelf behind the till and riffled through a few pages making annoyed noises.

'What do you want?' she asked at last.

I bit back the impulse to ask for cod and chips twice.

'A bridesmaid's dress. For me. The wedding is three weeks today. Sorry.'

Miss Dell ruffled through a few more pages and huffed a bit while the woman in the dark blue dress dusted a china cake topping of a startled groom and watched me over the top of her glasses.

'Well, it's not very convenient,' Miss Dell said, 'but typical I suppose.'

I was hustled into the fitting rooms with all speed in case I was planning to escape and encouraged out of my jeans and shirt and into what Miss Dell described as a modesty robe. As I did so I fell back several decades.

Outside the fitting room India sat on the brocade chair trying not to snort with laughter, her ankles neatly crossed like a 1950s model.

Far from sneering at my figure, Miss Dell was, in her own way, rather excited.

'*Hmm.* It makes a change,' she said, writing down a few alarming-looking numbers. Were those my measurements or was she playing bingo?

'I have *something somewhere*,' she said at long last. 'You should have come in months ago. We could have made something more ...' She waved her hands, trying to express something.

'Yes,' I said, chastened. 'I was hoping to lose weight. I kept putting it off.'

'Hmm.'

At last she said she had a couple of ideas and was going to *look for something* but first she sent her assistant off to *the other room*. The woman wandered off and Miss Dell closed

343

the door firmly behind her. Evidently we could not be left alone with her, but whether she was concerned about our safety or her colleague's I wasn't sure. Then she went upstairs and left India and me sitting looking at each other.

'What do you think she's gone to look for?' India hissed.

'Heaven knows. A length of rope and some gaffer tape?'

'And what do you think is in *the other room?*'

'A spare bridegroom? A fossilised cake covered in cobwebs?'

I pulled the modesty robe around myself a bit tighter and India went to look at the eclectic mix of bridal ephemera laid out on the glass shelves behind the till.

'Look, a tiara! Who was it who said you had the face for a tiara? Someone on the ship, wasn't it?'

'Put it down!' I hissed. 'She'll be back in a minute and she'll catch you!'

'Are you sure you couldn't get into that pink dress in Monsoon?' India said. 'It was so pretty.'

'Not unless I can organise a breast reduction in the next couple of weeks,' I said, trying on the tiara and squinting at my reflection. 'Or I don't mind every bloke in the reception staring at my chest all evening.'

'Well, it's a reasonable question. Would you?'

'Yes, I would, India,' I replied.

'God, you're so difficult sometimes.'

Miss Dell was coming back downstairs so we both straightened up like a couple of naughty children. She was holding several dresses over one arm.

'I have four,' she said, 'and a small bet with myself.'

'Whether they'll fit or not?' I said.

'Hmm. Which one you'll buy. Of course they'll *fit*.'

And they did.

In fact two of them were rather lovely and in the end we chose a blue one that was floor-length, with lacy sleeves and a floating satin ribbon bow on the back. The most exciting part was it was a size twelve.

I gasped with excitement on seeing this. Miss Dell fixed me with a beady eye.

'Of course it's a US size,' she said with a humorous twist to her mouth. 'You mustn't look at labels.'

I started trying to work this out and quickly decided it would be to my disadvantage so I stopped thinking about it.

We watched as the silent woman in dark blue reappeared and packaged the dress into several layers of tissue and then stuffed it unceremoniously into a crumpled supermarket carrier.

'Right,' India said a few minutes later when we stood outside the shop, 'we deserve a drink. How about a cocktail?'

Chapter Twenty-Five

Especial Day

Blackberries, Rum, Martini Rosso, Pineapple Juice,
Crème de Mure, Bitters

The week before India's wedding day I descended into a funny sort of mood. Obviously I was thrilled for my sister and loved seeing her so happy, but at the same time I felt quite numb inside. Just sad I suppose.

I'd spent quite a long time looking at that selfie of me with Gabriel, wondering what he had been thinking and why he had sought me out for those magical few days. But of course life had carried on. There was always work, there would always be irritating clients and unexpected successes, but for the first time in a long time I wasn't fretting, nagging or overeating. Even with the wedding coming up, India was working harder and not making as many mistakes. Maybe we'd both needed a holiday to come back and feel fresh. It was almost fun

346

working with her in the office now. Tim seemed happier too since India and I weren't sniping at each other over doughnuts.

My parents came home from Australia with sunburnt arms and all sorts of tales. Mum seemed especially surprised to find no mess in the house and pretty much all of her food still exactly where she'd put it. India and Jerry bickered happily about his stag weekend in Wolverhampton (no, I've no idea why he went there either), there were last-minute hitches and choices to be made about the wedding. The traumatic decisions regarding hairstyles and shoes. None of it seemed to touch me deep inside. It was as though I was pining.

Yes, that was it – I was pining for Gabriel.

How ridiculous. I wasn't thirteen and in the throes of my first crush; I was nearly thirty and behaving like a complete prat.

I owed it to India to buck up a bit and join in. I would not think about Gabriel Frost again. I would jam my memories of him into a metaphorical canvas bag and sling it somewhere deep and dark. To make up for my neglect I made her take a few extra days off work so she could get her head around things and really concentrate on the last-minute wedding details.

Charlie Smith-Rivers from the Exeter office oiled his way over the Wednesday before the wedding. He was due to take over from me for a couple of days anyway, and he never missed an opportunity to: 1) stress his importance in helping out the 'girls' and 2) stare at my chest.

'So you'll be next,' Charlie said smoothly.

'Next what?' I asked distractedly as I searched for a brochure on my tidy but somehow still not perfectly ordered desk.

I'd been stressing about some floor plans all week. Never particularly accurate, it was a wonder the clients hadn't dispensed with our services. I wasn't in the mood for Charlie's banter.

'Next into the blessed institution.'

'You're going into a home?' I said, being deliberately difficult.

'No, the institution of marriage,' he said patiently.

I waited, resigned, for the punchline, which wasn't long in coming.

'But who wants to live in an institution? Hahaha! Twenty-eight years I've been married to the little girlie. Or it might be twenty-nine. The Great Train Robbers got less.'

God, Charlie, don't give up the day job.

'I can't understand why a lovely girl like you hasn't been snapped up long ago,' he continued, rubbing his hands together. 'I can't think what the matter is with young men today.'

'Me neither, Charlie,' I retorted.

'So, not got any nice young chap to take to the wedding as your plus-one?'

Why were people so obsessed with this? Why did it matter if I went on my own?

'No, I'm in charge of three flower girls,' I said. 'That's far more fun than watching some random boyfriend get plastered, isn't it?'

'If you say so.'

Charlie went and looked out of the window at the traffic. 'What happened to that chap you were shacked up with? Jack or Jim?'

'Ryan,' I said, bristling a little at the term shacked up, which we weren't because I never moved in with him.

'That's the fellow.'

'He wanted to marry me but I said no. So the next day he went and walked into the sea off Woolacombe.'

Charlie wheeled round. 'Good God, really?'

'Absolutely.' I nodded, keeping my face as honest as possible.

'What a dreadful tragedy!'

'No, not really. He did have a wetsuit and surfboard at the time.'

'Oh.'

Behind him Tim snorted his amusement and I carried on typing at high speed, hoping to put Charlie off. By the middle of the afternoon I'd had enough and was checking my watch every five minutes.

Even Charlie noticed.

'Look, why don't you hop off home? I'm sure there must be lots to do. I'll hold the fort for the last hour or so.'

'Would you?' I felt a sudden burst of relief; perhaps I should try and be nicer to him. 'Really?'

'Sure, off you go. I mean I'm sure you have things to try

on –' he looked a bit misty-eyed for a moment '– stockings and the like.'

I collected my things together and put my coat on. Outside the afternoon was dark and miserable with rain pelting down the window. What had possessed India to have a wedding in December?

As I opened the door to leave, the phone on my desk rang and I hesitated.

Charlie waved me off. 'I'll get that, don't give it a thought.'

He picked up my extension. 'Fisher Estate Agents, Charles Smith-Rivers speaking, how can I help? Yes, that's right. Yes, she does. Yes, indeed. No, can I help?'

I raised my eyebrows at him and he imperiously waved me away again with his spare hand, mouthing *it's okay*. So I opened my umbrella and fled.

*

The weather on India's wedding day was slightly better but we still woke to grey skies and blustery winds. Thank heavens India had been talked out of having a marquee on the lawn or we would have been chasing it down the valley as it ripped from its moorings. Anyway, The Manor House was all ready for us and the church was decorated with as many hothouse flowers as the florists could jam into it. All we had to do was get India to the church.

Luckily the ceremony wasn't until two-thirty because, as

I've said, India is not a morning person. We'd been up quite late too as she'd decided she wanted us to share a room on her *last night of freedom*. Her words not mine. You would have thought she was going to prison in the morning, not getting married.

After we had spent an hour trying to remember India's past boyfriends in chronological order, she decided she needed some champagne 'to help her sleep' and crept downstairs to find some. She returned a few minutes later with two glasses and a bottle with a very important-looking orange label that I'm sure she shouldn't have taken.

'I think it's about time you got married too,' India said a few minutes later.

'Okay, I'll try harder,' I said with a laugh.

India sipped her champagne and looked thoughtful.

'I know I've been a cow to you sometimes. I don't mean it, not really. You've been a great sister.' She sniffled a bit at this as if she was getting emotional. Perhaps it was the champagne. 'I mean I'll never forget that fight you had with Lou Beddard, remember? When she chucked my packed lunch on to the gym roof.'

'Lou Beddard?'

'You must remember! I was in year eight. She'd been making my life a misery for ages until you sorted her out. My friends thought you were like a *god*.'

'Lou Beddard?'

'In my year, spotty, incredibly hairy legs and arms. When

we went into summer uniform she looked like a werewolf in a frock. And I'm sorry about that time when I locked you in the cupboard under the stairs.'

'That was about twenty years ago,' I said. 'I'd forgotten that.'

'I know, and I'm sorry. And I did lose the bits out of your *Polly Pocket*.'

'You swore you didn't!'

'Well, I did,' India confessed.

I thought about it. 'If we're in the mood for confessions, remember your imitation pink pearl necklace?'

'Yes, I never did find out what happened to it.'

'The string broke and I hid the beads under the carpet in the spare room,' I said.

'You rat! You swore blind you didn't take it! I thought so!'

We sat in silence for a few minutes and then India hopped out of bed and went to fetch something from the wardrobe. She handed me a carrier bag inside which was something wrapped in tissue paper.

'What's this?'

'I thought you should wear this tomorrow. You're supposed to give the bridesmaids something, aren't you? I saw it in the shop where we bought your bridesmaid's dress and I remembered what Ike said. Or was it Marion?'

I unwrapped the parcel. I gasped. It was a tiara. Quite small and pretty with a fair amount of twinkle involved and two tiny enamelled bluebirds in the middle.

'Oh gosh, Indie, thank you!' I put it on and went to admire it in the dressing table mirror.

'It suits you.' India giggled. 'Especially with your Bagpuss pyjamas.'

'Perhaps I should wear these tomorrow?'

'Perhaps you should!'

'Thank you!' I was quite overwhelmed for a moment.

I went across to give India a hug, both of us rather stiff and a bit awkward. It felt nice, like it should feel when you hug your sister, and we both laughed.

'S'okay,' India said.

I got back into bed still wearing it.

'So. Are you ever going to tell me what happened at Laura's party, with Ryan?'

I don't know what made me ask it, but somewhere deep inside I still needed to know. I'd been so mad at her after Ryan had said she'd made a pass at him, but now I could see how stupid that was. He was a lying, cheating bastard. Why should I ever have trusted him?

India paused, her mouth open.

'He made a pass at me. He did a bit of back rubbing, you know? The way he did? And then stuck his tongue down my throat and his hand up my skirt. He really was a shit. What did you see in him?'

'I can't remember.'

'And what about Gabriel Frost?' she asked, a cheeky grin in place.

I tried to sound vague. 'What about him?'

'He was nice. I don't know what might have happened that day with Liam if he hadn't been there. You liked him too, didn't you?'

'Yeah, I suppose so,' I said, topping up her glass and wondering how to change the subject.

'I'm sorry,' she said.

'Not your fault. What's important is that you and Jerry are happy.'

'Oh, we will be happy,' India said confidently, draining her glass. 'I've no doubt about that.'

We settled down to sleep soon after that. Just before I fell asleep India rustled about for a bit, and I could tell by her breathing she was still awake.

'I do love you,' she said, very quietly.

And I smiled. Yep, we were sisters and nothing was going to change that.

*

The following morning I dragged her out of bed at seven o'clock and she went to shower and pull her dressing gown on before the hairdresser arrived with enough boxes of brushes, rollers and hairpins to style the Miss World entrants.

'I can't think straight,' India said. 'I'm starving but I can't eat anything. Do you think this is last-minute nerves?'

'Yes, probably.' I was trowelling on my make-up in an

attempt to look less weary. 'I pity your poor husband; you snore like a rhinoceros.'

'Ha! You can talk,' India said.

I thought about this as I layered on mascara. I stopped and looked rather sadly at my reflection. Maybe my lack of self-discipline and untidiness and general sloppiness regarding getting the ironing done was too much for any man to tolerate? Perhaps Marnie's *Spring-Cleaning* business had something going for it. But on the other hand ...

I took stock. I was okay – I think I was anyway. If I snored and couldn't get to the bottom of the ironing basket, so what? If I didn't always make my bed properly and was a teeny bit overweight then so be it. It meant there was more of me to love. I was me: unstructured, a bit crackers, prone to excessive chocolate consumption on occasion, and well known for crying at Christmas films.

This was going to be an exciting and happy day. Today was my sister's wedding. I was going to be her bridesmaid and chief helper. For the first time in years we were getting along. I just needed to keep it all together. I had flower girls to marshal. I had a nice blue dress to wear that flattered my figure and hid the damage caused to it on the *Reine de France*. Lots of our friends and relations were going to be there. It was quite possible some of them wouldn't ask why I wasn't married yet. There was going to be cake. (Albeit slightly bashed about. We'd had to repair it when it fell over in the van on the way to The Manor House, crushing some of the sugar roses.) I did not need to obsessively google Marnie Miller any more to find out what she was doing (holidaying in Gstaad). I had absolutely no need to look at the picture of Gabriel Frost on my phone again.

Well, perhaps just once.

*

If I'd had to guess what sort of wedding dress India would choose it would have been something sleek and sort of cool. I never imagined she'd choose an off-the-shoulder, retro vintage one with a froth of underskirts, petticoats and a nipped-in waist that made her look rather like Audrey Hepburn in *Roman Holiday*. (The bit when she's dressed as the princess, not the bit when she's on the back of Gregory Peck's scooter.) She looked fabulous and when I saw her coming downstairs with Dad I'll admit I teared up a bit. And I'd been there when she chose it so it wasn't as though I'd never seen it before.

She came and stood next to me and, without looking at me, grabbed my hand.

'You should find someone nice now, Al,' she said.

'Oh well, never mind!' I said, trying to sound confident and jolly. 'You're the clever, pretty, thin one.'

'I do mind. I mind because you're nicer than I am,' India said. 'You always have been.'

We looked at each other and I think we both would have

burst into tears if the prospect of redoing our make-up hadn't stopped us.

'Oh, shut up,' I said.

India grinned. 'You shut up.'

'Million times more than you ever say,' I said.

'Plus one.'

*

The church was only half a mile away from our house and on a good day I guess we could have walked it, but it was raining, the lanes were muddy and by the time we'd wedged India and her petticoats into the car she was almost mute with nerves.

This was not something that happened. I mean the being mute bit. India was always the loudest voice in the playground, the one with the annoying laugh at the cinema and the first one to start singing at a birthday party.

We got to the church to see some of Jerry's barrister friends hanging around under the lychgate smoking, just like they did outside court. Honestly, they were supposed to be intelligent – they should have known better. When they saw us they stubbed out their fags in the fire bucket and scarpered inside pretty quickly to tell Jerry that his bride had arrived. Then there was just time for a few photographs, with Dad looking startled by the whole thing, before we went in. There we found our cousins Cathie and Leila trying to control their flower girl daughters. I straightened India's skirts, adjusted her bouquet so the elderly aunts wouldn't think she was pregnant and got the flower girls into a reasonably straight line behind her before we set off towards Jerry and her date with destiny.

The church was almost full. There was a wonderful scent of greenery and perfume and a terrific display of hats and fascinators just as India had wanted. At the front I could see the extravagant riot of lilac feathers that marked where Mum was sitting. I walked slowly forwards, trying gamely to hang on to my shoes, which were very slightly too large, keep the three flower girls together so they didn't dash off when they saw their mothers scuttling down the side of the pews, and keep my own bouquet of white roses and blue hydrangeas the right way up.

We all took a collective deep breath and India looked round at me and winked.

'Okay, kid?' she said, and I almost wanted to cry. I was suddenly so happy for her.

At the front of the church I could see Jerry's narrow head with his dark hair sleeked back and next to him his crazy best man, Mark. As the 'Wedding March' began, Dad and India started forwards and mercifully the three flower girls were sufficiently overawed to follow without making a fuss.

I looked around the congregation, recognising school friends, aged aunts, India's university chums and some of our many cousins who were all bobbing about and turning to see her. Over by the font I could see Tim, and Charlie and his wife. At the end of one pew I recognised Mum's sister, Fiona, under an alarming green feather fascinator, and just beyond them Dad's brother, Paul, with one arm in a sling following a recent argument with a brick wall.

There was a large woman in pink I didn't recognise, smiling and nodding at me, and next to her was Gabriel Frost.

Chapter Twenty-Six

Looks Familiar

Single Malt, Silver Tequila, Agave Syrup, Angostura Bitters

It took me a moment to process this information and I walked on for a few steps, hardly breathing.

I looked again. It was him. It was definitely him. It was Gabriel.

He was wearing a dark suit, a white shirt and a beautiful crimson tie just as stylish and gorgeous as I'd imagined. Our gazes locked for a moment and I felt a quite astonishing thrill of excitement run straight through me. *Why and how was he here?*

India had reached Jerry by this point and I had to spring into action, stopping the flower girls from trampling on the back of India's shoes and herding them towards their mothers so that I could take India's bouquet.

'Dearly beloved.'

I stood in a sort of stupor behind India while the vicar went through the service.

'Do you Jeremy St John Cholmondley Sinclair ...'

Cholmondley?

Gabriel was in the church, just a few steps away from me. But what was he doing here? How did he know? How had he got here? Why was he here?

'Do you India Mary Fisher ...'

It was surreal, it was incredible, it was wonderful.

'... to have and to hold from this day forward ...'

I wanted to turn round; I wanted to look at him again to make sure he was still there, that I hadn't imagined it. I could feel his eyes on me, I was sure of it. Why was he here?

I forced myself to concentrate; my sister was getting married. It was a special and wonderful moment.

I shouldn't be thinking about Gabriel Frost and remembering the feel of him. That moment when I thought he needed me, that I loved him. My mind carried on recalling more and more erotic details.

I shouldn't be standing in church remembering how Gabriel had gently bitten my neck, run his tongue over my breast, how he had tasted, smelled.

Ashamed, I looked up at the disapproving face of St John the Baptist in the stained-glass window in front of us and waited to be struck by lightning.

By now the vicar was rousing himself to a veritable pitch as he held India's and Jerry's hands between his.

'Those whom God hath put together, let no man put asunder.'

There was a sudden cheer from the herd of barristers and applause echoed around the church and grew in volume as Jerry beamed down at India and kissed her.

I shouldn't think any man would put this couple asunder; they were so perfectly, wonderfully matched. They each thought the other was wonderful despite knowing their faults and having lived together for over a year. Jerry knew India couldn't be left alone with a box of chocolates and as he had trouble remembering his own birthday he would probably never remember hers.

One of Jerry's friends from his chambers came forward to play something rather lovely on the piano while we went into the vestry so the newlyweds could sign the register. India was wild with happiness and couldn't stop grinning while Jerry was obviously a bit emotional and kept dabbing his top lip with his handkerchief and saying 'Gosh' as though he couldn't believe his luck.

I stood watching them as they posed for the traditional signing-the-register photographs and India looked up at me with a wicked grin.

She came over and hugged me and I congratulated her.

'You okay?' she said.

'You knew he was going to be here, didn't you?'

India laughed. 'I told him where I was getting married and when. Then I left it up to him. Apparently he spoke to Charlie the other day, in the office.'

I remembered it now, Charlie waving me off early as he answered the phone.

'*Yes, that's right. Yes, she does. Yes, indeed.*'

Well, blow me down! Surely he hadn't come back from America just for this?

Hang on, I had been angry with Gabriel, hadn't I?

Should I be this pleased to see him again? No, I shouldn't. And yet I was giddy with wanting to get back into the church, this time facing the congregation so I could see if Gabriel really was there or if I'd imagined it.

He was there.

It was true.

Jerry and India fairly skipped down the nave of the church, India waving her bouquet triumphantly above her head. Happily the two bigger flower girls had stayed with their mother as she had produced cartons of squash, and the smaller one, Maudie, was busy lying on the floor having a tantrum because she only had water. I walked out next to Mark, the best man, my arm linked through his, and Gabriel's was the first face I saw.

Thank heavens it was raining. It meant we would have to go straight to the reception rather than stand in the churchyard having photos taken. Anyway Maudie was now red-faced and howling because she had seen the other two having crisps, so Jerry and India nipped into their posh car and were driven away.

I felt a hand on my arm, warm through my lacy sleeve, and I turned.

'Can I give you a lift?' Gabriel said.

I looked up at him and couldn't think what to say. I mean not even a vague sort of hello. I was suddenly aware my mouth had dropped open and I probably looked like a complete moron.

He steered me gently out of the church and put up a huge black umbrella to shield me from the rain. Then we got into his car (dark blue Aston Martin, pale leather seats, my absolute dream car) and he started the engine.

As we waited for the other cars in front of us to move he turned to me.

'You look wonderful,' he said. 'You're even more beautiful than I remember.'

'Oh,' I said, wondering for a split second who else was in the car with us.

*

The Manor House was a gorgeous old place, once home to a family who had slept with the right people and fought on the winning side in the seventeenth century. Now it was a beautifully refurbished and very elegant hotel. We swished up through the gates in fine style. Gabriel dropped me by the front door and went to park the car. A line of waitresses waited in the marble-floored hallway with glasses of champagne and trays of canapés. I skirted round the nibbles, even though they did look rather spectacular, and took two glasses of champagne. I knocked one back in record time and hid the glass behind a clock on the mantelpiece before anyone noticed. I knew India and Jerry were already in the dining room because I could hear India exclaiming how lovely everything looked and Jerry laughing like a lunatic. I sipped my other glass of champagne and went in.

'Looks absolutely fantastic,' I said.

India span round. 'You've not lost Gabriel already?'

'No, I bloody haven't! He's gone to park the car.'

'Nice surprise?' She hunched her shoulders at me in delight, the same way she used to when she watched me open my birthday presents.

'I think so. Yes, just a bit of a shock,' I said.

'Well, I got fed up with seeing you so miserable. At least this way you can talk to him and see what's what. Doesn't it look great in here? I mean *so pretty!*'

We stood side by side looking at the array of round tables covered in pale blue cloths, the silver cutlery glinting in the lights from the candelabra overhead. There were white flowers threaded with fairy lights on every table and sparkling silver confetti scattered round each place setting. It looked magical.

'It's wonderful,' I said, sliding my arm through hers, 'really beautiful.'

'I'm so happy,' she said, with a funny little bob of her head. 'Everything is fabulous. I'm bubbling inside! I'm married to the most wonderful man in the world. I just want everyone to feel like this! And I want you to be this happy too.'

'I'll do my best,' I said.

'Do better than that,' India said. 'Ooh, look, Aslan is on the move. Gabriel's back. Over there by the cake. My word, I suppose he's not bad-looking, is he? Hang on, Mum's coming over. I'll head her off as long as I can.'

Not bad-looking? There wasn't a woman in the place who didn't turn and look at Gabriel as he walked across the room. In his gorgeous dark suit and with his hair shining under the lights he looked fabulous. Three waitresses nearly collided with each other in their haste to serve him and I even saw Mum and my Great-Aunt Audrey give him the once-over before India took them both away to help her with something. What the hell was he doing making a determined beeline for me?

Anyway.

He scooped up two glasses of champagne and got to my side, his movements graceful and unhurried. He held out a glass to me and I took it, wondering if I was going to last the afternoon without dropping my meal down my dress, bursting into tears or saying something embarrassing.

'You look fabulous,' he said with a smile at India. 'Congratulations.'

'Thanks,' India said. 'Oops, I'd better go and ... you know ... um, do that thing we were talking about.'

'What thing?' I said.

'That *thing*,' India said, hurrying off as fast as her high heels would allow.

'Well, cheers.' Gabriel and I clinked glasses and he took a sip of champagne.

'I didn't expect to see you here,' I said. 'India says it was her idea.'

'It was mine actually,' Gabriel said. 'She just gave me enough information to track you down. I never did ask for your phone number or address, did I?'

'No, I assumed you didn't want them.'

'Always a risk to assume that sort of thing, Alexa,' he said as he bent towards me so that his breath stirred my hair. 'I wanted them a great deal.'

His voice was low and slightly husky and I felt the most incredible clench of lust.

I was going to fall over; my legs were suddenly weak.

I gave a little whimper at the back of my throat.

He touched my arm. 'By the way, you have no right to be more beautiful than the bride. It's not done.'

I couldn't speak for a moment and busied myself straightening a knife on one of the tables so I didn't have to look at him. I wanted to be cool and sensible and not draw attention to myself. But at the same time it would have been nice to start a sophisticated and interesting conversation that would make him laugh so that other people would look over and see me with this amazing man. Then I wouldn't be the gooseberry on the Smug Marrieds' table as I was fully expecting to be.

Out of the corner of my eye I could see people watching

us. It was only a matter of time before someone cracked, came over and asked to be introduced. From then on I would have to share Gabriel with all the other women who were probably dribbling at the sight of him.

Unfortunately it was proving very difficult to be cool and sensible because I was having the most startling flashbacks. Remembering being in bed with him, the feel of his breath on my neck, his hands on my skin. I didn't want to introduce Gabriel Frost to anyone, or make small talk about the hotel or the flowers or the meal. I wanted him to kiss me. I wanted to go upstairs with him. I wanted to completely abdicate all my bridesmaid's duties and spend the rest of the day in bed with him. Preferably in one of the fabulous, four-poster rooms with the vast en-suite bathrooms I'd seen on the hotel website. The sort of rooms that are so gorgeous you know you'll be comfortable and have a lovely time in them. There would be beautifully co-ordinated cushions all over the place and massive tassels on the curtain tiebacks. The sort of room where you were guaranteed fantastic sex and would probably lose a dress size as you walked in through the door. One of those rooms.

He touched the small of my back with his hand and I melted towards him in a pathetically unsophisticated way. Let's be honest, he was the sexiest, most fabulous, most gorgeous man I'd ever seen and I couldn't wait to …

Hang on a cotton-picking moment!

There was something I was forgetting, wasn't there? There was the shadow of Marnie Miller standing next to him with

368

that pleased cat smile she had. I'd been furious, hadn't I, when I saw her with him? And miserably jealous. The divorce. Her dear friend Gabriel. What was he doing here, in a small country house hotel, with me at my sister's wedding? I mean it wasn't as though we had royalty among the guests. I wasn't aware India had struck a deal with *Hello!* magazine for the photo rights.

I stiffened my spine and steadied myself.

'So, last time I saw you was in the papers with Marnie. Her divorce from the perfect Leo? How's that going then?'

His face clouded. I'd said something wrong, something that had spoiled the mood between us. But I didn't care. I didn't want to be a fool, not again.

'I told you I was her lawyer.'

'And it's all going well?'

'It depends what you mean by well,' Gabriel said. 'No divorce is fun.'

No, I thought, particularly when it turns nasty.

'So introduce us, why don't you?'

I turned to see Lola, one of the PAs from Jerry's work, standing with a hungry expression directed at Gabriel. She looked a strange mixture of drag queen and nun and had come to the wedding in a flowing grey and white dress accesorised with blood-red nails and lipstick.

'Lola, this is a friend of mine: Gabriel Frost.'

Lola shook Gabriel's hand with a white claw and manoeuvred herself in between us.

'Oh, you're American? I love that special relationship between our two great nations,' she purred.

'Well, I'm not actually American, but yes,' he said, 'great, isn't it?'

'I must introduce you to a friend of mine.' She looked around the room. 'Her name's Georgia and she loves everything American.'

'How wonderful.' Gabriel moved smoothly around behind her and took my arm. 'Perhaps later – we should go and give our congratulations to the groom first.'

We went over to where India and Jerry were standing by a glorious flower arrangement, accepting compliments and kisses from their guests.

India's face lit up when she saw Gabriel.

'All going well?' she asked.

I interrupted quickly. 'So, India, is there anything you need me to do?'

'No, I don't think so.' She looked around vaguely. 'Just look after Gabriel. He's on your table, by the way, under the name Captain Hornblower.'

Jerry leaned forward and shook Gabriel's hand.

'So *this* is the famous Gabriel Frost,' he said. 'We meet at last!'

Oh, great.

'Aren't you going to introduce me?' It was Mum, standing with her most inquisitive look on her face. 'Is this the chap India was telling me about?'

Mum, don't …

'She's been almost unbearable because of you. She thinks I don't know but I can tell. I hope you're going to bring a smile to her face?'

Mum, shut up …

'I hope so too. This is a beautiful wedding,' Gabriel said. 'Thank you for inviting me.'

'Oh, it's always nice to meet Alexa's friends.' Mum gave him a slightly hard look. 'We'll have a really good chat later.'

'I'd like that, thank you,' Gabriel said, and mercifully Mum was dragged off to have some more photos taken.

Jerry was watching Gabriel with a rather penetrating gaze that I bet he'd perfected in court.

'Thank you for inviting me,' Gabriel said, shaking Jerry's hand.

'Our pleasure,' Jerry said, thankfully distracted by one of his fellow barristers who was bringing him a present that was beautifully wrapped but very obviously a wheelbarrow. Why would they need that? They lived in a second-floor apartment without so much as a window box.

'Sebby! You old git! Just what we need,' Jerry said, obviously delighted.

'So tell me what you've been doing?' Gabriel asked, leaning closer to me than was actually necessary, but it was deliriously nice.

We had gone out of the main room into the conservatory where it was quieter and there was even more champagne.

I tried to think what I had been doing for the last few weeks. Could I make up something exciting? Bungee jumping? Being able to fold a towel into a pterodactyl?

'Well, there's been the wedding to organise of course. That's taken up most of my time. There was a problem with the hydrangeas at the florist's being pink instead of blue, which had to be sorted; bridesmaid's dress to be bought.'

I swept a hand down my dress to indicate how successful we had been.

'You look wonderful.'

'I do?' He'd already said it, but I felt like I needed the confirmation.

Gabriel nodded.

A waitress came towards us with a tray of canapés. Mushroom something. I picked one up and wondered if I could manage to eat it without dropping it down the front of my dress. Of course the only way not to do this was to eat it in one go.

'So apart from the shopping and wedding, how are you?' Gabriel asked again. 'Done any *Spring-Cleaning*?' He grinned down at me.

I made sort of hmm-hmming noises as I chewed frantically. I swallowed and took a gulp of champagne rather too quickly so I spluttered a bit. My word, I was excelling myself in the *cool and sensible* behaviour stakes.

'Catching up on work – I've not really had time to do much else.'

A flake of pastry had stuck in my throat and my voice was high and squeaky.

Actually I had mislaid my seagull-decorated notebook. I thought it might still be in my suitcase along with more sugar sachets, nicked biros and free shampoo from the cabin bathroom.

Out of the corner of my eye I could see Lola and Georgia edging towards us. I turned and looked at them and they stopped. Only to start moving again when I looked away. It was like a sort of Grandma's Footsteps game for grown-ups. Outside the rain was hammering down; there was no way I could escape out there.

'That's a pity,' he said. 'I thought you might have a lot to write about.'

'You did?'

'You're certainly very imaginative as I recall.'

I looked up at him and his grey eyes twinkled. I bet we were both remembering the same thing. I'd found a blindfold by the side of his bed and some ... well, never mind; now that *had* been fun.

I stifled a giggle.

Just as Lola reached us there was the sound of a gong being struck and we were saved from her because we were all called in for the wedding breakfast. The December afternoon was dark outside now and the fairy lights on each table were sparkling. It looked wonderful.

I found my seat and gave a little excited jump inside when Gabriel took the seat next to me.

A few minutes later, at the front of the room, my father banged on the table with a spoon, calling for silence before he introduced India and Jerry and the two of them swept triumphantly into the room to loud cheers.

It was a lovely meal. India and Jerry had haggled over it for weeks. We were sharing the table with two couples from Jerry's work who India always referred to as the Smug Marrieds. They all kept up a loud, cheerful stream of chatter, helped by the steady flow of wine.

At last I began to relax but of course the Smug Marrieds weren't called that for nothing and, sensing some easy prey on the table, they started to tell us how they had met (Internet for one couple and blind date for the other so hardly ground-breaking), then one of them – a Very Smug Married in a tight purple satin dress that showed just how bony her chest was – turned her gimlet gaze on me.

'So how did you two meet?'

Deadly question. Luckily Gabriel took up the challenge.

'Drawn together by a love of literature,' he said.

'*Rahlly?* How fascinating! Do tell!' Mrs VSM said, leaning her chin on her hand and fluttering her eyelash extensions at Gabriel.

'I was in a high-security jail and Alexa was a prison visitor.'

Mrs VSM backed away a bit, her eyes like saucers. '*Rahlly?*'

Gabriel took pity on her. 'No, we met on the *Reine de France*.'

'The transatlantic liner,' I added.

'Oh yes, I always think that must be the most tedious of holidays. I had a nanny once who went on them with her boyfriend. Tattoos, wife-beater vests. It sounded ghastly.'

Mr and Mrs VSM turned to each other with knowing looks.

'I don't think we've met,' said the man sitting next to me, holding out a hand. 'I'm Buzz Aldrin.'

He couldn't be. I'd seen Buzz Aldrin on TV only recently advertising porridge and he was about eighty.

'Basil actually,' said his wife, sensing my confusion, 'but everyone calls him Buzz. I'm Angie. Doesn't India look a picture?'

'Gorgeous, so happy too.'

'And married so young! What is she, twenty-four? Twenty-five?'

'Twenty-six,' I said.

'You'll be next then,' Mrs VSM put in, with a knowing look.

'You married, Gabriel?' her husband said.

'I'm divorced. Still looking for the right girl.'

'Me too.' Mr VSM guffawed, earning himself a poisonous look from his wife.

I almost stopped breathing.

Chapter Twenty-Seven

The Last Word

Dry Gin, Green Chartreuse,
Maraschino Liqueur, Lime Juice

I took a deep breath. It didn't matter. I had almost been over him anyway. Hadn't I? I didn't care that he had turned up again with his smooth lies, throwing me into a hormonal spin like this. Did I? No. I could deal with this in a sensible and adult way. Who cared if he was gorgeous and sexy and at that moment touching my hand with his to attract my attention?

'What do you think?' he said.

I had no idea what he had been talking about so I took a sip of my water and shrugged.

'So?' He looked confused.

'Sorry, what did you say? I wasn't really listening,' I said.

He laughed and my heart did a funny little flip at the way his eyes sparkled.

'No, I didn't think you were. I asked if I could take you out to dinner tomorrow.'

'Oh well, yes, no, yes, actually I'm not – you know how it is after a wedding. There's always a lot to do. Things to clear up and stuff.'

I was feeling rather hot and bothered by this point and growing intensely aware of his hand on mine. He'd left it there and was now very gently stroking the backs of my fingers with his. I gave a tiny whimper and pulled my hand away, pretending I needed to top up my full water glass.

A waiter took my plate away. I think it was a smoked salmon thing for the starter and a moment later he brought me a lamb thing. It really did look rather splendid, with all sorts of jus spots and tiny gel cubes on the plate. It reminded me of the meals we had enjoyed on the *Reine de France* and I felt suddenly very nostalgic for those few days when I had been so confused and yet so happy at the same time. I don't think I had slept properly or felt quite normal since.

'So, what do you do, Gabriel?' Angie said.

'I'm a lawyer.'

'Goodness, how thrilling. Do you do trials and send people to prison?'

'Well, not often. I specialise in divorce.'

'I say, I couldn't have your card, could I?' Mr VSM said smoothly. 'Ow!'

I think his wife kicked him under the table at this point.

'And have you done any famous people's divorces?' Angie asked.

'No, not really. Most of them are pretty run of the mill. Anyway, if I did, I wouldn't be able to tell you about them, client confidentiality being what it is,' Gabriel said, winking at them. 'But tell me about you, Angie. What do you do?'

'She pretends she's my PA,' Buzz said, 'but in fact she's a personal shopper with one client. Herself.'

'Oooh, someone's grumpy,' Angie said, not at all offended. 'I do have the house to look after and the children. Three of them,' she said, reaching for her phone and flicking to her photos. 'There, aren't they absolutely divine? Mila is ten, Winifred is eight and Ena is four. My girls are so amazing.'

I looked at a photograph of three fairly ordinary-looking girls covered in chocolate, pulling faces at the camera.

'Wonderful,' I said, 'and unusual names.'

Angie smiled while Buzz rolled his eyes and said *Ena, honest to God … why not just call her Old Lady and be done with it?* under his breath.

They then proceeded to have a tense and very quiet argument about their children's names, which resulted in Angie stalking off to the ladies' loo, her mouth in a grim line of fury.

Mrs VSM threw her napkin down on the table.

'Honest to God, Buzz, can't you let it drop?'

She went off after Angie with a martyred expression, wobbling slightly on her stilettos.

'You're right not to rush into getting remarried, Gabriel,' Mr VSM said, watching her go. 'They promise you the earth to get you to marry them and then they turn into their mothers. Women are a frigging nightmare.'

'Not all women,' I said, indignant.

'Oh, present company excepted,' Mr VSM said with a vague wave of his hand.

'Some men can be a nightmare too, especially the ones who lie.'

There was a moment's silence around the table.

'That was mistaken identity,' Mr VSM said rather heatedly. 'I explained that at the time. That woman was absolutely barking. It wasn't me and it couldn't have been because I was away in Nottingham at the time. For fuck's sake, is she still banging on about that?'

He got up and stamped out of the reception, fumbling in his pocket for his cigarettes. That just left the three of us and after a moment Buzz went off to the loo.

Gabriel and I looked at each other.

'What was all that about?' he asked.

'I have absolutely no idea,' I said. 'Evidently I touched a nerve.'

'Evidently! More wine? We seem to have plenty between us.' He topped up my glass. It was jolly nice wine too, very cold and dry Pinot Grigio; I took a sip, enjoying the iciness.

'But you knew he'd been cheating?' Gabriel said.

'I had no idea!'

'So the comment about men lying?'

'I meant you,' I said, draining my glass and reaching for the bottle. If we were going to have an argument I might as well do it pissed.

'Me?'

'All that *never met the right girl* business. It's not true, is it? I know about Elsa and the nasty divorce.'

I looked at him, waiting for him to explain, crumble, or at least look a bit guilty. He did none of those things.

'Sorry?'

'Yes, all that pretence, all that smooth talking so you could get me into bed. I know all about the divorce and how you're never going to get over her.'

'What are you talking about?'

'The nasty divorce. And the children having to go into therapy.'

'Children? Therapy?'

'Will you please stop repeating everything I say? It's very annoying,' I snapped.

The waiter was back and he cleared our plates away. When he left Gabriel leaned towards me.

'I have absolutely no idea where you've got these ideas from,' he whispered.

'No, well, you would say that.'

The waiter brought us bowls of profiteroles and at the same time the four others returned to the table looking rather shamefaced.

'Sorry about that,' Buzz said with a hearty chuckle. 'Mmm, this looks scrummy. My favourite.'

'I think you and I need to talk,' Gabriel said quietly, but in a tone that I didn't think meant I had an option.

'Yes,' I said, pushing my profiteroles around the plate with a careless spoon. There was no way I could eat them. Inside I was all sort of clenched and excited in a really odd way. What emotions was this reawakening in me? What had I started?

Then of course there were speeches. Dad, very brusque and a bit weepy, describing India and how she had been a joy and delight all her life.

At this India snorted with laughter. 'You're thinking of someone else, Dad.'

And everyone chuckled in that sort of good-natured way they do when they're happy and slightly drunk.

Then Jerry, overexcited and emotional. Introducing 'my wife and I' and grinning at the huge cheer from everyone. Proposing a toast to the bridesmaid and flower girls. By now two of the flower girls were making a den under a table, their silk dresses crushed and grubby. The youngest – clutching a blue rabbit in one hand and a bread roll in the other – was asleep in a buggy next to her mother. Which of course meant everyone turned and stared at me. I could feel myself blushing.

India's sister.

Who is that with her?

Very nice – why isn't she married yet?

I could feel my cheeks burning. I wished I could have slid under the table with Poppy and Scarlett. Next to me, Gabriel was joining in the applause with a broad grin on his face as though he could imagine my embarrassment, our tense exchange seemingly on hold for now.

Then it was the turn of Jerry's best man, Mark – tall, dapper and excruciatingly funny. Everyone turned in their seats to watch him as he asked for the lights to be dimmed, brought out a laptop and proceeded to give a very professional PowerPoint presentation on Jerry's character, behaviour in chambers and stag weekend in Wolverhampton. I still couldn't understand why they had chosen to go there when they could have gone to Vegas or Monaco or anywhere for that matter.

I felt Gabriel reach for my hand. I turned to see him watching me. His eyes were bright in the shadowy light.

Mark's speech went down brilliantly. I think he must have been really funny because everyone was laughing. Angie was wiping away tears of laughter at one point and Buzz Aldrin was slapping his palm down on to the table and rocking back and forth.

Then there was the cake cutting and bouquet throwing to be done, and then there was a blessed pause when Jerry and India went to their room in the hotel, apparently to get ready for the evening party, but there seemed to be a lot of giggling going on.

*

With a sigh of relief I went to my room, kicked off my shoes and lay down on the bed. I just wasn't in the mood to finish that conversation yet. Too much champagne and wine – I couldn't be trusted to say things clearly. I needed time to think.

I think I stayed there for about half an hour until I could hear people rushing about in the corridor outside my room like a load of kids playing tag.

The party was due to start at seven-thirty; maybe there was time for a shower?

There was a thump on the door and when I opened it India was there, still wearing her wedding dress, a glass of champagne in one hand and a slice of wedding cake in the other.

'This is for you,' she said, putting it on the dressing table. 'It's really scrummy.' She flopped down on my bed and gave a happy sigh. 'I'm looking forward to the party, aren't you? Are you going to be long?'

'No, just going to freshen up, and then I'll come down. Had a good day?'

'The absolute bestest day ever,' she said. She stood up, came over and gave me a hug, rocking slightly. 'I'm a bit pissed but who cares? I'd better get back to *my husband*.' She giggled. 'How weird is that? *My husband*. This is my husband, Jerry. This is Jeremy St John *Cholmondley* Sinclair, my husband.'

I laughed. 'Did you know his name was Cholmondley?'

'I had no idea before we started organising the wedding. He told me about the St John bit but *Cholmondley*? I mean really! I think there was an uncle somewhere. I'm going to put some flatter shoes on. These stilettos are killing me, and this dress is so heavy – that doesn't help.'

She tottered out and I closed the door behind her.

I freshened up my make-up and went back downstairs. The rooms that so recently had been filled with chattering people were nearly deserted and eerily quiet after the excitement. There were just a couple of people sitting at a table in the corner finishing their drinks. Then a couple of young men came in through the doors from the car park, wheeling heavy disco equipment on a couple of trolleys. They started to set up their kit ready for the evening party and some of the hotel staff came in to move the tables off the dance floor area.

I walked out of the room and into the deserted conservatory nearby where there was a large table filled with lovely-looking presents for India and Jerry.

We had done it; India was married and, by the look of her, blissfully happy. You couldn't ask for more than that for your sister.

'Alexa.'

I turned to see Gabriel had followed me, watching me from the doorway with an unfathomable expression. Suddenly I couldn't meet his gaze and I turned to straighten up a couple of the presents, tucking a gift tag in under the ribbon.

'We need to talk,' he said.

He closed the door behind him and the noise of the

chattering guests milling around in the hotel faded. It was just him and me alone.

'Yes,' I said.

'I came back to find you.' Slowly he crossed the room, his footsteps behind me getting closer with every moment.

'I want to tell you the truth. I told you; I'm divorced, reasonably civilly. It wasn't my wish but Elsa wanted more than I could give her.'

I remembered my thoughts: what more could any woman want but him? And yet there was that lingering doubt. It was so long since I'd taken those memories out of their dark bag that I couldn't quite remember them properly.

I wasn't cold but I shivered.

'I met Elsa at university. She was bright, ambitious; we were married for seven years. At first we made a good couple. I thought we wanted the same things. Then somehow things drove us apart. My work, travelling, the pressures of trying to keep everything together. And then she found someone else. Someone she thought could give her what she needed. So she had an affair. It went on for a long time – I don't quite know how long, but long enough to make me understand I wasn't what she wanted any more. I think I could have forgiven her but she didn't want my forgiveness; she wanted him.'

'Really?' I so wanted to believe it was this straightforward.

There was a long silence. I could hear my heart beating, thumping in my chest. It was getting warm in the conservatory.

Gabriel took off his jacket and looped it over the back of a chair. Then he loosened his tie.

'Are you all right?' he said.

'Yes.'

He ran one hand through his hair and came to stand in front of me.

'You're not making this very easy,' he said.

'I don't know what you want me to say.'

'Alexa, I thought there was something very special between us,' he said at last, 'something I've never felt.'

'What do you think it was?'

He laughed and turned away, standing with his hands in his pockets. God, he had a fantastic bum. *Stop it, stop looking*.

'I came here to see you,' he said. 'I mean it was lovely to see India getting married too – weddings are great occasions.'

'I thought you didn't believe in marriage,' I said.

He turned round. 'There, that's what I'm talking about. This business with marriage and men lying. What do you think I've done?'

'Lied to me about things. About your terrible divorce, about your children. The ones who had to go into therapy after your divorce.'

'What? Where did you hear this nonsense?'

'Marnie Miller.'

'Oh, for heaven's sake! And you believed her?'

'I didn't know what to believe! Why wouldn't I believe someone who was a friend of yours? She said you had a history of seducing women, that you took what you wanted and then –'

'Look, Alexa, firstly I'm not a friend of Marnie Miller, and I never have been. I'm her lawyer. Well, I was. I think it's time she and I parted company on any level if this is the sort of nonsense she's going to spout. My daughters are well-rounded, happy little girls. I thought I explained ...'

'Beatrice and Amelie,' I said.

'You've got a good memory,' he said. He was beside me now, just a touch away from me.

'I remember a lot of things,' I said.

'So do I,' he said, his voice very low. 'My divorce was as amicable as these things can be. Elsa has remarried and has the life she wanted. My daughters spend their holidays with me and are not in therapy. I swear on my mother's life.'

'Is your mother even still alive?' I asked stubbornly.

He fought a smile. 'She is alive and well and living in the house I told you about. Her name is Lynnette Mary-Beth Frost, she's sixty-seven, although she wouldn't thank me for telling you that, and she's been happily married to my father, Victor, for over forty years. She nags me to visit more than I do and worries that I'm still unmarried.'

'No significant other?'

'No significant other,' he said, trying hard not to laugh.

'It's not funny!' I said.

'No, I know it's not funny.'

He came towards me and ducked his head to look at me.

'So why would Marnie say such things about you if they weren't true?' I asked, feeling my heart start to race again.

He reached out and traced my collarbone with the tips of his fingers, making me shiver.

'Why do you think?' he said.

I shook my head, not knowing what to say.

'Because she could tell that I was attracted to you, that you were attracted to me.'

I looked up at him. His face was so wonderful, his expression so kind, that I almost wanted to cry. He pushed my hair off my face and took another step towards me so that we were almost touching.

'Because she knew I looked at you in a way I would never look at her. That I wanted you in a way I would never want her.'

His voice had dropped to a whisper.

'Oh,' I said, looking up at him.

He ran his thumb over my lower lip and I licked it with the tip of my tongue. He gasped. Then he held my head between his hands and kissed me.

'Perhaps that's why,' he said. 'I've found someone wonderful. Someone I never thought to find. Someone I couldn't forget. A beautiful, funny, sexy, sweet girl I could love.'

'Oh, and who's that?' I said, wondering how my legs were still holding me up.

'You, you daft thing,' he said and then he kissed me again. And after that we nearly missed the party altogether.

Acknowledgements

My third book – as always – owes much to the help and hard work of several people.

So thanks go to the team at Avon UK, especially Victoria Oundjian, Helena Newton and the clever Diane Meacham who provided such a lovely cover.

Also to my agent, Annette Green.

Thank you to the readers and bloggers who have been so generous with their time and lovely reviews of *The Summer of Second Chances* and *A Year of New Adventures*. I hope they enjoy this one just as much.

Thank you to the Literary Lovelies who never fail to encourage, cheer and sympathise when the need arises!

In no particular order: Jane Ayres, Kirsten Hesketh, Catherine Boardman, Susanna Bavin, Chris Manby, Kaz Coles, Christina Banach and Vanessa Thornton Rigg.

They are all talented and hardworking writers and good friends.

To James, Beth, Claudia, Jon and David, and also the wider family who have been so encouraging.

Finally, to my wonderful and exceptional husband, Brian, who helped inspire me with two transatlantic crossings on the lovely Cunard liner *Queen Mary 2*, purely for research purposes of course.

Love *Come Away with Me*? Then we think you should try
Maddie's first book, *The Summer of Second Chances*.

...even when you think you've lost everything, hope and
romance can be just around the corner

A brilliant romantic comedy that will have you
crying with laughter...

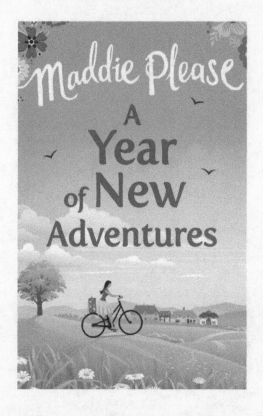

...because sometimes all you need is a second chance!